His eyes glittered and Abigail's hand rose without direct consent to her lips.

"You can see me," that familiar silky, deep, masculine voice said.

Her eyes tightened. No one there. A figment of her imagination. She would not look.

A tall, darkly dressed man moved into her vision. Stood before her, dark eyes piercing her.

"You can see me," he repeated forcefully.

Her lips parted. A tingle brushed down her arm, a bone-deep shiver followed in its wake.

Rainewood circled her. "Talk to me," the commanding, sensual voice said against her ear.

"I know the look in a woman's eye when she has noticed me, I know the look in *your* eye when you've seen me."

She shivered again . . .

Romances by **Anne Mallory**

ATTENTION: ORGANIZATIONS AND CORPORATIONS
Most Avon Books paperbacks are available at special quantity discounts for bulk purchases for sales promotions, premiums, or fund raising. For information, please call or write:

Special Markets Department, HarperCollins Publishers,
10 East 53rd Street, New York, New York 10022-5299.
Telephone: (212) 207-7528.   Fax: (212) 207-7222.

Anne Mallory

For the Earl's Pleasure

AVON

An Imprint of HarperCollinsPublishers

This is a work of fiction. Names, characters, places, and incidents are drawn from the author's imagination or are used fictitiously and are not to be construed as real. Any resemblance to actual events, locales, organizations, or persons, living or dead, is entirely coincidental.

AVON BOOKS
An Imprint of HarperCollins*Publishers*
10 East 53rd Street
New York, New York 10022-5299

Copyright © 2009 by Anne Hearn
ISBN 978-0-06-157914-1
www.avonromance.com

All rights reserved. No part of this book may be used or reproduced in any manner whatsoever without written permission, except in the case of brief quotations embodied in critical articles and reviews. For information, address Avon Books, an Imprint of HarperCollins Publishers.

First Avon Books paperback printing: July 2009

Avon Trademark Reg. U.S. Pat. Off. and in Other Countries, Marca Registrada, Hecho en U.S.A.
HarperCollins® is a registered trademark of HarperCollins Publishers.

Printed in the U.S.A.

10 9 8 7 6 5 4 3 2 1

If you purchased this book without a cover, you should be aware that this book is stolen property. It was reported as "unsold and destroyed" to the publisher, and neither the author nor the publisher has received any payment for this "stripped book."

For The Gudge

Acknowledgments

Thank you, as always, to Mom, May, and Matt, the wonder M's. ☺

For the
Earl's Pleasure

Chapter 1

He was a magnificent animal. Dark and deadly in both looks and wit. Most would describe Valerian Danforth, Lord Rainewood, in terms of a lean strong predator—a panther or a wolf. Personally, Abigail Smart found him to be the worst kind of bloated ass.

"Stupid donkey," she muttered as, all sinewy grace and confidence, he matched her step for step around the nearly empty balcony surrounding the crowded ballroom below.

"Ill-tempered shrew," came the lazy reply.

She watched the dancers move sinuously across the parquet floor, oblivious to the drama that swirled above them—society ever unaware of the tension that gripped her around Rainewood.

He made sure of that.

For even though he was deliberately walking beside her, provoking her, anyone observing them from below would think he was merely passing her by—a gnat to his social Goliath.

"Lousy, holier-than-thou, miserable, good-for-nothing, donkey."

"I withdraw my previous statement," he said

in a voice smoother than the best whiskey—and twice as dangerous when overly consumed. "So cruel a comparison for the shrew."

As if bored by the entire conversation, he flicked a pocket watch to check the time. Only the twitch to his fingers as he flipped the piece open said otherwise. With another smooth flick of his wrist the watch closed and disappeared into his expensive jacket.

A long look beneath longer lashes challenged her to a response as they continued on their somewhat aimless circuit. His loping grace vied with the lofty tilt to his head. As if he too couldn't decide whether he was the apex hunter or the sitting king. Then again, to her he was a little bit of both.

Abigail looked away to glare at the ballroom's occupants and at the patterned floor shifting beneath their feet as they danced. The alternating dark and light inlay perfectly reflected her moods where he was concerned.

"Don't you have something else with which to occupy your time?" she finally bit out. "I think I counted at least five young ladies flailing about in your path, their eyes as big as the large china saucers our hostess favors."

A splinter. He was like a large, long sliver of mahogany she could never quite rid herself of. A splinter which had become such a part of her being that it was rooted beneath her skin, permanently overgrown, and now she couldn't bear to remove it.

Otherwise, she would have stayed below, amongst the herd, safe in the knowledge that he wouldn't deign to spar with her in the crowd.

"I'm flattered you noticed," he said. Damn intoxicating whiskey. "Are the ghosts and ghouls, spirits and beasties, not holding your attention anymore? It must have been a crutch to focus on something other than your world of make-believe."

Abigail's fingers curled into her palms and she resolutely kept her eyes on the crowd below. Had she stayed near the area where the unmarried women waited patiently for a dance partner, she too could have been out there on the floor, losing herself in the ritual, feeling the flowing air and the touch of a warm gloved hand against hers . . . instead of the coiled heat and anger buried beneath her breast, seeking outlet as it always did when she separated from the pack and "bumped" into the most virile and biting man in attendance.

He never failed to find her alone, even for the briefest of moments. And she never failed to separate from the pack at least once an evening, despite her knowledge of what would come.

"Be still, my baited breath, as I await your answer. I might come to think you care, Smart."

Fingers brushed her bare elbow. A touch that could be completely accidental coming from someone else. Dark, sultry eyes met hers—sure in their intent. Fire licked beneath her skin. A signal of danger wormed its way through her and activated a sudden need for flight.

"You will be waiting a long time, Lord Rainewood."

"Will I?" The hair on her arm stood on end as his fingers trailed lightly along the underside and then lifted.

Flight. Most definitely.

"Donkey, donkey, donkey," she muttered as she stepped to the side, out of the path of danger. She skillfully negotiated a route between couples and groups gathered at the top of the stairs leading back down to the floor. She bypassed the stairs, trying to shake him free of her shadow, and turned as if heading to the retiring room.

He fell behind as they merged into a highly trafficked area and became part of the milieu once more. Ladies chattered and flirted, gentlemen postured and boasted. A sharp turn down the stairs was all it would take to be free. It was the smart move. There was something in the air tonight. A change. And rarely did those favor her.

Her elbow tingled.

Abigail threaded back through the throng and bypassed the stairs again, making another casual turn to head to the other side of the balcony ring to continue her seemingly aimless circuit.

"Donkey," she repeated for the tenth time, irritated with him and angry at herself for not taking the steps. For feeling the pull to continue.

"Talking to yourself again, Smart?" Rainewood drawled lazily as he pulled alongside her once more as they entered a path of columns that would interrupt the view from below enough that anyone observing would not be able to tell they were talking as they walked.

His long strides easily overtook her shorter, overly energetic ones, allowing him to be relaxed and in control while she always appeared to be in perpetual retreat. A peerless prince of ice and grace to her frenetic and plebeian bearing. She repeated her assessment of his character like a litany of prayer in her head.

"A better option than the alternative, considering the company," she said aloud.

A cool smile lifted his mouth in direct contrast to his suddenly hot, chocolate eyes—the only window to the real Valerian, who presented himself as even-tempered and remote, but was anything but. "Madness, talking to oneself. Should I send for the wardens? Put an end to your metaphysical games once and for all?"

Her limbs froze and she partially tripped on her suddenly leaden legs. The cool smile turned mocking and revealed even, white teeth that only enhanced the rich color of his eyes, his dark hair, even his flawless skin, which held a much healthier hue than the paste most of the men sported. She had long since assumed that his pact with the devil must have included abnormal dental and physical health.

"For yourself, perhaps. For continuing this farce." And she had allowed it—was encouraging it even now. She cursed herself internally. "Leave me be, Rainewood."

"I think not. It has been obvious for years that you require a keeper. I'm simply making sure that the rest of humanity is safe from you."

She stepped sideways, closer to him, changing her path so that he would have to move or hit the next column.

Instead, he pushed against her, pressing into her side. She stumbled at the contact.

"Pardon me, Miss . . . Smith, was it?" he said

to her in a falsely felicitous manner as two older women heading in their direction peered their way. Upon his statement, the two women looked away and began conversing again, deciding there was no gossip to be had.

It was maddening really that for all of the time they spent arguing at events that no one seemed to *notice*. By Jove, they had just spent the last ten minutes walking near each other in partial view of observers. Granted, he made it look like they were apart. But was she that invisible?

As far as the ton was concerned it would be surprising that Rainewood would even manage two correct letters of her name. He was elevated too far above her socially for anyone to think it odd that he completely ignored her, and he enjoyed the private game he played with her far too much.

He gave a sly smile under his lofty false concern as the women passed from view.

Her heart thumped in her chest from the shock of his bump and in renewed anger with herself. Frankly, one of these days she would probably start screaming at him in the middle of a gathering. The wardens would surely be called then.

She narrowed her eyes as she took in his patrician features arrayed in distant coldness and his eyes in heated derision. Someone needed to cut him down to the level on which the rest of society resided.

And she needed to stop playing his game. Needed to resist the pull that had existed between them for half of her life.

She turned and walked away from him.

"You are turning into a veritable stodge, Smart."

A note of irritation crept into his usual smooth drawl as he easily caught up with her. "Trying to limit my amusement."

"Your amusement could use limiting, Rainewood," she said. "Now scurry off to the rock from whence you crawled."

"You first, Smart." Smooth fingers traveled down her arm causing every hair to stand on end again. She forced herself to continue walking straight and not to lean in or jerk away. Either reaction would show too much.

A deep chuckle met her right ear as he leaned in instead. She had obviously not succeeded in keeping her face straight.

"Leave me be, Rainewood." She shrugged him off. No one in the ballroom below, or the scattered guests around the balcony, would have seen the touch. He was much too clever to allow that. And if for some reason he failed to be discreet, the damage would be turned upon her. There was a very good reason Rainewood ruled a large part of the ton.

She stopped at the small refreshment table set out for the guests seeking a break above stairs, and gathered her wits enough to pour a perfect cup of punch—controlling her shaking fingers just enough to do so. Through the years she had learned to hide her anxiety behind graceful gestures. Gestures that she had practiced over and again until they were natural.

"I don't think I will, Smart." He popped a cracker in his mouth and leaned forward against the table, negligently putting himself back in her sight. "Since you didn't answer my question—

shouldn't you be off scaring the locals with tales of ghosts howling in the night, spirits beseeching them for favors, calling out dire warnings, inhabiting their domains?"

Brittle past hurt crackled along the edge of her skin and she rubbed her arm.

He continued, apparently quite content to ridicule her without response. "And how in the world did you manage to secure an invitation to this event?"

She fought a grimace as her eyes swept the crowd below. Her mother, with her eagle eyes and never-ending social-climbing enthusiasm, was tracking her from the sidelines of the ballroom. Her mother's brow furrowed as she saw Rainewood standing so close. She waved a hand, obviously wanting Abigail to return to the action below. Worried that her only child would do the unforgivable.

Worried about what Rainewood would do to their social standing if he took it upon himself. Or vainly wishing that perhaps he would take a blow to the head and realize he was desperately in love with Abigail—and that all of these years of coldness were merely a poor cover to hide his deep and abiding desire.

She snorted derisively at the thought. Her mother never had been able to figure out what happened all those years ago—even though she had tried quite hard to get it out of Abigail once Rainewood had become heir. All of a sudden an earl, the heir to a dukedom? Her mother wasn't stupid and she played the social game harder than she had any right to.

"A deal with the devil, Smart?"

Abigail kept her eyes away from her mother and their newly procured companion and tutor—the woman hired to open doors for them among the members of the ton. Doors that would otherwise be closed if highfliers like Rainewood had his choice. "I don't remember making a deal with you, Rainewood. No, this invitation was nothing out of the ordinary. You'd be surprised at how boring people find the current members of society. Hungry for fresh blood and new perspective."

She gave him a tight, all-encompassing glance, taking in his fashionable attire; the enviable style he carried off without looking as if he tried. "So boring to just be fashionable these days. Much more interesting to have genuine content to one's character. So rare in present company."

She raised her cup to her lips and kept her eyes wide with innocence, as a pair of gentlemen stopped next to them to secure refreshment.

Rainewood's eyes tightened and he popped in another cracker, responding to the men as they obsequiously acknowledged him, then waiting for them to move away. She thought about moving away first, but there was something about Rainewood that never failed to draw her in, even as it repelled. A leftover sentiment from childhood. That intangible something that caused her to stay that extra few seconds to watch the bee sting even when she knew she should swat it and run far away.

She blamed childish flights of romantic fancy for the stupidity inherent in the poor battle tactic. Rainewood had far more maneuvers in his arsenal than she could ever achieve. And socially he was capable of completely destroying her. She was continually surprised when he didn't—instead, he preferred to dangle her on the edge of destruction, like a cat playing with a half-starved mouse.

The two men finally left, carrying their liquid prizes.

Rainewood leaned in, the crisp smell that clung to him—the whisper of forbidden nights and unending challenge—wafted over her. "That's the thing with you, Smart. Always trying to play above your status."

She finished her sip and tried to keep her fingers relaxed around her cup as she lowered it. A sharp slap to remember the past and never confuse it with the present. Unending challenge was all she would ever receive from Rainewood now. That and the coldness and biting sarcasm that she had never felt she had earned.

"I learned the hazards of playing above my status at a young age. The actions and knowledge gained me little truth or regard. But joining that status will secure me *justice*." The tenuous grip of the forbidden broke its hold and she embraced the loud, crackling sounds of the ballroom. She walked backward, not breaking the hold between their eyes as she communicated her desire. "I hope when that happens that you choke on it. Have a pleasant evening, *Raine*."

His dark eyes went black at her reminder of their intertwined pasts, secrets, and the moment their paths had unraveled beyond control.

"You will never achieve that goal," he called out as she started to walk away, shattering his rule of publicly ignoring her. His voice was far more calm than his eyes had indicated.

She turned, walking a few steps backward once more. "Don't bet against it, Lord Rainewood. Our tally is still in my favor, I believe."

"That tally was wiped away."

She tilted her head. "Perhaps by your arrogance, but not by my account. You destroyed it, not I."

A loaded statement that meant far more than just the implication that at one time they had kept friendly running bets. The hurt, dulled, but still there, crept under her skin and she turned, unwilling to let him see it creep into her eyes. He always could read her. There was too much ammunition between them.

To her surprise, he didn't follow. Didn't try to score the last taunt. Didn't publicly ruin her with the secrets that would close every door to her.

Chapter 2

A bigail descended the stairs and skirted the slim path between the chatty groups collected around the edges of the floor and the whirling dancers. A ribbon loosened from a young woman's dress as she twirled to the music. The thin thread lifted and snaked through the air toward Abigail. She caught the supple blue satin and continued forward, threading it through her fingers. The woman had already disappeared into the throng with her partner, not noticing that the hem of her dress contained one less accoutrement.

Abigail gripped the freed ribbon tightly in her hand. Freed like she would never be.

She resolutely moved to her mother's side. It was not her favorite place to be in the middle of a crowded ballroom, but far safer than other options. Such as walking the rope with the devil.

"Abigail, chin up. And do fix your collar." She could see her mother's fingers itching to touch the lace.

She stepped back to free her mother from the temptation. Mrs. Gerald Smart practiced the social graces religiously, but she sometimes forgot herself in her zealous need to ascend. Her mother wanted the end result too badly, fought the battles too aggressively, and missed the subtle, internal steps it took to win the war.

"And your hair. It looks dreadful. What did you do?"

Abigail touched the lock that never quite stayed in place no matter how many pins she or her maid used. She caught the sharp eye of their companion, Mrs. Browning, who was observing them from the matrons' chairs with a tight, disapproving crease to the sides of her mouth, as usual.

"Oh, never mind now," her mother said. "Here comes Mr. Brockwell. Pleasant. A thousand pounds per year. Healthy stock. Look smart." Her mother chuckled at her own joke, and Abigail withheld a flinch. She could never quite hide what an avid social climber she really was, with communication skills that at times hearkened back to a past life.

Sometimes Abigail wished with all her might that her present life was a dream, and the past could become possible once more. No *Lord* Rainewood, no *special* gifts, no fear of discovery.

Phillip Brockwell ambled over, all spindly legs and awkward motion.

"Mr. Brockwell," her mother said with a quick head-to-toe perusal. "What a pleasant evening for your company."

"Mrs. Smart, yours is by far the lovelier. And Miss Smart's too."

Her mother nodded and Abigail smiled at Phillip's aplomb. He was not the most graceful or grace-filled man, but he tried quite hard.

"How kind of you, Mr. Brockwell," her mother

said. "Abigail was just speaking of you and saying how much she enjoyed your conversation and company."

With difficulty Abigail kept her own smile firmly on her face as Phillip went pink.

"A lovely evening to enjoy both," her mother pronounced, obviously satisfied. "Oh, I say, I do think our hostess is waving me over. Do pardon me."

She waved a hand, bequeathed Phillip with one last bright smile, said "Stay sharp, Abigail," in a voice that was embarrassingly above a whisper, and walked to the other side of the room, far from their hostess.

Abigail wondered if there was a way to shackle her mother to a wardrobe later.

Without a murmur of protest, Abigail had gone along with the entire plan to firmly plant themselves within the belly of the ton. But sometimes her mother made that difficult.

Phillip shuffled his feet, cheeks still pink. "How are you, Miss Smart?"

"I am well, Mr. Brockwell. And you? Have you tried the punch?" She lifted her cup, trying to put him back at ease. "I was told it was a new recipe Lady Malcolm brought back from her last visit to the islands."

He gave her a wry, crooked smile, his shoulders loosening from their tight hold. "Twice." His shoulders suddenly tightened back up.

Abigail turned to see Edwina Penshard hurrying toward them. "Miss Smart, Mr. Brockwell," she said brightly, blowing out a breath as she jolted to a stop. Edwina was like the bright full tulips in her lovingly tended garden—all golden curls, red cheeks, and plump frame. She never failed to brighten Abigail's evening.

Edwina's brother, Gregory, a fair-haired man with sharp green eyes and a rapier tongue, strolled after her, greeting them as well. The Penshards had the distinct displeasure of being related to Rainewood and the two men got on like tigers circling the same food source.

Gregory gave her a tight smile and nod. He had been acting peculiarly for the last week. She wasn't naïve enough not to realize that he possibly had some intentions in her direction. The question was whether she should encourage the attention. There had always been something about Gregory that had reminded her of Rainewood's deceased older brother. And that was something to be avoided.

Rainewood had neatly filled his brother's shoes after his death. And the ton could only stand one absolute ruler.

Edwina's naturally joyful smile widened, and Phillip's face pinkened in reaction. Poor smitten Phillip.

"Lovely party," Edwina gushed. "I do so hope to catch our host at some point this evening. He spoke at the gardening society about how plant growth can be enhanced by the benevolent wishes a gardener harbors. Fascinating."

Phillip tugged his cravat away from his increasingly sweaty neck under Edwina's bright regard. "He spoke on the topic to the Young Scientist's Society as well. I thought of you and your benevolence." Poor Phillip.

"Oh, how lovely, Mr. Brockwell." Edwina

smiled happily. "And you joined the Society! That is excellent!"

Phillip's face flushed in pleasure, then pinched as he looked at something over Abigail's shoulder. "Yes. Though there is a faction that is trying to change the society into something else entirely."

Abigail followed his gaze to the group prominently on display at the other edge of the floor. The most fashionable of the younger set—clustered around their star.

Donkey.

"Has one of them been giving you trouble, Brockwell?" Gregory asked.

"It's nothing," Phillip responded, a mite too quickly.

Across the room, Rainewood whipped his head to the left, a strand of hair falling *just so* across his haughty brow, showing his best side as he shared in a joke with one of his cronies. Abigail pushed against the pull and tried to focus on the delinquent faces of the white-gowned, dreamy women also looking in his direction.

A cold prince each young, unmarried woman hoped would bestow his blessing upon her, and her alone, as if his attention would ensure her success and self-esteem. The problem was that in most cases, it would.

Abigail turned back, irritated. "Don't let them bully you or the society, Mr. Brockwell. Who gives a thought to what they think?"

Phillip gave her a disbelieving look. Gregory's eyebrows raised in dark humor.

"Well, *I* don't," she said a mite defensively.

"Me neither," Edwina said loyally. "And I think

you make a grand addition to the society, Mr. Brockwell."

"And it is only a matter of time before one of the instigators drops," Gregory said in his dismissive manner. "With all the talk today, I wouldn't be surprised."

Edwina sighed. "I would that we'd never heard of the corruption list. Such a negative thing."

"The corruption list?" Abigail asked.

"You haven't heard?" Gregory raised a brow. "It's been scorching the room like wildfire."

She had been too busy creating her own blaze with Rainewood. She shook her head.

Phillip glowered. "Came out this afternoon during our Society meeting."

"It would have come out anyway, Brockwell," Gregory said.

"But that was the most inappropriate place for it. Another example of how they are trying to change the scientific forum into another betting club. Gossipmongers attempting to be fashionably interested in mechanics. They should take their indulgences to White's or Boodles where they belong."

"Yes, well, I heard there have been some heavy bets placed. One of them is sure to be ruined in the crossfire." Gregory smiled unpleasantly. "I can't wait to see which one. I hope it is Rainewood himself."

"Now, Gregory—" Edwina started.

"A comeuppance on par with perfection," he said with relish.

"Gregory, that is hardly kind," Edwina said chidingly. "Lord Rainewood has done nothing to deserve that type of venom."

As the heir to a duke, Rainewood had inherent social power. As a clever ass, he knew exactly how to use that power to his best advantage. Being born with superior looks and a wealth of charm—should he choose to employ it—made him unstoppable socially. And completely in control of whatever he desired. The serpent toying with its prey.

One had to play with the serpent in order to be placed in Eden's garden though.

"Are you defending him? He is a complete waste of human material, and you know it, Ed. How many times do you have to be struck by one of that group, meant to feel beneath their regard, before you will fight back?"

Abigail had been crushed by the king snake long, long ago and hadn't even attempted to enter the popular group upon her debut. Following Rainewood's lead, as always, the group had firmly and neatly placed her beneath their notice from the outset. A move that just made her determined to prove them all wrong.

"But Lord Rainewood is not responsible."

"You are delusional, Ed. He could stop them with a word. Why he doesn't participate in their antics is the question you should be asking." Gregory's eyes turned to Abigail. If the ton took no notice of Rainewood's attention to her, Gregory was not included in the group—his past knowledge combined with his keen observation gave him an edge.

His eyes constantly mocked, but his lips stayed sealed.

"Oh, Gregory, he is your cousin," Edwina said.

"Distant, *distant* cousin."

"Not so very distant in ton terms," Edwina

pointed out. Gregory was sixth in line. "You are far too interested in old grudges. You should try to extend an olive branch."

"And you are far too kind. I'd as soon extend a pitchfork, tines forward."

Edwina opened her mouth, but Abigail quickly jumped in. "The list?"

Edwina shook her head. "Oh, some crazy notion of a secret dialogue that lists those with insanity in their heritage, scandals not previously acknowledged, and impostors in the ton."

"Impostors?"

"People claiming to be who they are not," Gregory said unhelpfully.

Abigail frowned. "I know what an impostor is. Someone has a list of these things written somewhere? How would they have discovered such a wide variety of information?"

"Who knows." Gregory shrugged, but his eyes were pinched at the corners. "All the rage though. The ton loves a good scandal. The juicier the gossip, the more the rage, of course."

"Well, I think it absurd," Edwina said. "That all of this energy is being expended to stir the pot."

"Please, Ed. Where have you been hiding? You were born to this."

"I don't have to acknowledge it." She sniffed. "Mother is completely consumed by it, of course. Anxious to 'expel' those on the list from society."

"As if you are surprised. Mother is insufferable. She loves a good witch-hunt. Don't be foolish."

Phillip looked fairly ill as he anxiously glanced between the squabbling siblings. He always shied from conflict.

Edwina sniffed again. "I only hope Lord Raine-wood does right by his knowledge and destroys the thing so that she doesn't have a chance."

Abigail stiffened. "Lord Rainewood?"

"He is said to have purchased the list. Keeps it on him at all times, or so they say," Gregory said. There was something dark in his eyes as he looked Rainewood's way.

"There is a lot of damage that can be done with such an item." Edwina tutted. "When father returns from his trip I hope that he will have a positive impact on turning things around."

Gregory didn't respond, but his eyes darkened further.

"Yes, when is your father planning to return?" Abigail was eager to change the conversation. Their father had been visiting his plantation in Ceylon for over a year.

"He didn't say, just that things were going well. I wish he would let me visit," Edwina said a little wistfully.

Phillip shot her another anxious look. "Surely there are things to amuse you here, Miss Penshard."

"Oh, of course, Mr. Brockwell. But I do miss father, and I've always wanted to visit the islands."

Gregory's fists knotted and Abigail shot him a questioning look. He smiled tightly and turned his head away.

The orchestra struck up a new piece.

"Oh. I *would* miss London though." Edwina's face took on a dreamy cast. "I love this reel."

Phillip shuffled his feet. "Would, um, would you care to step to it, Miss Penshard?"

She brightened. "I would, Mr. Brockwell. Thank

you." She held out a hand and Phillip nervously wiped his gloved hand against his trousers before offering his arm.

Abigail watched them take to the floor, Edwina bobbing and Phillip awkwardly moving them into the first form.

Gregory watched them with his usual mocking expression. "Brockwell better do well by my sister."

"He will be a most loyal beau." Abigail smiled. She couldn't imagine a couple better suited. Phillip but needed to make his intentions known. "He just needs to snag her before she takes off to faraway lands," she joked.

Gregory's eyes tightened. "No need to worry about that. Edwina isn't going anywhere."

"You can hardly keep her here if your father approves."

"He won't." Gregory brushed a forceful hand over his trouser leg. "Would you care to take a turn about the room. I find myself suddenly in need of movement."

"Of course." She held out her hand, uncertain as always about Gregory's mercurial changes.

They passed by a group of women chattering.

"I can't wait to see who is listed," one said, waving her fan.

"Oh, but what if there is a mistake?"

"Are you worried about your lineage, Lettie?"

"I'm just stating the fact that we don't know how this list was generated."

"Well, I personally don't care how it was generated. The Connages go back eight generations and we haven't a nut in the tree."

"But they have plenty of scandals," a woman whispered loudly and the chattering turned cattier.

Gregory looked at Abigail. "I can't believe you hadn't heard of the list. What have you been up to, Miss Smart, that you were completely unaware of the overriding gossip tonight?"

"Oh, this and that. I agree with Edwina. Petty things to discuss."

"Society thrives on such things."

"Hopefully Lord Rainewood destroys it." She smiled as best she could. It was like wishing on a rainbow. No one destroyed something with that much power. Least of all Rainewood.

Gregory scoffed. "Have you gone mad, Miss Smart? You know better than most—he would use it to crush those in his path. He is the reason society is declining like a London gutter rushing toward the Thames."

She shifted her eyes between Gregory and Rainewood. She had never seen the two friendly, even as children, but the amount of acrimony blazing from Gregory's eyes was even more pronounced. She wondered what Rainewood had done this time.

"Has Rainewood done something lately of which I am unaware?" She knew why she had trouble with him. But the increased venom from Gregory . . .

As if he knew she was thinking of him, Rainewood's head turned and his gaze locked with hers. One eyebrow lifted, and she could see the light flow into his dark eyes.

"Nothing that I can't deal with."

One of Rainewood's cronies noticed his gaze in

their direction and said something in his ear, before striding toward them, eyes dark and malicious.

Rainewood smiled slowly at her and pushed away from the wall, sauntering forward. And even though he was behind his friend, he still appeared the one to be leading, prodding. The others started to follow behind, like the sheep they were, until a lazy hand waved. She could almost hear the group bleat as they stopped at Rainewood's command.

Abigail opened her mouth to alert Gregory, but he stopped suddenly and smirked darkly. "Rainewood will be knocked from his perch soon enough."

"Still setting your sights on the prize, Penshard?" A dark, silky voice said. Abigail stiffened.

"Eavesdropping, Rainewood? How plebeian," Gregory responded, turning sharply. "But then that is to your level."

"Level? One to talk, are you? From the bottom of the barrel, really," intoned an unwanted second voice—a strident, staccato with a predatory edge that perfectly matched the looks of the man uttering them. Rainewood's favorite lackey.

"Now, Templing, it is considered rude to point out one's station," Rainewood's silkier and much more deadly voice replied, a bored tone underlying the rich quality. Her entire body stiffened under the contact of the auditory waves, even though she had been subjected to them no more than thirty minutes before. "Especially when the other party is so desperate to have it changed."

If Gregory had access to a pike she knew without a doubt that it would have been hoisted and planted firmly in Rainewood's chest.

Rainewood's eyes slid briefly to her, silently including her in the taunt. Something in her broke loose, the ribbon wildly whipping free. Through the anger, she was only partially aware of another of Rainewood's friends joining their taut circle. Piranhas banding together to destroy.

"Do you only seek out people in order to attack them?" she demanded. "Do you require the diversion to satisfy your boredom?"

Rainewood looked at her as if he'd never seen her before and raised a brow. "I beg your pardon, Miss, but have we been introduced?"

"Why, yes," she replied sweetly. "I think I managed to receive a 'charmed' response from you once."

Templing snorted. "More than you deserved, obviously."

Abigail didn't even bother looking in the lackey's direction.

"I say." Templing stepped toward her, putting him in her line of sight, obviously irritated at her dismissal. "Who do you think you are speaking to?"

"I believe I was speaking to Lord Rainewood."

"He doesn't wish to speak to the likes of you."

"Oh, my apologies." She put a hand to her chest. The freed ribbon swung wildly, detached from any semblance of good sense. "I didn't realize that Lord Rainewood required someone else to speak for him. Why, I had forgotten that as an heir he need not fight his own wars just to get noticed."

Rainewood's fingers gripped his glass more tightly. She smiled sweetly with just the slightest batting of her eyes. Fighting dirty worked all the better when you had a childhood arsenal at your behest—and frequently people seemed to forget that Rainewood had once been the forgotten middle son.

No, now that Rainewood was at the top of the social heap, he was nearly untouchable. Which meant that she was doubly stupid to say a negative word to him in front of others.

Her mother was going to kill her, although Mrs. Browning was going to draw and quarter her first.

The third man who had joined them laughed softly. "Such cheek in such a petite package," Aidan Campbell said, giving her a long, considering look. She caught Rainewood's dark glance in his friend's direction, but Campbell seemed oblivious. "I am enchanted by your daring, Miss Smart."

She said nothing, staring at Campbell, waiting for another taunt or some form of disapproval. Neither appeared.

"Perhaps a lesson in manners is required." Rainewood's voice curled around the space and darted toward her.

"I am sure one of the matrons would be happy to help you. Two weeks and they say that they can turn any lowly peasant into a prince." She tossed sense firmly to the wind and looked him over in a gesture that she hoped managed to convey how lacking she found him to be.

"You seem familiar with the drill. Perhaps further lessons are required?"

She narrowed her eyes.

"Rainewood . . . so hard on the lass. She seems quite spirited. I wonder why I haven't noticed it before." Campbell studied her.

Templing snorted and Gregory verbally attacked. The three quickly fell into heated argument.

Abigail turned to Rainewood. "Did you have a reason for joining us? I'll start to think you fancy me, Lord Rainewood, if you keep following me in such a manner." She kept her voice low so that the others wouldn't be able to make out the words, but her action in talking to him at all made the interaction public.

A suffocating tunnel formed, connecting Rainewood's dark eyes to hers. He leaned in and gave her a slow perusal from the wisps of escaped hair on her forehead to the hem of her dress. Hot eyes that promised pleasure and pain.

Lowering his voice above a mere whisper, he murmured, "Fancy a crazed woman with a mother who is nearly a leper—one social finger falling off at a time? Do you think yourself enough of a catch? Your beauty, charms, and *spirit* so great, that I would even deign to breathe in the same space as you?"

The low, seductive, mocking voice wrapped across the tunnel, squeezing it. The emphasis on that damned word crushing tightly. Just by his status he could ruin her in the higher levels of society with a few choice words—that had always been true. But he could do so much worse, should he finally decide to play his trump.

It was hard to breathe, to swallow, when everything inside turned to rock. Neither air nor spit could erode the diamond walls, the dark cavern.

Anger burst again, sharp and as hard as the diamonds lining the walls pierced her. "Is that so, your lordship? And yet here you are breathing my air." She leaned into him. "Coming closer to inhale more." She tipped her head to the side and lowered her voice to a mere wisp of sound. "And as for my mother, she is what she is and twice the person you will ever be. I recall a boy desperate not to be anything like his brother, yet so close have you fallen to that tree."

Hot rage licked from his eyes and everyone else in the room disappeared in the searing heat that flowed from him toward her. "Funny that you should mention my brother. A special topic for you, isn't it? What was it you once said?"

He was going to do it. She could see it in his brittle whiskey eyes. He was about to announce her secrets to the world. Tell everyone that she was raving mad. That she claimed to see ghosts. They would call the wardens. She'd be carted to Bedlam. Or worse. Her mother might intervene. She might call . . .

Her mind rejected the thought. She felt lightheaded, separated from her body as she watched the darkness and anger in his eyes.

Suddenly he jerked away from her. "I think we are done here." He stopped one movement short of giving her the cut direct. The resulting action, somewhere between hot heat and freezing cold, held the room in silence for a long moment.

It was at that moment that she realized the others had stopped arguing to observe them—and that they weren't the only ones.

Gregory opened his mouth to say something, but Abigail put her hand on his sleeve, nearly shaking. Her simmering anger completely overwhelmed by the notion that Rainewood could have simply raised his voice to normal tones. Could have announced anything he pleased in his silky drawl and everyone would have heard and listened. Accepted his word as gospel, especially with the gossip concerning the list. Even if he *didn't* have it, that people thought he did was what counted.

Her social status was important, but had never mattered to her even half as much as her freedom.

She could have sworn he was looking away, but Rainewood's eyes tightened imperceptibly and his gaze switched back and narrowed on Gregory. "As for you, save your social gasps for things you might actually be able to grasp."

He looked at Abigail's hand resting on Gregory's sleeve, raised a scathing brow, and then walked away.

Her mother hurried over, a flurry of harried brown silk as the noise of the crowd reached new heights with the latest on-dit—she could already hear voices loudly whispering about what Lord Rainewood had found interesting and infuriating about Miss Smart, a woman barely on the social gossip wagon. Mrs. Browning walked just as quickly as her mother, but with a much more militant manner.

She was as good as a mouse crushed beneath a carriage wheel.

Gregory's eyes followed the group of men, deadly in intent, then he excused himself and walked away.

Valerian emerged from the second hell that night. The ball had only made him antsy to do something else. Something that would distract him. Damn woman. *Damn her.* With her honey brown hair, blue eyes, strong features, and sharp tongue.

He had snapped at a minimum of ten people who had tried to ask what the interaction with *Miss Smart* had been about.

"Can't believe we are down three hundred. Campbell would be in dire straits."

Valerian looked at Templing stumbling out next to him. They were down three hundred because Templing could barely stand up on his own. The man was a gambling twit when he was drunk.

"Campbell needs to clean up his finances," Valerian said dismissively. The state of their friend's pocketbook was a boring one. Aidan Campbell bet too much and won too little. He was going to be in to Valerian for ten thousand pounds soon. He had bet against the list.

Damn list. Damn woman. Damn friends.

Valerian had no notion of calling in the bet, but he wasn't going to let Campbell know it. The future viscount needed to learn sooner rather than later that he could only extend himself so far before there were dire consequences. Better that it be a lesson from which he could return, than from a shark lender on the east side.

And Campbell needed to stop looking at Abigail Smart in the way that he had taken to doing. Valerian didn't like the looks at all. They produced a bone-deep urge within him to pummel something. He would have to make it clear that Abigail Smart was off limits in every way.

He had a lot of practice in doing so.

"No way Campbell is going to manage it unless he hooks himself to an heiress," Templing slurred.

"In too deep. Heard he was seen with men from the east side."

The admission surprised Valerian, but his attention was focused on a man standing alongside the walk. Everything about the man screamed not to disturb him, which was fine with Valerian. The younger pups just out of school liked to play at walking on the wilder side of town—Valerian had done so not so long ago. But even though most of the more deadly elements refrained from attacking a member of the upper class—knowing the higher priced punishments such actions would bring—one always had to be on guard.

That Campbell was indebted to someone from the east side was very bad. There were many who claimed dubious reputations and endless resources. Dangerous. Men who would collect on their money regardless of the means.

His mind temporarily wandered as he thought of the multitude of reasons Campbell would be interested in Abigail. "Idiot."

Templing huffed to keep up, stumbling behind as he did. "Now, Raine, not everyone has—"

The sound of a body hitting the ground behind him caused Valerian to sigh. The night was obviously over for Templing. Idiot. Valerian turned to help Templing and call for a hack. He felt like corralling a bottle of fine whiskey at home and brooding on blue eyes anyway.

A swift movement, a flash of green. Pain exploded in Valerian's head and all went dark.

Chapter 3

Men's trousers appeared much easier to unfasten these days than in the past.

"Isn't it simply delightful of what society is capable?"

Abigail absently nodded to the flesh-and-blood man standing in front of her and watched the more interesting ghostly spectacle in the corner.

An upstairs maid by the look of her thirty-years-old outdated clothing had wrapped herself quite indecently around a footman—pressing together so closely that the air between them nearly whooshed out in an audible breeze. The man hitched the maid higher on his leg and pushed her against the wall. His fingers worked to undo his old fashioned trousers in frenzied motions.

Two matrons walked by, chatting behind their fans and pointing long fingers to different attendees at the Grayton House ball, identifying anything noteworthy. If the servants' clothing hadn't given it away, the complete inattention by two of society's dragons to the moans, groans, and squirming of the two copulating in the corner reaffirmed to Abigail that she alone was seeing the spectacle.

Her *talent*.

With Rainewood absent from all activities for the past two days, the tension that had always gripped her in society had gradually diminished. And the timing between his heated interaction with her and his disappearance had her name on many lips, which ironically was helping her social stock. Sending more than one sneaking glance her way.

She should be securing a quality husband—quickly. So why was she concentrating on things she usually tried to ignore? The very things that had destroyed a cherished friendship and turned her life upside down.

It was almost like *she* was the spirit languishing in nostalgia—attached to the physical plane, doomed to repeat the same movements over and over.

And unfortunately not memories as entertaining as the scenario being played out in the corner.

She stared more inquiringly at the physical mechanics required to attain the position that the footman was rocking the maid into. She wondered if it was a true memory she was seeing, and if so had the gilded wall sconce dug into the woman's bared shoulder? Had her head knocked into the fresco of satyrs at play? Or was this an unfulfilled act that their spirits could only indulge in after death? Whichever it was Abigail felt her face heat.

"Miss Smart?"

Abigail focused on the slight man standing across from her. He was looking at her worriedly while Mrs. Browning glared. "My apologies, Mr. Southertonmonsmith . . ." She let the last part trail into a mumble as she couldn't quite remember *what* the man's name was. Her senses had dulled as soon as the donkey had gone missing.

"Mr. *Sourting* was inquiring as to whether you would like to take a ride in the park tomorrow. I think it a lovely idea." Her mother smiled widely at Mr. Sourting, who smiled tentatively back.

Sourting. Right. He had popped up in what seemed a bid to court her weeks ago, then abruptly dropped the suit. She was used to the quick changes—the lure of the Smart fortune bringing the men forward, then something about her changing their minds. Her oddness or ambivalence, she didn't know. Easier to deal with the hit to her pride by forcing herself to forget the mercurial suitors entirely.

Mr. Sourting looked to her and Abigail worked up a smile. "Of course. How lovely that would be."

"Excellent. I shall see you on the morrow." He looked rather relieved, then quickly excused himself. She absently wondered at the man's change of heart.

"Abigail! What have you to say for yourself? What were you doing?"

She could be honest and say that she had been watching a couple of spirits copulating in the corner, but she didn't think that would please her mother, nor Mrs. Browning.

Mrs. Browning sniffed. "Yes, do bring her in line Mrs. Smart. I will speak with a few other gentlemen and return for a hopefully more respectable performance."

"Well, Abigail?" her mother asked as Mrs. Browning strode off.

"Just thinking, Mother, my apologies."

"Thinking? No man wants a future wife who *thinks* instead of listens! You know better than that."

A lady in a one hundred-year-old flat-bosomed dress drunkenly swayed through the crowd singing a bawdy ditty. With a downward swipe of her hand one breast spilled over her bodice, and she caterwauled at the top of her ghostly lungs about meaty paws and suckling maws.

Abigail tore her eyes away as the woman stepped through her mother, who shivered and waved her fan.

Abigail swallowed. "Of course that is true. I will do better, Mother."

Her mother's brows furrowed as she glanced around furtively, letting go of the rigid persona she tried to play and reverting to the more natural flighty, paranoid bird that she was. "You don't have need of Dr. Myers, do you?"

Ice crackled down Abigail's spine. "No, no, definitely not, Mother. I am completely purged. Fine. Wonderful even." She smiled brightly, the ice cracking even at the corners of her mouth. "I have just been speculating on the whereabouts of Earl Rainewood and Mr. Templing."

"Well, I don't believe those two are where you should concentrate your marriage efforts, dear." Her mother's face took on a dreamy cast. "Of course, the heir to a dukedom would be magnificent. And if you had worked your wiles on him properly long ago before he was heir . . . or if you had secured him afterward instead of letting him slip away . . . but Lord Rainewood is all but be-trothed to the Malcolm girl."

"Yes, of course." The very idea that she would concentrate "marriage" efforts on Rainewood was so laughable that it wasn't even remotely funny.

"Let us speak with Mr. Farnswourth while Mrs. Browning is off on her mission—lovely catch for us to secure her," her mother gushed. Abigail thought it more a case of their deep pockets nicely lining their dragon companion's own. "I have seen Mr. Farnswourth send more than one speculative look in your direction. A steady stream of invites there, and seventh in line to an earldom. Seventh in line is nothing to scoff at. You never know, dear, you never know!"

For a second her mother held out a hand as if she would take Abigail's arm, but her mother seemed to recollect herself in time and her face changed from eager excitement to a more rigid, controlled expression. She woodenly waved Abigail forward. "I expect you to make an afternoon appointment with Mr. Farnswourth as well, if you can. The end of the season will be upon us soon, and we do want to have a number of good options."

"Yes, Mother." With her head held high and a cheerful smile plastered on her face, Abigail pushed aside the insidious thoughts about when her mother had become so reserved in her physi-cal affection and instead followed her through the crowd. She had survived for years without any pur-poseful physical contact from her mother—she'd survive another few hours, days, or years as well.

* * *

A half orchestra played enthusiastically as couples in full ball attire danced merrily around the Grayton House ballroom. Valerian allowed himself a rare moment of shock. What the devil had just happened? One minute he'd been walking from a gaming hell with Templing, thinking of home and *her*, and the next he was standing in his father's house in the midst of an immense party. Grayton House should have been devoid of guests. Servants should be scurrying around making last minute preparations for the party in two day's time. A party didn't simply just *happen*.

Which meant he must have spent the last two days in some sort of alcohol induced stupor. Damn. He thought he'd left those days behind. He looked down at his evening clothing—yes, this shirt, jacket, and cravat were exactly what he had been wearing to the Malcolm's fete and to the hells afterward. Dear God. He would never live this down. Abigail Smart would rub it in his face for all eternity.

He couldn't allow her the upper hand. Not after what she'd done to him so many years ago. He needed to change quickly, hide in one of the anterooms, or practice his verbal barbs.

An underbutler skirted the edge of the crowd, staying watchful but apart from the proceedings.

Valerian detached himself from the column rooting him and approached just close enough to be seen and heard by the servant. "Fetch me Samuels, and hur—" Astonished for a second time, he watched as the servant sauntered right past him without a lick of acknowledgment. Cheeky bastard. No one ignored him, especially in his father's home.

He reached out to grab the underbutler's shirt, but his hand cut cleanly through the man. He stared for a moment before his hand dropped like a cleaver to the block. What devilry was this?

He reached for the next person who passed him, a pretty little debutante with upswept hair and a virginal white gown, and that too was like grasping a dream, fair and fleeting, his hand passing right through like a waterfall that kept flowing. He backed away. He was in a madhouse. Or a dream. He concentrated on waking up, but the scene continued to unfold. He drew back into the alcove, his feet taking him back as far as he could go.

Something passed over his body, and the next thing he knew, he was staring at a dark paneled wall.

He crouched and rotated, searching for threats. The interior of the mahogany and gold-encrusted study came into focus. A memory of his grandfather filling ledgers with numbers and ordering men to his bidding flickered through his head, then fled down the waterfall.

Two men strode through the door. "I don't need this now, Reston. You promised it would be done. And we can't meet here." Gregory Penshard threw something on the desk. Valerian's father would have his head for the treatment.

"And so it is. The doctor wishes to conduct more experiments. You don't escape from the doctor." The other man, unfamiliar to Valerian with his dirty blond hair and muddy brown eyes, spread his hands.

"Yes, but closure is more important."

"And closure you will have." The unfamiliar

man suddenly went from conciliatory to threatening. "We provide a service. You pay the fee. Do you want to take it up with the doctor? Make a visit yourself? Provide a target for wagging tongues to ask questions?"

Penshard's lips tightened and Valerian could see his distant cousin's hands turn white. "No. Just see that it's done."

A crooked-toothed smile ringed the blonde's mouth and he looked affable once again. "Excellent. I will take this nice draft and be on my way." He tipped an imaginary hat. "Your *lordship*."

Penshard's tightly clenched lips fully disappeared from view. As soon as the other man exited, he swiped a hand along the desk, scattering the papers.

His father would have his distant nephew's ballocks in a vice for that. And for presuming a title when he had none.

Valerian had never liked Penshard. That he had somehow wormed his way into Abigail Smart's good graces just made him more irritating.

"Fool," Valerian said scathingly. "What the devil do you think—"

But Penshard strode from the room as if Valerian weren't there. The shock at being ignored once again turned into something much closer to unease.

How had he entered the room without using the door anyway? He turned and stared at the wall behind him. It connected to the ballroom, from where he'd just come.

He put a tentative hand against the wall and felt it give way. He stumbled through to the other side.

For everything that was holy and wise . . . he stared into the crowded ballroom as a man passed right through him.

"I say, Norton, damn breezy in here," the man said to his companion as they maneuvered the edge of the crowd.

Valerian stared at his fingers, then at the rest of his body. A sharp look verified that everyone else seemed quite capable of touching each other—couples embraced on the dance floor, a flirtatious tap with a fan, a warm shake of a hand.

He . . . he was the odd one. He wasn't . . . real.

The orchestra played a cacophony of notes and jarring chords, the high-pitched cackles of the matrons, silly giggles and whimpers of the girls, the crowing of the men—Valerian lifted his hands to his ears, only slightly reassured that he could touch himself.

What had happened to him? He tried vainly to remember, but events and memories started to slip and whirl faster, flowing into a miasmic whirlpool, sucking him in, drowning conscious thought in the rushing tide.

He frantically tried to grasp hold of the important ones, his eyes desperately searching for an escape.

And that's when they met a brilliant blue pair watching him from across the crowded room.

Abigail watched in shock as Rainewood appeared suddenly, completely out of sorts, on the other side of the ballroom.

And was he wearing the same clothing from two nights past? Yes, definitely. When it came to Rainewood, her memory was chisel-sharp.

Where had he popped in from? A forty-eight-hour binge of women and alcohol, no doubt.

His eyes caught hers and held *much* too long. There was something primal and unfocused in his dark eyes. Then he started toward her. Her thoughts straightened and her attention strengthened as she prepared for war. He never approached her in full view of the ton, save for the incident two days past. Why would he now be heading her way as if hell-bent on a personal vendetta? Had she finally pushed him over the edge?

She paused suddenly as her mother's face caught in her periphery. No matter what his desire, Rainewood wouldn't taunt her in front of the elders, not even her social-climbing mother.

She took a deep breath, ready to face whatever it was head on, as she watched his tall broad-shouldered frame advance through the ballroom, the careless gleam in his eyes gone for once, his usually perfectly groomed hair messy and rakish.

He was advancing on her with remarkable speed, the usual path that flowed around him even more accommodating. And then suddenly, she watched one of the matrons pass *right through* him.

Her heart stopped beating.

"Miss Smart?"

Dear God.

She shook her head to clear it. Surely she had been mistaken . . .

Rainewood passed through two men without breaking stride, without a single pause. His eyes glittered and her hand rose without direct consent to her lips.

"Miss Smart?"

Panic licked her spine and she jerked her eyes from the terrible sight to concentrate on Mr. Farnswourth. "Yes, Mr. Farnswourth?" She wiped suddenly moist and clammy hands on her dress and tried to catch her breath.

"I say, are you well?"

Her mother was looking at her sharply and Abigail pasted on a smile—the hundredth such time she had done so tonight—but much, much more strained than ever before. She tried to ignore the man, *ghost*, *oh god*, striding her way. "I am, thank you. You were saying a—. About the musicale next week?"

Dead, dead, dead. The word continued on an infinite loop. Speculation about where he had been for the past two days froze, cracked, then shattered in her head. Surely she had been mistaken. Valerian—no, *Rainewood*, she corrected—wasn't dead. She had seen something, somebody, *anything*, else.

She refused to turn her head to look again. To confirm the bone-deep certainty that she would never mistake Rainewood for anyone else.

"Oh, yes, jolly good time it should be," Mr. Farnswourth said. "My cousin is quite proficient at the pianoforte. I would most enjoy—"

"You can see me." That familiar silky, deep, masculine voice said at her elbow. Her eyes tightened. Nothing there, no one there. A figment of her imagination. She would not look.

"—if you would join me," Mr. Farnswourth finished.

A tall, darkly dressed man moved into her vision. Stood before her, dark eyes piercing. "You can see me," he repeated forcefully.

Her lips parted and her brain froze. Rainewood was standing there, caught in the circle of the surrounding bodies; he had just spoken, and *no one had noticed*. She closed her eyes and inhaled a shaky breath, then took another.

A tingle brushed down her arm in a parody of his usual taunting touch, and a profound shiver followed in its wake. Not the usual maddening shiver he produced in her, but one equally as unnerving.

She hesitated a second too long over the feeling. She had to pull her thoughts together.

If she ignored the situation, maybe she would wake to find it the day after the Malcolm's fete and nothing out of the ordinary. "Mr. Farnswourth, that would be superb."

"Most excellent. I was just saying to Father the other day, Father, don't you think we should—"

Rainewood circled her. "Talk to *me*, Smart," the commanding, sensual voice said against her ear. "I know the look in a woman's eye when she has noticed me, I know the look in *your* eye when you've seen me, and you possessed just such a gaze."

She shivered again, but not from a touch this time. She sneaked a quick look to her right, and her eyes met shocked dark golden brown.

"You *can* see me. And you can hear me." His voice darkened and intensified. Repeated tingles ran through her as he tried to connect his hand to her body. "What madness is this? What have you wrought against me? Why can't I touch you? Why can't I touch anyone?"

Unable to stand the stirrings of panic in his voice, she glanced away, her eyes moving toward the couple copulating in the corner. Her color automatically rose.

"I did nothing," she blurted, flustered. "And it's not possible. The laws prohibit it."

"That is exactly what I said!" She jolted to see Mr. Farnswourth nodding eagerly at her response. Sheer dumb luck had her answer to Rainewood in agreement with whatever Mr. Farnswourth had said.

Luckily her mother was chatting with another lady in their carved-out space and was not paying attention. If she had been, her mother would *know* her infirmity was back. Not that it had ever disappeared, no matter what Abigail had pleaded and assured them of. Her mother would know. She'd call Dr. Myers to sort her out again.

Everything in Abigail shuddered, and she tried to block Rainewood from view.

"It isn't against the law to touch someone," he said. "And no one else can see me. I'm invisible. Why can *you* see me?"

At any other time she might have responded with something along the lines of how he deserved to be invisible for once, but she was too numb. First, that he was dead. Secondly, that he even remembered her postmortem. Spirits almost *never* took notice of anyone who didn't directly affect their environment.

Unless . . . unless he was like . . . Lightning ran down her spine and she smothered the thought. Only two spirits had reacted similarly to her and both situations had ended badly.

She tried to concentrate on Mr. Farnswourth, a proper beau, one who would make her mother proud. A man with whom she could have a nice, unfettered life, free from the threats of being sent away, and freed from desires that could never be.

"Why don't the counselors see it, do you suppose?" Mr. Farnsworth asked, completely oblivious to her distress.

"Tell me why I can't touch you or anything else, Smart. Answer me." A ghostly hand traveled over the bare flesh of her arm, making every hair stand at attention. "Why are you the only one who can see and hear me?" Rainewood demanded.

If there was one thing she knew about Valerian Danforth, now Lord Rainewood, it seemed even in death, he would stubbornly try to beat her down until she admitted defeat. She tried to answer him while not cluing Mr. Farnswourth into the fact that she was two pence shy of a full pound. "It—it is a consequence of living, I'm afraid. That we are made to see that which is for mortal eyes alone. And those outside of the system often do not have the same advantages."

"Living? What the devil do you mean?" Rainewood's voice lowered and took on a much deadlier tone.

"The judicial system is in place for a reason, Miss Smart," Mr. Farnsworth said cautiously, as if she were sane and answering him instead of speaking to a dead man at their side.

"Yes, but that hardly helps when one dies." She looked directly at Rainewood.

His face froze. "Dead? I'm not dead. This is just a bizarre dream."

"That is quite morbid, Miss Smart," Mr. Farnswourth said, sounding slightly unnerved. "But I take your meaning. The good minister said just the other day—"

She let Mr. Farnsworth natter on while she carefully observed the changing expressions on Rainewood's face.

"Never," he said dismissively, though his jaw moved as if it took effort to do so. "This is more of your hokey talk."

She bit her lip and shook her head woodenly.

Anger suffused his face. Rainewood channeled all feelings he couldn't deal with into anger—he always had. "Stop this. Whatever this is. You are mad."

She swallowed around the stone columns of her throat. It was as if the hurt would never heal. She heard the echo of a long summer past—*You are mad. Never speak to me again.*

She nodded tightly and concentrated on Mr. Farnsworth. Perhaps if she concentrated hard enough, she would wake up to a more pleasant day.

Mr. Farnsworth's lips moved as he actively nodded along with whatever he was saying. A life with Mr. Farnswourth—or Mr. Sourting. Thirty long years of comfort and sweet boredom. She could run a home of her own. Start fresh with servants who didn't think she was eleven shy of a dozen.

She could evade the constant threat of being sent *there*.

Her mother would be pleased. Perhaps she would even embrace her at the wedding. She could banish all of her abnormal qualities with a fresh start.

All in all, Farnsworth was a decent prospect,

not too high on the instep, no one with whom she could taunt Rainewood . . . she briefly shut her eyes against the thought of him . . . but a solid husband, and she should be cultivating the opportunity of his suit instead of—

"This is ridiculous. You will tell me how to get out of this nightmare," the dark voice said, now with a hint of a bitter whiskey. "Come with me. Now."

—instead of thinking of a man who had ridiculed and crushed her and was now far beyond her help.

"No."

"Pardon me?" Mr. Farnswourth gave her a quizzical glance.

She smiled as brightly as her turmoil would allow. "Would you care to take a walk around the room, Mr. Farnswourth?"

He puffed out his chest. "Of course, Miss Smart." He held out an arm and she gratefully took it, keeping her gaze away from Rainewood.

She kept her fingers loose on his sleeve, fighting the instincts that screamed for skin-to-skin contact, especially now in the face of Rainewood's demise.

Although the balls and routs and endless gatherings were tiresome in their consistency, she always had a chance to dance with men on the lower end of the social scale. She could brush by people in the crowd. She could accept the hand of someone new to meet. There was always a chance for physical contact when she went out. It was the only thing that kept her involved in the marriage game.

Mr. Farnswourth maintained a steady dialogue that allowed her to nod continuously while keeping contact with his sleeve.

Rainewood shadowed them, striding through people apace, leaving people shaking and shivering in his wake.

"Come with me, Smart." That horribly demanding voice was closer, more insistent, just behind her ear, the tenor of it raising the hairs at her neck and sending shivers down her spine. Shivers changed in substance, but that had been ever present companions around him since she had turned thirteen. Since everything had changed.

Anger suffused her from multiple directions—Rainewood's behavior, past and present, and her own.

"For years you have ridiculed me about this exact type of behavior you are demanding," she said as quietly and scathingly as she could from the side of her mouth while Farnswourth nattered on, oblivious. "Deal with this on your own."

Valerian fumed as he watched her take another turn about the room, then two. He had always known that she liked to walk with people and touch them. He had used the knowledge too often against her. Just the feel of her skin beneath his fingers, always shivering a bit, as she visibly fought with herself to lean in for more, made him hard. Made him irritated with anyone seeking the same. Made him angry at his own reactions.

He tried speaking to everyone he knew in the room. He tried Abigail's friends, thinking that

perhaps they were in on the secret. He even tried
Penshard—surely the man would smile evilly if he
knew.

Nothing.

It was as if . . . as if what she had begged him
to understand years ago had merit. No. Never.
That would mean he had been wrong. It wasn't
possible.

Ghosts. He wiped the thought away. He'd never
believed her. Had used her words to taunt her, to
hide the past hurt. He wouldn't believe her now.

A movement of blue caught his attention. He was
so used to keeping an eye out for her, that it was
nearly second nature. She moved away from her
new beaus. Finally. If only he was able to interact
with the others in the ballroom. The hell he would
generate for her attendance to those two . . .

Piled dark hair atop a blue dress—he'd know
that neck anywhere—followed an even shorter,
more energetic form to the door.

To the *door*?

An emotion that felt uncomfortably close to
panic washed through him. Abigail was leaving.
His only source of information and sanity was
walking right out the door.

He bounded after her as she crossed the threshold. He tried to skirt around bodies at first, then
closed his eyes, gave up the notion that he had to
skirt around others, and strode through the throng.
Through Aidan Campbell, Mr. Farnsworth, Celeste
Malcolm. Through anyone who crossed his path.

Just a nightmare. A simple nightmare. As soon
as he caught Abigail Smart, he'd wake up. He was
sure of it.

He made it to the door just as the footman opened it again—and smacked right into something solid. The solid feel of hitting something sent a thrill through him. Perhaps he was already waking. But no, people continued to pass through him, and he could not follow in their wake.

He reached out a hand to the open space between the door and its frame on the other side. Solid air. He swallowed. Rainewoods didn't panic. He pushed against the barrier. Nothing. It was as if something was seeking to keep him trapped inside.

More guests passed through him, and he gave an involuntary shiver at the disquieting thought of it all. He looked up in time to see Abigail enter a carriage in the drive. He needed to be in that carriage.

He backed up and ran toward the door. A shock reverberated through him as he bounced back. How that could be so, he didn't know, since he was otherwise not even physically present.

The carriage started to roll down the drive.

He pushed against the barrier with all his might and thought of blue eyes and shining chestnut hair. More than anything he needed her to tell him what was happening. More than anything he knew that she was his link to the truth. More than anything he wanted to be in the carriage with her.

And all of a sudden he was.

Chapter 4

"Continue to encourage Mr. Farnsworth," Mrs. Browning said in her usual bossy fashion. "Mr. Sourting as well. Given favorable circumstances and due diligence, you will be married by the end of the season. Both are solid choices."

"And that nice Mr. Brockwell," her mother said.

"Mr. Brockwell is also acceptable. But Mr. Penshard . . ." Mrs. Browning frowned. "You have encouraged him. A more radical type of man. You'd do well to choose one of the others."

"Mr. Penshard is not radical."

"I think I have more notion of men's characters, especially those on the mart, than you do." Mrs. Browning raised a brow. "Heed my words. We want someone pliable."

Abigail wasn't sure why she—*they*—wanted someone pliable, but since her hire, Mrs. Browning had always insisted on that as the foremost quality in a suitor.

"We should take Mrs. Browning's advice, Abigail," her mother said. "You have a finite window to make a match."

"And you can't be too finicky," Mrs. Browning added, giving her a once-over that clearly stated that she was found lacking.

"Oh, no, finicky is not good. Your father used to say—"

Abigail nodded absently at her mother and Mrs. Browning. Abigail was too used to the words and dire glances to really register them. Mrs. Browning had come highly recommended, and she had fulfilled her reputation so far, so Abigail tried not to let the woman upset her. After a while, all the jibes started to blend together in a sort of unending diatribe. And she had more important thoughts on her mind.

"And your hair," her mother tsked, bringing Abigail's attention back. "It just *hangs* by the end of the evening. That maid of yours needs to secure the pins more tightly. It is absolutely unconscionable that you look so sloppy."

Mrs. Browning nodded sharply in agreement. Abigail tucked her one loose wisp of hair behind her right ear self-consciously. Not even four dozen strokes of her favorite brush could get it to behave.

The thought of her brush—and its origin— brought pain. She tried to keep it from her face and shoved the emotion deep.

"Mr. Farnswourth was kind enough not to say anything, but I could tell by the way he was looking at you that he noticed," Mrs. Browning said. "A man wants a wife who takes pride in her appearance. He needs a woman who will run his household, his servants, and"—she jammed a finger into the leather seat—"someone upon whom he can depend to uphold the family image and honor. You must project that."

Abigail nodded along. It was always less tiring to do so.

"And you need to stop taking so many turns about the room. It is fine if you are encouraging a specific suitor, but you seem to find an excuse to do so at the most unreasonable of times." Mrs. Browning's brows drew sharply together.

Abigail could hardly justify why she had done so tonight. She sent a surreptitious glance to her mother. Had her mother watched her carefully enough to question her actions? She would be aghast. And more determined then ever to break Abigail of her tactile need.

But her mother simply frowned at nothing, sitting, as usual, as far away from Abigail as the interior of their rented coach allowed. But one knee was tantalizingly close to hers. And the stress of the evening begged for some physical reassurance. If the carriage hit a large rut in the road, they would brush.

At that moment the carriage shuddered slightly, and Abigail overly lurched forward in her seat. She bumped Mrs. Browning's knee instead.

"I say, Miss Smart." She drew herself up and put her knees to the side out of reach. "Have you no more grace than an infant?"

"My apologies, Mrs. Browning."

"I noticed that you displayed some *strange behavior* at the end of the night too." Abigail looked resolutely back, trying to ignore the widening of her mother's eyes to the right of their paid companion. "I thought you understood the consequences of—"

Abigail jumped as Rainewood appeared on top of Mrs. Browning, Mrs. Browning's flapping mouth somewhere near his chin. His face melded with the older woman's in a grotesque fashion so that it looked as if she possessed an extra pair of features.

The mouth superimposed over Mrs. Browning's forehead spoke. "Tell me what is happening."

Abigail felt her lips part. How on earth had he come to be in the carriage?

The lower mouth continued moving with words like consequences, trouble, marriage, and duty.

"Why did I have trouble leaving the house?" The deep voice demanded, too masculine and intimate to come from her strict companion. "What forces am I facing? What are you?"

"Abigail," her mother said sharply. "Are you paying attention to Mrs. Browning?"

"Of course I am, Mother," she said automatically.

Mrs. Browning's eyes were narrowed in the middle of the horrific display of combined features. "And we will need to take advantage of Earl Raine wood's notice of you the other night and the stir it created. Secure the affections of a few other well-chosen men, before he has a chance to retract the attention."

"Ha. You *do* have something to do with this, I knew it," he said, Mrs. Browning's forehead grotesquely delivering the scathing indictment, a male hand reaching out from her body to point accusingly at her.

"I didn't have anything to do with it!" Both sets of lips on Mrs. Browning separated in shock.

But for the clicks of the wheels on the cobblestones outside, the carriage grew silent.

Abigail swallowed. "With Lord Rainewood's notice, I mean."

"Abigail dear—" Her mother's volume was soft and soothing, but her tone was unnerved and scared.

"No." Abigail rubbed her forehead and focused on her lap, unable to watch the strange spectacle across from her, unable to believe what she had almost said. "I have the headache, Mother, please. I can barely think straight as you can see. Can we discuss this in the morning? I apologize for any odd behavior, but the megrim came upon me so quickly at the end of the night, that it's hard to think."

It was partially true. Rainewood's appearance had given her a headache for sure. And now . . . well, now she just wanted to go to her room and have a good cry.

"Your megrims are becoming more common," Mrs. Browning said tightly, regaining her composure. "Don't think I don't know the trick, Miss Smart, because I assure you that I know them all."

"Yes, Mrs. Browning." She honestly didn't care at this point if her mother or their entrée into society was displeased. As long as they partially bought the story. As long as her mother didn't think to send for *him*. As long as she could convince them she was fine in the morning.

She just wanted to trudge to bed and never awaken.

Rainewood stayed surprisingly quiet as they pulled up to the rented house on Hanover Square. The door opened and with the help of the footman, Abigail exited after Mrs. Browning and her mother. It wasn't until they entered the foyer, that she realized Rainewood wasn't behind them.

She craned her neck to see the carriage rolling down the street, harsh lines from the gas lamps outlining his face in the window.

"I want to see you first thing in the morning," Mrs. Browning announced, handing her shawl to a waiting servant. "We need to prepare for Mr. Sourting's arrival."

Abigail gave one last look at the retreating carriage as it rounded the corner, then turned and jumped in alarm as Rainewood suddenly appeared in front of her.

"Abigail," her mother admonished.

She watched Rainewood for a moment, trying to hold back a hysterical scream. "Yes, Mother. Mrs. Browning. First thing. Good evening to you both."

Mrs. Browning's eyes and lips were pinched, but she turned and retired to the drawing room with Abigail's mother. They would likely go over her many foibles and draw up a new plan of conquest. Mrs. Browning was her mother's ally, though there was always something strained about her face when she looked at Mrs. Gerald Smart. Why Mrs. Browning was harder on Abigail, considering all of her mother's occasional mistakes, she had yet to unravel.

And for all of the time Mrs. Browning, with her eagle eyes and wolf ears, had spent with them in the past few weeks, Abigail was surprised that the woman hadn't guessed their secret.

Abigail straightened her sagging shoulders and headed for the stairs. She would not pout. She would not scream. She would get through this just like she always did.

Great Aunt Effie floated along beside her as she ascended the two flights. "I have tea. Hot and piping. Two lumps. A twist of lemon. So hard to get good lemons in winter."

Abigail nodded, hardly surprised about mythical lemons in wintertime after six years of repetitive conversation and endless winter with Aunt Effie.

"Dolores and Francine are coming by. I have the most scandalous news. Miss Turnbridge is with child, *unmarried*." The elderly woman leaned in. "And, I'm telling you this before I tell them, but the *king* has suffered a *breakdown*." Her hand went to her mouth.

Abigail closed her eyes for a moment, then opened the door to her room. Effie floated through the wall on her right.

"Aren't you the least bit shocked? I say!" Effie went off to a huff in her corner.

After a daily dose of the same thirty-year-old bits of gossip it was not as much of a shock anymore. Some days Abigail played along—most often during especially trying days with her mother or Rainewood, when any social contact was appreciated.

But tonight she couldn't participate, and she couldn't even work up the guilt. She threw her reticule down on the coverlet. Effie would be back with the same gossip tomorrow and wouldn't remember a thing about tonight's brush off. A blessing, if she was in poor spirits like tonight. A curse in any other imaginable way she could think of.

She shut her eyes again.

"Are you going to speak to me *now*?"

She opened one eye to see Rainewood leaning against the doorframe, one brow lazily cocked, but the edges of his body thrummed in agitation. She fell backward onto the bed in one ungraceful thump. She'd regret the position in a second, but for the moment she was just too exhausted.

"You aren't really here. I'm having a nightmare. Go away."

There was no pressure on the bed, but she looked up to see him looming over her, one hand and then the other falling to either side of her shoulders in a thoroughly dominant position. Her heartbeat increased as she recognized the posture from any number of ghostly liaisons she had observed. Were he physically present and able to touch her, she would be in deep trouble. All he would have to do would be to lean down and kiss her, to connect them below and claim her.

He shifted the intimate position and leaned on his side so that he was lying alongside her on the bed. One hand propped up his head as he watched her. She had a feeling that, spirit or not, he had seen her reaction.

He always did. He never ceased to use those weapons against her.

She took a deep breath, determined not to let Rainewood, a *spirit* of Rainewood no less, get the better of her. "How did you manage to exit Grayton House? Then the carriage?"

His eyes sharpened. "You knew I would have difficulty?"

"All spirits do. There are barriers that keep you inside. A type of haunting, if you will."

"I'm not a spirit." His teeth clenched on the word. "This is merely a dream from which I cannot wake. But you hold the key, I can feel it. I want to wake up now, Smart. Do it." He waved an agitated hand imperiously.

Something vindictively satisfied rushed through her at the notion that soon he would have to accept that she had always been truthful. "No, you are not a spirit. You are a *tenacious* spirit. Though I shouldn't be surprised. You were a bloody ass in life." She passed a hand over her eyelids, closing them. It was unreal. This was no more than a passing dream. How could he be dead, when he was lying next to her on her bed, alert and seemingly in full control of his faculties?

It only made sense that Rainewood wouldn't even *die* properly.

"I'm not a spirit." But there was something off in his tone. A question. A remembrance of a conversation so long ago. "This is a dream. A rather disturbing one, since I'm stuck with you."

The reminder of their present bleeding from the past angered her again and she swiped a hand through his body. "No?" When he didn't respond she waved it around his rib cage. "What are you, then?"

He didn't answer.

She sighed and rubbed a hand along her forehead, the pain there lashing twofold against the sides of her skull.

"One of *those* spirits. You'd just have to be, wouldn't you."

"What are those spirits?" All coaxing had left his voice. She knew he still didn't believe her, but that questioning, that remembrance . . . it was there in the hesitation he never possessed in life.

"Miss Abigail. How was your evening?" Her maid saved her from answering by entering the room, as silent as if she too were incorporeal.

"Pleasant, Telly." She forced a smile over the lie.

"That is good, miss. I look forward to hearing all about it. I have a warm towel for you."

"Thank you, Telly."

Her maid placed the towel on Abigail's forehead and just over the upper half of her eyes so that she could still see. Her fingers only lingered long enough to make sure the placement was secure, skillfully avoiding any contact with her skin. Abigail pretended not to notice and breathed a sigh of relief as the warmth soothed away some of the discomfort and stress.

Telly removed Abigail's slippers and stockings in an efficient fashion.

"While I will have to gouge my eyes out after that peek at your ankles—" Rainewood's gaze traveled downward. "We are not addressing the issue and this is my dream. *Nightmare*. What are the spirits to which you refer?"

She pinched her lips, but answered anyway. "Some spirits have a quest that needs to be solved. Something that must be resolved before they can move on. While others just imprint themselves on the living world instead."

"Do you have a new one, miss?" Telly asked as she brushed her stockings.

"Yes, Telly, a most tenacious spirit that followed inside."

Her maid nodded and put her slippers away. She would never ask unless the information was volunteered.

A dark voice at her ear said, "A most tenacious *man* who will continue to follow you until you help him."

"A cursed man who will rein havoc upon the land, unless I stop him from seeking his vengeance against all who have betrayed him," she said in the most dramatic and hushed tone she could manage.

The expression on Rainewood's face was worth every bit of guilt.

"Then you must stop him, miss." Telly looked all too serious.

"Do not worry, Telly, we will impede his mad plans." She jabbed a closed fist into the air. Rainewood's mouth turned downward, his eyes dark, missing the sparkling mirth they used to contain so long ago. Lost in the past.

She closed her eyes to block the view.

"'Tis a true gift," Telly whispered in the reverent tone that told of her Gypsy roots. It was the only reason Abigail could think of for why the maid hadn't run screaming the first time she had caught Abigail talking to what appeared to be dust mites in the corner. She'd proclaimed that Abigail had her grandmother's sacred gift.

Gift? Abigail shook her head, her headache reviving a notch, and she pushed the towel from her forehead. "Just a questing spirit, Telly. We will be rid of him shortly."

"Over my dead body," he said.

"That is the case now, isn't it?" She rose and walked to her dressing chair, sitting so that she could still watch him. Telly removed the pins from her hair and began to ease a brush through the brown strands.

"I don't see the humor, Smart. And moreover, I'm not dead."

"You are in fact dead, Rainewood." The brush snagged in her hair, prompting a wince that had *nothing* to do with how she felt about her nemesis being dead. He was still sitting on her bed, speaking to her. It was almost as if he wasn't really dead.

Telly murmured a quick apology and began brushing again.

"I don't believe it," he murmured, and she had the feeling that he truly believed he was in a dream for a second, otherwise he would never have used such a soft tone near her. "Something . . . something happened." He screwed his eyes shut, as if he too was pained by a terrible headache. "I . . . I think I'm in danger. I need to wake."

He rose and started pacing soundlessly across the curling ivy rug. She said nothing as he continued to silently pace, his eyes tightening, his hands fisting. The only sound was the gentle swish of the tines brushing through her strands.

Telly set the brush back on the dressing table and Abigail rose.

Rainewood looked up.

"Go out in the hall," she commanded.

He simply lifted a brow. "No."

"I need to prepare for bed. Go haunt someone else for the night."

He flopped down at the edge of the bed and crossed his ankles, hands splayed behind him. "I think I will stay right here. I'll wake soon, and far be it for me to miss the show in my own head."

"Miss?" Telly said, a bit nervously.

She pointed at Rainewood again. "Leave."

"No."

"Yes."

He raised a brow. "Are we going to argue childishly all night?"

"When do we ever do anything but?" She wiped an agitated hand along her skirt.

"Miss?"

Abigail considered her options. She could continue arguing. She could go to another room. She could simply change in front of him. See what his reaction would be.

She shook her head violently. "Absolutely not."

Now both Telly and Rainewood were looking at her as if she'd lost her mind.

Going to another room would generate all sorts of suspicion as to her mental stability. Arguing was their forte, but not something that she cared to do for hours in front of her maid—the one person who knew that she could see ghosts and accepted it. She needed Telly on her side too badly.

Which left . . .

Abigail strode over to the wardrobe door and opened it, stepping behind to hide her mostly from view. "I'm ready."

Rainewood snorted.

Telly looked unsure, but walked over and lifted her dress to position it so she could get to the buttons. The other layers briefly lifted too.

"I can see your ankles, Smart. And a good deal of your legs. Still have knobby knees, I see."

She could feel the sweat tickling her hairline and the heat pool in her face as Telly lifted the outer layer. "Do shut up, Rainewood." At least he couldn't see more.

She was jerked to the side as Telly suddenly yanked the outer layer over Abigail's neck, covering her face and catching her ear. Within the cocoon of the confining material, Abigail quickly tried to yank back—knowing without a doubt that she was completely free of the door's protection. Underthings exposed to Rainewood's gaze.

The garment became further stuck. Abigail shut her eyes as they began a tug of war trying to get her free.

"Telly!"

The layer pulled free and Abigail dove behind the door, but not before she caught a glimpse of dark eyes.

"Forgive me, miss! I am clumsy tonight." Telly's hands anxiously wrung the hem as her face appeared to the side.

Abigail shut her eyes. It was a nightmare. Plainly and simply a nightmare that had invaded her waking hours.

She usually ignored spirits when changing. For they usually ignored her. And after her first episode of watching the spirit of an innkeeper during an overnight in Bristol tup no less than four ghostly women, Abigail's modesty around the dead had never quite been the same.

Really, spirits were a lusty lot. Reliving things they had enjoyed, or wished they had enjoyed, in life.

She swallowed at the memory and told herself firmly that Rainewood was no different. He was not real. Not in the true sense.

But that couldn't stop her from feeling completely naked in his presence as her maid unbuttoned and then stripped one piece of clothing and then another from her in what had to be the longest changing session in history. She never realized how blasted long it took to change. Each button, each tie, each fastening, one layer after another slipping from her and then being handled and put away before Telly moved on to the next.

She had no idea what Rainewood was doing or thinking behind the door. She expected more verbal mocking at the very least. Perhaps he had simply fallen asleep in boredom. If spirits slept. She had never thought to inquire.

But the thought that he might be staring at her nearly unclothed ankles instead . . . staring at any peek of skin around the door . . . staring in a way that meant a man admired a woman . . . She had always wondered what it would be like to see a man look at her in that way.

Not that she needed *Rainewood* to do it.

Something inside her mocked her own stupidity.

Her maid's slow but efficient motions in helping her undress meant that she touched Abigail as little as possible. It was designed that way, for unlike her mother who didn't touch Abigail for specific reasons, her maid couldn't bear to touch someone she felt was too worthy and revered to paw.

Gift? No. Nothing about her life was giftlike.

Finally she was down to her shift. Nearly naked. She hastily grabbed her nightgown from Telly and shrugged into it, getting bunched at her shoulders and hopping to the side just long enough to produce a deep chuckle from the direction of the bed. She righted herself and kept her chin firmly set.

"Miss, would you like some warmed milk after you read?" Telly still looked as if she was pacifying a spooked horse.

"Yes, that would be wonderful."

A bobbed head and softly closed door left her alone with one too attractive dead man and one crazy dead aunt who was still chattering to herself in the corner about the merits of Martin's cha blend versus Gates's hardy leaves.

A quick look at Rainewood showed that he seemed much more relaxed. As if he too continued to think this was some strange dream and had therefore lost his prior urgency.

"Why can I lie on the bed, walk on the floors, yet in Grayton House I fell through walls?" Rainewood poked a finger at the wall. It disappeared through the surface. He quickly pulled it back, then ran a hand over the coverlet.

"The more time you are a ghost, the more you will recognize this reality as your own. You will no longer fall through things unless you mean to. You will feel their"—she waved her hands—"energy, I suppose. Or you will convince yourself that you do. I know not. I know only what I have observed."

"I have always wondered about your imaginings. Since this is my dream, I might as well inquire."

"It's not a dream, Rainewood."

"Mmmmhmmm." Dark eyes observed her beneath his perfect fringe. "So why do you only know what you have observed? Haven't other imaginary dead people told you how your fantasies work?"

"You're an ass, Rainewood." But she said it without heat.

There was a strange calmness to the exchange. They hadn't had a rational conversation in a long time. It spoke to the suspicion that he might truly think the whole thing unreal.

She cocked her head, deciding to keep the keel even. "There are few that interact with me in this way, actually. Usually the spirits are much more self-contained and absorbed." She thought of another spirit who had spoken to her in the way that Rainewood was able, but she held back from saying anything more. It would shatter any peace in the room.

"I think you just complimented me."

"I wouldn't dare."

He pulled a finger along the coverlet and just watched her with his dark eyes.

She hesitated, letting the comfortable silence stretch for a moment more. "I'm going to give you some well-meaning advice." She bit her lip. "Let go."

He raised a brow and his hand. "I'm not holding on."

"No, let go of any belief that you are still alive."

"I have to agree with that erstwhile suitor of

yours—Farnswourth, was it?—quite morbid of you, Smart. I think I prefer to think myself alive, thank you."

"The more you let yourself go, the more your imprint will collect and the happier you will be. Some hang on very tightly if they have left something undone, but they eventually let go and disappear when their mission is complete. Quite happily let go, might I add."

"How lovely for them."

She frowned. "You don't believe me."

"You don't think?"

She balled her fists but gamely continued. "Is there anything that you feel has been left undone?"

He looked into the air and ticked off his fingers. "There is a bill in Parliament, a horse to buy at the derby, and my favorite boots require a shine."

"Amusing."

"I like to think so." He spread his arms. "It is why everyone loves me."

"I think not."

"Oh, Smart, you have been dying for my regard for decades."

"Seeing as I only possess two, I think you overestimate."

"Never." He rose and began poking around her room. "Now, what shall we do until I wake? I will even be pleasant to you for once."

"Lovely." She tapped an annoyed finger and walked to the bed. "Do what you wish. I'm going to sleep."

"You aren't going to try and convince me that I'm really dead?"

"You are really dead."

"Smart, you aren't very entertaining tonight. If I'm dead, then what happened to my body, oh all-knowing one?"

"It's lying somewhere," she said, as she tucked her feet under the covers. "Probably in some brothel."

"I take back the comment on the quality of your entertainment."

But then . . . why wouldn't he be haunting the brothel?

Unease sifted through her. That she could be forever stuck with an imprint of Rainewood unnerved her—especially since if it were true, some of his true being would soon fade away.

"What ails you, Smart?"

"Nothing." But she said it too quickly.

"Tell me."

Those that lingered left an indelible imprint, even if it turned into a false one with time. She shoved the thought away.

"Nothing. Your memories will slip away soon. They will just be a bothersome reminder."

He turned suddenly and pinned her with his eyes. "How did you know my memories were being affected?"

Her breath caught. "They are?"

He stared at her a moment more, then shook his head. "A dream. Of course you would know more than you should."

She pulled the covers into place. "Even dead, you tax my patience."

His eyes narrowed. "Just wait until I discover how to make this dream bend to me, Smart. I will have you unclothed and begging on the floor in front of me."

She thought that he just might be trying to accomplish such a thing too with the way he was concentrating. The image of her on her knees in front of him brought forth scalding cheeks.

"I hardly think you will be thinking of me, Rainewood." She put her chin up. "Soon you will get to enjoy all that you want to remember best. Those memories will arrange themselves to you. Allow you to relive your favorite things." She waved a hand, trying to project ambivalence. "Taunting people, wenching, making others miserable."

"Oh, believe me, Smart." He smiled slowly and slid into a chair, propping up his feet. "If there is one person that I'd haunt after death, it would be you."

Chapter 5

Valerian tapped a soundless finger against the four-poster pole behind his head and stretched his legs on the bed. He watched her sleep—even breaths lifting her chest, then softly falling.

He had never encountered a nightmare that had lasted this long. Or at least, upon waking his dreams had never seemed quite this lengthy or detailed or painful. And there were just too many things that were normal—that weren't out of the ordinary. Why would his brain have conjured up this state?

And whatever cursed state he was in, why were parts of it so dreadfully *dull*? He had been simply sitting, tapping, and watching her sleep for *hours*.

Well, perhaps parts of it hadn't been dull, but he was unused to being idle.

Needing no sleep would have been far more useful before being hit in the head and losing two entire days of life. He grasped the thought before it could sieve away into the dreamscape. He had been attacked. By whom? He gripped and tried to keep hold of the slippery tendril of thought.

Abigail's presence seemed to make his memories

stick, but as soon as she left him or he left her, his thoughts would slowly start to shift and fall like sand sifting through a disengaged lump in the throat of an hourglass.

He had walked around her house for a while after she had fallen asleep, but the need to return to her had plagued him the entire time.

He remembered Templing falling behind him. Remembered pain as he turned to help. Were their bodies lying in a gutter somewhere blissfully unaware? Who had attacked them? Footpads? Or something worse?

And why couldn't he wake?

He soundlessly tapped harder.

A soft sigh fluttered the brim of Abigail's lace nightcap and one naked finger curled around the equally girlish coverlet—not a style that he would have associated with her. Another queer invention that he had dreamed up obviously.

There was something rather insulated about the way her four-poster drapes drew together in a protective embrace. The rest of her furniture was rather cold and stark, but the bed presented a cocooned safe haven.

He had never thought her to have girlish tendencies. She usually eschewed pinks and other pastels unless they were at the height of fashion—something even Abigail Smart could not deny.

But here in her cocoon, a strangely softer side was on display. Not the girl who climbed trees or raced the boys. Nor the woman who shredded foes with her sharp tongue. In repose she was all feminine and demure. He narrowed his eyes, recalling her in her state of undress last night—or at least the last night in his dream—smooth, silky skin, teasing breasts pressed against her shift, narrow waist, and long, slim legs. He found this new side fascinating. Good thing it was all in his head. As it was, long ago he had made a pact with himself to cease thinking of her in such terms.

The gray beams of early morning illuminated the cracks between the fabric panels. He concentrated on making his finger tap an audible sound against the four-poster pole. Nothing.

She had said he needed to accept this reality as his own. He could do that. It was his reality *for now*. Not permanently. A grim thought. And of everything his mind could conjure, having Abigail Smart as his dream guide seemed insanely normal. His brain would completely trick him like that.

Tap. Nothing. *This was his reality.* He concentrated. Tap. A small ping of sound emerged and he smiled. Tap, tap, tap.

"I didn't think it was possible for you to make an even more annoying spirit." She groaned and turned over, her cap going askew in a rather endearing manner, her hair tousled. There had always been something rather fey and fetching about her despite the thorns. The kind of a damsel that men, who were far more chivalrous than he, loved to save.

He tapped harder.

She groaned again and buried her head into her pillow. "Can't you haunt someone else?"

"No. You are by far at the top of my list."

"You are such a cur."

"Did you know you curl your lip in a brainless way when you blow the hair from your face?"

He took her silence as assent instead of the sleep-addled fog that was more likely. "Besides, I need your help. I want out of this dream and you seem to be able to trick my mind into doing what you want."

The idea of requiring her assistance irritated him and he gave the poster pole a bang with his fist instead. The resounding thwack was darkly pleasing.

She startled, her cap falling to the side where it drooped disconsolately, then struggled upright with one hand behind her, and clutched the sheet to her chin. "You are still here."

He gave her a patronizing look. "Obviously."

"And you remember me."

"Hard to forget." He frowned.

She chewed her lip. "Surprising."

"You are surprised that I remember you?" He raised a brow. "While I find you irritating, that is not a characteristic that would lead me to forget you."

"I thought it some mad dream." She played with the lace at the edge of the clutched coverlet, obviously paying his words no mind. He frowned again.

"It is. And you fell right to sleep without a second thought for my well-being. I am sure that requires no interpretation."

But that wasn't true. He knew she had stayed awake long after crawling under the covers, ignoring him. Had heard small, uneven breaths from behind the drapes and wondered at them as he'd paced around the room trying to wake from his nightmare.

And the darkened circles under her eyes spoke to the way she had tossed and turned until he had settled on her bed to watch her and brood. She'd fallen into a deep sleep then.

"I can't believe it."

"Me neither. I can't recall a nightmare more dull than sitting for hours with nothing to do."

Watching her lips curl as she dreamed. Hearing her soft breaths. Thinking about things better left to the past.

Nothing good could come of an admission that she had been truthful so long ago. Not only would it mean he had made a major mistake, it would also mean he really *was* dead.

"Is it leftover spark? Or *are* you on a quest?" She looked at him, examining him from his feet stretched out near her seated hips to his head propped against the pole. "What quest though?"

"To wake up again and have this all be an unfortunate nightmare." He gave her a dark look, which she ignored.

"How are your thoughts? Your memories?"

He watched her for a second, unnerved by the question. "My memory is . . . hazy," he reluctantly admitted.

"As I said last night, it should become easier to forget."

His hands turned cold. "Forgetting should *not* be easier!"

"Soon you will forget even me," she said, a falsely bright smile on her face.

"That's not possible. I simply need to wake from this madness. But even in a dream, who watches

someone else sleep for that long?" he asked somewhat absently.

Abigail inhaled sharply. The admission caused a
strange feeling to surge inside her.

"The tea is hot and the scones are perfect," a
fluttering voice said from the corner of the room.
"Come have a sip and let me tell you about
Mabel."

"Yes, Aunt Effie," Abigail said automatically, as
Effie would chatter about Mabel no matter what
response she gave. Abigail was too concerned with
watching Rainewood—*who was lounging on her
bed*.

Rainewood frowned. "What?"

"I was just answering."

"I didn't ask you anything."

"I wasn't answering you."

He stared at her. "Who were you answering?"

"Great Aunt Effie." She pulled back the hang-
ing and pointed to the bright tea set in the corner.
When he continued to look blank she stared back.
"You mean you can't see her?"

He looked to the corner, his expression uneasy.

She peered at him, trying to decipher this new
puzzle as the morning shadows filtered through
the slits in the bed hangings and flickered across
his face. "I thought you would be able to see the
others, since you are in my reality."

The two spirits from her past who had been
somewhat like Rainewood had seen the others.

"This isn't your reality, it's mine. And there's no
one there," he said tightly.

She blinked and looked at Aunt Effie who hoisted her tea cup and continued to chatter.

"There's no one there, Smart," he repeated, his voice dark.

She didn't like the implications in his tone. She gave him a pointed look. "Were I to question Telly, she would say there is no one else on the bed either."

He watched her for a long moment, his face unreadable. "I can't wake."

She held his eyes for an equally long moment. "I know."

"I'm not *dead* though. I'm in danger of some kind. I need to wake."

She didn't know how to respond.

"I'm not dead. This is a dream. You lied."

She knew he wasn't referring to anything said the previous night. She stiffened at the dart to the past.

"I remember leaving a hell and being attacked. Perhaps if I go there, it will cause me to wake."

Really, the term donkey had been too kind.

He looked her in the eye. "Perhaps if I go there, it will cause me to wake."

"Then go," she said woodenly.

He looked back at Effie's corner, the edges of his mouth tight. "Don't you want to accompany me?"

"Heavens no. Why would I, a liar like me? And even if I wanted to, as a *lady* I could hardly do so, as you so often remind—*reminded*—me." The thing with darts was that they could always be thrown back.

Dark eyes pierced her. "Well, now things are different. Get dressed so we can go."

"No."

"Why?"

"Because I don't follow orders from you." She punched her pillow, making it more comfortable behind her back. "And ladies don't walk or drive around the parts of town you frequent. *Frequented*."

"That wouldn't stop you. You are pretending to possess far too much sense."

"And you are far too ready to ruin my reputation. As usual."

His face changed from irritation to dark amusement. "I don't think that is physically possible at the moment." He leaned forward and brushed a tingling finger through her arm. "Why can't I touch you? It's my dream—or nightmare—I should be able to ravish you."

She stared at him, the tingles and words leaving her heart still.

"If I *chose*," he said narrowly, obviously reading something in her face. What sort of dark cloud had she been born beneath to have this man toy with her endlessly, even in death.

She sat still, clutching the covers, unable to answer.

He looked away. "Fine. You need to come because I can't seem to leave the house without you."

She continued to stare at him.

"I tried last night." He picked at the coverlet, his fingers going through the cloth. "Nothing I did worked."

"Well," she threw back the covers. "That sounds more in the vein of what other spirits say and what

you always said as well. Self-indulgent ass." The
sudden fury pressed up her throat. But why should
she get upset at what always just was?

"I—"

She ignored him and yanked the cord for Telly.
"Don't trouble yourself with a response. I understand perfectly. But I'm not going to a gaming hell,
so you'll have to discover a way to attach yourself
to someone else."

Telly bustled in. As she changed behind the
wardrobe door and readied for the day, Abigail
tried to pretend it was just Telly and Effie in the
room with her.

She left Rainewood stewing on the bed and
ate the breakfast Telly had brought while trying
to concentrate on planning how to make the best
impression on Mr. Sourting. Luckily it didn't
take too much thought. If there was one thing
spirits had taught her, it was how to listen and
ask questions. People liked to hear themselves
talk.

She touched the waist of her dress. It would be
nice to have someone listen to her for a change.
Truly listen. Telly tried, but the separation between
them socially and the worship that Telly insisted
upon made it difficult, and in the end there was
little difference between talking to someone who
would never dare argue as to talking with someone
who didn't care to reply.

Mrs. Browning interrupted her increasingly
sulky thoughts, striding into the room precisely
fifteen minutes before their appointment with Mr.
Sourting. Her mother breezed in behind the starchy
woman. Hands on hips, Mrs. Browning inspected

Abigail shrugged. The routine was standard. Mrs. Browning always found something wrong. She'd learned to live with it—from her mother as well—and retreat into her own world when it became too hurtful. "She is not so terrible. She does secure the best invitations."

Her mother had somehow found the woman and engaged her services at the beginning of the season. Many times Abigail regarded their money more as a curse than a blessing. It had gotten them into this situation, given her mother ideas and plans. Opportunity.

He stared at her. "And?"

"And nothing. You are hardly unaware that the correct invitations are everything."

"Remove her."

She perched on her dressing seat, suddenly finding the whole situation absurd. "Remove her? And do what exactly afterward? I have no clout of my own and few prospects, in case you haven't noticed. Which I know you have." She crossed her arms.

He shrugged and continued his infernal tapping against the dressing table—sound that only those who were the most sensitive would be able to hear. "So? Banish her from my dream. Tell everyone to go to hell. I would expect it of you. Go see the world. Make your fortune or spend time chasing dreams—fantasies." There was a dark look in his eye, as if his own suggestion irritated him.

Dreams? Her eyes pinched. "Tour the continent and beyond with no clothes, no money, no protection? A woman alone?"

He stopped tapping for a second. He cocked his

head and a strange expression crossed his face, as if he was seeing her for the first time.

"Yes? You were saying?" she asked sarcastically, unnerved by his changing gaze.

He started tapping again. "You could dress like a boy. Get work and go adventuring. Not be a woman on your own."

She closed her eyes. "How enlightening. I see that you have a plan for my complete destruction well in hand." A sigh worked its way up from deep within her chest. "You are a penance of some sort, aren't you? I finally proved them right and did something unforgivable and was saddled with you."

"That is hardly charitable, Smart."

"I feel little need to be charitable to you, Rainewood, even in death." She felt a twinge at saying that, but refused to linger on the feeling. She looked at the mantel clock. "I must meet Mr. Sourting. The requisite time has passed since he entered."

"Let us go then and see what witty conversation Mr. Sourting brings to my head."

She held out a hand. "No. You stay here."

"I want to see how you deal with your lackluster suitor."

"Lovely. No."

He raised a brow and she interpreted all of the ways in which he was going to ruin her chances. Her day. Her life.

"If you stay here, perhaps we can work on your quest later," she said, dangling a carrot.

"I would rather work on it now."

"Then stay here and think about it."

"No."

"Why?"

"Because I want to know what you are up to, and what I need to do to ruin it, so you will do my bidding instead."

She simply stared at him slack-jawed for a moment. "I never need worry that you will hide your selfish motivations behind coy assertions."

"Thank you."

"That was hardly a compliment."

"I think you just called me honest. From you that is about the best compliment I am likely to receive."

Her patience was eroding as fast as the morning shadows were giving way to the hot rising sun.

"Stay. Here."

"No." He proceeded to stick a hand through the wall. "And furthermore, I'd like to know how you are going to contain me? This *death* thing, as you deem it, has advantages."

She gripped her fingers into tight fists. Why did she always feel she lost when it came to him? "I won't help you, if you continue to be such an ass."

"I'll just haunt you forever, then." He seemed quite pleased with himself, despite the note of unease running beneath.

She knew with everything in her that he would do exactly that. A lifetime of Rainewood at her elbow, incorporeal and irritating. Driving her to Bedlam. Or someplace even worse.

She swallowed. "I can't speak to you while I'm with someone else. People eventually notice the oddity."

Something flashed through his eyes, but then he smiled broadly. "Then perhaps you should cancel the appointment."

"No." She rubbed a hand under her elbow. "Come along, then. I can't stop you."

He gave her a dark, weighted look. "I will say nothing . . . *if* you take me to the east side afterward."

"No."

"But—"

"Absolutely not!"

"Then I won't stay quiet." He started humming loudly, looking quite pleased with himself as he leaned back against the wall. He only slipped through the wood an inch before regaining his insouciant position.

"Miss?" Telly's head appeared around the door. "Your mother is becoming agitated."

"I'll be right there, Telly."

"Yes, Miss." She disappeared.

Her mother. She'd *know*.

"You must be quiet, Rainewood." Abigail looked away. "If I slip and talk to you . . . they'll lock me up." She bit her lip. "I do not say that in jest. You of all people should know what the reaction would be."

She remained facing away from him, not wanting to hear the echo of his thoughts that she deserved to be locked up. The silence stretched further than the shadows on the mantel.

"We will see how things go."

His tone was unreadable. Abigail nodded. It was a better response than she thought he would give. She smoothed her dress and gave the escaped wisp on her forehead one last tuck before striding from the room and down the stairs to face her fate.

Mr. Sourting rose upon seeing her. "Miss Smart, you are looking well." There was obvious relief in his voice, and she wondered how such a man would deal with having a woman like Mrs. Gerald Smart in his life. It looked as if her mother had been sweetly grilling him in Abigail's absence with the help of Mrs. Browning.

"Thank you, Mr. Sourting." Abigail nodded and perched on the edge of the seat nearest him, watching Rainewood settle into a lazy position against the wall. "How are you this morning?"

"Rather well." He retook his seat. "We were just discussing the weather. A nice time for a walk through the park."

She inclined her head, waiting for the cue from her mother as to whether to accept or politely decline. Accepting would provide an opportunity to get out of the house and away from Rainewood.

"Abigail would be delighted to walk tomorrow, Mr. Sourting. We have a rather full schedule today, unfortunately. Mr. Farnsworth already asked for her accompaniment in the park for this evening's ride." Ah, so that was her mother's game. A little competition to up the stakes. "However, if you are free on the morrow . . . ?"

"Yes, of course." He pulled himself upright. "I would be honored to walk with Miss Smart in the park tomorrow."

There were a number of volleys that had just been lobbed. Mr. Farnsworth was in possession of an open carriage for a tour around the park—a decided bonus in the marriage hunt. Mr. Sourting would have to bring himself up to scratch to compete. But there was enough hope with her mother's phrasing to make him rise to the bait—which he had.

"You can't tell me you want this namby ponce courting you? My God, I think he is even worse in my dream than in reality." Rainewood's low voice issued from the wall.

Abigail kept her smile in place and her eyes fixed firmly on Mr. Sourting. He would make a steadfast, respectable husband. His uninspired responses, his matte brown hair and watery eyes— were they blue, green, gray?—weren't things on which to refuse a suit.

Steadfast, respectable, kind. Those were the qualities that mattered. She had all the excitement she needed in her life from right inside her head.

She watched Rainewood from the corner of her eye as he went to the window and tried unsuccessfully to poke a finger through, the digit bouncing off of an invisible barrier.

"Miss Smart, what did you think of the play the other night?" Mr. Sourting asked. The conversation washed over her, as she automatically took part.

"This is worse than tending a sick horse," Rainewood muttered in disgust. "I thought I had gotten rid of this one a few weeks ago. Why are my thoughts bringing him back up?"

Abigail's mouth dropped. So that was why Mr. Sourting had dropped his suit and then reappeared after Rainewood's disappearance from the circuit.

And quite possibly, that was why *all* of her past mercurial suitors had acted in such ways. Maybe it *hadn't* been her after all.

Her mouth opened and closed a few times, trying to figure out how to respond.

"Easy enough to threaten the man again with your acid tongue though," he continued to mutter. "You display it often enough."

Something in the very thought that she wasn't the sole reason for her suitors' abandonment had her back straightening. And her ire at Rainewood increasing. The man couldn't just ignore her in public or berate her in private, no, he was actively ruining her marriage chances behind the scenes. Or had been.

She curled her hands into fists. He smugly looked back, one brow raised as he played with a button on his expensive evening jacket.

"Why would you want such weak-kneed specimens anyway? I'm doing you a favor really."

He offered similar opinions several more times over the course of the afternoon. He seemed to have no notion or care that he was spilling all sorts of things to her that she had never realized.

At a visit with a potential suitor—"Just like that idiot Banning. Easy to dispatch."

And at an afternoon musicale where the son of the house sat next to her, with Rainewood tweaking him in the head mindlessly—"Desperate. Too in hock to even know what to do should he find money lying on the side of the road. One good threat will do it."

And at the last visit before promenade—"Sister compromised by Campbell, and he didn't have the ballocks to defend her. Weak."

Every time they would have a caller or go on a call, Rainewood would tag along, somehow adhering himself to her as she left and entered each building. By the time she returned to the house, she had only a brief period to collect herself before her appointment with Mr. Farnsworth. Frankly, she was exhausted and she could see Rainewood was beyond irritated. He had taken up pacing across her floor as she laid down for a brief nap. She closed her eyes trying to pretend to sleep—anything to save her sanity from the endless torment of her new *companion*.

"I don't understand you. You don't enjoy any of this. You aren't any good at it either. Bored stiff," he said ungraciously. "And I need you to help me wake."

"This is *my* life. You are dead, not asleep. I'm quite good at conversation, should I wish to be. And right now I'd be willing to help *anyone* other than you."

Her maid's cap peeped around the door. "Miss Smart, Mr. Farnsworth will be here in ten minutes."

She sighed and closed her eyes briefly again, a headache pressing against the edges of her skull. "Thank you, Telly."

"Another damn outing," said a voice that definitely did not belong to her maid. "We'll see how this one holds up. I'm coming along," he said almost defensively.

She gave him a dark look. "As if I could stop you."

He frowned at her weary tone and something inside him twinged, even in his dream state, before he pushed it away. He needed to have her help going to the gaming hell. He felt it—that is where he needed to be. He didn't understand why he couldn't force her to go. Damn nightmare. Even more annoying than the standard fare where his legs wouldn't run or his arms wouldn't move. If she would only go with him, maybe then he could remember what he'd seen and finally awaken.

The memory of what happened lit, then slipped away, right there on the edge of his consciousness, eluding him once more. He whacked his fist on the table with enough force to move it. Of course, it didn't budge.

And he had annoyingly discovered that only Abigail could hear the sounds he tried so hard to make.

If he could find a way to detach himself from her without getting stuck inside something else. . . . He had stayed in her family's carriage during one such trial and been stuck there until her return from the call. He hadn't been able to budge from the carriage and had nearly gone out of his mind with boredom verging on panic that he'd be stuck there for his dream's eternity. He didn't plan to do that again. He didn't understand the boundary situation at all. Abigail had said that she'd seen spirits—*dreamers*, his mind forcefully inserted—wandering the streets. Surely he should be able to do that too?

But as soon as he had tried to separate from Abigail, his thoughts had started to sieve loose again. The waterfall seemed to be there ever ready to catch him in her current and sweep everything that remained of him away.

It was incredibly frustrating.

Then there was the tug. He hadn't said anything to Abigail, not that she would care. But it was like a snag in his jacket caught by a sharp hook. There was something definitely wrong. Well, there were many, many things wrong at the moment, but a creeping sense of dread was upon him. He needed to find out what it was and why, before some rogue monster alighted from under the bed.

As Abigail entered the room, Mr. Farnsworth greeted her like an overly excited puppy panting around her legs. A dozen scathing comments popped into Valerian's head. He had cultivated quite a repertoire when it came to Abigail's suitors—not that she had ever been able to observe or hear them all. And he had done well to make sure that society wasn't any the wiser to his attention.

But when she was away, any suitor was fair, fair game and he had delighted in dispatching most of them.

Fifteen minutes later they were roaming around the park in Mr. Farnsworth's barely adequate carriage and Valerian practiced poking the man between the eyes while Abigail pretended oblivion.

"Isn't the weather just dandy today?" Farnswourth said as he shook the reins with a bit too much gusto, causing the team to lurch forward.

Valerian snorted and gave him another invisible poke—this time with two fingers right in the eyeballs. *Dandy* described a lot of things today.

Abigail continued to ignore him and responded to Mr. Farnswourth instead. She was completely bored by the man, it was obvious in every automatic response she uttered—displaying none of the fire or brimstone that she possessed when fully engaged.

A man walked along the edge of the Serpentine. He looked reflectively into the depths and tossed an acorn. There was something familiar about the man, but he was too far away to recognize.

Valerian would never admit that glasses made everything in the distance clearer. He'd never worn the blasted things, and as a result he had never been able to best Abigail Smart at shooting because of it.

He couldn't believe that even in his dream he was poor-sighted for distance. What a stupid thing.

He looked back at Abigail. Mr. Farnswourth was sitting entirely too close to her and his foot was inching closer to hers still. Valerian narrowed his eyes and instinctively ran a finger down her arm, urging her to move away from the man. To his complete shock she shifted, moving her body an inch away. His mouth parted and he scrambled to sit up from his lazy position. He touched her again, wishing that she would tell the man to move them into the more heavily trafficked lanes.

"Mr. Farnswourth, would you care to show your beautiful carriage in the promenade?"

The idiot man straightened proudly. "Of course, Miss Smart." But Valerian had eyes only for Abigail. Her brows drew together, pinching in thought. He moved his hand away, whistling as all sorts of delicious possibilities presented themselves.

If only he could touch her for real . . .

Abigail frowned. The thought had just popped into her head. Not that she wouldn't have ignored it if she hadn't been getting more bored with the outing. Still . . .

She looked at Rainewood, but he was merely staring out toward the other horsemen. She wondered what he was thinking.

Mr. Farnswourth moved them into the more well-traveled lanes. They made the standard circuit, promenading, then stopped to speak with a number of other carriages, collecting together. Carriages joined for a few minutes, then moved on to other groups, a constant stream of rotating groups. Women showing off their finery, men showing off their companions or horseflesh.

A chill went through her as Rainewood brushed her and she got the urge to walk.

"Mr. Farnswourth, would you like to walk a bit?"

"Of course, Miss Smart."

She could see her mother and Mrs. Browning ahead, gathered in a group on foot that was chatting amiably.

They joined the group a few minutes later and a number of younger people did as well. A man that she didn't know well joined them and gave her an encouraging look. He had always been nervous around her before. Had Rainewood really ruined so many relationships for her? She sent him a dark look. She couldn't seem to send him anything but.

"Miss Smart, so good to see you."

"And you." She nodded to the man, a little surprised by his eagerness.

"Grandfather's taken crazy," Rainewood muttered. "Confirmed on that blasted list. Not enough sane thoughts in that family to rub together and make a quilt."

A chill—from the cold, from his words, and from his touch—rocked through her as his fingers skimmed her arm. "Crazy thoughts seem to be going round though," Rainewood continued muttering. "Ask him if his father has recovered from his recent bout of insanity himself."

The fingers skimmed her arm and her lips moved without her consent. "How is your father? Has he recovered?"

Abigail watched, appalled at the question she had just asked, as the man's eyes widened and he stuttered, "Yes, he is doing much better, thank you."

Standing at their side, observing the interactions, Mrs. Browning's lips parted an inch before pinching tightly. The poor man took off no more than twenty seconds later to parts unknown.

"Miss Smart," Mrs. Browning hissed, under the earshot of the surrounding people. "What was the meaning of that?"

Abigail swallowed, horrified at herself. Rainewood looked smug.

"I had just heard that there was some turmoil in his family and wished to inquire after his father's health."

Mrs. Browning tutted. "Bad form. But obviously there is something there," she said in a fashion as close to mulling as Abigail had ever seen. "Can't have bad stock like that. I must make inquiries."

Abigail turned dark eyes on Rainewood. He shrugged. "She's right."

It took everything in her to bite her tongue and not respond. The evening only went downhill from there.

She excused herself as soon as they returned home. She threw her reticule onto her coverlet. She didn't know whether she wanted to follow the collapse of her article now that the day was over or give in to the ire that had grown to a boil.

She pointed at Rainewood. "You ruined my outing. My evening!"

He snorted. "I did not. I was simply trying to spice them up a bit for you. That man is dreadfully boring. And the others . . ." He waved a hand in disgust.

She poked a finger at him. "I need him. Them."

His face turned unreadable. "Need them? Whatever for? An early death from complete boredom? If I hadn't helped you along you might have succumbed."

The suspicion that had been brewing all evening gelled. "You, you *made* me say those things!"

Rainewood crossed his arms. "And how is that?"

"I would never have said something about that man's father! I don't even know him!"

"But you asked the question, so you must have," he said, a smile working the edges of his mouth. "Unless you are claiming that I have some power over you?"

She sputtered.

"Maybe I can make you do other things while I'm in this state." He reached out fingers and she skirted them wildly, half afraid he was right.

He looked smug again. "I'm figuring out how to control this dream. Excellent. Soon I will have you begging, Abigail." His eyes slid half shut and her fear increased. She feared that was all too true.

"Only if you suffer a complete reversal in personality, Rainewood," she said instead, lifting her chin. "You are hardly someone to whom I will bow."

"Oh, don't be too sure, Smart." He reached across just enough to brush ghostly fingers against her cheek. "So many possibilities in a dream where one can start fresh."

She wished her mind weren't just conjuring up the wistful tone to his voice, but this was Rainewood. He didn't get wistful.

"That is wonderful for you that you can start fresh—be anything you want in your dream state." She laughed bitterly, because she could never start fresh with him on her own terms and because he still viewed himself in a dream from which he would wake. "But I need those men."

Need those men? Over his dead body.

"Need them for what? Target practice?" He examined his fingertips. "You are a veritable ogre. Or are you only rude to the men you *want*?"

Hot red—rage or embarrassment?—suffused her face. "You know, I thought it might have just been me who wanted you dead, but obviously there are others out there too! And you really do, *did*, have that bloody list everyone is talking about. You used it on that poor man today. Made *me* use it against him. If only I could give you a good knock on the head," she said, the color in her face blazing, her chest heaving. "Might put you out flat for a while, and give me some peace!"

The stunned sensation of a missing key fitting into a lock clicked through him. He had no idea what his eyes showed, but he saw her face change from outrage to confusion. The hot color drained to her normal peaches-and-cream complexion. Concern flashed across her face, and she reached out a hand.

Before her hand could make contact, he flickered and was gone.

Chapter 6

His eyes violently ripped open. But the pain of the candlelight two inches from his eyes and the tear of skin and lashes that hadn't been opened for days dwarfed under the agony slashing through his body. Pain tore through him again as something crushed his smallest finger on his left hand. His back arched up and he tried to pull away.

"Awake and fighting," a voice said. "Excellent. It does show some evidence. But can't have you fouling my work yet. Can't have that at all."

His bleary eyes tried to focus on the speaker at his left. Something blocked the sun of the candle, hot liquid poured down his throat choking him, and he knew no more.

Chapter 7

Abigail strode up the stone walk and heavy steps of Grayton House.

"Miss Smart, stop fidgeting with your pelisse. You are the one who made me beg for this invitation. If Henny and I hadn't debuted the same year, it hardly would have been possible. I expect you to be on your *best* behavior. I swear that if you . . ."

Mrs. Browning left the threat undefined as the door opened. The butler greeted them, relieved them of their wraps, and showed them to the tearoom. Abigail glanced around the hall, trying to locate her quarry. The insatiable servant spirits chased each other toward the ballroom, and she could hear the echoes of a bawdy ditty as well as see the frittering motions of an older woman dressed far too young for her age. Reliving her days as an ingénue.

But there was no stupidly handsome man with a cutting smile.

Mrs. Browning gave her a sharp pinch in the side as she passed by Abigail and entered the drawing room first.

Abigail knew she had taken a risk coming here.

She now owed Mrs. Browning multiple unnamed favors that would undoubtedly be painfully repaid. But she'd been unsettled ever since Rainewood had disappeared.

He was gone. Truly gone. He had disappeared from her bedroom two days before. The whispers in the ton concerning his whereabouts and missed invitations had grown to a dull roar, but there wasn't a peep of anything other than speculation and dismay. He was just . . . gone. That fact unsettled her in a way she hadn't come to grips with upon seeing him as a ghost.

What if he . . . what if his spirit had moved on? She tried to convince herself that his passing would be a good thing. She stumbled over the words in her mind. He was out of her life for good. He had achieved peace. He had moved on.

He was out of her life.

Her ears strained more desperately. The house echoed with the sounds of activity, but none of them what she hoped to hear.

"Welcome," the Duchess of Palmbury, their hostess, said as she motioned them into the room. The dowager duchess gave Mrs. Browning a firm embrace on the forearm before they sat. She wasn't nearly as cordial to her mother. Bad luck that the two had met before Mrs. Gerald Smart had perfected some polish.

"It's been nearly a week since I've seen you, Mrs. Browning. I'm so glad you could stop in." The dowager gave Abigail a sidelong glance. "And Miss Smart, how pleasant to see you again."

"Likewise, Your Grace. It is a most favorable occurrence to see you once more."

They exchanged the lies with vapid smiles.

"Undoubtedly." The dowager's pinched lips formed a point. She was a hag of the worst sort.

The woman had disliked her from their first meeting—when she had caught her by the back of the dress running through the kitchens, giggling riotously, sticks in her hair and a muddied duke's son in her wake.

The animosity from that exchange had never disappeared. Had in fact grown worse with every scrape undertaken and new meeting discovered.

Her mother, as usual, was oblivious to the undercurrents. She was leaned forward in her seat, eagerness in every movement and a smile that could light the entire west side of London. Abigail loved her mother dearly, despite their problems, but why couldn't she see . . .

No.

Abigail rubbed the ribbon running through the middle of her skirt between tight fingers. She just needed to secure a husband. Then her mother could have some social security. Maybe then she would settle like a basset hound instead of bob like a chirping westie.

Rainewood's grandmother steered the conversation into increasingly inane topics to which Abigail and her mother continuously failed to submit interesting tidbits. There was a sort of clear victory in their hostess's eyes, as if everything she had ever thought about the Smarts continued to play forth. Abigail could only wish that she hadn't had the insane urge to come here and search for Rainewood.

"Your other charges, Petunia, how are they?" the

dowager asked Mrs. Browning. "I must commend you again on the wonderful matches they made. A viscount for the first, to boot. A complete success all the way around no matter what happens."

Abigail took a sip of her tea, not tasting the liquid. Not needing to see the significant look that was assuredly being passed from their hostess to Mrs. Browning. A look that said even if, *when*, Abigail failed, Mrs. Browning would still be a success. And at least she'd have a much fuller purse for having gone through the trial of the Smarts.

"Yes, Viscountess Berston is a lovely title and match." Mrs. Browning touched her hair with her palm, then took her cup in hand. "Your grandson is quite the catch as well. Too bad that he was away when my niece Violet made her debut."

The dowager inclined her head, tension forming about her eyes at the mention of the missing earl. "Yes, that would have been a splendid match. Violet is such a dear. And already two sons for Mr. Sestner. She would have made a fine duchess. And the fertile nature of the stock is a point in your family's favor."

Abigail coughed violently, her cup sloshing a drop of tea over the side.

The Duchess of Palmbury's pinched features grew more pointed. "But some things, alas, cannot be overcome by—"

"Duchess, Mrs. Browning, Mrs. Smart, Miss Smart. Heston just informed me you had arrived."

Abigail admired the timing of Rainewood's younger brother in absenting himself for five minutes of their fifteen-minute visit. Though it was slightly bad form to appear so late, he was able to stretch protocol with a charmed smile. Not finding much use for protocol herself, she had to respect his escape from the inanity.

She gave him a firm nod with her greeting. One groomed brow rose in acknowledgment. Despite having known each other as children, they usually ignored one another out of the discomfort that arose from her feud with his brother.

He was greeted by the other women in turn and he sat down to make quick small talk for the time they had remaining. Lord Basil Danforth, sickly throughout his youth, had turned his frequent convalescences into extreme cleverness. Seemingly, the time that he had spent abed had allowed him to plot out his own future apart from his domineering father and grandparents.

Because of his illnesses she had never known him well. Instead she had spent her days with the unruly, forgotten middle child who had been abandoned by his father—for the heir—and by his mother—for the sickly second spare.

But now it seemed as if the sick child, who no one had expected to make it through childhood, would have the last laugh.

Basil would do well as the future duke. Affable with pleasant features. The type of man who didn't raise men's hackles, and who was a conversational hit with the ladies. If there was something entirely too calculating behind his eyes, then most seemed not to notice.

Heston, the butler, silently approached the dowager and whispered something in her ear.

"Invite them in, Heston. I'm sure Mrs. Browning will be charmed to speak with Lady Malcolm."

Abigail withheld a wince. That meant that Raine wood's group, or at least part of it, was in the foyer. They often traveled with Lady Malcolm, the mother of Rainewood's rumored betrothed.

Mrs. Browning inclined her head in a neutral manner. A sideways glance warned Abigail against doing anything odd.

She felt Basil's eyes on her as well, but no one said anything as the footsteps clicked through the hall, until Lady Malcolm in all her vibrant rose glory entered the room. "Your Grace." She clasped the dowager's hand. "Forgive our impertinence in calling, but we just couldn't wait."

She handed the dowager a box. "We found these on Bond Street and they are simply too delightful to keep to ourselves."

The dowager opened the box of sweets as the rest of the party filed into the room.

"These are lovely, Lady Malcolm." The dowager gave her a smile—though even her gracious smiles appeared like a barracuda about to devour her next meal.

Celeste Malcolm, Aidan Campbell, and Charles Stagen followed behind. Brows uniformly rose at seeing the Smarts. Celeste Malcolm's eyes narrowed. The gossip concerning Rainewood's interaction with Abigail was still fresh in the rounds.

It took a minute for everyone to exchange terse greetings and be seated. The fifteen shades of purple in the room became even more overwhelming as matched and complimentary chairs were drawn together.

Aidan Campbell's chair was a mite closer to Abigail's than she was comfortable with.

"We were just speaking of the balloon demonstration next week on the green," Charles Stagen said to Basil before addressing the dowager duchess. "Campbell is just mad for them. He has been up in two already. Still trails Rainewood in number of lifts though."

"Solid fun," Campbell said, though his eyes tightened briefly. Worry over his friend? "Just the other day I said to Rainewood, 'Raine, quite a future in the—'"

Her attention keeled as a more commanding presence, and the current topic of conversation, strode through the door. Something in her chest jerked in response and relief. She barely spared a glance to the others who continued the conversation without her.

Rainewood stopped abruptly when he saw her. He looked as if he'd been running, breath heaving in the way that it had when they'd been small—though without the laughter that had always accompanied it. The stray thought that he hadn't learned he didn't have to breathe crossed her mind.

"I thought it was you." Rainewood took a step forward, then another. "I heard you from the study above, but couldn't get here until someone opened the damn door. I couldn't remember what was on the other side and there was a barrier again." The words tumbled out in a fashion completely opposite from his usual controlled drawl. "I thought perhaps I'd dreamed your voice."

Her own breath caught.

"I don't even know how many moons have risen since I last saw your face."

Her heart could have stopped beating in that

moment and she wasn't sure that she would have cared. Not only did he still remember her, something she had been unprepared for, but he was looking at her as if the sun rose only on her express permission.

"My focus only returned when you did." He stepped around a chair.

"Miss Smart?"

She batted away the annoying voice that was attempting to divert her attention. Rainewood continued toward her, more quickly now with forceful steps. "I have barely been able to breathe without you. And here you are."

Her heart vibrated her chest, reminding her that she was still very much alive, and she joined him in his race-worthy furious breathing.

"I could take you in my arms and kiss you senseless right now."

"Yes," she murmured.

"Miss Smart?" The voice retreated further from reality.

He reached for her and she closed her eyes. If only she could convince herself to feel the real touches—to feel the tingles turned into solid caresses.

She nearly dropped her cup when partially solid fingers, warm and firm, and *nearly real*, curled around her wrist. The fingers froze and her eyes tore open to stare into shocked chips of brown. Perfect lips pulled apart and a low breath emerged.

"Miss Smart?" Urgency laced the unwelcome voice. She watched the unmoving lips in front of her wishing it were Rainewood speaking instead.

His hand gently squeezed, calloused warmth caressing the underside of her wrist—not quite there, but not quite *not* there either. A question in the action and a stake of some type of claim. Her lips parted, completely undone by the feeling and intimacy.

"Miss Smart?"

The foreign feeling of intimacy made her nervous and something in her finally responded to the outside demand. She tore her gaze away. "Yes, Lord Basil?"

"I've been calling your name for many moments. You look as if you've been taken by fright."

She gave a nervous laugh. She hadn't truly expected to find Rainewood here, even though she had come expressly to see if he would be present. She definitely hadn't expected that he would recognize her. And to *feel* him . . . what in the heavens . . .

She darted a look around the room, cold settling in her bones that perhaps this was all a trick. To think that Valerian would actually care and would touch her with anything other than manipulation . . .

But she could count on her own mother, in this instance at the very least. And her mother had plastered a friendly smile on her face as she watched with nervousness, awaiting Abigail's answer. No exclamation was forthcoming about the earl's sudden presence. No looks sent in his direction.

Mrs. Browning's eyes reflected the normal shades of disappointment and demand for Abigail to behave properly. The others seemed equally oblivious to what had just occurred. All eyes fixed on her for explanation. Campbell was positioned like he might have been considering reaching over to shake her for good measure.

Rainewood truly was still a ghost. One who could nearly *touch* her.

She grasped for the first thing she could. "I was just admiring your vase there in the corner. The colors are exquisite."

Basil gave a vacantly charming laugh. "Thank you. I believe Great Uncle Alfred Pennyton picked it up in his travels. Tenth-century Ming."

Rainewood's eyes were fixed on her, but he automatically said, "Yuan."

"Yuan?"

She cringed at speaking aloud and looked over just in time to see Basil's eyes sharpen.

"There is a great family debate over that piece straddling the dynasties. How did you know?"

"Oh." She laughed uncomfortably and smiled as brightly as she could manage. "I must have heard it somewhere." Ghostly fingers caressed the underside of her wrist and then moved up to explore the delicate untouched skin of her forearm, making her nearly forget the thread of the conversation and where she was.

"I had nearly forgotten the lovely feel of a woman's skin. And yours is softer than any I've felt before," Rainewood said. "Beautiful."

"Of course," Basil murmured at her explanation.

"Well, we were speaking of the races while you were woolgathering." Celeste Malcolm looked down her pug nose.

"Yes, the next race," Stagen said. "What a lot of good it will do us if Rainewood doesn't show his pretty face." It suddenly seemed quite obvious that everyone was trying to suss out where he was without asking straight out. "Where did he store the filly?"

"Oxting Stables," Rainewood said automatically as he continued to stare at Abigail like she was something rare and precious.

"Oxting Stables?"

It took her a second to register the stunned silence. She looked around in dread to see what she had done this time. The males in particular stared at her with expressions ranging from complete surprise to deep mistrust. She withheld her nervous laugh this time and just pretended that she was in full possession of her faculties.

"I mean, that is where some people store prime cattle, is it not?" She had never even heard of Oxting Stables, so she could only hope that she hadn't said something completely unforgivable— like the name of a house of prostitution. Filly could mean anything if one were to rely on the cant that the younger bucks loved.

Aidan Campbell's eyes were narrowed upon her, a darker light there than she was used to seeing. Charles Stagen just looked considering.

Rainewood stroked her arm again causing her to shiver. She had to remember that he had some strange way to influence her. She put up a blocker in her mind.

Stagen looked at Basil and something passed between them. "Good suggestion, Miss Smart. We will look there indeed."

Basil picked up a small plate. "Biscuit?"

She nodded and accepted the offering, trying to focus on the least unnerving of the room's inhabitants instead of the one *petting* her.

"I haven't met a woman who is so interested in ancient pieces and horseflesh. Perhaps we may discuss it more in the future?" Basil said.

Her mind was too full of his brother and how he could almost fully *touch* her, *was* touching her as he continued to stroke each bit of uncovered territory she possessed, to formulate a mother-approved, appropriate response. "Oh, I'm n—"

"Abigail is interested in many things." Her mother waved an excited hand and smiled. "She would be delighted."

Abigail noted that the Duchess of Palmbury's mouth turned down as she looked toward her youngest grandson. Likely wondering what in the heavens he was thinking to encourage any sort of attention with her.

"Yes, that would be . . . wonderful," Abigail said to Basil.

Something about the exchange snapped Rainewood back to himself and he jerked his hand back, gazing around the room with narrowed eyes. "What is happening here? You can't go on an outing with *Basil*."

She swallowed and tried to pay attention as Basil set a meeting date. Campbell's eyes were remote and unnerving. Stagen's were unreadable. The three other women—Celeste, Lady Malcolm, and Mrs. Browning—were clearly displeased. The duchess just looked furious.

Rainewood started muttering and pacing around,

trying to touch the others and inspecting everything—crouching and staring up into their faces, poking fingers through them.

The dowager shivered as his fingers fell through her. She put on a good face as they all rose, but in contrast to the warm greeting she had given Mrs. Browning, she offered a much more stilted send off. She barely acknowledged Abigail. She gave her the bare minimum attention that she could engender while still maintaining a veneer of the polite hostess.

She was obviously displeased with the youngest member of the family.

"I look forward to seeing you again, Miss Smart." There was a wealth of warning in the dowager's tone. Abigail knew exactly what the warning conveyed, and it wouldn't be kind for her if she captured any more of Basil's attention. One outing far exceeded anything that the Duchess of Palmbury would allow.

"Likewise, Your Grace."

Abigail had only taken two steps before Rainewood was striding next to her, his gaze more focused and sharp. "Stop. Where are you going? I can't speak to any of them. Tell them about me."

His voice had lost the slightly dreamy, worshipful tone and had returned to its more demanding notes.

She continued following her mother and Mrs. Browning through the long gilded hall.

"Turn around," he demanded. "Tell my grandmother."

"Tell her what?" she whispered. "That you are a ghost? No."

"Turn around." His voice grew sharper.

"Are you mad?" She whispered harshly, looking around to make sure no servants were observing her. "They will think I've gone round the bend permanently. Your grandmother would love to have that type of ammunition."

"So?"

She tightened her lips. "I *have* gone round the bend to have come to find you once more."

That shut him up, but only for a second. "You did come for me, then."

She covered her mouth and pretended to cough as they reached the entrance hall. "A momentary lapse, I assure you," she said behind her raised hand to hide her moving lips. "I will happily leave you behind next time."

A light finger brushed her arm and she shivered. "No, I don't think you will, Abigail." The finger continued up to her elbow, her skin shivering beneath. "And isn't my ability to touch you an interesting development to this continued dream?"

She tried to ignore both his words—stupid man still thought he was dreaming then, did he?—and his questing fingers.

There was a moment's hesitation at the door as she wondered if he would be able to follow her out. His mahogany gaze grew more intense as he looked upon her and he walked right through as if it was nothing. She stared for a moment before proceeding down the walk several paces behind Mrs. Browning, as usual. Rainewood kept pace closely next to her, so close that if others could see him, tongues would be set to wagging. His footfalls fell silently on the stones.

A boy hawking papers called out loudly from the walk crisscrossing the front of the property. He threw a paper onto the pavement. It disappeared as soon as it touched.

Rainewood's finger brushed her arm.

Impetuously, Abigail pulled away and walked over to the newsboy. She extended her hand. The boy paid her no mind, continuing to try and sell his papers with his slightly desperate air and frayed cuffs. She slowly reached out to him, her fingers inching toward his, which were curled tightly around the paper he held aloft.

She swallowed as her first finger touched him. But then it almost immediately dipped through, the rest of her fingers following suit as her hand fell back to her side.

Nothing had changed, then.

Except that *Rainewood* could touch her, which meant *everything* had changed.

"Miss Smart. Stop dallying. Now."

She walked back to the carriage, unnerved, noting Mrs. Browning's irate look, her mother's nervous one, and Rainewood's unreadable expression.

Rainewood held out a hand to assist her into the carriage. She reacted without thinking, barely catching the footman's surprised glance as her arm hovered two inches above his outstretched hand as she ascended.

She closed her eyes, frustration and immediate regret running through her. The servants would be gossiping again, but at the moment that wasn't the important thing. Her entire world had turned on end.

"What are you?" she whispered to Rainewood as he settled next to her on the seat, pressing his leg into hers. So comforting to feel the slightest weight against hers. A terribly dangerous thought.

"What did you say?" Mrs. Browning asked sharply.

"I told you, I'm not dead," he said. He looked away, his eyes narrowed on the window. "Well, not yet," he said tightly.

There was a part of her starting to believe him, though Mrs. Browning's next words laid that to waste.

"Miss Smart, cease your mad mutterings. That recreational visit to Bedlam addled your head. Only the weak-minded allow themselves to be addled thus."

Her mother's eyes widened and she looked fearfully between Mrs. Browning and Abigail. But Mrs. Browning couldn't know anything more about her. Her mother had kept the doctor and his visits secret. The one thing that Abigail could count on since her mother was so determined to succeed in society.

Abigail pushed away the nightmarish memories of the doctor and the recent visit to Bedlam—all the rage to go and gape at the patients—and turned her head. "I am not addled, Mrs. Browning. I was simply commenting on Lord Basil. I didn't finish my thought. I want to make a good impression. He is second in line to a dukedom, after all."

Rainewood jerked as if burned.

"I was merely wondering at what qualities he's looking for in a wife," she finished. She suppressed the memory of a distant, bitter conversation and kept her gaze firmly away from the ghost at her side.

"Someone not addled!" Mrs. Browning yanked the hem of her dress from where it had become caught beneath her. "And someone with social polish and grace. I don't know *how* you managed to interest him."

"It matters little," her mother said as brightly as she could, though her eyes said that she would be watching Abigail more closely for mind weakness. "Just do not toss away this chance like you have the rest."

Abigail smoothed her skirt and tried to put an inch between her leg and Rainewood's. He simply moved his closer again, though there was a promise in his eyes that he was going to punish her for the thought about his brother. And for her words.

"I have not tossed away any chances, Mother. I can accept the fact that some men are simply not interested in me, why can't you? I do not possess a magic wand to entrance a suitor. If I did, I would assure you that I would not *toss* them aside willy-nilly."

The prolonged contact with Rainewood was making her antsy.

"You are growing more impertinent, Miss Smart," Mrs. Browning growled. "I do not know if I will allow much more."

Rainewood touched her again and her lips moved without her consent. "Allow it, Mrs. Browning? I do not find plain speaking about my marriage chances to be impertinent."

Normally she wouldn't give in to her irritation

in front of her mother or their companion—especially the companion who could drop them and claim them "unmanageable" while still collecting her presentation fee. She blocked Rainewood's influence from her mind.

"Impertinent, Miss Smart? Why, I'd say—"

"What a troll. I'd say, good riddance." Rainewood lazily swatted a hand toward Mrs. Browning's arm. Abigail's breath caught, but his hand passed through and Mrs. Browning shivered, the action seeming to derail her from a full-blown rage.

"—I'd say you'd just better mind your tongue."

It was nowhere near the type of tantrum the woman could normally manage and Abigail had a feeling it was completely due to Rainewood jabbing repeated fingers into sensitive parts of Mrs. Browning's anatomy. Mrs. Browning shuddered and turned to focus on something through the window, her lips pressed together, the line of them almost disappearing completely into blanched skin.

A silent vigil fell upon the interior for the rest of the carriage ride. Rainewood seemed uninterested in conversing. He stopped tormenting Mrs. Browning and instead repeatedly reached over to touch Abigail.

Fleeting, butterfly touches as if to reassure himself that she was real. Then bolder strokes along the skin of her cheek, her throat—still light touches, not quite real, but there all the same. Pulling the capped sleeves through his fingers, then sliding down her arm, into the crook of her elbow and firmly circling around. *Bare* fingers, not gloved and removed.

She couldn't keep the vibrations of her body hidden as he continued to touch her, and she couldn't tell him to stop with her mother and Mrs. Browning waiting to pounce on any mention of insanity. The feelings coursed through her and as his bare fingers moved along the sensitive skin of her throat she tipped her head back.

"Miss Smart!"

She wrenched her head forward at Mrs. Browning's outraged call and swatted Rainewood's hand away. "I find myself quite tired, Mrs. Browning, Mother. I nearly fell asleep. I believe I will rest before we call on the Barretts."

Mrs. Browning's lips pulled even tighter, and Abigail felt no small amount of relief when they pulled up to Number Forty-seven. Abigail didn't make the mistake of accepting Rainewood's hand this time as she scurried out of the carriage and into the house with as much bearing as she could muster.

"Miss—"

Abigail bypassed her maid on the stairs. "Telly, wake me in half an hour to freshen up."

"But, miss, do you—"

"No, nothing, Telly. Half an hour."

She didn't turn around to see Telly's reaction. She could feel the press of Rainewood's presence behind her, vibrating with energy for her to move more quickly.

She slammed the door behind her as soon as she entered her room, intent on keeping him out. He simply strode through the wood.

Against her better judgment she held out a

shaking finger and pressed it into his chest. The pressure held for a moment, as if pressing into a real body, before her finger fell through. "How are you still able . . . *What* are you?"

His head slowly shook from side to side, his eyes never leaving hers. "I don't know."

"You can touch people."

He caught hold of her hand against his chest in another butterfly-soft touch. "No. Only you."

She stood stock-still as he held her forefinger and pulled it from socket to tip between three of his. Captured. Then his fingers seemed to lose hold and they disappeared through hers.

"But I don't understand—"

"You came back for me."

It was a statement, not a question. She swallowed. "I thought maybe there was a chance that you might be there."

"And you came."

"I—I . . . you just disappeared. I was simply curious." She lied.

"I'm being held somewhere. My body. One moment I was with you and the next I was there. I need to return."

A jolt went through her, but from his words or his actions as he slid her finger against his soft, full lips, she didn't know.

"What? Where?" she managed to utter.

"You taste like strawberries." His voice went strange, and his eyes grew more intense. Her captured finger brushed his bottom lip.

"What?" she asked in a strangled voice. "I haven't had a single strawberry."

"Strange, isn't it? My favorite fruit."

"I—I think you might have been damaged while disappearing."

He raised a brow, his eyes clearing, and stepped back. "No. The only damage that is being done is to my body." His gaze sharpened. "I must find where I'm being held and return so I can escape. There is a strange tug and a dreamy cast to things, but I can feel it."

She bit her lip, not entirely believing in this new Rainewood who seemed much more *attentive*. "Where then?"

"I don't know. I wasn't there long enough. They are keeping me drugged."

Spirits were wild storytellers. Sometimes she thought the most eccentric of the bards deliberately left an imprint of themselves as a last huzzah of entertainment for the world.

"But now you are here," he said. One hand curled into the hair at her nape. "Or I am once more with you. And you can help me. I can feel that too." He slowly pulled her closer. "The fair Abigail Smart with skin like satin and lips like roses."

She felt drugged herself as he continued the slow pull. *Wrong, wrong! Right, right!* her mind screamed.

She pushed away from him, the conflicting feelings converging into certainty. She quickly stepped back until she bumped into the wall.

"You aren't Valerian Danforth, Lord Rainewood. Who are you?"

Chapter 8

A deep chuckle emerged and he was in front of her in a flash, fingers again seeking the hair at her nape. "I assure you I am."

"He would never say such things to me. You are some sort of strange imprint of his on the world come to torment me."

It was a frustrating admission. One that the real Rainewood would grasp and use mockingly for all it was worth.

"No. I have to admit to some belief in your fairy tales now, but I can't be dead. Not if I can touch you." His thumb caressed her lip. "Perhaps even taste you."

The feeling of his semi-solid chest made her breath catch. She pushed away from him and put her dressing chair between them. "Don't come any closer."

He crossed his arms. "You aren't being very accommodating, Abigail."

"Since when do you call me that?" She narrowed her eyes and began sorting through her options. They were few.

"I used to call you something else." He prowled

closer, the curve of his lips taking on a much more rakish slant. "Didn't I?"

The sound of low, quick breaths reached her ears, and she realized she was panting. The feeling inside of her increased. Knots of tension and desire. He skirted the chair and came within a few feet of her.

"You call me Smart."

One finger raised and brushed the stray wisp from her brow. The gesture too intimate. "There was a time long ago that I called you something else."

The knots grew larger. Too large, as though she would explode from them.

"Before your brother died."

The skin at the corner of his eyes tightened and he stepped back an inch. Relief and distress ran through her in equal measures.

"Yes, before Thornton." His voice was several shades colder.

A part of her withered at the loss of intimacy, but this was firmer territory—a battlefield she knew well. If he played on this ground she could better believe it was the real Rainewood—or at least a real spirit of him—in front of her and not just her own imagination making a copy of the Rainewood she used to wish for.

She fingered the brush on her dressing table. "You suddenly believe in my fairy tales, do you? And now you desire my help."

His eyes narrowed. "I was transported somewhere. I could *feel* again." The ardor in his voice mixed with anger. "Mostly pain. I need to escape from there. I need you."

She curled her lower lip in and nibbled on it as she moved her ivory brush to and fro. Touching the brush gave her equal measures of comfort and distress, as usual.

"You don't believe me." His voice was clipped.

She looked up and tried to decipher the expressions flickering across his face before his features retreated into the icy mask he had worn for nearly a decade. "The boot is on the other foot now then, isn't it?" She said it as simply as she could, but the underlying anger and past hurt crept through the words.

His face went blank. They stood in a parody of a standoff for several moments.

"Believe what my eyes and body told me when I woke."

"But I'm not even sure I can believe what my own eyes or skin tells me—and I am fully awake."

He reached out a hand, but dropped it when she shrunk away. "And what do they tell you?"

She shook her head, pressing her lips together. "Do you know where your body might be?"

"No."

"Then we have a dilemma, regardless of the issue of trust."

"You will find me." His voice held the same old arrogance, but the core confidence behind the assertion made her look at him more sharply.

"Will I?"

"You have the uncanny ability to manipulate things to your advantage, especially when it comes to me." There was a touch of darkness to his tone.

"I do not share your confidence." Nothing was ever to her advantage when it came to him.

"You found me at Grayton House."

"Only because that is one of your homes. And it's where I first saw you like this," she said pointedly.

"There's a reason you can see me when others can't. To help. Everything in me says that you will make me whole."

The phrasing made her heart clench and she angrily shook the feeling away.

"I have tried to tell you—multiple times and at multiple points in our lives"—she didn't back down under his suddenly closed look—"I see everyone like this. Yes, you are an anomaly in many ways, but I assure you that I've been seeing spirits since . . . for a long time," she finished lamely.

She still remembered her first spirit with the crystal clarity of a nightmare come to life. A likeness of the man standing before her.

He didn't respond, which irritated her.

"What about Mr. Templing? He disappeared with you."

"Yes." He nodded and seemed more than ready to grasp this new thread and veer from the previous subject. "We should go to his house. Break in. And to the gaming hell. There is something there. I know it. I feel it."

She shook her head. She didn't have the first clue how she could break into Templing's house, no less a gaming hell. And then to find a clue to Rainewood's whereabouts?

She shivered at the thought of finding him in some shallow grave instead.

"Speaking of your friend . . ." She grimaced. "Where is Oxting Stables? No, a better question, what is Oxting Stables?"

"It's a stableyard between London and New-market."

She closed her eyes in relief. "Oh, thank goodness. I thought perhaps I had said something worse."

"It couldn't have been too much worse, Smart." He shook his head. "No one knows of Oxting outside of an elite group of men. That you would know the name is highly strange."

Well, that explained the looks, then. "You volunteered the information!"

He shrugged.

"I know what you've been doing." She shook a finger. "I won't let you make me say things anymore. No more touching."

He was in front of her before she saw him move. Fingers sliding down her arms. "You don't want that, Smart."

"You are using me, Rainewood," she said in a voice far more calm than she felt. "You always have. And now you demand I do your bidding. Finally forced to believe the *tales* I've always told."

"I am not forced to believe you, Smart. This could all be some crazed dream still."

"Then in that crazed dream you are going to be vastly disappointed when I fail to comply."

"Visit Templing's tonight, Smart," his voice was low and coaxing.

"You have hardly given me incentive to do so. One, you are an ass. Two, you are using me once again when it is convenient to do so. And three, you are *dead*."

"I'll give you something in return."

"I don't want a nagging ghost following me

around for the rest of my waking hours, thank you."

"I'll help you find a suitable husband."

She stopped twitching the brush. "Come again?"

He crossed his arms, eyes dark. "I will help you secure a husband. I'll make sure that certain *facts* stay hidden in your marriage quest. I'll even give you a highly sought-after *nod* in the middle of a gathering."

She swallowed. "I could do without the sarcasm, thank you." But the offer was tempting. "If I help you regain your form, should you truly still be alive somewhere, in return you will not only stop hindering my marital state, but will help further it?"

"That is what I said."

"It would help me believe you more if you didn't sound so irritated."

"Fine." He smoothed his lips into a smile that most would find quite pleasant, indeed charming, had it reached his eyes. "I would greatly desire to help you marry one of your wretches, if you would but do me the honor of bloody helping me out of this situation."

"You are terrible at making deals sound tempting, Rainewood." His eyes narrowed. "But. . ." She lifted her fingers from the brush and folded her hands primly in front of her. "I accept."

The deal had the further incentive of allowing her to pretend that he wasn't dead yet. She wasn't quite ready to give in to the thought that he would disappear for good at any moment.

"Fine."

"Fine."

They stared at each other for a long moment and she wondered how he could brood so well even as a spirit.

"We start at Templing's," he said.

She crossed her arms to mirror his. "Fine. I don't know why I'm worried. This is going to fail from the outset. I'll never gain entrance to his house."

"Hardly a problem." His face relaxed and he flashed a smile that made her heart pick up a few beats.

"I don't see how you can say that. His butler is hardly going to let me in to search with impunity."

"No, but I know where he hides his spare key."

Going to Templing's house—sneaking away in general—was as hard as she thought it would be. Why had she ever agreed to this stupid plan? A handsome face, some charming words, a pretty deal, and an internal tension she couldn't deny—all of it spelled trouble.

She released an oof as she tumbled from the top of the short, vined wall and tripped into the bushes outside of the Carters' sortie.

Rainewood snorted as he stepped through the wall. "Graceful."

"Shut up, Rainewood." She brushed her skirt, trying to dislodge the greenery from the fabric and not to think about what the devil she was doing, *why* she was doing it, and *how* she had been talked into the actions. If she reentered the ball with bits of leaves and twigs, she doubted even Mrs. Browning's reputation would be able to save her. "We have fifteen minutes to do this, and I'm completely unamused so far."

He snorted again and started down the street. She looked furtively in both directions before following him. Templing's house was only half a block from the ball. Her slipper caught on a rough patch of the walk and she tripped.

"Smart, my god, you have to be the most graceless, most incompet—"

She caught up with him and poked him in the chest. Her finger held for a moment before sinking through. Just enough of a moment to stop him dead.

Well, perhaps that wasn't the best way to describe it.

"I do not have to help you," she whispered harshly. "Remember that, Rainewood. Remember that I am the one with the power now. So shut . . . up."

His eyes narrowed, but he continued forth, silently this time.

They reached Number Ninety-two a minute later. She had a moment of stupid clarity as she realized something far too late.

"Anyone could leave the party early, drive by, and see us." She frantically shook her head, trying to dislodge some of the panic that was collecting there. "See me, I mean!"

"Yes, yes, right, right. Your spotless reputation will come to ruin."

"Rainewood, don't be more of an ass than you already are. You know perfectly well what—"

He touched her arm, the light force sending a shiver through her. "Your reputation is under more

stress the longer you are about. The key is in there."
He pointed to a bush in a large planter at the right
of the door. "Dig around a bit and you'll find it."

"Dig around?"

He waved his hand. "Well, come on, we haven't
all night, as you said."

She furtively looked in all directions. The street
was blessedly devoid of activity for a block or two.
Thankfully, no one seemed to be around, but all it
would take was one inquisitive neighbor peering
through a window or a carriage rolling down the
street to catch her out.

Stupid, thy name is Abigail.

She gave Rainewood a dirty look and plunged
her hand into the soil at the base of the bush. To
her relief, her fingers touched something solid and
coolly metallic. She retrieved the key, gave one
more furtive look to the street, and inserted it into
the lock.

As soon as it turned, she pushed the door open
and hurried inside. Rainewood slipped in after her,
but his face was creased in concentration, and he
shivered as he crossed the threshold.

The lights were out in the house, just as they had
appeared from the outside. Rainewood pointed to
the stairs, seeming to forget for the moment that
she was the only one who could hear him. She
nodded and walked on slippered feet to the base.
The servants would be abed below stairs. She
briefly wondered how they were taking their mas-
ter's absence.

The first stair creaked as she put her weight on
it. She winced.

"Good one, Smart. Way to sneak around and

be discreet." Rainewood seemed to recall that he could speak, unfortunately.

"Not all of us are ghosts, you donkey," she hissed and took another step, one closer to the banister. When that yielded only the sound of her slipper, she tentatively took a few more. It seemed like an age, but she finally made it to the second landing.

"One more level up."

She withheld a groan and continued the slow pace upstairs, following Rainewood until they reached a chestnut furnished study. Rainewood walked toward the desk, giving her a look when she didn't follow. She was too busy eyeing the sculptures and strange art on the walls. Who knew that Mr. Templing so enjoyed the ballet? Naked ballerinas, to be sure, but ballerinas all the same.

"Smart, get over here and paw through these."

She absently obeyed, still examining the art.

"Smart, you are going to get caught. Stay on task."

"I'm sorry that I was not better trained as a housebreaker. I will endeavor to up my game in the future."

"Good."

She wanted to kick him. If he were corporeal, she just might give in to the urge.

She started sifting through the papers. Markers and debt logs dotted the surface. "Your group engages in entirely too much betting," she murmured. "Why here is a marker made out to Mr. Templing for twenty thousand pounds."

He leaned closer. "From whom?"

"Aidan Campbell."

Rainewood shook his head. "Fool."

"Oh, are you trying to say that you don't engage in the same behavior?"

"I don't lose those types of sums."

"But you make the bets."

"Of course."

She shook her head. "You are the fool as well, then."

There was a creak and every muscle in Abigail's body stiffened. A furtive little man came into view mumbling about debts and mergers. He walked over, checked some invisible books on the desk, then walked through the wall. She breathed a sigh of relief, her muscles struggling to relax. If it had been someone real . . .

"Rainewood, go watch for the servants."

He gave her a disbelieving glance. "No. You don't know what you are looking for."

"Neither do you! And you can't touch anything."

"That's a low blow, Smart."

"But a true one." She poked a finger at his chest. "And if I get caught you are out of luck."

"But—"

"No buts!"

He hesitated for a moment, shifting on silent boots. "You are looking for a dark green ledger."

"What?" she asked sharply.

"It's a book."

"I know what a ledger is."

"Then look for a green one."

"What is in it?"

"Are you going to nag all night, Smart? I thought you wanted me to keep watch?"

His words were normal for their exchanges, but his eyes were shifty.

She'd definitely have to have a look in that book once found.

"Fine. Shoo!"

He gave her a dirty look but walked out into the hall and, she assumed, down the stairs. She stared at his retreating back for a second before he disappeared. It was the first moment he had left her alone since reappearing. He had been stuck to her like a marriage-starved mama to a prime bit.

It felt strange to have him gone.

Not good. She shook her head to clear it, and resumed searching with added vigor.

Five minutes later she had found plenty of information about Rainewood, Templing, and their friends' habits, but still hadn't found the ledger. She was starting to feel like there was nothing to find.

She plopped into the chair behind the desk and leaned back. Her toe hit something. She leaned down to see the edge of a book sticking out from under the shadows of the desk. She pulled it up, flopped it on the desk, and opened the cover.

Rainewood burst through the wall panting.

"Butler up. Hurry."

She scrambled around the desk toward the front stairs, but he stopped her. "Too late to go that way. Use the back stairs."

"But the door—"

"No time. I know another way."

She started toward the back stairs, but a ghostly hand gripped her wrist for a moment, before sliding through. "Take the ledger."

"But—"

"Just take it! Hurry!"

She grabbed the book and sprinted toward the back stairs. There was a definite sound of footfalls coming up the front. She hurriedly descended, wincing as she produced yet another squeak on the bottom riser. The footfalls abruptly stopped, then suddenly began again, moving three times as quickly. Another set of footfalls echoed from the front foyer. The front door was definitely out, and the back doors in most of the houses in this neighborhood let out to walled yards. No escape there.

Rainewood waved her to a small room off the back, then motioned for her to move quickly to the drawing room in the front. A large draped window beckoned. The second set of footsteps paced around the front foyer, so close to where she stood. The first set descended the back stairs. She unlatched the window, pushed out, and tumbled through.

She spit out a mouthful of leaves and pulled her dress from the gaping maws of the evergreen bushes. Rainewood was frantically waving her toward a tree in the neighbor's yard. She stumbled to it and stepped behind just as the front door of Templing's house opened.

She crouched behind the tree, panting, as Rainewood watched the door.

"Damn it. He's coming this way."

Her panic spiked. She'd be caught for sure. She clutched the ledger to her chest. She was a thief now. Rainewood had told her to take the book and, unthinking, she had. They'd throw her in prison.

"When I tell you to move, scoot around the tree."

She heard the footsteps coming her way.

"One foot, go."

She stepped to the left.

"Another. Another. Stop."

The click of boot heels on the pavement stopped on the other side of the tree. If another servant were to look from the door, he would see both the butler and Abigail separated by the girth of the giant oak.

The butler swore. "Damn villains," he muttered.

"Smart, step back the other way, quickly," Raine wood demanded.

She shimmied around the tree as the butler returned to the house at a fast clip, his boots clicking.

"He's going to call the watch." Rainewood swore. "Come. Hurry."

She hardly needed Rainewood's direction to start running down the street. A carriage rolled past and she lowered her chin against her chest and the top of the book as she continued to run.

When she finally made it back to the Carters' house, she chucked the ledger over the wall and used the heavy curling branches to climb back over. She reached the top and vaulted down, the loud sound of ripping fabric in her wake. Footsteps in the garden broke through the sound of the blood beating in her ears. She closed her eyes and shook. She didn't want to assess the damage to her dress, what her hair currently looked like, or who might have observed any part of her vault over the wall.

This was a nightmare. That was all. Any moment she'd wake.

When no one exclaimed over her state, she tentatively opened an eye. Rainewood stood in front of her, scanning the area. "You need to rejoin the party."

"No." She closed her eyes again, fatigue replacing the broiling blood that had been pumping through her. "I'm going to lie here and pretend I've fainted. It will make for less of a scandal."

"Smart, you need to get up. Someone is walking this way."

She held back frustrated tears and levered herself up with one hand, the other grasping the back of her dress. It felt perfectly intact. She looked behind to see part of her under dress hanging from a prickly vine. She shakily unwound it, lifted her skirt, and tied it to her leg. She couldn't leave it behind.

"Excellent thinking, Smart. You can use that to tie the ledger to your leg as you leave."

She didn't even look at him as she double knotted the fabric. "I'm as good as ruined, Rainewood. I might as well just carry the blasted thing through the house. You won't need to carry out your end of the bargain after all."

"Don't be such a worrywart. You look presentable enough." A ghostly finger brushed the fringe away from her face.

Voices came closer. "What do you expect from him? He has always done as he pleased."

She kicked the ledger under the hedge and looked over her dress in order to catch any grass stains. The voices materialized around the surrounding greenery and rosebushes as Charles Stagen and Basil stepped into view. They stopped abruptly upon seeing her. She attempted a smile, but knew it was a grimace at best, the edge of a sob at worst.

Both of the men scanned the surrounding area, as if searching for someone who had either attacked her or tupped her.

"Merely lost my footing. Forgive me, but I must return to the party."

Stagen's hand shot out and gripped her wrist as she tried to move past him. "Be that as it may, Miss Smart, perhaps it would be better to remove that twig from your hair?"

He reached up and when his hand reappeared in her view a spindly branch was held between gloved fingers.

"Yes, thank you, Mr. Stagen." She wobbled past him.

She only made it halfway back to the terrace, thankfully passing no one else, before she leaned against a statue to calm herself. She looked longingly behind her. She could just vault back over the wall and run. Just keep running and running until she could run no more.

"Smart, you need to get back to the party now," Rainewood said. "That hatchet-faced woman is looking for you and she does not look pleased."

Abigail closed her eyes. "I don't care. I've gone crazy. They will lock me up somewhere. The hospital. Prison. What difference does it make?"

"Smart, calm down." His fingers curled around her nape and pulled her an inch toward him before his fingers slid through her. She shivered. He looked at his hand in annoyance. "Where is the girl that climbed the tallest trees?"

She laughed humorlessly. "Dead. Stamped out. Resigned."

He didn't say anything, and when she looked at him there was a strange expression in his eyes that she couldn't read. "I don't believe that. And I can't believe you do either. Now get moving."

She pushed away from the statue, straightened her dress and hair one last time, and stepped onto the terrace as if she had nothing to hide. She made it through the door before a clawed hand gripped her upper arm.

"Miss Smart. Would you care to explain where you have been for the last half an hour?"

Her mind went blank as she looked at Mrs. Browning's irate features, her mother's nervous ones, and the inquiring looks on the faces of the guests surrounding them.

"She was dancing and then speaking with us in the garden, Mrs. Browning." A voice behind her said smoothly. Basil tipped his head to Mrs. Browning. "Unfortunately, she took a spill on the wet grass. No harm done, but Mr. Stagen and I wanted to make sure she was well."

Abigail wasn't sure which was worse, the speculative looks on the surrounding faces, wondering whether she was having a liaison with one of the men, or the downright dubious expressions that these men would be attending to her at all.

"I also saw Miss Smart fall. There should be a warning sign near the hydrangeas," Gregory's strident voice said. "I have seen more than one lady lose her footing."

The looks on the surrounding faces changed. Gregory Penshard would never agree with Charles

Stagen or anyone of Rainewood's group unless it was the truth—or he was forced to at swordpoint. He would definitely not save her reputation if she had been cavorting with one of them outside. That the ton understood this fact made the whole social system seem childish.

But it did save her.

"Mr. Stagen, Lord Basil, and Mr. Penshard have been all that is kind," Abigail said as calmly as she could. "I believe I just need to freshen up. Thank you again, gentlemen."

They tipped their heads, all three sets of eyes regarding her in different manners—none of which she was sure bode well, but at least she might get out of this alive.

Mrs. Browning and her mother extended their thanks as well, then followed her upstairs to the retiring room hot on her heels.

Mrs. Browning checked to make sure the retiring room was empty before turning to Abigail. "I don't believe a word. What were you doing?"

"I fell. Truly." And it was the truth. She had fallen multiple times, in fact.

But it was apparent on both of their faces that they didn't believe her, and for the rest of the night, both women stuck to her like a glove stuck to skin too moist.

"You are very nearly wearing them," Rainewood said as if reading her mind.

"This is your fault, Rainewood," she muttered, then regretted saying so as Mrs. Browning gave her a sharp look.

She finally shook her mother and Mrs. Browning partially free when she moved into a group and began speaking with Edwina, Phillip, and Sir Walter Malcolm. They were discussing modern technical marvels and she smiled and nodded along, relieved to be on safe ground for once that night.

Gregory joined their group a few minutes later. He looked bored with the conversation and somehow positioned himself so that the two of them were slightly separated.

"Miss Smart."

"Mr. Penshard."

Rainewood made a mocking little gesture at her side.

"Would you care for a refreshment?" Gregory asked.

She could see that he wasn't going to let her go without saying something. And with Gregory, not letting someone overhear his sometimes scathing invectives would be most opportune. "Please."

They walked to the table, which was blessedly free of people loitering.

"Since I helped you," he said, pouring a glass. "I feel quite free in asking what you were really doing in the gardens."

She smiled brightly as he handed her the glass. "Just grabbing some fresh air."

"That is hardly a wise thing to do without someone with you." He poured another glass and took a careless sip. "Edwina would have accompanied you."

Abigail tried not to watch as Rainewood circled Gregory, eyes narrowed. "I know," she said, wiping her free palm against the skirt of her dress. "I won't make that mistake again."

"Wait a moment," Rainewood muttered, eyes dangerous. "He mentioned a doctor in the study."

She tried to ignore him as Gregory continued. "Good. I don't like seeing you exploited by men of their ilk."

"Penshard spoke about a doctor and tests at the Grayton House ball," Rainewood said darkly. "In a room he should not have been using."

"Uh, yes," she said, her concentration broken as two sets of deep brown eyes narrowed—one pair focused on her, the other on the first pair. "But Lord Basil and Mr. Stagen were quite kind. It could have been disastrous. Thank you as well."

Gregory tipped his head. "Of course. Just be cautious, Miss Smart. You never know who is lurking about." He drained his glass, set it on the table, and strode away. She swallowed at his statement.

"It's Penshard. Penshard is the one behind the attack."

"What?" She glanced around to see if anyone had seen what appeared to be her asking the punch bowl a question. She scooped a glass, trying to keep her chin tucked enough so that no one could see her lips move. "What are you babbling about?"

"Penshard. He hired someone to be 'taken care of' by a doctor. It's obvious. And he hates me."

"Gregory is hotheaded, but not the murdering type."

"I'm not dead yet, Smart. I'm not saying that someone didn't try though. And my head says Penshard did it. Perfect motive and it is completely something he would do."

"Gregory would not."

"Of course he would," Rainewood scoffed. "He is not far out in line to the title. And he is a little codswallop. Always has been."

"Just because you don't like him—"

"Not only that." Rainewood looked away. "He is on the list."

She swallowed. "You really do have it, then."

He said nothing and was saved by a group of partygoers descending upon the table.

It wasn't until the end of the evening, when her wardens were speaking to their hostess, that Abigail slipped away from them completely. She hurried outside to retrieve the damn ledger and tie it to her leg. Damned if she was going to leave it here after all the trouble she'd gone through to obtain it. She searched through the hedge. Nothing. She squatted down, but there was nothing there but dirt, twigs, and leaves.

Someone had taken it.

Rainewood swore.

Abigail shrugged. "I can't say that I'm pleased to have it missing after going through so much trouble to obtain it, but it's hardly a momentous loss."

"You don't understand, Smart."

"You are correct, *Rainewood*."

"Part of the list was in that ledger."

She closed her eyes, weariness pressing against the back of her lids. She opened her eyes without responding, wiped her hands, and strode back inside. The trip to the garden had cost her another set of pinched lips, but she didn't much care as Mrs. Browning railed at her, her mother whined, and Rainewood repeatedly impugned

Gregory's parentage, convinced he had taken the book.

Throwing herself beneath the carriage wheels had never sounded so good.

They arrived home to even more good news from their frantic, wide-eyed servants.

"Mrs. Smart, we've been robbed!"

Chapter 9

A constable took statements from the servants and tried to calm Abigail's mother.

"If only dear Geor-Gerald were still alive," her mother said. "This would never have happened."

Abigail looked sharply at Mrs. Browning, but she didn't seem to have caught her mother's slip. Her pinched eyes were too busy assessing the damage to the parlor. Likely racking up gossip tidbits.

"Try to stay calm, ma'am," the constable said. "We'll get the miscreants. What time did you leave this evening?"

"Gerald would never have allowed this. He was always so brave and competent."

If her mother wasn't careful, she would slip again. And in front of Mrs. Browning that would be truly disastrous. Abigail tightened her fingers into fists. She had warned her mother not to come to London.

She touched her mother's arm. "Come, Mother; let me take you to your room. I think the good constable can get everything he needs from Worston."

The butler gave her a tight nod. He thought her

as strange as the rest of them did—but he was a proper servant.

She trudged up the steps holding on to her mother's elbow. Her mother seemed to recall herself halfway up and pulled her arm away. Abigail thrust aside the hurt and continued to ascend the stairs with her, just in case she faltered. She could feel Rainewood following behind and Aunt Effie floated ahead, chatting as usual.

"I have tea. Hot and piping. Two lumps. A twist of lemon. So hard to get good lemons in winter."

Abigail shut her out. She wanted to do the same to everything and everyone.

Her mother uttered a nighttime farewell and listlessly shuffled toward her room. Her mother's maid ushered her inside, sent Abigail a long glance, and closed the door.

It was dangerous to leave Mrs. Browning downstairs with the constable and servants, but at the moment Abigail was too exhausted, emotionally and physically, to care. She resolutely walked the few steps to her own room.

The room was a disaster. Clothing was strewn across the floor, and drawer and table items had been scattered. Telly was rushing around in an attempt to put everything back into place.

Abigail felt more than a moment's unease. Her room looked far worse than the parlor. "Were the other rooms this desecrated, Telly? You said downstairs that you didn't find anything missing, so I thought . . ."

"I don't know, miss, I think so. It will take me another few minutes to get everything back in place, I'm sorry."

"Do not worry yourself, Telly, it looks as if you are doing a fine job." She chewed her lip. "I just didn't expect this type of damage."

"I don't know how it happened, miss. All of the servants were present downstairs." She looked as if she might start crying at any time.

"It's not your fault, Telly." The servants had all been at Templing's too and yet she had somehow avoided getting caught. She stooped down and picked up her favorite, cherished brush, pulling the ivory inlaid handle through her fingers and checking for damage. "I think I'm going to have a lie down, if you don't mind."

Telly put down the pile of clothing in her arms. "Let me help you ready for bed."

"No." She waved her hand. "I'm just going to slip in for a few minutes. I think Mother will require me again."

She needed to prepare herself to run interference with Mrs. Browning, if necessary. She crawled under the top cover, still fully dressed, and closed her eyes.

"Smart, we need to talk."

"I don't wish to speak with you right now, Rainewood."

Something crashed against the wall and Abigail peeked an eye open to see Telly wincing as she picked up a fallen hanger. "Sorry, miss. Got away from me."

Abigail closed her eyes again and heaved a sigh. The bed didn't depress next to her, but she felt him sitting there, hovering. Her heart picked up speed.

"Smart, someone took that ledger."

"I know."

"It was Penshard." The distaste was evident in his pronouncement.

She smoothed her fingers over the inlay on the brush's handle and then pushed it further beneath the coverlet. "Perhaps. In a minute." She trusted her maid to a point—she had to trust her as her only ally—but something made her hesitate.

Telly slipped from the room minutes later, promising to be back to help her to bed when she was ready.

"Why do you think it was your cousin?" she asked as soon as the door shut.

"He hates me. He'd love to see me dead."

"But that doesn't mean he tried." She looked at him, leaning over her, fiddling with the coverlet as if he could touch it. "If you truly think you are still alive, why is someone keeping you in that state? Why not just dispose of you? That would make more sense with what you are accusing Gregory of—if you think he is after the title."

Brooding eyes met hers. "I don't know. Perhaps they are selling my perfect body for pleasure."

She closed her eyes. "Rainewood—"

"It doesn't matter. The fact is that they are keeping me in this state."

"There *are* no facts here." She turned over to her side, leaning up on one elbow to face him. "Why would Gregory pick up the ledger? How could anyone know that I'm helping you? It's more likely that some servant found it while cleaning up during the party."

"I don't believe that. Perhaps someone saw you leave the party and go to Templing's."

Her eyes narrowed. "That isn't amusing. I should have made you stay behind me to watch. No, no I shouldn't have gone at all."

Why had she developed a penchant for trouble again now?

The man in front of her stretched then pinned her with rich brown eyes. Right. That was why.

"And now your house has been turned inside out."

The unease that had been sifting beneath her skin bloomed. "What makes you say that?"

"Don't be stupid, Smart. You know as well as I do that it is extremely convenient that the night you rob Templing someone robs you."

"I didn't rob anyone. I merely borrowed Mr. Templing's ledger." When his brow rose she pushed up on both hands. "Under your direct orders, might I add."

"Yes, the man that isn't even here."

She tried to untangle herself from the covers. Better to endure Mrs. Browning downstairs than to deal with Rainewood and the idiotic decisions she made around him.

Fingers curled around her wrist. "No. Listen, Smart." He gave a sigh. "This means that we are on to something. The thread of events makes me think that we are making progress."

She said nothing.

"And that progress is dangerous." His fingers lightly caressed the underside of her wrist for a second, then slipped through. "You need to tell someone. Someone who will help and do these tasks instead. Like searching Penshard's place. Or having him followed."

"And just who am I going to tell? And what will I tell them?"

"Basil. Or the constable downstairs. Tell them exactly what you see."

"Absolutely not." She threw back the covers and rose, pressing through him the slightest bit.

"You have to, Smart."

"Do I? I've only told three people willingly about being able to see spirits and every time it has gone horribly wrong." She couldn't help the tears that formed. She turned away. "My maid is the only one who doesn't think me a freak."

"I don't think you a freak, Smart."

"Oh?" She gave a harsh chuckle and turned around. "Really? *Stay away from me. Never speak to me again.* Those ring any bells in your empty belfry, Rainewood?"

His eyes tightened. "I didn't believe you."

"Didn't or don't? Let's be honest here, Rainewood. You still aren't entirely convinced this isn't a dream. And I've seen the looks you've given me when I mention other spirits."

"You don't know me as well as you think you do, Abigail."

"I know you *very* well, Valerian." She gave him a smile without humor.

"And I know you."

"No. No, if you *knew* me, you wouldn't have turned against me. Wouldn't have let Thornton play his game. You knew exactly what your brother was made of."

He shoved away from the bed, fueling her ire.

"See, even now you can't admit your mistake." She stomped over and pushed him in the arm, making him turn. For some reason she seemed to be able to touch him longer and more fully than he could touch her. "I won't go through it again. I won't tell anyone else."

He grabbed her arm for a fleeting instant before it fell through like so much dream smoke. "Why? You are in danger. You need to tell someone."

"No."

"Yes. I need your help, Smart, but it can't be you doing these things."

"Why do you even care?"

He looked down at his shirt and flicked something invisible from his sleeve. "I don't. But don't be stupid."

"Fine. Find another way for someone to know. Find something tangible."

"Tell Basil," he said as if she hadn't said a word in disagreement. "He will help."

"Maybe Basil is the one who took the ledger, have you thought of that?"

He stared at her. "Yes, yes I have. It is not a kind thought to have. No one wants to think ill of their brother."

She let her shoulders slump. "I can't, Rainewood. You don't know what they did to me."

He narrowed his eyes. "What who did to you?"

Damnit. She had not meant to say that. Never. To anyone. "Forget it."

"No, tell me."

"No, Rainewood. You don't want to discuss your brother, *brothers*, and I find myself unwilling to discuss this."

They stared at each other, wills raging, both of them too stubborn to give in. It had made them an unbeatable combination when getting into trouble so long ago. It had become somewhat less of an asset later.

"I'll find out, Smart."

Something inside her tightened. "You can't do much at the moment, Rainewood."

He stepped forward and his hand brushed down her arm in just that taunting way that he loved. "I will find out, Smart."

His hand slipped through a half-second later, thankfully. She hated it when he touched her.

Hated how it made her want for things she could never have.

She stepped away from him, putting some distance between them in more ways than one. "I'm not going to your family, Rainewood."

"Then the constable—"

"And say what exactly? People think you are either gallivanting around the countryside or kidnapped. I would think you were off wenching too, were you not standing in front of me in all your ghostly splendor. Everyone will assume that I did you in should I reveal knowledge of you in this state."

"I'm not a ghost. My body—"

"Yes." She put a hand over her forehead. "As you keep reminding me."

A soft touch made her arm tingle. "Listen, Abby. Just give in."

Her throat choked. A rush of emotions overtaking her for a moment at his words before she could speak. Feelings she had kept locked down slipped from the box before she could restrain them.

"What was the last gaming hell that you visited, Valerian?"

There was a strange look in his eyes. Satisfied and conflicted. "St. Thomas's. Down by The Stout Hearted Goat Tavern."

She nodded her head resolutely and walked over to pull the cord for Telly. The box refused to close.

"You will tell Basil, then?" He loped behind her.

"No. We will go to the hell tonight. You can look yourself."

"What?" He tried to pull the cord from her hand, but it simply slipped through. "You can't go there."

"You wanted me to go before, if you recall." She spread her hands down her dress. "You are changing your tune."

"Damn right, I am. Don't be stupid, Smart."

The comforting old lick of anger crept over her. "It's a better option for me than telling someone straightaway that I'm crazed. Do you want to go to the hell or not? I assume you've tried to haunt Basil already to no avail."

Pressed lips gave her affirmation.

"Then you either come with me or you don't find whatever it is you think you'll find there." She strode to her closet and started rummaging through her things. "I am not without my resources. I can take care of myself."

"Against forest creatures—squirrels and rabbits. Not here. Not in the city."

She swung around. "I don't know why you suddenly care, Rainewood," she said a little viciously against the old hurt. "You hardly gave a care for my well-being before."

His eyes tightened. "I gave a care for your well-being."

"Once? Yes. Perhaps. Though I find it hard to reconcile your recent behavior were those past feelings true."

"Don't talk to me about feelings, Smart. You—"

Telly chose that moment to pop in. "Yes, miss? Are you ready for bed?"

"Is the constable gone? Mrs. Browning?"

"Yes. They both left."

"Good. I need you to acquire an outfit for me." She swallowed as she thought back to an earlier conversation. "Male."

"What? Bloody—"

She tuned out the deep male voice and concentrated on Telly's confused, and slightly alarmed, face.

"Telly, can you acquire a footman's outfit or the like for me?"

"I suppose I can, miss."

"Excellent. I'll need it within the hour, if possible?"

Telly tentatively nodded. "I will do my best, miss."

"And don't say a word to anyone, Telly. If they ask, say you are making repairs to the cloth."

Her maid blinked. "Very well, miss." She stood there for another second, as if she was waiting for Abigail to change her mind. Abigail gave her a shooing wave to get her moving.

Telly turned, shot a look over her shoulder, and exited the room.

"Even your maid thinks you are barmy."

She gave a brittle laugh. "I am barmy, Rainewood. You've been right all of these years."

Silence greeted her and she went back to her closet to see what she could find to aid in their, *her*, mission.

Telly returned a half hour later with a clean young footman's outfit. She reluctantly handed it over. "Miss, I have a bad notion in my gut."

"Telly, if someone asks for me, tell them I'm sick. Casting up my accounts." Her mother would never enter her room under those circumstances. "I'll be back before you know I'm missing."

"Then you truly are leaving dressed in this? Miss, let me travel with you, at least."

"Yes, Abigail, don't be a goose." Rainewood leaned against the four-poster pole, arms tightly crossed. "If you are going to be foolish, at least take your maid."

"She needs to cover for me in case of Mother."

"Your mother is asleep, miss," Telly said quickly. "She was most distressed and took one of her pills. She won't wake until the morning."

And she won't care anyway, except for your status as her ticket to society.

"Why are you doing this, Smart?" Rainewood's voice was low, questioning, shielded.

Abigail felt the urge to weep creep upon her again. Why was she? Rainewood had touched her, *looked* at her in that way, and she'd up and set upon this path. Thrown her lot in with him just like any other foolish society girl who thought she might have some chance with him *if only*.

Stupid, stupid.

He'd called her Abby.

She could ignore him. She could spill the entire tale to someone who might be able to help—if the person she chose weren't the party responsible for his disappearance in the first place—and get a first-rate opera ticket to a sanitarium in thanks. Or even if they didn't commit her right off the bat—or accuse her of doing in Rainewood herself—at the very minimum her mother would hear the story, and regardless of the ton's off-and-on fascination with the paranormal, Abigail would be put under the doctor's care again.

And she couldn't allow that to happen. She had done everything to get away from him. She shuddered.

He'd called her Abby.

But going out into London on her own with a spirit as her lookout was folly. Taking her maid wasn't much better. But at least she could have an extra pair of eyes and ears.

"Very well." She ignored Rainewood's question. "But you have to dress differently too, Telly."

"Yes, miss." She bobbed. "I will be back in a thrice." She ran from the room.

Telly was true to her word, and she came back with a boy's outfit ("my brother's, miss, just like yours"), quickly donned it with help from Abigail ("couldn't have anyone seeing me on the way"), then helped Abigail dress.

The trousers stretched between Abigail's legs—an odd sensation as her skin rubbed against them from the inside. She pushed a leg forward and examined it.

"It's a pair of common trousers, Smart, not the latest fashion from Paris."

"They feel . . . strange. Clasping around my legs, hugging them almost." She stood and took a step forward, holding on to the top of the trousers that Telly, who was rummaging through a bag, promised a rope would cinch. The lack of layers was disconcerting. "I feel naked."

"You walk around in those dresses with nothing beneath. And now you feel naked?" Rainewood asked in disbelief.

"There is plenty beneath my dresses," she said, irritated that her cheeks were hot thinking about him peering under her clothes every time she changed.

"Miss?" Telly looked anxious. "We should go before it gets too late. Unless you've changed your mind?" She asked hopefully.

"No, let's go."

They cleanly escaped from the house with the help of Rainewood acting as a lookout ahead of them. Abigail hailed a hack down the street and they were off, caps firmly in place to help shade their features and hide their hair. Telly had a bit of apoplexy when she heard the direction Abigail gave the driver, but Abigail ignored her pleas to turn back.

She already knew she shouldn't be doing this. It was dangerous and stupid. She blamed the donkey and that *look* upon his features when he had said something about protecting her.

And he'd called her Abby.

Stupid man. Stupid thoughts.

The driver stopped down the street from the gaming hell. It was located in a shady section of town. Not completely beyond the pale, but also not like walking down Bond Street in the middle of the day either.

They exited the carriage and she chanced a look at Rainewood. Anticipation and perhaps a touch of unease graced his handsome, pale features. Telly paid the driver and the hack swayed away across the stones, clippity-clop.

Rainewood started walking, energy in his usually languid gait. Abigail followed, trying to keep her eyes averted and at the same time sharp to her surroundings. It was an exercise in futility. She decided that the risk of discovery was slightly less worrisome than being unaware of what was going on about her. Men of all shapes and sizes prowled the streets and walks engaging in all matters of side betting, copulating with hard-looking women in the unlit corners, and urinating in convenient places.

Abigail tried hard not to stare. This was the type of place that you couldn't separate the spirits from the real folk. Everyone seemed to be dancing to their own tune of hedonism. She couldn't believe Rainewood frequented this area.

She peeked in his direction—his bearing full of long lines and confidence. Not the wickedly humored but kind youth she had once known. Instead he was the ultimate man about town she had become used to.

Telly missed a step after they heard a particularly lusty moan from one of the women in a side alley.

"Miss, you shouldn't be here," she whispered, her tone more insistent and edged with panic.

Abigail completely agreed, but decided against saying so to her maid, who would likely try to shuttle her off. Rainewood looked increasingly animated, and she wasn't going to up and leave him.

He stopped suddenly at a small shallow corridor. "Stay here with your maid. I'll come back to collect you."

She put a hand out to stop him. His eyes locked with hers. Her hand fell through his after a long second. "Where are you going? You can't leave without me."

"We were attacked just around the corner. You will be far safer here tucked away." He cast a glance in all directions. "Just pretend like you are having a debate or argument with each other." The edges of his mouth curved. "Shouldn't be too hard for you."

"I—"

But he was gone.

Telly looked at her worriedly. "What is it, miss?"

"He said we should pretend to have a conversation and then left."

Telly watched the people passing. "How long will we be here, miss?"

Abigail shook her head, feeling as if malevolent, watchful eyes surrounded them on all sides. "I don't know. I don't know."

Valerian couldn't believe she had actually come to this section of town. Well, that wasn't true. The girl he had known would do such a thing for him. The woman she had become wouldn't dare. Not for him. Not after the way their paths had diverged.

He tried to repress the insidious thoughts of why those paths had split. If he opened that box, all sorts of Pandora's curses would fly at him and deep down he knew he would be the loser. He tried to ignore the forbidden box completely, but it grew ever closer to the forefront of his mind each day he spent near her. Whatever world he was in was obviously not good for keeping hidden one's desires.

And the desire to make amends with Abigail was becoming stronger each day. Each second. To go back to the way things were before girls were women and boys were men.

No, he shook his head as he rounded the corner and passed through a man in a top hat. That wasn't true. It was a deeper desire forming—one that had always been lurking around the edges those last few summers together. A feeling that had frightened him with its intensity so long ago. To have her. To become more than friendly allies with Abigail.

And then Thornton had passed and everything had changed. Everything.

He pressed his lips together as he neared the hell. It was useless dwelling on the past. He wasn't even in full control of his present—his body somewhere far less safe than the den of iniquity he neared. And when he regained his life he was fully expected to marry Celeste Malcolm—or someone of equal standing. Everyone expected it. He was the heir. His father, so removed from his life until Thornton had passed, was becoming increasingly demanding on the subject.

Diddling with Abigail Smart was not the proper or wise thing to do. In any way, shape, or form. No matter what his body said, what his hands tended to do—touching her in a taunting manner, pretending that it was just to unnerve her rather than to satisfy some overwhelming urge within him.

No, better to concentrate on the task at hand—getting back to his body—and to forget the side pleasures that he might find with Abigail.

He grit his teeth. Easier to swim upstream of the waterfall than to forget.

A group of young men emerged from the hell, chattering and swaying drunkenly. Stupid not to have at least one man in control. Not that it had helped him, he thought in disgust. He watched a pickpocket cleanly remove a handkerchief from one man's pocket, and a watch from another's, before slipping back into the shadows.

A man stood just under the dim light shed from the hell's windows, a low-brimmed cap further shading his features. There was something familiar about his stance. Warning bells rang in Valerian's head.

The man had been there that night. Watching. Right before Templing had fallen behind him.

Another man approached. "Good haul tonight, Evans. Thought there might be a drop off in business at first, but if nothing else, we've had an increase with the fancy lickers trying to take the place of the old ones—or to find them." The man looked extremely satisfied, his hands on his hips. "Have to say that I didn't think the plan would work. Thought we'd be inhabiting fair Newgate's cells for it."

"You have a fat mouth, Burns." The voice was low and dark. "Leave now before I remove it permanently."

Burns gave an uncomfortable laugh and dropped his arms. "Now, no need for dramatics. No one around to see or hear. Just the gulls going about their way, filling our pockets."

Burns received no response and his uncomfortable laughter became laced with something resembling fear. "I was just having fun with the notion that we might burn for it. The fancy man will take the fall, if it comes to that. We melt into the shadows, we do."

A hand reached out and clasped around the flunky's throat. "*You'd* do well to remember that. No one would miss you, Burns."

The hand released and Burns stumbled back. "Yes, well then, I'll be going back to my business. Boys have done fine tonight." He moved back a few steps, keeping his eyes on the more dangerous man, and then turned and fled to the other side of the street.

Valerian walked closer, trying to see the man's— Evans's—features. Eyes sharpened and looked in his direction, and for a moment Valerian's nonbeating heart metaphorically stopped, thinking the man could see him. But then Evans's gaze again switched off to the side, to a new group emerging from the hell, and he slipped into the shadows. Valerian stepped after him, but the pull became stronger with each movement further away from Abigail. He cursed and stepped back.

The other man, Burns, was already across the street yelling at a pack of boys—pickpockets and runaways. Likely taking his fear out on his underlings—finding a release in rage. Valerian stepped closer so that he could hear what they were saying.

"I want you to find out everything about the fancy man who did the deed on those two blokes. There's money to be made, I know it."

Valerian reeled. Here it was within his grasp. Proof of who had taken him. "Say the name, damnit," he demanded, even knowing no one could hear him.

Burns pointed to two boys. "Jimmy, Tony, Golden Square. Keep tabs. And I still want your daily take, you hear me?"

The boys nodded sullenly.

Golden Square . . . Penshard lived there, as did a wide variety of other acquaintances. Even Basil had a temporary residence on the square.

Jimmy and Tony moved away on stealthy cat feet, blending into the crowd. Valerian started to run, desperate to follow them, but just like with Evans, he didn't get far before the tug pulled and pressed too hard, before his memories started to slip.

Abigail. He needed her. Needed her to follow the boys so that he could.

And if that yielded nothing, he was going to need her to search the outskirts of the underbelly of London. Even more dangerous territory.

He cursed.

Violently.

Then cursed again.

Chapter 10

"**Y**ou want me to do what?"

The shock of his request made Abigail momentarily forget that she was in a dark alley, shallow or not, and dangerous-looking men were passing by.

"I need you to follow two boys."

She stared at Rainewood for a second. Telly pulled on her sleeve. "Miss, what is it?"

She ignored Telly for the moment and concentrated on the greater foe. "Follow them where?"

"To Golden Square. Far better to get you out of here anyway."

She caught sight of a man with a low-slung cap watching her. There was something entirely wrong with the way in which he was doing it.

"Very well. I'd rather leave anyway, as it were."

She heard Telly give a relieved sigh. "I will find a hack, miss. Please, let's go."

Abigail kept her head averted as they passed a few men that she recognized as the more adventurous men from the ton. She panicked and ducked her head entirely when Gregory passed. Rainewood's eyes narrowed.

"Penshard's finding new stomping grounds, I see. Yet another strike pointing his way."

"What happened between you two?" She had always wanted to know, but Gregory hadn't been forthcoming and his cutting personality had discouraged questions.

"He's always wanted the estates for himself. He was Thornton's little dog. Doesn't think I will run them well. A bit hypocritical for him to set foot down here." His eyes narrowed further. "Or further proof that his actions mean ill."

She had known of Gregory from his visits to the estate. As children they had never formed any sort of attachment though, and had barely crossed paths, as Rainewood had held the man, then a boy, in contempt. Gregory had always liked to follow Rainewood's older brother, Thornton, the heir, around instead. "Trying to be a little duke," Valerian had mocked.

Telly pointed to a hack resting at the corner and hurried in that direction. Abigail felt for her money pouch in her pocket, secure that they would be on their way home soon. What problem could they encounter with one measly stop on Golden Square?

Her total ruination if seen by someone in the ton notwithstanding.

Rainewood seemed to read her thought. "We will stay in the carriage."

She nodded. Telly had already talked to the driver and nervously shifted from foot to foot before hopping up into the carriage in a way that no man would. Abigail turned to the driver, a man with droopy lids and a large mustache.

"Circle Golden Square," she commanded gruffly. "Slowly. Want to observe the uppers at play."

The driver shrugged and jerked his shoulder toward the interior of the hack. She climbed up, trying to mimic a gentleman's actions, consciously tapping down on her urge to grip and lift the imaginary dress that should be pushing in front of her.

The trousers still felt foreign against her legs, but she had to admit that it was easier to enter a carriage without having to worry about gripping yards of material, no matter how ingrained the gesture.

The carriage traveled west through the streets toward Mayfair. Abigail distracted herself by watching Telly's hands mottle red and white as she clutched them together, then clutched her shirt, the handle of the door, and the worn material of the seat.

Rainewood looked just as antsy, though he displayed it in less obvious ways. Brooding, dark eyes, fingers that silently tapped the seat, slouched position that was just a little too languid to be anything other than forced.

The hack turned onto Golden Square and Rainewood straightened, peering through the open window into the center park as they passed each house at a leisurely pace. She watched through the window facing the houses, but withdrew to the edge when she saw more than one face that she recognized.

Edwina and Gregory lived in the square on the north side. Phillip's aunt lived somewhere in the square as well. It was a busy address, full of society members and social climbers.

They rounded the first corner. The faces of the

buildings were shrouded in shadows or blooming from internal light, condemning or gawking at her as the hack passed.

They rounded the next corner.

"Stop." Rainewood's voice was harsh.

She jerked from her trance and thumped the carriage wall behind her. The hack pulled to a stop. She scooted over next to Rainewood.

"There." He pointed at two men talking in the park. They were trying to blend into the foliage, trying to appear as if there was nothing strange about their presence in the square. However, they were much less nattily dressed than the people walking by, and on second viewing she could see they were younger than she'd originally thought. No more than boys—street rats at that. Still, had she been walking along the street in her finest, she doubted she would have paid them any mind with the way they were shielding themselves.

A constable, on the other hand would notice. And a man who was obviously part of the watch was walking along the path a dozen paces away. The two boys disappeared into a copse of trees. The constable walked by, greeting a couple passing him. As soon as he was a respectable distance away, the boys appeared back in their places as neatly as if they hadn't moved at all.

They stared at a house across the street, waiting. For what, she didn't know.

She looked at the facade. Number Eighteen. She wracked her brain. Who lived in Number Eighteen? Her mother had drilled the numbers into her upon their Town descent. Eighteen, eighteen. She took in Rainewood's hard lips and unreadable expression.

Eighteen. Her hand went to her mouth. Oh no.

She automatically put a hand out to Rainewood's arm, but he simply lifted it so that her fingers dropped right through. She withdrew her hand into her lap as he signaled for her to have the carriage continue. She thumped the wall again and the carriage started its slow lope around the square.

Rainewood never took his eyes away from the facade of the row house.

It felt like an eternity until they reached the point down the street where they had agreed to disembark. Telly led the charge, shooing Abigail forward in her eagerness to get back to the house. Rainewood simply walked alongside, lips tight.

They reached their house ten minutes later. "Telly, crack the door, but don't enter yet," Abigail said.

Her maid did so and Rainewood strode through, returning a moment later with a nod that the foyer was clear. Shadows swirled in his eyes.

With the help of Rainewood they crept through the house and her room as stealthily as they had left. Telly quickly had her stripped of the footmen's outfit before Abigail could even work up the embarrassment to change in front of Rainewood—this time with far fewer clothes on. Just as well, since he was preoccupied, prowling about the room, stepping through Aunt Effie as she chattered.

Abigail knew what ailed him, but she thought it better for him to admit it aloud. "What ails you now?" she asked as she helped Telly dress—refastening the back of the maid's standard outfit. Telly quickly slipped from the room as soon as she was done, promising to return with a hot cup of tea.

Rainewood hit the pole of the four-poster—a blow that would have made the wood vibrate had he been physically present. Instead his hand merely sank through after a moment of inattention. "I can't believe Basil would do me in."

She bit her lip. "You don't know for sure that it was his house they were watching." But Basil held a lease in Number Eighteen for when he desired independence from the heavy thumbs of the dowager and the duke.

"Who else's could it be? If it had been Penshard's, I wouldn't have been surprised. But Basil . . ." He gave a humorless laugh. "You were right about not going to him, Smart."

"I . . . no, not because of that. I can't believe that Basil would—"

He hit the four-poster and this time produced a thud of sound to her ears. "So what next, is the question. Shake it out of Basil?" He gave a self-deprecating laugh. "Not much I can do there."

"Have you thought that maybe it is someone who is staying at Basil's? Do any of your friends stay there? Or his?"

Brooding dark eyes turned to her, but there was a slight lightening around his eyes. "Perhaps. Perhaps, Smart." He turned away. "You have a full day tomorrow, do you not?"

She self-consciously picked at her rail. "Yes."

A day full of suitors, appointments, and an outing with Mr. Farnswourth.

"Sleep, Smart," he said softly. "I'll keep watch."

* * *

Unfortunately the mellower Rainewood who had been present when she'd fallen asleep had been replaced by the side of him she saw more frequently about town—brooding and whip-edged.

She hadn't thought anything could be quite as miserable as her first outings with Rainewood tagging along, but she had been grossly mistaken. He sliced and diced everything, from the cut of Mr. Farnsworth's cloth to the lack of intelligent conversation to the way the clouds were moving in the sky.

After a particularly cutting tirade in which everything from the man's parentage, lineage, and manners were dissected, she let her reticule fall to the ground and whacked Rainewood in the forehead with her palm as Mr. Farnsworth bent down to retrieve her bag. "Stop that," she hissed, unable to concentrate on anything but Rainewood's less than dulcet tones. "You promised to help, not hinder!"

She had the feeling that her reaction was precisely what he had wanted. He touched his forehead and smirked.

"What, what?" Mr. Farnsworth asked as he drew upright and handed her the bag.

"Thank you, Mr. Farnsworth. That was most gentlemanly of you. You are an asset to your lineage." She smiled winningly and let the edge of her lip curl when Rainewood glowered.

She gloated for a second at this response and opened her mouth to jab at *Rainewood's* lineage, when her arm was given a sudden jerk. Pain radiated up her limb as her newly retrieved reticule was ripped from her grasp. The shock of the feeling was enough to keep her twisted in position from the force of the motion before her body and mouth kicked back into action.

"Thief!" Her feet went from still to racing as she ran after the man, no boy, dodging in and out of the walkers, bag clutched against his chest.

"Thief!"

A man ahead made an attempt to grab the tow-headed boy, but the boy nimbly sidestepped and disappeared into the crowd.

Abigail stopped to scan the area and heard a wheeze as Mr. Farnsworth caught up to her.

"Miss Smart, I say, are you well?"

"That boy stole my reticule! Of course I am not well," she said irritably. "I had a new handkerchief in there that I rather liked."

Mr. Farnsworth looked uncomfortable. "Are you hurt?"

She sighed and shook her arm to loosen the tension that had gathered there. Having her bag ripped from her grasp had not been pleasant. "I am fine, Mr. Farnsworth. Thank you for your concern." *And for running after the perpetrator,* something crabby inside her wanted to add.

"We should contact a constable, Miss Smart."

"Yes, Mr. Farnsworth. That is true. Luckily I didn't have much in—" She broke off as she saw a blond head peer from between two stalls, then disappear. "There he is!" she pointed.

She took off running again, surprise and ire giving her added speed. She broke through the crowd, running as fast as her slippers and skirts could manage. Blond hair darted between one stall then another as she continued the chase.

Rainewood appeared at her elbow, running alongside. He seemed to have finally realized he didn't need air though, as he wasn't winded. "Stop, Smart, I thought I saw—"

A hand gripped her arm, yanking her into a secluded alley at the back of the stall she had followed the boy into. She was immediately pinned to the wall, unable to see her attacker, but it was definitely a large man who held her, not a slip of a boy. Panic rushed through her, and she took a deep gasp of breath, the stench of the alley washing over her as the bricks bit into her cheek.

A grimy hand covered her mouth. "Got ya'," a rough voice said in her ear.

She could still hear the bustle of the vendors along the street. Surely someone would see them. Would come to help. She was in a safe part of town.

Her arm twisted and she gasped another foul breath.

"The infamous, Miss Smart. I've been looking forward to meeting you," a rasping voice said to her left—not the man holding her, a second man then. His speech was not that of a longshoreman though, the voice was more cultured, though the tone was uncivilized. "Imagine my surprise when you turned up last night. What were you doing slumming in that section of town, Miss Smart? A bit out of the way for someone like you."

Panic spiked in her further that the man seemed to know her. Valerian appeared at her elbow, eyes a bit wild as he tried to pry the man's fingers away from her arm to no avail. "Damn it, Smart."

She tried to calm her fear. Surprisingly, having Valerian near helped.

Something sharp pressed into her side. "I wouldn't attempt a scream, if I were you," the cultured voice said. "We will be long gone before someone finds your corpse."

The first man's fingers slid away from her mouth, leaving a foul feeling behind. She concentrated on Valerian and his frantic movements, finding courage.

"I don't know what you are talking about, sir. But please tell your friend to release me."

"Perhaps. Eventually." The now amused voice whispered in her ear, closer. "What were you doing near the St. Thomas hell?"

Panic worked through her again, and Valerian's eyes grew wider and his fingers worked harder—never connecting to the man, slipping right through his flesh. "I've never heard of it."

"Oh, no?"

The other man gave her arm a twist and pain shot through her. Her cheek scratched against the grit of the mortar. She tried to move away, but was neatly trapped between the man and the unforgiving bricks. The man was far too strong and he had placed her in a hold designed to use less than half of his strength—her body position and the wall doing the work for him.

Valerian continued trying to grip, punch, and grapple the man unsuccessfully, his eyes darting above her head to the other man as well. He let out a string of curses, and then touched her instead, his cool fingers soothing the skin of her cheek pressed against the wall as his hand dipped through. Fingers trailing down her neck, stroking, petting.

"Damn it, Abigail," he whispered. His forehead

pressed against hers for a moment before he disappeared through her. Reassuring, ghostly fingers pet her on the other side. It gave her strength.

"Let me go. I don't know of what you speak, and your friend is hurting me. I won't call the watch, if you just let me go," she said into the space of the trash-filled alley, her lips brushing the mortar with each word.

"So sure of yourself. Perhaps other tactics are needed in order to get answers?"

Her captor pressed against her and she struggled again, her actions merely causing him to chuckle foully in her ear. "Oi, that helps me right out, lady."

"I'm not sure you want to continue to struggle, Miss Smart."

Tears filled her eyes as she went limp. Prayers, one after another, went through her mind that someone would see them.

The man holding her laughed again and his free hand drew down her hip and grasped her dress, lifting it, bunching it.

Complete panic overtook her. She didn't even feel the shiver as Valerian appeared in front of her again. "Damn it, Abigail, move, leave!"

She wanted to demand how exactly she was to accomplish that, but she was too terrified to produce the words.

"Now why were you in that alley?" the cultured voice asked.

"Tell him!" Valerian demanded.

"I, I was looking for a friend."

"I don't think so. No friends of yours down there, are there lovely?" The other man's hand continued bunching up her dress, exposing her knees, almost to her thighs.

"A friend who was lost."

There was a sudden movement behind her and the hand stopped. "Keep talking."

Everything stubborn in her wanted to tell him to go to the devil. Everything that was terrified and instinctual told her to tell him anything that he wanted to know.

"Tell him, damn it." A ghostly hand touched her shoulder, shaking it an inch before disappearing.

"I . . . there was a rumor that someone I have had bad dealings with in society was last seen there. I, I wanted to find out if he had finally received his comeuppance."

"Ah, so just there for a little gossip, is that what you are trying to tell me?"

"Satisfaction. The man is a menace. I, I just wanted to see. But it was a bad idea. I didn't stay. Didn't talk to anyone. Surely if you saw me you know that." Desperation and fear laced her words, but she tried to inject just the right amount of sincerity. It was true, she hadn't talked to a soul other than Telly and the hack drivers.

Silence followed her words. "Clever girl. And yet, you followed two boys to Mayfair. Odd that. Who would have given you such direction? Almost as if you had unseen help."

Complete terror overtook her as she realized that somehow this man hinted at a knowledge far exceeding what he should know. What anyone knew.

"Almost as if you had someone beside you telling you where to go. I think you are going to have to be more forthright, Miss Smart, or perhaps I will just let the man holding you take what he will."

The man holding her seemed to take that as permission. Abigail struggled, lashing her foot out in any direction she could while pressed against the wall. He used his feet to spread her legs further apart, immobilizing her as his thighs pushed into her rear, pinning her there.

"Such spirit," the smoother voice said. "What a rare treasure you are. Too bad your *friend* didn't see it that way. Or didn't see it sooner, should I say?"

She went still.

"Oh, poor thing, are you just now coming to understand?" Fingers, not the calming ones of Valerian, but the calloused, crooked ones of the unseen man, stroked her exposed cheek, pressing her other cheek more firmly into the mortar. "I need to be sure now before taking you in for further questioning. The state you arrive in is completely up to you. You have twenty seconds, Miss Smart."

"I don't know what you want!"

"Tell me why you were really in that alley last night."

"I told you why."

"Partial truth, Miss Smart. Partial truth. And not the truth I desire. I think for that I will let my friend here have partial payment."

She squished her eyes closed as her dress was hiked all the way up.

Frantic ghostly fingers touched her face and she opened her eyes to see Valerian looking completely panic-stricken. She had never seen him in such a state. Not even when he had come to tell her about the death of his brother and his own involvement.

"No, no, no, no, no." Something dark and deadly came over Valerian's face as the sinister promises of the man behind her jarred her ears.

Valerian pulled his arm back and swung violently at the man. She closed her eyes as he did so. A strange calmness overtook her, even as she felt the man behind her press closer, the movements slowing to a crawl as her thoughts far outpaced the actions. There was a kind of calm bearing that filled her. That Valerian actually cared enough to do battle for her with that look upon his face—one that went deeper than simply a gentleman defending a lady. That there was an attachment that still existed between them. The world had tilted into something she was having trouble processing, and the stark thoughts were strangely comforting in the barren numbness that was overtaking her.

A crack sounded and she was pressed into the bricks further—as if the man's body had recoiled behind her—than released. The skin of her hands tore against the bricks as she pushed away and turned.

The man who had been holding her was splayed on the ground holding his nose, the other man stared down at him in shock. Some preservation instinct caused her to act without thinking, and she bent down and picked up a small wooden plank and swung it at the leader's head. He keeled over and lay there motionless. She repeated the action on the man holding his nose.

Valerian clutched his stomach and forehead, crouching over next to the fallen men. "Run, Abby." Then he blinked out of existence, and she ran as if the devil were upon her heels.

Chapter 11

The sounds of screaming punctured his dream and he jerked awake. Light flared above him and he squinted, that same terrible feeling that his eyes hadn't been opened in days washed over him once again as he ripped them apart.

He opened his mouth to call for Abigail, but his lips wouldn't part. A sound at his left echoed and he turned his head that way, the force required to move just those few inches made him squint further. When his eyes opened back up it was to see Templing straining on a table a few feet away, a man in a dirty coat leaning over him with some sort of ungodly implement in his hand.

Valerian tried to move, tried to help, but his hands wouldn't obey. His arms strained and he wobbled his head enough to see bands stretched across his wrists, tethering him to the surface. Templing gave another cry and Valerian pulled at the bonds. A meaty fist gripped his chin and yanked it up.

Something was poured down his throat and all went dark once more.

Chapter 12

Abigail's spine was much more rigid when she dragged her mother and Mrs. Browning to Grayton House for the second time. The dowager and her snide looks could go to the devil. She would collect Valerian and then leave. She couldn't countenance that he wouldn't be there, couldn't think about such a thing. And as far as this visit was concerned, as long as she didn't reveal her real purpose for being there, she would recover from the embarrassment of returning where she was unwanted.

Truthfully, at the moment she didn't care what anyone thought of her actions. She'd tossed and turned all night. Haunted by the way Valerian had looked right before he'd disappeared. Plotting a way to gain entrance to the house. Unable to think that he wouldn't be here when she came.

Mr. Farnswourth had been nearly apoplectic when she had darted out of the alley. She hadn't wasted time with him, however. She had asked him as politely as she could manage to return her to her mother, explaining that she had fallen while chasing the thief.

Embarrassed, most probably at his lack of athleticism, he had bent over backward to help her. He was a truly nice man. But she had been too worried about Valerian, and about what the other men had nearly done to her, to show Mr. Farnswourth the appropriate regard. They had reported the theft of her reticule to the nearest constable, but she had no delusions that she would see it again.

And she had said nothing to either the constable or Mr. Farnswourth about the attack. Too many unanswerable questions lay there.

She didn't even know the answers herself.

"Miss Smart, I do not know what you hope to achieve by visiting Her Grace again."

"I merely wish to give her my regards, Mrs. Browning. And they extended the invitation." Abigail lifted her chin and squarely met the eyes of their guide. Hopefully Basil wouldn't reveal that *Abigail* had sent him a missive asking for the visit. Who knew what Basil thought of the request, but he had replied with a simple yes and an invitation had appeared an hour later.

Mrs. Browning's eyes narrowed, but she gave a single nod and led the way once more into the drawing room with its magnificent, but cloying purples.

Abigail's mother trailed behind looking preoccupied, as she had for the last few days. Casting strange looks in Abigail's direction. Abigail tried not to let the fear manifest. Her mother didn't know for sure. She was biding her time, watching and waiting.

Which also meant that Abigail had to sit on every urge she had to yell out for Valerian. To see if he was somewhere in the eerily silent house, waiting for her.

The dowager coolly welcomed them into the drawing room, in much the same manner as she had dismissed them last time. She gave Mrs. Browning a receptive greeting, but barely worked up the social smile to greet Abigail and her mother.

"You have been much on the lips of those around me, Miss Smart," the dowager said, showing her sharp teeth. "Lord Basil has a kind word for you, as do some of his friends."

"Thank you, Your Grace." She inclined her head, knowing that the woman wished to say more, wished to lay bare everything she thought of Abigail, but society's strictures were too well ingrained.

"I find myself most curious as to your future plans."

"Oh, I am merely interested in a fulfilling season, Your Grace. I am honored by any kindness extended our way." Abigail gave a demure nod.

The dowager smiled in her vampirish way. "You are a resilient lady, Miss Smart. I daresay you will find a fulfilling end to your season. I hear that both Mr. Farnswourth and Mr. Sourting have a care in your direction."

But no one with the name of Rainewood or Danforth—nor would there be—was left unsaid, lingering in the air to curl around the teacups that were automatically lifted and sipped as the volleys continued.

She inclined her head. "Thank you, Your Grace."

Basil appeared in the doorway. "Ah, Mrs. Browning, Mrs. Smart, Miss Smart, so good to see you."

He walked through the door and gave a courteous bow before taking a seat. She watched him, slightly unnerved. Had he really done something to his brother? It was hard to countenance Basil doing such a thing—not with that affable smile in place.

"I am looking forward to our outing the day after tomorrow, Miss Smart."

But he had always maintained depths that he kept hidden from society.

"As am I, Lord Basil." She purposely held his gaze and did not look at the dowager, knowing the displeasure she would find.

"It will be a bright spot in this otherwise rainy week."

She had barely noticed the rain, so used to it, but the temperatures this morning had taken an unpleasant downward spiral. She blamed Valerian's absence for her lack of attention.

Or perhaps she had finally just noticed the weather based on her own feelings of depression and anxiety now that he was gone and might not return.

"Abigail."

A rich voice heavy with meaning. The very fabric of it sent ripples of emotion through her, like the raised pattern on a particularly fine piece of silk.

She turned automatically to the sound, half rising from her chair to meet that voice, to hug it, to stroke the fabric in order to be sure it was real. She remembered herself a second later and sank back into her seat.

But her eyes said that her ears did not deceive. There Valerian stood, looking thinner, the planes of his face sharper, but the relief on his features could only be matched by the nearly violent physical loosening of pressure in her body that made her feel lightheaded and shaky.

"Miss Smart, are you ill?" asked the dowager in a sharp tone.

"No, I am rather well. Happy in fact."

She knew she sounded mentally inept, but as Valerian strode through the furniture and the Duchess of Palmbury, she found that again she didn't care a wit for the others' regard.

"Are you well? Did you get away?" He extended a hand to stroke her face, and she wanted to alternately laugh and sob in relief.

"I am well," she repeated. "I do believe Lord Basil is right in that the weather is about to take a turn for the better."

She couldn't stop staring at Valerian though, and as his extended fingers touched her, shock punched her in the gut. Real fingers touched her cheek like an unexpected wave washing over her toes at the beach. Refreshing, shiver inducing, heightening all senses.

"What . . . ?"

Her shock was reflected on his face, and then an even more intense look came over his features. He extended his other hand and began to touch her everywhere—her neck, her hair, the cloth of her poofed shoulders and sleeves.

"Madness," he whispered, but continued to explore, his eyes nearly black as he touched the lace at her neck, the satin of her sash, always returning to her bared skin as if seeking reassurance from the heat beneath.

"Yes, Miss Smart?" Basil prompted.

It was assuredly madness that held her. She tried to pull her thoughts together. "I, I was wondering what you had planned for the outing, Lord Basil."

"I hope to surprise you, Miss Smart. Nothing unpleasant, of course. I daresay Mrs. Browning and Mrs. Smart may also find the activity interesting to watch, if not participate in, at the least."

Abigail nodded, unsure how else to respond. Valerian's cool fingers glided down the hollow of her throat.

"I do hope you like surprises, Miss Smart," Basil said.

Abigail wasn't sure she liked the entirely too watchful set of Basil's eyes.

"Some surprises, Lord Basil. Those that are favorable."

Valerian's fingers touched her cheek. Surprises seemed to be haunting her as much as he was.

"Favorable is always preferable," Basil said with a smile. "It is hard to determine which way the coin might fall sometimes though, I do concede."

"Your own actions precipitating that concession, Lord Basil?"

Basil's smile grew more charming. "Of course, Miss Smart. And I have found it exceedingly interesting to watch your actions and how you deal with difficult situations."

His words could mean anything from the more benign aspect of dealing with Valerian when he was physically present in society to a more nefarious meaning entirely.

Valerian's hands stopped their movement. "It was after we visited Basil's house that those men

appeared. They saw you, Abigail. Followed you."
He suddenly appeared in front of her, eyes narrowed, voice turned harsh. "What are you doing here? It's not safe."

She looked at him in shock. She couldn't very well answer him outright. Her need to stay out of a madhouse reasserted itself now that she had found what she had come for. Him.

She turned back to Basil. "I am flattered, Lord Basil. I hope that I continue to impress you."

"I am sure that you will, Miss Smart. I look forward to watching your next move."

Valerian took a step toward his brother and slapped a hand toward him but it slipped right through. "Do not go anywhere alone with Basil, Abigail."

Abigail hadn't planned on it, but she kept her lips pressed together.

Mrs. Browning shifted the conversation to the dowager and other inane topics. The visit lasted the standard fifteen minutes, thankfully, and she escaped with a repeated vow to see Basil in two days and to also see the Duchess of Palmbury and Basil at the Louddon's gathering that evening.

"That wasn't as poor a showing as I expected from you, Miss Smart," Mrs. Browning conceded once they were safely ensconced in their carriage. "Lord Basil seems to be more interested than I can countenance—and it would be silly to look seriously in that direction—but it may help with your other suitors."

Her mother smiled absently. Along with the strange looks at Abigail, she had been generally off since the break-in.

Changes.

Her mother. Valerian. Mrs. Browning. Valerian's friends.

For good or ill?

Valerian touched her again, his expression mixed, as if he too couldn't believe that he could touch her and at the same time couldn't stop himself from doing so. Instead of the previously fleeting touches, his strokes grew bolder. As if he was afraid that should he touch her less she would slip away. She couldn't comprehend what strange force was at work to allow her to feel him, to allow him to touch her.

The carriage ride grew more tense as bolder strokes turned into completely dominating exploration. She barely kept herself from gasping and squirming on the seat in front of her mother and their starchy companion. She barely kept her head enough to pitifully answer the questions posed by Mrs. Browning. She barely made it into her room, breathily dismissing Telly before Valerian was touching her everywhere, clutching her to him as he ran fingers down the back of her dress.

"I can't believe you are real," one or both of them said. She didn't know which, couldn't separate her thoughts from her words as his fingers swept her hair to the side and lips dragged down her bare neck.

She tilted her head back, gasping. This was something that she had only experienced through watching others. Always watching, never participating. Never experiencing the wonder of another's touch upon her bare flesh. Starved for the smallest amount of tactile need from those of her own household.

Rainewood, no, Valerian, pulled fingers along the edge of her full dress sleeves, skimming the side of her neck, touching the delicate lace and making it flutter just a bit. He pulled his fingers along the soft ribs of the weave and although it lifted as if caught by a slight breeze, the fabric didn't release.

The action broke the spell. "Can you feel it?" she asked.

Can you feel me? echoed in the silence.

"It is like a touch through a glove." He flexed his lean, strong, bare fingers and ran them down the satin waist of her dress, skimming fire beneath. "Like the waterfall, smooth but dangerous."

"The waterfall?"

"My memories, me, *I* slip down the waterfall when you are not near. It's something I can't touch, can't grab, can't feel." His hand moved to her bare flesh and she shivered as they skimmed the skin at her throat. "But you, everything is alive and bright the moment I set my fingers to you."

She struggled to form thought, to catch her breath as his fingers curved around her nape and into her hair. To remember that he was acting like this because he needed her—that she was the only one to whom he could turn.

"You physically hit that man yesterday."

His fingers stopped their exploration. "He was hurting you. You got away without harm."

It wasn't a question. It was a demand. As if he wouldn't accept any other answer.

"Yes."

He nodded and pulled her to him—a delicious warmth covered by a cool edge. His body was hard against hers, but leaner. He had always been lean and muscular, perfectly fit for his height, but feeling him against her, he was thinner by a noticeable degree.

"Those men. I don't understand."

He stilled against her. "Nor I. I saw them at the hell. I don't know the name of the one who held you, but the man talking was called Evans by another. I don't know who they are, but at the hell a man named Burns was ordering around the man who held you. Burns sent the two boys to Golden Square. He hinted at knowledge of me."

She shivered. "The one talking seemed the more dangerous, even with . . . even with . . ."

A hand stroked down her back, then up again and into her nape. "Yes."

He didn't say anything else for a second, just stroked her neck, but he said softly into her hair. "It is my fault for putting you in the situation."

No, it had been her own choice. Not the smartest one, but her choice all the same. "What happened to you? After?"

He tensed. "I returned to the place where they are holding me. Templing is there too. I saw him strapped down."

Shock shot through her. "Strapped to what?"

He let go of her and stepped away. "A table. I think . . . I think someone is performing experiments on us."

She swallowed and took in his form. "And you are reflecting that in your present state. You are thinner."

"Weaker," he shot back, prowling toward the dresser and concentrating before flicking a comb. It didn't move. "I couldn't get up. Couldn't fight. My hands are strapped as well, and I can do nothing before they knock me back out. Then I wake once more in Grayton House."

She swallowed thickly again. "It sounds like a hospital."

"I've been to Bethlehem. It's not Bedlam, or at least not a part to which I'm familiar." He hesitated before turning to her. "Have you visited any of the others?"

She looked away. "One. But it was a small asylum."

"Did they use straps?"

"Yes." Dozens and dozens of straps ready and waiting to clamp her down and never let her back up. The doctor had whispered in her ear that the straps were always a possibility in her treatment were she to step out of line. She had read in his eyes that he relished the thought. The only thing that had stopped him was the threat of her mother, who had asked him to perform other tests before resorting to the less savory treatments. Like . . .

No, no she wouldn't think on it.

"But it is doubtful that is where you are being held," she said after realizing that she had been staring, frozen like some small woodland animal on the wrong end of a hunt, for a few seconds.

"Why do you say that?"

"I just do. Were there identifiable smells or sounds? Can you describe the building at all? There are dozens of hospitals, and who knows if you are not in a confined space that looks remarkably like one."

"Yes." He ran a hand through his hair, ruffling it before the strands settled back into place. "White walls, few windows. Two men at least."

"That isn't much to go on."

"I need to keep disappearing, returning to gather more information." He closed his eyes as if concentrating on doing just that. "But I can't seem to do it without some provocation from you."

"I don't know if it is wise for you to disappear again," she said uneasily.

"Why?"

"You look worse each time you reappear." And the fear kept increasing that he wouldn't return at all.

"Thank you, Smart." His moody voice was full of sarcasm. "I will endeavor to look my best the next time I return from torture."

She fought the urge to reach out and touch him, but all of her insecurities concerning him kicked back into the fore and she kept her hands at her side.

He looked toward the partially opened drapes. "There was something. Letters through the one window. M-A-L."

"Like a sign across the street?"

"Yes."

"I can ask Telly. Have her look into it."

He slowly nodded.

"I am to attend the Louddon's party tonight," she said. "All of your cronies will be there. Perhaps now you will be able to talk to or touch one of them as well." He hadn't been able to touch Basil, so she didn't think that was likely, but who knew. He had been able to hit that man.

She hesitated. "Basil will be there. And if we don't learn more from him tonight, I will try and drag information from him the day after tomorrow. Perhaps we can settle the matter of his—"

"You are meeting with Basil in two days?"

"Yes, didn't you hear the conversation?"

"I wasn't paying attention to that part."

"Oh, well I am. Meeting with him, that is."

"No."

She blinked. "I assure you that I am. My mother and Mrs. Browning will be there. It is hardly as if we are having a liaison. Or that he could harm me in the middle of Hyde Park."

"Just like someone couldn't have harmed you in the middle of the fair yesterday?" he said darkly.

"That—" She licked suddenly dry lips. "That was different."

"All it takes is for someone or something to separate you from your companions."

"I will hardly choose to run after a footpad again."

"There are dozens of other ways."

"Valerian, I can't stop living just because I'm scared." Which was a darkly humorous statement. She had determined her life over when the doctor had finished with her. Had remained in a state of shock for months before pulling herself together and saying that she would never again give someone that power over her—to put her in such a state. She would not let fear rule her. At least not to that extent.

She still had to live within the strictures of society. Still had to make sure that she kept herself out of the hands of people like that.

But caution was different from fear. And choices were different from dictates.

She continued, "People who want to do harm can always try and separate one person from the pack, but I am in a better position now that I know to look for it."

His eyes grew darker, but there was something unreadable in their depths too. "You called me Valerian."

She fiddled with her lace cuff. "That is your name, is it not?"

"You never call me that without sarcasm." *Anymore*, went unstated.

Her hand went to her waist. "And you never call me Abigail, if you'll remember."

He shook his head, but she continued before he could say anything. "Back to the situation," she said, trying to get the conversation away from more uncomfortable topics. "It is unreasonable to avoid Basil in public spaces."

Valerian's eyes tightened.

"We will go to the ball tonight and see if there is anything we can glean about Basil or Number Eighteen."

There was a tentative knock on the door. As she invited Telly in she felt a light touch at her neck—reassuring, demanding, claiming. Which Rainewood would win at the end? The old one, the new one, or a combination of the two? Or was each incarnation designed to torment her forever?

Chapter 13

Abigail wound through the dense ballroom crowd with a heightened sense of purpose to her movements. Valerian prowled behind like a large pet cat impatiently waiting for her to fill his dish.

She smiled at the image. She might be uncomfortably turning into one of the young women who groveled for a word from Valerian and preened with confidence when in his good graces, but he was equally cursed at the moment.

"Feeling good tonight, Smart?" His fingers pulled down the exposed skin of her arm, then continued and curved beneath the shoulder of her dress to pull her against him. She tried to cover the fact that she had awkwardly moved an inch forward from no apparent cause, but her heart was beating too quickly and her breath gusting too fast.

He hadn't been able to touch or talk to anyone else in the room, so he seemed to have concentrated all of his ability to do so on her once again.

There was an ironic aspect that their conversations were still private—even though they took place in the belly of the ton.

He leaned forward and whispered in her ear. "I could do all manners of things to you here in the ballroom, and no one would notice."

Heat, searing and forceful, burned her.

"Miss Smart, might I remark that you are looking quite lovely tonight."

She jerked away from Valerian and turned to see Aidan Campbell standing before her, the look that he had been sporting whenever their eyes met during the last week was deeper and more urgent.

"Thank you, Mr. Campbell," she said politely, carefully looking around to make sure there were others near. "It is a pleasant evening, is it not? I find myself succumbing to the pleasure of the teasing weather that states summer is nearing."

He smiled. "How lovely, Miss Smart. I too find summer to be most pleasurable." A dance struck up—a waltz. He bowed to her. "I wonder if you would do me the honor?"

"Don't do it, Abigail," Valerian said darkly, his eyes narrowed slits as he looked at his friend.

She looked into the crowd to see shocked or unreadable expressions on the faces of most of Rainewood's group.

"He's up to something," Valerian said more insistently, but there was a tinge of something else in his voice. She almost dropped her fan in shock when she recognized the emotion.

She smiled widely at Campbell, fanning the green flames. "Of course, Mr. Campbell, it would be my pleasure."

She was on the lookout for oddities in behavior, and Campbell's definitely qualified as such. Nothing could happen in the middle of the dance floor though—besides threats. And in that case they would be one step closer to the truth. One step closer to finding Valerian's body.

To her losing him again.

She shut down that train of thought and accepted Campbell's extended arm as he escorted her onto the floor.

The violins struck their opening measures and Campbell competently began the three-beat rhythm. He was a good partner. Confident and practiced.

"You are a very good dancer, Mr. Campbell."

"As are you, Miss Smart. I daresay I have missed a keen opportunity to partner you all these months."

She tilted her head to regard him. "You could have asked me to dance, Mr. Campbell. Though I am surprised even now that you have."

"Raine wouldn't much have liked it, would he have?"

Shock rocked her. But judging by the explosive expression on Valerian's face as he paced alongside, she was pretty sure that was an accurate statement.

"I don't know to what you refer."

"Don't you?"

"No. But if I did, do you always do what Rainewood wants?"

A false smile appeared upon his lips. "Usually, yes. And I have long suspected more between the two of you."

Her posture tightened. "Oh?"

"Yes. It's in the way you interact. Or strictly don't, I should say. I can't put my finger on what it is, but the other day it shone brightly."

"Lord Rainewood was quite unpleasant the other night. I found myself equally unpleasant in his company, unfortunately."

A dark melody whispered in her ear as she passed. "We'll see how unpleasant you feel later, Abigail," Valerian's voice darkly promised.

"Are the two of you lovers?"

She missed a step, then another as Campbell shifted to help her back into the rhythm. "Pardon me?"

"I asked if the two of you are lovers." There was a pinched look to Campbell's expression. "It would be just like Raine to cover an indiscretion so boldly."

"I think I am finished with this conversation, Mr. Campbell. Thank you for the dance." She tried to extricate her hand, but he held tight.

"No, forgive me." There was an almost desperate air to the plea. "My lips run away. I admit to maddening jealousy."

She stared, hard, but allowed him to continue to lead. "I find that hard to believe, Mr. Campbell. With how often you associate with Rainewood and the rest, it would seem you are on the same page as they in how I am viewed. Invisible."

"And yet, I am but a simple coward, Miss Smart. Only with Raine gone do I now come forward to dance with you."

"I admit to thinking you must have an ulterior motive, Mr. Campbell."

There was a sudden sparkle in his eyes—not the darkening that she had imagined would take place. "A very keen one, in fact. It is possible that I wish to turn our dance into two and perhaps two dances into a carriage ride through Hyde."

She missed a step again. She could hear Valerian behind her swearing up, down, and around about everything from Campbell's stupidity to his parentage. He seemed to find exceptional fodder with one's parentage she'd noticed.

"I don't know whether to be amused or ashamed that you seem to think so little of me that you would miss a step, when all of the rest of your footwork has been so graceful," Campbell said.

"I confess I find myself at a loss, Mr. Campbell. You have taken me by complete surprise."

He looked over her shoulder. "And that is to my detriment. I should never have relied on the grace of my compatriots to define my actions."

Pretty words. Earnest eyes. Abigail didn't believe a bit of it.

Her mother, however, would have a fit were she to turn down such a lucrative possible match, a future *viscount*—her mother would be over the moon. She had seen in the ledger the amount of money Campbell owed—especially to Valerian. At the very least it would be interesting to make him confess his motivation for pursuing her so suddenly.

"Should you choose to call, you will not be turned aside." She tilted her head in the other direction to observe him, watching his shifting expressions. Satisfaction, joy, darkness, surprise. If only she knew which emotion to trust. It could all be a lark.

Though—she looked at the group gathered along the side—most of them looked quite displeased.

"Have you lost your sense? Tell him you want nothing to do with him," Valerian demanded.

She smiled at Aidan Campbell and let him twirl her away from the darkening face of her ghostly companion. Sometimes decisions had more than one effect, for good or ill. Valerian's reaction struck something deep and satisfying within her. She had scoffed at females for such actions before, but now . . . a warm giddiness overtook her as she saw his outrage as she twirled again. She could almost understand the addiction.

"That is quite wonderful to hear," Campbell said with a satisfied edge to his voice. "I will make an appointment."

She inclined her head.

"He's either dangerous or after your money," Valerian insisted, leaving a trail of shivering dancers in his wake as he passed through, trying to stay with them.

Money—their blessing and curse. It was the one thing that had kept them in decent stead in the ton. The Smarts had fallen from society two generations ago, destitute. Renewed fortunes had provided them entrance once again.

Those renewed fortunes had bought Mrs. Browning and an audience at court. Her mother had used their money liberally to ensure their base success. If Rainewood had given them a modicum of good will, they would have secured their standing.

She gave him a dark look over Campbell's shoulder. She recalled her debut as clearly as if it had occurred yesterday.

Campbell seemed to be on the same train of thought. "I remember when you made your debut. Every eye was on you that night."

She wanted to ask Campbell when he had

become possessed of a suitor's tongue. Instead she laughed lightly. "That is kind of you, Mr. Campbell, but hardly true, I think."

He tilted his head. "No, it was quite true. I believe the crowd went silent in contemplation of where you would take your place in the social milieu. You are a beautiful woman."

"That is very kind of you," she repeated, not knowing what else to add—such as how one's deep pockets always made one more attractive.

"What did you do to Raine to make him react so negatively to you on the evening of your debut?"

She hadn't expected the question. No one had been brave enough to ask it. They had just taken their cues from whichever side of the social circle they resided.

"Perhaps Lord Rainewood was just having a bad night. Unlucky for me."

"Perhaps." He sounded entirely unconvinced. "Raine sometimes has his piques, it is true."

"I would say so." She glared at the topic of conversation.

Campbell swiftly turned her. "How did you come to know of Oxting Stables?"

She almost missed another step at the abrupt topic switch, but held together and gracefully glided forward. "I must have heard someone mention it in idle conversation." Partially true.

"Mmmm. I confess that you intrigue me, Miss Smart." He twirled her competently for the final time as the violins pulled their last note to a close. "You always have."

The twirl put her back in view of Valerian's face, which was dark and deadly. His eyes met hers and he stepped forward through Campbell, placing himself between them, his height obscuring Campbell from view.

She gasped as his fingers curled possessively around her waist.

"Miss Smart, are you ill?" Campbell asked from somewhere behind Valerian.

She seemed to get asked that an awful lot in the presence of Valerian. "No, it is just rather warm in here, is it not?" She fanned herself with her gloved hand, wishing she'd brought a real fan, trying to cover up her deepening color, her parted lips, and the sweat collecting on her brow as Valerian pulled a hand up her back and around her nape, massaging the skin there.

She tried not to react. To step away from him. To avoid the pull.

She stepped left, removing herself from his grip and putting Campbell back in her sights. Campbell's eyes had darkened, and she recognized the signs of a man who was partially aroused. She had seen the burgeoning look too many times in the faces of spirits. What had appeared on her face to have made Campbell react that way?

"Thank you for the dance, Mr. Campbell."

He bowed, eyes never leaving hers. "Thank you, Miss Smart. I look forward to seeing you again, in perhaps a less formal venue."

She tipped her head and allowed him to lead her back to the sidelines. He walked closer to her than he had before they'd stepped onto the dance floor. Seeing some of Rainewood's other lackeys heading their way, and feeling unnerved in more ways than one, Abigail excused herself as quickly as she could and walked over to where Phillip, Edwina, and Gregory were conversing about technical marvels with Sir Walter Malcolm.

"Sir Walter, how good to see you," Abigail said. The man had been unfailingly kind to her since her debut, even in the presence of Valerian's dismissal and the coldness of his wife and daughter.

"Likewise, Miss Smart." He smiled good-naturedly. "Your mother mentioned that you were going to watch the balloon competition in a few days' time."

"I am."

"Excellent! Mr. Brockwell will make a good showing, I am sure. I look forward to seeing his design."

Phillip flushed beneath the praise. "I aim to do so, Sir Walter."

"Excellent. I shall see you both upon the morrow. And perhaps Miss Penshard as well?"

Edwina nodded, blond curls bobbing above her cherry cheeks.

Sir Walter took his leave.

Edwina turned inquiring eyes on her. "I saw you dancing with Mr. Campbell."

Gregory's disgusted look spoke of far darker thoughts than Edwina was expressing—Edwina was always a bright light, willing to forgive any slight or indiscretion. Phillip simply looked uncomfortable.

"He asked," she said simply.

Edwina looked thoughtful, but nodded. Gregory was hardly as kind.

"After the Malcolm's ball, you danced with him because he asked?" Gregory narrowed his eyes. "He has ignoble intentions."

From the corner of her eye, she could see Valerian's darkly satisfied look.

"Would you not be curious as to what they are?" she asked Gregory.

"No. I know what they are. I would have publicly cut him. Given him a taste of his own behavior."

Edwina put a hand on his arm. "Now, Gregory, I am sure that is not true. We can forgive those who hurt us."

If it had been anyone else, Gregory would have assuredly shrugged off the hand, but he simply pursed his lips. "You are foolish in your forgiveness, Edwina. I thought Miss Smart more intelligent."

"I am sorry to disappoint you, Mr. Penshard," she said tartly.

Phillip looked increasingly uncomfortable. But then he had always hated confrontation, unlike Gregory.

"Be careful with whom you choose to associate, Miss Smart. We have always been your allies. Don't annoy me." His green eyes were nearly black.

"Gregory! Apologize this instant," Edwina declared.

"I will not. If she thinks to take up with them now that Rainewood's out of the picture, then she deserves our scorn."

Valerian stepped forward, eyes narrowed on Gregory. "He knows something. I knew it."

"What do you mean, now that Rainewood is out of the picture?" Abigail demanded.

Edwina and Phillip also looked at Gregory in question. Phillip's eyes darted between Abigail and Gregory anxiously.

"You should be relieved he's gone," Gregory said.

"Or is it as I suspected—and you never dropped that heavy girlish torch you carried for him?"

Her mouth dropped. "Pardon me?"

Gregory laughed darkly. "I suppose if you are dancing with Campbell and dancing on Danforth, then perhaps I am mistaken."

It wasn't a surprise that Gregory would be irritated by her outing with Basil or dance with Campbell, but she was still taken aback by his acidic tone.

She narrowed her eyes on him. "I challenge you to live as a woman in this society. To see how well you deal with turning down such invitations," she said as calmly as she could manage.

Even Valerian's eyes looked at her in an assessing manner, unreadable.

Gregory's eyes pinched, the look in them flat and unsympathetic.

She squared her shoulders and prepared for war, recalling an earlier conversation with Valerian. "Why do you require a doctor, Mr. Penshard?"

"Mother is looking for you, Ed." Gregory firmly took Edwina's arm and gave her a push. "Hurry."

Edwina gave him a questioning glance before dutifully shuffling off.

Gregory turned back to her. "Watch yourself, Miss Smart." He strode off in the direction he had pushed Edwina.

Unnerved, Abigail looked at Phillip, whose besotted gaze focused on Edwina's retreating back. "Mr. Brockwell?"

Phillip looked like he might throw up in the potted ferns at any moment from anxiety. "Yes?"

"Do you agree with Mr. Penshard about my

new association with the members of Rainewood's group?"

Phillip twitched. "I, I don't know, Miss Smart. They have hardly been kind to us. But, you must do as you wish. Pardon me, but I must go."

He quickly walked away leaving her standing on the sidelines, a bit lost.

Campbell and Mr. Stagen suddenly appeared next to her before she could say anything to Valerian. "That is hardly an expression I wish to see upon your lovely face, Miss Smart," Campbell said. "Let us cheer you up."

Valerian's hands fisted at his sides.

Phillip, Edwina, and Gregory had left her and Rainewood's crowd had taken up residence. Her world had tilted, and she didn't know which side was up.

Valerian was a bear for the rest of the party and through the ride home—irritated that Campbell seemed to be extraordinarily attentive all of a sudden.

"Perhaps Campbell is simply interested in me." She threw her wrap on the bed. "There is nothing so horrid about me, I'll have you know." Other than the slightly crazy bit, of course. "And Campbell can offer social security and companionship," she couldn't resist adding.

"There's nothing you can get from Campbell that you wouldn't get a thousand times better from me."

Her lips parted, but before she could form a response, his lips descended hard upon hers.

Chapter 14

The actual feel of her lips shocked him even as he knew that he'd be able to kiss her. But thinking about touching his lips to hers and actually doing it were two entirely separate things. They had shared one kiss in the past, one mistaken glorious moment before all had crashed down.

This kiss was nothing like that. Except for the fact that everything in him seemed to shatter as her breath caught, her lips parted, and she kissed him back with just as much force as he was kissing her.

Her lips felt like the softest blanket, but the strength beneath them, her vibrant personality, was even more intoxicating, drugging. Somehow his fingers found their way into the back of her hair, curling at the top of her nape, bringing her closer still. She made a little noise and his body responded, wanting to press against hers as hard as he could, to push her back toward the bed and complete the pieces that begged to be interlocked.

He drew his hand down her neck instead, around the curve of her collarbone to the cloth at her shoulder, the satin rippling beneath his fingers as they sought for the sweeter feel of more deliciously bared skin.

He could spend hours running his fingers down the back of her arm, soft as velvet, smooth as silk, her skin composed of the finest materials found on earth. It was one of the reasons he always indulged in taunting her, but now, open to him, starved from touching her for the days, weeks, that he'd been disallowed physical contact, touching her was what it had to be like to touch the moon when it was low slung and full, glowing and silky.

She broke the kiss, her cheek level with his as she panted in his ear. "Valerian, I'm not sure that—"

"That this is a good idea?" he said into her ear.

She nodded jerkily.

"You are right." Her neck was so near, the scent of her mild, breezy soap tingling every sense he had feared lost to him. "It is a great idea."

His lips sought the spot of her neck just beneath the side of her chin where the skin curved and her pulse beat a mad tempo. Her breath caught and her head arched back allowing him greater access. The hand around her nape moved down her back, down her spine, down the edges of her hips to curl around her rear and hike her against him. Her body responded automatically and one leg bent and lifted to fit them together.

God, she drove him mad. Even in this, something with which she should have no experience, she fired his blood, tempting him to take more and more until she conceded.

He continued to stroke the lovely skin of her arm with his other hand, pulling downward to her gloved fingers. He gripped the edge of the glove in one hand, determined to remove the barrier, to remove each barrier between them. To rid himself of whatever demon had resided within him since he'd turned old enough to know the difference between the girl he had romped with as friends and the woman she had started to become.

There was something so symbolic in removing her glove. As if it represented all that had become wedged between them. Children playing, little adults trying to fit their roles. Changing circumstances and bad choices that had irrevocably driven the division.

Removing the glove was a little like removing the wedge. Opening his heart back up to something that he had closed it to long ago, too hurt and confused to do otherwise, then too proud and stubborn to recognize any fault of his own.

He gripped the glove more firmly and just before he could make the final decision to remove it fully, his fingers slipped through. He paused for half a second. No, they must have slipped *from* the fabric instead. He pulled his suddenly free fingers back along her arm, lifting his head from her neck to look at her, eyes hazy and half closed, head tilted back.

His other hand moved along her backside, hiking her closer still, making her eyes flutter shut for a second before opening again to stare at him, challenge him, as always.

There was nothing he could do but kiss her again, maneuvering her against the back of the dressing chair, using the force to keep them pressed together below as his fingers once more sought her nape, bringing them closer, deepening the kiss, tasting every part of her mouth.

Everything in his body urged him to remove the layers between them. And the analytical portion of his mind was silent for once, not weighing the decision, too distracted by the wonderful feel of her. Feeling he had been denied since falling into this dream.

He moved his hand back down to her glove and gripped the edge. He gave a tug and his fingers fell through the fabric.

He pulled his lips from hers and looked down at her wrist, only the heavy breathing and constant tick of the mantel clock making sound. He traced a finger around the top of her glove, around the soft, strong skin, then dipped beneath the glove to trace the untouched flesh there. She unconsciously arched against him with a gasp.

He could feel the edge of her glove on the sensitive top of his finger, just behind the cuticle. It was a muted feeling of silk, not the vibrant edge that her skin possessed. He rubbed against the fabric to try and gather more feeling.

His finger pulled through.

His body went still.

"What? What is wrong?"

He could hear the uncertainty in her voice, could feel her body tense. The edge of battle always there, waiting for him. He was too long practiced at watching and reading her to know that there was a part of her waiting for him to finish the game. The game that she thought he still played. To do something irrevocable.

He stepped back, unnerved. Unnerved by more than the fact that he was completely able to touch her skin, but still unable to touch much else. Unnerved by his thoughts on what lay between them, wedged still.

What he had placed there. What she had built upon.

He opened his mouth, but the colder part of his brain came to his rescue. "I can't touch your clothing. For very long, that is. I can't remove it."

Her cheeks, already bright, blushed a deep rose. A beautiful color next to her vibrant eyes and kiss-puffed lips.

"Oh." She tugged self-consciously at her shoulder sleeve.

"Why?"

"I don't know." Her cheeks took on a brighter glow, one that made her look even more delectable.

Telly bustled inside. It would have been decidedly awkward had she entered just one minute earlier.

He watched Abigail run a hand down her hair in an attempt to calm herself. Sometimes he felt as if he knew her better than he knew himself.

Telly helped Abigail remove her clothing, which although a magnificent sight, left a bitter taste in his mouth. He could touch her, miraculously, but not enough. Not enough to forget what or where he was. Where was he? Would he be in this cursed state forever? Or once the men who had taken him finished doing whatever it was they were doing, would he disappear as Abigail had said that some spirits did?

Spirits like his brother's.

The shoulder cuffs of her dress caught on her wrists as Telly tugged the gown from her. Straps of cloth tying her in. He rubbed his wrists. How was he going to discover where he was being held without putting Abigail in more danger? Abigail seemed determined to help him even considering what he had done to her for the last few years.

He watched her, absently rubbing his wrists. Shackles that bound him in life, death, and in between.

Abigail's eyes met his and her gaze shifted to the wrists he irritably stroked, her emotions reflected in her eyes. Pity, determination. He dropped his hands and paced to the window, pressing into the drapes in order to look through the panes, his back to her. He ignored the low conversation behind him, instead absorbed in his own morbid thoughts.

He heard the door close and a light hand ran down his back. "Telly said that she identified more than a dozen places that start with M-A-L or have that letter sequence in the name. Mostly pubs and taverns. We can search tomorrow."

He wondered if tomorrow would be too late, but he simply nodded, the innate concern for her that had never disappeared—instead overlaid with anger and bitterness these past years—blossomed fully again.

"She said that neither she nor the man who helped her read the signs were aware of any hospitals or asylums being near, but we can take the carriage around to check at some point when mother and Mrs. Browning aren't aware. They would ask too many questions otherwise."

"Why do you put up with her?"

"She's my mother."

He turned to her. "No, not your mother, though she is unfortunate for you as well. I meant Mrs. Browning."

She stepped back and returned to her dressing table, lifting a brush and running the tines along her palm. Something tickled at the edges of his mind. "She has provided us with entrance to society. I think most would ask why she puts up with us."

"You could do better."

A mocking little smile worked along her mouth before she turned her back fully to him, hiding her face. "No, we couldn't. Mrs. Browning is far more than we could hope for."

He frowned and she dropped the brush, meeting his eyes in the mirror.

"Do you seek to argue?" she asked.

Did he? Yes, he usually did when it came to her. Far better to argue and be angry than to give in to other, more insidious feelings.

"Don't you tire of it?" She wiped a hand along the looking glass, and he could see her reflected face, lost and searching, sad. "Wish that things could be different?"

"Things are different," he said automatically.

She laughed without humor. "Yes. But for how long?"

"What do you mean?" He narrowed his eyes at her. "Do you know something about what will happen to me?"

Perhaps she had been lying this whole time—this dream-like incarnation of Abigail—stringing him along, knowing exactly what would happen to him. Her tales of spirits echoing the real Abigail, merely hiding the fact that his body was already dying. That he would disappear to wherever it was that spirits disappeared.

He had never been fond of the notion of death, personally. It seemed like giving up, of failing. Of something he couldn't control. Like his brother's death. Unnecessary. A circumstance he should have been able to change.

Her eyes closed and she once more fingered the brush on the table. "I merely meant that nothing stays the same. Everything changes. Nothing can be counted upon."

"Plenty can be counted on. Prestige, ancestry, that Parliament will always produce brilliant men and jackasses."

"You are so caught up in lineage. You use it at every opportunity to degrade or to compliment."

"It is a vital component in our world. That should hardly be a surprise to someone who walks within it." He leveled a look at her through the shifting glass, the slight imperfections of the glass causing her reflection to ripple.

"Don't be a boor, Valerian." She looked down at the table.

The spike of pleasure from her use of his name caught him by surprise again. The spike turned sour as he pondered a response.

"What difference does it make?" He grit his teeth, lying. It had made all the difference in the world between them. "You should hardly be worried about your lineage. It is safe enough."

Her head shot up sharply.

He pretended to ignore the reaction. "Or perhaps your mind is telling you to wait. Saying you are not ready for marriage. In which case"—he wiped a hand along his leg—"I think you should listen to that instinct and not get betrothed so spuriously."

He thought that quite brilliant actually. He himself had been pushing away his betrothal for more than a year. He sometimes felt as if he could continue to do so indefinitely, though he knew his father might try to force him one of these days.

She laughed again, and once more her voice held no humor. Her eyes dropped to the brush so that he could not read them through the glass. "Mother would be supremely unsupportive of that plan, of course."

"She can't make you marry." A silly response as he recognized that he would do his duty eventually as well. Every man of his circle must.

"No." There was something about the hitch in the word, as if there were an unstated "but" attached.

"The last time I checked, the bride did need to consent."

"Consent to marriage," she said darkly.

He narrowed eyes at her. "Yes, what else?"

She waved a hand. "Marriage, of course."

"What are you hiding, Abigail?"

"Nothing."

"Then why do you continuously hint at something as if you want me to know."

"Want you to know? That is rich. You are the last person with whom I'd care to share my secrets."

"Why? I've kept them, have I not?"

She walked brusquely to the bed. "We will go searching tomorrow, see Basil the next day, and hopefully figure out what the devil this is all about—to borrow your phrase. Perhaps find your body, set you to rights once more, and allow you to continue your one-man terror campaign of the ton."

"I don't know if I should feel pleased by your compliment that I can terrorize the ton single-handedly or annoyed that you are ignoring my question." The spike of anger that covered another emotion caused him to cross his arms.

She said nothing, didn't turn around.

"Abigail—"

She turned tired eyes to him, cutting him off before he could formulate what he wanted to say. "No. We can argue tomorrow. Please. I can't do this now. I need to sleep."

Anger combined with the stranger, soft emotions she always provoked, and jumbled the words in his head.

"Very well."

He watched her fall asleep, and when her breath evened, he moved next to her and curled around her heat, feeling her even breaths against his unmoving, deadened chest.

When Abigail woke, Valerian was gone. Skulking about the house, no doubt. She stretched and then stared pensively at the ceiling. He had kissed her last night. Actually kissed her.

The kiss had been much better last night than the first time he'd kissed her. Though the first time she'd only been thirteen, and he fifteen, so she didn't think it quite a fair comparison. It was hard to countenance that the emotions evoked at thirteen had been less confusing than her emotions now. She had thought her world turned completely on end then.

She lifted the covers and swung her feet from the bed. She was surprised Telly hadn't been in to wake her already. The light had already started to seep past the drapes—around the edges that hadn't been tightly fastened.

She paused for a moment to listen to the bustling of the servants going about their tasks, a muted conversation somewhere in the hall, the birds chirping a violent melody outside.

Aunt Effie sat in her corner, an almost pensive cast to her face as she raised her teacup. She usually was chattering incessantly by this time of the morn.

"Is something amiss, Aunt Effie?" she asked absently, not expecting an answer as she pushed from the bed to the floor.

"No."

Abigail landed heavily on her feet, jerking to stare at the apparition who suddenly smiled battily and waved her teacup. "Just thinking about my lemons. Dreadful winter. Spring is coming though. The blooms are so lovely. The lemons so tantalizing. And soon, soon it will be summer."

Abigail continued to stare. Aunt Effie had a very rigid routine—she had since the day Abigail had moved into the house years ago and adopted her as an "aunt." Never had she said the like.

"I've always loved summer," Abigail carefully replied, not knowing what type of response she might receive, if any.

"Oh yes, dear." The spirit looked directly at her. "I'm sure that you have. Lovely memories, yes?"

Through her shock Abigail acknowledged that most of her summer memories were good ones. Romping with Valerian, and then waiting for him to return from Eton those few precious years between his start there and the end of their friendship.

"I'm sure that you will have many more, dear." Effie raised her cup to drink, watching her over the edge.

"I . . ." Abigail wet her lips. "Why are you suddenly chatting with me like this, Aunt Effie?"

The spirit tilted her head and opened her mouth to answer.

Valerian burst through the door. "There is a man downstairs asking for you. I dislike the look of him."

"Really, Valerian, you promised to help me with my suitors—"

"He's not a suitor, Abigail."

Something in his tone made her pause.

"Dreadful winter." Aunt Effie shook her head and started chatting about tea and Mabel, the same words she'd always used, the same actions she'd always performed. As if nothing had changed.

Abigail frowned, but turned to Valerian. "I don't understand. You mean a man paying a social visit? Or a constable?"

She thought of the stolen ledger. Did it count if you only had possession of the stolen item for a few short minutes?

"Neither. Hurry and get dressed, then leave down the back stairs."

She stared at him. "Whatever for?"

"I told you, I don't like the look of him. Your mother sent Mrs. Browning a note saying you would not be attending your appointments this morning due to sickness. This man appeared soon after."

Fear trickled through her, but she clamped it down before it could spread to panic. "What does the man look like?"

"Small, brown-haired." He waved a hand. "Barely descript. I'd never notice him in a crowd. But I don't like his eyes."

"Does he carry a cane?" Please, no.

Valerian's eyes narrowed. "Silver-handled, shape of a snake."

The room tilted.

"Abigail? Abigail, what the devil?"

Yes, those were the appropriate words. She looked up to see Valerian holding her arms, steadying her.

"You know the man. Who is he?"

She laughed a little hysterically. "Oh, no one important."

There was a knock on the door. "Miss?"

"Tell your maid to help you escape," he demanded.

She opened her mouth, but the handle turned, and her mother appeared in the door instead, brows furrowed.

"Abigail, you must dress quickly," her mother said.

"No."

"Abigail!"

"Mother," she whispered. "Why?"

Her mother didn't ask how she knew. "Because you need help. If you already know who is below, then your problem never disappeared. You lied to me."

Abigail shook her head. "Please."

Her mother looked away. "It is for the best, Abigail. Believe me. Everything will be better. You will be happier. Remember when you were happy?"

"I'm happy now, Mother."

"No, you haven't been happy for a long time, Abigail. Let him make this right."

"You can make it right by making him leave." Her voice rose, a hysterical edge to the words. "You know what he wants to do."

Something passed over her mother's face. "I told him he couldn't. He's just going to speak with you. Maybe do a few exercises."

"Abigail, tell me what is going on. Right now," Valerian's voice said in her ear.

"No." She answered to both. "Send him away, Mother."

"No, Abigail." Her mother lifted her head. "Mrs. Browning has already begun to suspect something is off. She is asking questions that I cannot answer."

Coldness washed through her. "This was your idea, Mother. This whole thing was your plan. What are you going to do if I don't speak with him? Take us back to the country? Leave society? Your obsession, not mine."

Her mother's lips tightened and her eyes clouded. "It is for your own good. Can you not see what a better life you will have?"

Abigail wanted to sob. "Yes, I can see what you want, Mother. And it is working well enough as it is. Don't do this."

"It will help." The firm conviction in her mother's voice stopped her for a moment. "Believe me.

All you have to do is rid yourself of the curse, and
you will feel—"

"Much, much better."

Her heart stopped as the brown-haired, brown-
eyed, non-descript man moved around her mother
and through the open door. There was a sharp,
calculating look in his eyes, and in the confident,
slick way he moved, tapping his cane to a beat that
demanded attention and obedience.

"Who is he?" Valerian demanded.

"It has been a long time, Miss Smart, has it
not?" He placed a satchel down near the dressing
table and began unbuttoning his left cuff, curling
it up.

"Dr. Myers," her mother said softly. "You should
be waiting in the drawing room."

The doctor shot her mother an oily smile. "But I
know Miss Smart quite well already. I didn't think
she would mind."

"I do mind. Get out."

"Oh, so feisty still." He rolled his right cuff. "It
has been far too long, Miss Smart."

"Mother, tell him to get out."

"Now, Mrs. Smart, you know that this is for her
own good. She will be far better served if you left
us alone. I will keep to my promise." He smiled. It
was not a nice smile, but her mother nodded and
turned to leave, not meeting Abigail's eyes.

"Mother, I will never forgive you."

She hesitated in the doorway. "Someday, Abigail, you will thank me." She closed the door. The
lock turned on the other side.

"Smart, answer me, who is he?" Valerian shook
her arms, trying to gain an answer.

Effie gave a sympathetic wail in the corner and slipped through the wall.

"Dr. Myers, you should leave. I have not invited you into my bedroom, which is beyond socially egregious."

"Oh, but we must get reacquainted, Miss Smart. Far better for you to remember what you are missing out on by not giving yourself over to me for a full treatment." His eyes strayed to the bed, and she gripped Valerian's arm for a second before tearing herself away.

"I find your treatments foul, just as I find everything else about you." She strode to her dressing table, seemingly putting things in order on top while trying to find a useful weapon. Never losing sight of the intruder through the looking glass. It was always a very bad idea to take her eyes away from Dr. Myers.

"Shall we start with the most boring part of this intervention?" He walked toward her and she unconsciously backed away. He smiled and pulled her dressing chair away from the table and sat in it, leaning his cane against his leg and his bag on top of the table. "The questions?"

She said nothing, moving away to the other side of the room, looking for anything that might aid her.

"Are you still seeing ghosts, Miss Smart?"

"No, only jackasses."

Valerian circled the man, examining him. He looked up sharply at the mention of ghosts and wisely, thankfully, remained silent.

"That is not what your mother thinks. Seems

she believes that the treatments I used at our last meeting didn't cure you of the evil."

"Well, Mother has been quite stressed lately. The season will be coming to a close in a month. She is feeling the pressure."

"Ah, yes." He smiled. "Pressure for you to marry well. To secure a place in society."

She didn't answer.

"So interesting, your case." He opened his bag and began rummaging through the contents. "My father knew your mother when she was a child blooming into a woman. Lovely girl, I was told. Much like yourself."

Abigail spotted her shears on the bed table beneath her book and grabbed them, hiding them in her skirts.

He pulled something from the bag, a strap, long, leather and whipcord thin. "I did promise your mother that I would not perform the final test, but she knows it will eventually be necessary. She just couldn't bring herself to give me permission. Not that I require permission, necessarily." He smiled. "But then, if you admit everything to me, perhaps it will not be necessary after all."

"No. There is nothing to say, and I won't let you."

"Ah, innocence still. Lovely." He smiled, satisfied. "So, Miss Smart, did you ever stop seeing the spirits or did you just convince your mother that you had? You know that I never believed you."

"I know you didn't," she spat. "You didn't care anyway, just wanted to give the 'full' treatment. You are a deranged lunatic, far more crazy than I."

"Ah, so you admit your madness."

She laughed harshly. "I admit your madness only."

"Ah, but that—"

Valerian punched a hand through the man's head before she could say anything to stop him. "I don't like him. How do I get rid of him?"

Dr. Myers stopped and tilted his head. "Cool air. He is here now. In the room. Tell me his name."

Abigail couldn't stop her spine from going rigid. Those who were sensitive could feel the ephemeral touch of spirits—like a mist wrapping around the skin—rather than just the simple cold they exuded. The man in front of her had made it his trade to be able to feel them.

Dr. Myers smiled, satisfied. "Someone important? Or are you just nervous? Come now, Miss Smart, tell me who he is?"

Abigail said nothing.

"I see I am correct on all accounts without you having to admit a word. How did you pick him up? Is he haunting the house or you?"

"I don't know of what you speak."

Myers tilted his head. "Tut. It took *death* to finally snare his interest. You must have been ecstatic."

A thousand warnings fired. He knew. Somehow he knew. "You are mad."

"We fit so well then, do we not? I offered to teach you the many ways our madness could fit together, but you so prettily denied the offer." He withdrew another strap.

He withdrew a bottle of liquid and she went still. Her eyes met Valerian's and with everything in her she tried to will him to move. His eyes narrowed, and he moved toward the window.

"Do you remember what I did to your last spirit? Or at least the last one you admitted to seeing. Certain tools are so helpful." He uncapped the bottle and sniffed the contents. "You were such a sad girl, but it was for the best. No one can live a full life talking to the dead."

"How would you know? You don't even deserve a half life."

He smiled. "I think you like this one. But then you like all of them. Such a lonely girl. So sad after the duke's new heir was through with you. Turning to whoever would give you comfort. But you turned to the spirits, when you should have turned to me." He swirled the container. "Now point him out, Miss Smart, and we will make some progress. It will be easier for you if you cooperate."

"No. I told you, I don't see spirits."

His smile grew. "Of course you don't." He rose and began idly walking around the room. She tried not to react as he neared Valerian.

"What is that liquid, Abigail," Valerian asked, eyeing the bottle.

She couldn't afford to answer Valerian directly. "What has ever made you think that spirits disappear to hell when you douse them with that, doctor?"

"Experience, Miss Smart. Oh, and your lovely reaction when I killed your friend. She never returned, did she?"

"You are vile."

"I am quite brilliant actually."

Valerian stepped through the bed and behind

her. "What does he mean he can kill spirits? He killed your friend?"

"Of course, should you wish to let your new *friend* survive, we could discuss alternatives," the madman said. "I would be severely punished, of course, but it would be worth it. I offer you a better option, believe me. Finish the treatment, Miss Smart. It will cure you of"—he waved his hands around, a bit of the liquid spilling to the floor, steam rising from the drop—"everything."

"No." Her mind whirled at his words. Punished by whom? Why? How many people knew? What was happening?

"Tsk, tsk. Letting him go to hell."

"Get out." She kept her gaze on the doctor, but directed the words to Valerian. "Get. Out."

The doctor smiled in understanding. "Oh, but I have set up wards to disallow that. Fennel and onions, such a dastardly combination."

Valerian spoke lowly behind her. "I can't leave. There is a barrier. I feel it."

But Aunt Effie had managed to escape. There must be a small hole in the corner that the doctor had missed. Perhaps a break in the wall to the connecting room.

She addressed the doctor, trying to give Valerian more time. "So you already believed I had a spirit following me."

"I did." He glanced around with his eyes, his head staying perfectly tilted. "The reports confirmed that you have been talking to one for days. Confirmed everything."

Reports? Ice froze her blood like a lake in

winter, starting at the edges and shooting toward the center.

"Reports? Who would report to you?"

"That hardly matters. Would that they had told me more earlier. Tut, Miss Smart, but I'll think you not so innocent after all." He smirked. "I am here to extract information, but I believe I should start the process to end your part in this for good. I will accept the punishment from them, should they be displeased."

"Perhaps you should do what they tell you." She grabbed Valerian's hand behind her and maneuvered his finger to point toward Effie's corner, hiding the action with her body. "And escape unscathed."

"You think to threaten me? Marvelous."

"I can't leave you," Valerian whispered harshly, as if raising his voice would bring the doctor closer.

"Please," she emphasized. "Believe me that I will prevail."

"I won't leave you."

"Is he over there, Miss Smart? By you, perhaps?" He stalked toward her, and she dropped Valerian's hand, squeezing the shears in her other.

"I won't let you touch me. And you are foolish for believing me still afflicted. Why would I risk another visit from you? I loathe your very presence."

"You haven't missed me? I'm hurt. But everyone makes mistakes, Miss Smart. You lived up to your name until recently. What was it about this ghost that had you giving in and revealing yourself? I am most curious. I greatly desire to know. Do you fancy yourself in love? A substitute for the young lord's rejection so long ago?"

Any mortification she was feeling was covered by anger so deep and swirling that it threatened to drag her forever into the abyss. "You try very hard to play your games, *Doctor*, but I'm no longer the naïve girl I was."

"Gotten over your sadness and pain, have you? But it was so lovely to see. I wanted to cure you of that."

"No, you wanted to play."

He smiled and shrugged. "Alas, my weakness. Let's play."

He sent a ribbon of the liquid shooting from the bottle in Valerian's direction, and she threw herself in the way, the liquid burning her skin where it touched. Valerian shot through the man, cleanly slicing him, but leaving no damage behind. The doctor gave a little shudder with his shoulders and smiled more widely.

"Come here, spirit. Just a little taste, then I will cure Miss Smart of her affliction and damn the consequences." He started to loosen his cravat. "Unless you enjoy being a voyeur and care to watch me physically thrust it from her, before I banish you from her mind and from existence. I think the latter will be far more satisfying. There is a reason these ailments occur at the onset of womanhood, you know. I just need end that blissful phase and voila." He smiled. "I was able to witness Miss Smart's reaction to her previous friend dying, so I think I can make an exception this time. A different sort of satisfaction as I'm plowing you from her mind."

Valerian rushed through him, trying to connect, and the doctor flicked the top of the bottle as he passed.

Abigail screamed as the liquid sprayed, nearly touching Valerian, barely missing as he arched and fell. He leaped from the floor in a defensive crouch.

The doctor kept his eyes moving about the room, smiling that awful smile as he gripped one edge of a strap he had laid upon the table.

She moved toward him, shears gripped tightly in her skirt. "I won't let you hurt anyone else."

"Patience, dear, patience." He reached for her with the strap and Valerian literally flew at him. The doctor somehow anticipated the action and tossed another stream of liquid while grasping her hand and pulling her forward. She pulled the scissors out and shouted as the liquid arched toward Valerian. Valerian's hands finally wrapped around the doctor's throat and they fell to the ground, pulling her with them, the shears bouncing from her hand as her wrist whacked the floor.

She saw Valerian shove the man's head against the hard wood. Valerian's face contorted. And then he disappeared, a tendril of smoke from the burning liquid swirled through the room, pooling around the doctor's suddenly still form.

"No!" She shoved into a standing position and wildly looked around. But Valerian was nowhere to be seen.

A sob built in her throat and then she began screaming.

Chapter 15

He woke to screams. These screams were different though. Higher, like someone had lost something important. Not just the shrieks of pain and distress that he was accustomed to hearing upon waking to the madness.

The second thing he noticed was that he was lying facedown on a hard, cold floor. A cellar? Had they unhooked him and dumped his body? Energy surged through him. If he was back in his body, he could return to help Abigail. His last thought had been murderous anger, and the knowledge that he couldn't leave her.

He hadn't thought he'd been hit by that liquid, but perhaps he had and it had returned him to his body for good.

He pushed off the floor and rose to his feet, surprised with how well his limbs worked. Not atrophied at all. A large bundle of supplies and a casket of wine and other cooling items surrounded him. Definitely someone's cellar. Perhaps the cellar of whoever had kidnapped him in the first place.

He walked to the door, again surprised when he didn't stumble. The cold of the room barely registered. He reached out to open the handle and his fingers touched cold steel and relished it.

A woman yelled. Abigail. Dear God. They had her too. She was locked up as well.

He frantically turned the handle, and then stared mutely as his fingers slipped right through.

He was still a spirit.

Shouts punctuated the air upstairs. Running feet and banging. *He was still in Abigail's house.* And that man was still upstairs.

He concentrated and pushed through the door, then ran up the stairs to the kitchen. Servants were in varying states—some looked uncomfortable, some shocked or surprised, a few looked completely intent to ignore the hubbub abovestairs, stoically continuing their jobs.

"None of our business," an elderly matron said as she ordered the maids about. "Go about your tasks."

"But Mrs.—"

"No, none of that. We all know she's a strange one. None of our concern. Let them take care of it."

Valerian usually took little notice of the servants, but he considered the punishment he could mete out were he ever to regain his form.

He continued through the hall and up the next set of stairs, then the next. A servant fled down the stairs past him. Valerian finally arrived on Abigail's floor to see the door open and the man still lying on the floor. Cold satisfaction rocked him.

"Abigail, calm down," Mrs. Smart frantically said.

"No, Mother, I will not calm down. Get him out

of my sight. And if you ever bring him back I will run. You'll never see me again," she said harshly. "And I will no longer call you mother."

"Abigail." Mrs. Smart sounded deeply hurt, but Valerian held little sympathy for her.

"No! Leave." Abigail kicked the prone man in the side and her mother gasped.

"You are crazed."

"Of course I'm crazed, Mother. Isn't that what you've wanted to hear? Isn't that what you've been trying to stamp from me all these years?"

"No, I just want you to be happy."

Abigail gave an ugly laugh. "You put us on this path. This has to do with your happiness, not mine. I had little to say in the matter. Little to call happiness."

"But you have success. Look at your success now." Mrs. Smart extended her hands, her arms, her face begging.

"And how long will that last? A fortnight more?"

"Lord Rainewood is gone. He can't hurt your chances anymore."

"Mother," Abigail's voice was unnervingly calm all of a sudden. "Did you have anything to do with Lord Rainewood's disappearance?"

Shock rocked Valerian.

"He's off carousing. How would I have?" Mrs. Smart sounded genuinely confused as she pulled her arms back to her sides.

"You didn't hire someone to remove him from society? To murder him?"

"Abigail, you are scaring me."

"Am I?" He watched her run fingers down her

dress. "Remove Dr. Myers, Mother, or I will never speak to you again. You can commit me and lose your place in society. I'd like to see you try to maintain your position after that. Curious that I never thought through the ramifications to your position sufficiently to stop fearing being locked up. You stand to lose just as much as I do. Now? Now I find I don't care. What is the point?"

She turned away from her mother and faced the window.

The butler appeared in the doorway. "Mrs. Smart?"

"Yes, yes." Abigail's mother smoothed her hair. "Remove this man." She bit her lip and pointed to Myers. "Throw him in a carriage."

"Yes, ma'am." The butler snapped his fingers and two footmen appeared, grasped Myers under the armpits, and dragged him off.

Mrs. Smart turned back to her daughter. "Abigail, we have a later meeting with—"

"Cancel it."

"But—"

"Cancel it."

Mrs. Smart seemed to be trying to calm herself, as if canceling had been her plan all along, instead of Abigail's directive. "Very well. I will inform Mrs. Browning not to return today, that you are feeling poorly still. We can speak later."

Abigail didn't acknowledge her. She merely waited for her to leave.

Valerian slipped through as Mrs. Smart clicked the door shut. He noticed that the lock was broken.

Abigail's shoulders gave a shake and she leaned

her forehead against the windowpane. Conflicting emotions ran through him—the desire to comfort her, the desire to yell and shake her, the urge to do more.

"Would you like me to go down and hit him again?"

Her head whipped around so fast that she stumbled. "Valerian," she whispered.

"Who were you expecting?" He tried to sound flippant, but it didn't quite work.

She ran toward him, arms wrapping around him, head buried in his shoulder. "I thought you gone."

"I was." He had thought himself back in his body, had felt the joy of being whole. The feeling slipped from him, leaving him numb. "I fell all the way into the cellar. Nasty places, cellars."

"No, really gone."

He frowned and then realized what her last comments to her mother had meant. His arms tightened automatically around her.

"No," he said.

"He didn't hit you with that poison?"

"No."

"Thank God," she said, her voice breaking.

He didn't know how to respond. Discomfort and fierce protectiveness twined together unpleasantly. "What was in that bottle?"

"I don't know. Something foul."

"He hurt someone before?"

"Yes," she whispered. "There was another spirit before, not like you, not one I could touch or speak to in the same way, but a companion. She made things . . ."

"What?"

"Less lonely."

His stomach twisted.

"He got rid of her," she said woodenly.

"What did he do to you?"

Her muscles tightened. "I don't wish to speak of it."

"Did he—" He swallowed. "Did he force himself on you?"

"No," she whispered. "He tried, he claimed that would cure me fully, pretended that only he could do so. But I held off long enough, convinced Mother that I was already cured. I don't know that she wholly believed me, but she turned him away anyway. I don't think she could bear it." She laughed harshly. "Though one wouldn't know it since she brought him back."

"You should have reported him."

"To whom?" She pulled back and narrowed her eyes. "Who would believe me? They would throw me into the nearest strapped cell. A creature to be gawked at by the hordes. To ridicule."

"Not everyone would."

She unwrapped her arms from him, but her fingers played with the stitching along his left cuff. "You did," she said softly.

"Well, I'm a bit of an ass."

That caused the edges of her mouth to lift.

"I'm surprised that you didn't just play it up," he said. "Make yourself into a spirit talker. People would line up to pay. It would also give you some level of security."

"The ton loves ghosts and fortune tellers as novelties. But someone who is trying to establish herself in their midst? Maybe an eccentric matron could get away with it, but a miss looking to marry? That doesn't go along with Mother's plan."

"You could make a fortune, then you wouldn't need to marry." He thought that sounded brilliant.

"We have a fortune already. It just doesn't seem to be enough." Her hand fell from his cuff and she walked over to her dressing table and righted the fallen chair. "I need to go outside. Let's leave. Let's search for your body."

"It's not safe—"

"It's not safe in my own home," she said harshly.

He shut up and watched her ring for her maid.

She fingered the tassels of the cord, looking pensive. "You hit Dr. Myers then fell through the floors and into the cellar."

"That's what I said."

"How?"

"I lunged for him—"

"No, how did you stay here? How did you touch him and stay here? That hasn't happened before."

He had thought of her—hadn't wanted to leave her. Desired to save her more than anything. Had pictured home and her face had appeared.

"I have no idea," he said glibly. "Isn't this your area of expertise?"

She frowned, but her maid saved him from further questions as she knocked, then entered the room.

"Telly, we are going out. Have the coach prepared. Mother will say nothing."

Valerian wasn't so sure of that, and Telly didn't look as if she was either, but she disappeared back through the door.

Surprisingly, Abigail was correct and the coach was ready for them in half an hour.

They sat securely inside, rocking toward their first destination. "How many places with M-A-L do you have on the list, Telly?"

"Thirty, miss. Right popular, those letters. Malfolk's, Malling's, Remallard's . . ."

"Well, we will just have to tick them off one by one. Perhaps section by section."

They broke down the list, Valerian adding his opinion and Telly twitching nearly every time Abigail spoke to or answered him. He watched the maid, watched the look on her face as she watched her mistress. There was something odd there. He'd have to keep track of her, perhaps follow her when they returned.

They made it through fifteen of the places on the list, stopping to have supper at a cozy hotel near the Strand. Valerian could nearly smell the juices of the succulent duck as Abigail chewed thoughtfully on each piece.

Food, top-notch cuisine, had always just been . . . inherent. He'd never questioned it or paid too much attention. A poor meal was an anomaly. The first meal he had when he was back in his body was going to be exquisite.

They ticked off ten more addresses before giving in to the pending darkness and returning home.

"We will tackle the last five tomorrow morning."

"But your appointment, miss—"

"We will make it in plenty of time, Telly. We looked at twenty-five sites today. Quite exhausting. But the last five are near one another. I am confident that we can get to them and still be on time."

"Very well, miss." Telly looked upset. "I just think that you should be concentrating more on the prospects you have and the—"

"Thank you, Telly." Abigail's voice was steely. "I plan to do that, do not fret."

Her maid remained silent the rest of the trip.

Mrs. Smart was waiting in the foyer when they returned. Probably sitting in the front drawing room, watching for them.

"Abigail, I'd like to speak with you about today and about the future."

Telly slipped away and Valerian was torn between following her and staying to watch the confrontation.

"Perhaps tomorrow, Mother."

But her mother blocked her way. "We can bring in someone else. Someone better suited—"

"Good night, Mother."

Abigail pushed past her and ascended the stairs. Valerian watched Mrs. Smart a moment more and thought about trailing her as well when she turned sharply and headed to the back of the house. But Abigail's stiff shoulders made him choose to follow her instead.

Abigail didn't say much as she put her things away. He opened his mouth to say something, he didn't know what, when Telly walked in and started to help Abigail change.

"To bed early, miss? Yes, I think it is a good idea too. Should I bring you some warmed milk?"

"No, Telly, I'm sure I will be sleeping soundly shortly. I'll see you in the morning."

Telly hesitated, then nodded and slipped from the room.

"Your maid is worried for you." Or something more, he still had to find out.

"She just wants me to find a nice young man. She says it often enough." Her voice was distracted.

A spike of jealousy, sharp and piercing in its intensity, struck him. "You have plenty of suitors, to my knowledge. I've been on enough outings." And tried to get rid of more of them than he could count before that.

"I know you hate the outings." She smiled, but it didn't reach her eyes. "Perhaps you will be able to see how tiresome they can be from the female perspective as well."

"Stop going on them, then."

She gave him a look full of exasperation.

He thought of the next day. The outing he truly dreaded. "You shouldn't go anywhere with Basil."

"We've talked of this already. My mother and Mrs. Browning will both be there."

"You don't know that he doesn't intend you harm."

"He is your brother."

"Doesn't that make it worse?" He grimaced, admitting his own fault in her circumstances.

She said nothing for a second, just watched him with her lovely blue eyes. "As much as Basil has been acting strangely, I can't believe he wishes you ill. He will likely be absolved."

And me?

"I don't share your confidence," he said instead.

"That is because someone is trying to harm you."

"Someone is trying to harm you too," he said pointedly. "Because of me. Unacceptable."

She fiddled with her brush as she was wont to do when she was near her dressing table. He paused for a second and looked more closely at the handle. He hadn't paid much attention to it previously, usually more interested in what she was saying when she fingered it then in focusing on the object itself. The familiarity of the brush clicked and he brought his head up sharply, but she was looking away.

"I am confident that once we find your body all interest in me will be lost."

A memory of a quaint Windsor shop filled with trinkets and personal items filled his mind. His third year at Eton. The scent of the tobacco pipes, the creams and perfumes. The shaving and dressing items for the men. The more delicate fripperies and expensive gifts for the women.

Her voice was hazy on the edges of his mind as she continued to speak. "It does little good to dwell on things that will not change."

A rosewood box with an ivory handled brush. Impetuously purchased in the inept and gawking manner that had overwhelmed him at that age between youth and manhood.

"I've been in worse situations," she said.

The embarrassment when one of his roommates had found it.

"And I feel as if we are close. You will be free."

He had considered throwing it into the Thames. Had considered throwing *himself* into the Thames. Had buried the brush deep beneath his clothes instead, vowing to dispose of it soon. Vowing to dispose of all the uncomfortable thoughts connected to it.

"Free to return to your life."

Had instead saved the damn thing and taken it home, buried in his trunk. Shoved awkwardly to the recipient on her birthday. A horrifying, tongue-tied moment. He had promised himself he would never to do such a thing again.

"And everything will be as it should."

He had stupidly purchased the matching comb that autumn anyway. It still rested deep in the bowels of his closet.

"I'm sure of it," she said softly, her voice breaking through the memory.

He looked at the brush, at the way her fingers stroked the handle.

"Abigail—"

One hand touched his chest sending all sorts of strange feelings through him—feelings tied to the memory, feelings new, and feelings old, but newly charged.

He looked at the desire on her face. A face that rarely withheld emotion from him. He loved to taunt her, to see the anger and passion. To feel something from her after all the barren years of not having her near. A purgatory that he had created through his actions. A gawky boy on the edge of manhood unable to deal with his feelings. A man at the top of his game unable to let go of his pride.

Her other hand played with the ties on her nightdress. "It is not tomorrow though. Tonight, tonight I want you to touch me."

She was taking a huge risk, she knew it. But she didn't care. She could see the desire reflected in his eyes, could read the lines of his body, and she couldn't deny that she had wanted him to touch her for the longest time.

"Just a little," she whispered. "Just to make me feel alive. To feel that you are still here."

His eyes darkened and she pulled the string of her gown allowing it to fall away.

"Abigail," he said, his voice hoarse. "What are you—"

"Thinking? I'm not." She stepped forward against him, her hand still between them. "I don't want you to think either."

He was here, with her. Still alive, at least within her madness.

She let her palm skim the edges of his never-changing shirt, still in the state she had seen it in at the ball. She had never given a thought to how he must have unconsciously kept it that way. Just as his appearance reflected his emotional state. More bedraggled when he returned from wherever he was being kept, more vibrant when he was passionate or enraged.

Her fingers caught in the edge of the material and glided over the button connecting the two sides. The material disappeared beneath her fingers, and all of a sudden, she was touching smooth skin, just slightly cool, as if it once had been a hot cup of tea that had warmed and then cooled to the room. A side effect of his state in the in-between.

His indrawn breath made her bolder, and she ran her hand along the curves of his chest, touching the curling hair there and the chiseled planes.

"My clothes?"

"You have discarded them," she said, not even glancing to the side, maintaining contact with his eyes, which were smoldering instead of cynical. "I've seen new spirits change clothing instantly. Sometimes in such a flurry that one outfit becomes the next ad infinitum until they settle."

One hand rose toward her in a more tentative gesture than she was accustomed to seeing him use. "Abigail."

"Are you going to touch me, Valerian?"

His fingers bent around the plait of hair that hung down her shoulder. He stroked the strands there. "I don't know. Is it real?"

"It's as real as we make it." She undid another tie of her gown, the material spreading so that more skin was bared.

His hand smoothed the ends of her plait and then lifted to her nape. He tilted her head back and drew her closer. "Like a dream." He pulled her to him and her eyes closed as his lips touched hers. As they drew careful strokes against the contours of her own, the smallest amount of resistance between them as they slid together.

Heaven. Perhaps she was in it. Perhaps this was her heaven, having Valerian all to herself, touching and depending on her. A wicked thought.

He deepened the kiss and traced the hollows of her throat. A trail of fire lit across the path, at odds with the cool touch of his hands. The coolness just intensifying her already burning skin.

His fingers descended down her throat and to the curves of her shoulders and collarbone, dipping to the valley below. She could feel her breasts tighten, an odd sensation that promised pleasure if she could just do . . . something.

He grasped the edge of the third tie, his fingers

lightly stroking along the edge of her left breast as he did so. The sensation grew and her nipple hardened. "I'm looking quite forward to seeing what is behind this tie. You have clung to that shift beneath. I'm going to unwrap you finally."

The tie fluttered between his fingers, then fell through, the same way that her glove had refused removal. He paused for a moment and she breathed heavily against his neck, eyes tightly shut, hoping that he wouldn't pull away like he had before.

Fingers, gentle, protective, possessive fingers, curled around the hand she held at his chest.

"If you only knew," he whispered and pulled her hand down. He pressed her hand to her own body, stroking back up, over her breast, circling the taut peak, causing her eyes to half close, using her own hand to do so. Her fingers touched the tie. His hand stroked up hers and took her forefinger and thumb between his, pinching them together around the ribbons. She looked up sharply, breath catching. His eyes were hot as he slowly pulled her pinched fingers away from her body, dragging the end of one ribbon from the clutch of the other, setting the edges of the fabric free.

Her heart thumped. He hadn't stopped. The look in his eyes said that he wasn't even considering the possibility. That she would be stripped naked before him if he had to have her undo and stroke every part of her body to do so.

"I don't know whether to speak to your surprise or just revel in the look in your eyes and the flush across your throat." He bent his head to her neck. "Beautiful."

She leaned her hips into him while tilting her

head back and giving him more access. His fingers took her hand and drew them down the valley between her breasts and to her stomach, to the next tie in the gown. He gripped her thumb and forefinger together again and pulled, more insistently this time. The gown parted further.

Another slow descent of her hand to her abdomen and then the vee below. Over the coiling heat and fire. He pressed her hand into her body and leaned back. "Have you ever touched yourself, Abigail? Watching the spirits as you say you do? Wanting to emulate their actions?"

She couldn't breathe, couldn't answer. She shook her head in the negative.

"I'm surprised. You are one of the most intrepid souls I've met."

But it had seemed so wicked every time her hand had gone near. Every time the lack of touch from others had impressed upon her. That somehow she was not worthy of touch, even her own.

He pressed her hand more firmly against the center of her heat, and his lips touched her ear. "I want to see you touch yourself, Abigail. But right now I want to touch you even more." He gripped her fingers firmly and ripped apart the tie, the gown parting as if by command.

He let go of her hand and it dropped boneless to her side. His palm was immediately upon her, cupping her through the shift, making her gasp and arch into him, partially in shock and partially because her body demanded it. Long fingers stroked a trail along her most intimate area, the cloth of her shift providing little barrier, and in fact urging the heat onward as it pulled against her. Her mouth parted on a silent phrase and her eyes locked with his.

He used his free hand to pull her head toward his and he kissed her with all of the passion that she had ever hoped for. His fingers continued their trail of fire, burning her, making something inside of her tighten and throb. He pressed two against her, nearly lifting her an inch, and then his fingers fell through the cloth, touching her skin, her curls, the throb that seemed to have blown into something tangible and physical.

A small sound worked from her throat and he swallowed it, pressing his lips more firmly, his tongue seeking entrance to her mouth and causing more of those sounds to work forth. One finger below imitated the action and curled into her heat, through the barriers, dipping inside. The sensation nearly undid her and her fingers wound into his hair, pulling him more firmly against her, the only thing that she could do in the increasingly deep, maddened frenzy to complete the action. To climb against him and make him undo the almost unbearable throbbing that had coalesced.

He broke free, and only the bright, swollen lips and heated eyes, his bare chest heaving to the same beat as hers and his hair gloriously out of place, caused her to stop from panicking. He leaned back against the pole of the four-poster, his eyes still hot, but some sort of tenuous reserve—held by tenterhooks—called to the fore. "Remove your shift."

"Pardon me?" she asked, unable to work up the correct words for what she really wanted to say, which was something more along the lines of asking why he had stopped touching her, demanding he continue, and perhaps adding a few curse words to the entire diatribe.

"Remove your shift."

She caught the light upon his darkened eyes, the way he was gripping his fists in the cross of his arms across his chest. She leaned down to the edge of her shift, looked up at him, and slowly began dragging it up her knees, her thighs. She paused, self-consciousness asserting itself as she reached the part of her that few had seen.

"Remove your shift, Abigail."

She met his eyes again; saw the challenge there, the soft mocking, not against her, not indicating that he was going to poke fun at her, but a challenge to see if she was really ready to do this. She took in his clutched fists and pulled upward, the fabric sliding across her belly, up and over the peaks of her breasts, causing them to lift and then fall as she did so, then finally over her head.

She held the fabric there for a second before reconnecting with his eyes. She took in his heated gaze, saw the way his body started to move toward hers before he regained control, and a different sort of throb, of pleasure, flowed through her, a womanly confidence and she let the cloth fall to the floor, pooling there in a reflection of her state.

He moved toward her swiftly, twirling her and pressing her down against the bed, lifting her leg and opening her to him as he kissed her again, more urgently, both hands reaching up to grip her neck, the kisses consuming her soul as he took, took, took. Then his mouth moved downward and he took her right nipple in his mouth. She arched off the bed with a silent scream, the sensation too surprising and overwhelming to vocalize. Strong tremors rocked her as he tugged her nipple and she arched against him and then bowed back straight repeatedly, her body unsure that it could withstand the treatment.

"Valerian," she gasped as he switched to her other breast.

Fingers drew down her ribs, stomach, abdomen and curled right back into her heat. The arch of her body grew more taught as one finger breeched her an inch, circled, and then stabbed again. Her fingers wound into his hair, her body spasming nearly uncontrollably as he sucked and stabbed, sucked and stabbed. The heat became more pointed, more focused, the coil straightening into an arrow, almost painful in its intensity.

His long finger circled just inside of her and she arched for the teasing stab, wanting it, waiting for it, but instead he pushed fully inside, a trail of heat pushing up that connected to the arrow, a crook of his finger knotting them together and everything exploded.

Chapter 16

Abigail woke, stretching. When she didn't see Valerian she instantly panicked.

"Lemons. I saw the first one on the vine. It must be cultivated or it will wither."

"Aunt Effie?" Abigail rose into a sitting position, alarmed by the look of the ghost. "What are you . . . ?"

The edges of Effie's old-fashioned dress crackled, faded, then crackled again. Abigail swiped the covers away and scurried over to where the apparition sat. "What is happening to you? Were you hit by the man yesterday?"

"No, dear. It is just lemon season upon us." Effie smiled gently. "Lemons are lovely, do not fear them."

Abigail sank down and held out a finger to Effie, but it slid through just as it always had. "Why is it that now you have started to converse with me in a real manner? Why can't I touch you?"

"You are at a crossroads and I am in your grasp."

"What do you mean?"

Effie sipped her tea. "I do not know. Only that you are at a crossroads. Lemons, dear."

"But why now?"

Effie continued sipping.

"Lord Rainewood?"

Effie tilted her head. "I am but a spirit, dear. I only see that lemons are within your grasp or in danger of falling, rotting, unpicked."

"Miss?"

Abigail turned to see Telly standing by the dressing table. She wondered how long her maid had been there.

"Yes, Telly?"

"Your mother wants to know whether you intend to keep the appointment today with Lord Basil."

Abigail looked back at Effie, who merely kept sipping. "Tell her that I do."

"Very well, miss. I will deliver the message then be back to help you change." Telly slipped from the room.

"You are up. Finally." Valerian had somehow slipped inside too.

She rose, feeling the color in her cheeks follow the movement. What to say to him?

She smoothed her hands down her nightgown, watching them, and thinking of other fingers touching the fabric. "I am."

Fingers touched her chin instead, lifting it. "Embarrassed, Abigail?" His eyes drifted past her to her dressing table. Something shifted in the dark brown. "Don't be embarrassed."

Telly returned before she could say or do anything truly embarrassing—like throwing herself at him or admitting secret thoughts aloud.

She changed into a morning gown and tried to

keep up thoughtless, easy conversation with both her maid and Valerian—a hard prospect when Telly kept twitching. She'd have to ask her about that later.

Abigail walked downstairs to where her mother and Mrs. Browning had gathered over steaming cups of tea.

She clasped her hands in front of her and said as calmly as she could manage, "I need to run to Bond Street to secure new ribbons."

"Absolutely not," Mrs. Browning said. "After your absence at all events yesterday, being tardy today will not do."

Abigail kept the smile on her face and her eyes focused on her mother.

"Be quick," her mother said in a quiet voice.

Mrs. Browning's head shot to the side in complete shock. She had never been overruled in the household before. "Mrs. Smart," she sputtered, and Abigail took perverse pleasure in the reaction.

"Thank you, Mother. I will be back in plenty of time."

She gathered Telly and walked toward the door. She turned back just in time to see Valerian, following lazily behind, smirk at Mrs. Browning and make a rude gesture. Abigail would have given her real ribbon money to have seen him do that where Mrs. Browning could see it.

They hailed a hack as soon as they could. She cursed her foolishness for taking the family carriage the night before. Not that the driver would know to say anything other than how odd she continued to act.

Of the last five places on Telly's list, the first two

were not possibilities, but the third, O'Malley's Tavern was located across from what looked like an abandoned building. A building with windows that faced the tavern sign.

"We could—"

"No, Abigail. I forbid it."

"But it's a possibility."

"And I'll figure out on your outing how I can search it, if needed." The edges of his mouth turned down. "You will stay away from that building."

"But—"

"There is no time anyway. Don't push your mother or that harpy you hired. Let's drive past the final two and return."

She gave in and told Telly to give the driver directions for the final two places, much to her maid's relief. The final two yielded nothing.

O'Malley's was the most likely candidate and she found her blood pumping a little more quickly, and her heart racing a little more erratically, at the thought that they might find him.

"I'll gather information on the tavern and surrounding buildings, miss."

"Excellent, Telly."

"Yes, let your maid do it." Valerian tilted his head back against the seat in a manner that stated he expected to be obeyed.

Abigail glared. Some things remained the same.

They returned home in time for Abigail to change and receive a reprimand from Mrs. Browning for her near tardiness. She grilled Abigail on what shops they had frequented and demanded to see the new ribbons. Thankfully, Valerian had suggested they purchase some.

Her mother kept silent throughout. There was still a slice of underlying fear that her mother would revert back to her former position regarding her treatment, yet the new sense of purpose that had bloomed in the wake of the tentative renewal of friendship with Valerian, and the quest to find him, kept the fear just below the surface.

Basil arrived in one of the open family carriages about half an hour later.

He greeted them with a jaunty gait and smile. "Miss Smart, I'm looking forward to our outing. I hope you like my surprise."

She hoped she did as well. She was taking a chance by going with him and she could hear and feel Valerian's displeasure.

"If you don't mind me asking, Lord Basil," Mrs. Browning said, "where are we going?"

"Hobbyhorse races in the park. There will be a number of familiar faces in attendance. And a chance to try the vehicles, should one desire. Though, perhaps not to race, unless one is daring enough." He smiled winningly.

Valerian snorted, circling his brother with narrowed eyes. Mrs. Browning looked less than ecstatic.

"Excellent, Lord Basil," Abigail said, smiling back. That sounded safe. Nice large crowd. Plenty of people she'd know in attendance. She smiled at Valerian, trying to indicate relief, but he continued to maintain his dark look.

"I do hope you are interested in the races, Miss Smart," Basil said after they settled into the carriage.

He began expertly guiding the team. She wondered when he had gotten past his childhood weakness and become so adept.

"I expressly thought it something you might want to see," he added.

She and her mother had left their house in the country and moved to London before Basil had fully recovered. A move that her mother had deemed the next step in establishing themselves. A move that had separated Abigail from the sorrow and demons of the estate. She hadn't put up a fuss.

If she had known what awaited her in London with the doctor, she might have.

"I am," she answered. "I confess that I have been most interested in witnessing how they work." She didn't add that Mrs. Browning found them plebeian and so they had abstained from the activity in the past. Only Lord Basil's standing and the fact that the invitation had been issued in front of the dowager kept the woman smiling grimly now.

"Capital. I am sure that we can get you on one as well. There's even a version for the ladies."

"No," Valerian said sharply from his seat inside Mrs. Browning. He seemed to enjoy making the woman shiver uncontrollably. It was still disconcerting to see their double features together, like some childish painting. "Do not attempt to ride one, Smart."

She smiled at Basil. "That would be quite the lark, Lord Basil. I do believe that it would give my mother a fright, however. She is a terrible worrywart."

Her mother simply nodded, but Abigail focused on Valerian as she said it. His eyes narrowed in promised retribution.

"Do you have a fondness for racing, Lord Basil? Or for the hobbies in particular?" Abigail hadn't heard of him being exceptionally prone to gambling or sport.

"Science. I find modern science completely enthralling. Johnson's design is masterful and I find myself excited for what might happen next. The rails and steel monsters that are all the newest whisper on science's lips are fantastic to contemplate. Can you imagine what we might accomplish with interconnecting rails—twice as fast as horses, with none of the stops needed?"

"You should speak to Mr. Brockwell. He is also a lover of all things mechanical."

"I have," he said surprising her. "Just because my brother chose—chooses—not to, does not mean that I have to follow," he said calmly, but his knuckles whitened around the edges.

Valerian muttered something inappropriate.

"That is too true, Lord Basil." She wasn't sure about his choice of tense, but let it pass, unable to say anything about it without bringing uncomfortable attention to the matter.

Mrs. Browning continued to adjust her shawl against the chill only she could feel while Abigail's mother stared from the side of the open vehicle, a latent sadness in her eyes. Basil continued speaking about the merits of Phillip's mind and the Young Scientist's Society. Valerian muttered something, his lips moving on Mrs. Browning's large forehead, his eyes dark in her high, knotted hair.

Abigail felt a sudden disconcerting notion that she had already entered the gates of Bedlam for the final time, never to return outside.

They arrived in the park to a sea of faces. All of Valerian's cronies were there as well as Basil's. She was surprised to see other faces as well—Gregory and Phillip, and a few other men and women that she wouldn't have associated with the event. Then again, dandy horses were all the rage and nearly everyone wanted to be in on the latest frenzy. And Basil had just finished his explanation on Phillip's keen mind and enthusiasm, so perhaps she should have expected it.

Gregory gave her a dark look as she stepped from the carriage with Basil's help. Phillip just chewed his lip.

She gave a wave, chewing her own lip when only Phillip tentatively returned the gesture. She tried to shrug off Gregory's snub as Basil helped her mother and Mrs. Browning from the carriage.

The crowd was gathered around five hobby-horses held by waiting servants. Curved smooth wood with perky saddles on top. One of the more daring ladies rode around the crowd on a modified horse fit for her skirts—her feet pushing along the ground in demure strides. Abigail would have loved to try one had circumstances been different. Had she been out of the eye of the public, and assured that no one meant her harm.

The lady preened under the attention of the rogues and dandies who were eyeing the machine, and eyeing the hem of her dress brushing her moving slippers—hoping for a bit of a show, no doubt.

Mr. Stagen walked toward them, an unreadable expression on his face, his walking stick thumping against the earth. "Lord Basil, Miss Smart." He acknowledged the two older women as well when they drew alongside. "A good day for racing, is it not? The skies seem to be holding to themselves."

Stagen had never been rude to her before, more a figure watching from the side, powerful in his own way, but more apt to keep his own counsel in public, at least. But he had never chosen to speak to or approach her before Valerian had disappeared either.

She gamely played along, as if it were normal for the two of them to converse informally. "Who is racing?" she asked, having not kept up with that aspect of the gossip, too many other things on her mind.

"Many of the gentlemen here, and even a few of the more spirited ladies, should you wish to join." He pointed at the woman still riding around on her wooden steed. "There is no one here that will gainsay you, should you wish to try it."

There was something probing in his eyes. Watching, questioning, accusing. Perhaps a combination of all of those things.

Valerian had been the natural leader of the group. Templing had been the witted viper. With both of them gone, the popular group was subdued.

"That is true." She met his eyes squarely. There was something about Stagen that said she could trust him to be on Valerian's side at the very least. That didn't mean he was on hers, however.

Stagen returned her regard, then tipped his head. "And there are a few individual races. Campbell and Penshard have a special bet."

She looked sharply at Gregory, who was examining his nails, seemingly bored.

"Why?"

"A challenge. I don't know the details," Stagen said, twirling his stick in the dirt. She narrowed her eyes. She'd bet every groat in every pocket in attendance that he knew exactly what the challenge was about and how it had come into being.

"I see."

"You should ask Penshard." Stagen's eyes still questioned, his head still tilted in consideration, but there was a less sharp quality to him than there had been when he'd first approached.

"Perhaps I shall. But a gentleman hardly enjoys speaking of his bets with a lady." She tested his new relaxed stance. "Or about other matters that he might find questionable."

"Abigail, Stagen will draw and quarter you," Valerian warned from somewhere behind her.

Stagen gave his stick another twirl. "That is true, Miss Smart. But someone else might be able to tell you—your friend Miss Penshard, perhaps?"

"Riders in the first race, line up!"

Abigail watched as the first five men stepped forward, pulling their hobbyhorses from the hands of the servants and into position at the makeshift starting line.

They mounted the wooden beasts.

Campbell walked toward their group, smiling. Valerian said something under his breath behind her. Stagen's stance changed again, more alert and wary as Campbell navigated the crowd.

"Go!"

The men kicked off, their legs racing along the ground. One of the men tried to run too quickly after kicking off and became entangled in his own momentum. He lurched forward, turning the wheel and veering to the right before toppling and crashing to the ground. The crowd laughed and the man's friend rushed over to see if he was hurt.

The other four vehicles raced down the slope, two of the men stretching their legs forward to ride with the gathered momentum while the other two tried to gain an extra burst of speed.

The crowd cheered and a knot of people surged forward to try and chase the contestants down the hill.

Campbell finished edging through the crowd to stand next to her. She saw a familiar hand reach forward and try to flick him before falling through. Campbell's brows pulled together before smoothing. "Miss Smart."

"Mr. Campbell."

"It is wonderful to see you here." He looked at Basil, who raised his brows. Stagen's were drawn and disapproving.

"And you, Mr. Campbell." It was as if she was living in a strange dream from which she could not escape. All of these men, friends of Valerian, had ignored her as if she had some interminable disease before his disappearance. "Are you prepared for your race?"

"I've been practicing at Johnson's for the past two days. I should be."

Johnson's riding school. She wondered if Gregory had done likewise.

"Laudable, Mr. Campbell," Mrs. Browning interrupted. "Better than riding through the streets like some of those other men."

Campbell bowed to Mrs. Browning. "Thank

you, Mrs. Browning." But Abigail noticed his shifty eyes. The man had obviously jockeyed with the horse traffic like so many other idiotic blades and Corinthians.

The crowd went wild and she looked to see that the first race had finished while she hadn't been paying attention.

Campbell stepped closer and Valerian put a hand on her back. "Get rid of him, Abigail. I'm telling you, he's up to something. I *know* Campbell."

Valerian had gone to school with all of these men. Had changed because of it. Something she shouldn't forget.

"What do you think of them, Miss Smart?" Campbell asked, one hand splayed out toward the hobbyhorses.

"They look like quite the adventure."

"Are you looking for adventure, Miss Smart? Would you like to try riding one?"

There was something about the way he said it. Stagen's eyes darkened. Valerian snarled behind her.

Basil had struck up a conversation on the matters of style between one wooden horse and another and was looking the other way. Mrs. Browning was speaking to a lady on her left. Neither appeared to have heard the comment.

"Perhaps some day, Mr. Campbell. I'm afraid I'm ill-prepared today."

"It is great fun though. A true adventure. I have heard that you are interested in adventure."

"I've already offered to procure a hobbyhorse for her, Campbell," Basil said, turning back. She noticed that Stagen's walking stick was slowly drawing away from the side of Basil's foot. "Shouldn't you be preparing for your race?"

"I should." Campbell tossed his head with a charming smile. "But I couldn't resist asking the fair lady for a favor."

She examined Campbell, whose eyes were wide and innocent. Basil waited, head cocked. Stagen swirled his stick through the dirt in a spiraled pattern as if he hadn't just alerted Basil to the conversation.

"I cannot in good conscience offer one when I've come with Lord Basil," she said as demurely as she could manage in this new situation under which she had little experience.

"Danforth won't mind, will you, friend? He's not racing, so he has no need of the luck."

Basil's eyes never left Campbell. "If you wish to give him a favor, feel free, Miss Smart."

Mrs. Browning and her mother were still chatting with another set of matrons on their left. Abigail looked back to the men.

"Yes, give Campbell a good-luck charm, Miss Smart. He needs it," came a voice to the other side. Gregory navigated the bodies around their crowd. "Can't win on his own."

Campbell smirked. "I will win this bet, Penshard."

"I doubt it, Campbell. Bad luck at the tables all around for you. Not sure you should be betting anything at all."

Campbell's eyes turned dark and he darted a look at her before narrowing his eyes at Gregory. "Trying to play with the men, Penshard. Never were much good at it, in school or out."

"I don't see any men around here," he said mildly.

"Gentlemen, is there some difficulty here?" Mrs. Browning spoke into the knot. The surrounding onlookers turned to see what was happening.

Abigail wasn't sure she had ever been as relieved to have the woman speak. All eyes moved speculatively from one participant in the tight knot to the next.

"I was simply asking for a favor from Miss Smart." Campbell smiled winningly.

"Well, give it to him." Mrs. Browning made a motion to Abigail with her hand. Abigail watched the looks on the various faces, unable to think beyond the state of immobility she was in. She woodenly extended one of the ribbons she had purchased that morning.

Campbell smiled and hoisted it. "A sure victory, then." He bowed to her and turned to go to the starting line as a loud voice called for the next group.

Gregory gave her an unreadable look, then turned on his heel and strode back through the crowd.

"What is your relationship with Penshard?" Valerian asked behind her, his voice dark.

She shook her head to indicate her confusion, but couldn't deny the friction.

Basil and Stagen watched her, as everyone else seemed to be doing. Basil smiled enigmatically. "Campbell will think his luck permanently turned. Little does he realize that his good fortune might not be what he thinks it."

"My apologies if you wanted—"

He held up a hand. "No, I'm not in the race. I have the pleasure of your company for the rest of this adventure, have I not? Something which Campbell cannot claim."

Abigail was at a loss. Basil couldn't seriously be wanting to court her. He didn't need her money, and other than seemingly neutral regard, he didn't seem enamored of her in any way.

And his father and grandmother would never allow the match. The Duchess of Palmbury would surely threaten to cut him from the bosom of the family, and perhaps even follow through on the threat.

That left few possibilities—including the distasteful one that he truly was involved in Valerian's disappearance.

The next five contestants took their places, Campbell included. Gregory watched with a dark, calculating look from the edge. Their individual race must be toward the end of the list, then. The riders mounted, sitting on the saddles.

"Go!"

The riders kicked off and a familiar hand wrapped around hers, pulling along her fingers—taking each one between, one at a time. Her breath caught, lost in the noise of the crowd.

Basil continued to watch the riders from her right, oblivious. She wanted to ask Valerian what he was doing, to whisper furiously, but couldn't afford to turn around to do so. No amount of whispering in the chattering crowd would go unnoticed if someone saw her talking to the air at her back or the tree behind.

"Enjoying the spectacle and attention, Abigail?

Talking with Basil, Penshard, Campbell, and the others?" he said into her ear, his lips brushing the lobe. "Seeing if you can gather even more suitors to annoy me?"

She felt his hand touch her waist, press, then slide beneath the material to her corset below, then to her shift, then to her bare skin. A neat trick. One she hadn't counted on when he'd been unable to remove her clothing. Her heart sped into a gallop faster than the fastest of the riders cresting the hill. Fingers ran along her stomach unhindered by the material of her clothing.

"Adventure. I'll show you what true adventure is," he whispered in her ear.

One finger curled inside her. She gasped, her body reacting automatically, just as if he had taken right up where they'd left the previous night. The crowd cheered, oblivious to her state.

She leaned back against him, partially arching as he swirled the finger and palmed her, his thumb rubbing against a spot that sent hot chills through her.

The crowd went wild as one of the riders broke out in front. People surged around her, craning to see more clearly. She used the movements to tug away from him, trying to get herself under control. She gasped as he stroked her again and involuntarily leaned back again under the caress.

His other forefinger and thumb gently rolled her nipple, tugging just the smallest bit. "Definitely not the type of adventure you can get from your dilettante Mr. Sourting or Farnswourth."

He tugged again, his thumb slipping over the

top. "And neither Basil nor Campbell, Stagen nor Penshard, can make you shiver like this."

Cool fingers stroked hotly inside and over her, full lips attached to her neck.

"Isn't that right, Abigail?" He sucked hard at the sensitive spot just under her jaw. "I'm about to make you come apart in the middle of this entire crowd. Make you beg for more than the trite little adventure that the others claim."

The riders reached the bottom of the hill and soared toward the finish line, legs fully extended, bottoms bouncing, rhythmic and nearly out of control. Heads back, savoring the experience.

Extended, arched, bounced, savored, screamed, gave in to the thrill.

The crowd cheered and Abigail gasped, raising her hands to cheer along with them, trying to cover her convulsions as she violently shuddered against and around him. As Valerian nipped her neck and sent her spinning. Spinning like they used to do in the meadows, laughing and free. No worries or concerns, no responsibility or death. Innocent and happy.

Her body tightened involuntarily around Valerian's fingers as he slowly stroked down, removing them and smoothing a proprietary hand over her hip.

She worked up a semblance of a normal smile as Basil gave her a grin, his lips forming words. Something about the mechanics involved in the race, or about Campbell winning, or about how her cheeks were flushed from passion.

She fervently hoped it wasn't the last. Long fingers stroked down her hips and pulled her back so she fit tightly against the man, spirit, *bane of her existence who was likely to torment her for all eternity*, behind her.

The men trooped back up the hill laughing—swatting at their trousers and sneezing as petite dust clouds formed and lifted into the wind. Servants scurried behind, pulling the wooden horses back up the hill for the next round.

Campbell brushed back his windblown hair, high color in his cheeks. The bottoms of his trousers and shoes were covered in dust and dirt.

Mrs. Browning sniffed and waited for Basil to turn toward Stagen before offering comment. "I suggest we leave soon. It feels as if it might rain. I wonder if those things will even work in the rain? Why you have always wanted to see them, I can't understand, Miss Smart."

Valerian stuck a hand into Mrs. Browning's arm until the woman shivered and moved a few steps away. Another body attempted to enter the space in the pulsing crowd, but they too muttered something about the cold and gave her side a wide berth.

Valerian moved next to her on the left. He smiled in satisfaction as he tipped up her chin and looked upon her face.

"Shall we try another adventure, Abigail?"

Chapter 17

Valerian watched in satisfaction as her already pink cheeks darkened further. With her lips parted and her eyes slightly glassy, he had no concern that she was thinking about anyone other than him at the moment.

He reached a hand toward her forehead and watched her eyes close as he brushed a coiled curl away. Fey and enchanting. He had thought her a woodland spirit when he had first seen her tromping through the trees at the estate so long ago.

She opened her eyes and the force of her gaze, the emotions within, punched him, threatened that part that he had kept sealed, ignored for so long. The image of a comb packed away, hidden and sealed in the same manner, flashed before him.

"Miss Smart," an unwelcome voice said. "Your favor was keen. I can't believe it took me so long to seek it."

Her eyes tore from his, and something in him felt stripped. Peeled like hot skin cooled against leather.

"Mr. Campbell, congratulations on your win."

Valerian didn't like the notion at all that she

had been concentrating on the race for one second. That she cared one iota for Campbell's placement. The man that he had long considered a friend suddenly seemed more and more an enemy.

"It was all due to your lovely good wishes."

As a future viscount right from the start of Eton, Campbell had been one of the boys who had run their age crowd from the beginning. Valerian hadn't cared—he was a forgotten second son uninterested in the social hierarchy, more eager for military and adventure, for exploring academic pursuits or taking to the high seas than for the stuffy chambers of Parliament and the rules of etiquette. Only interested in what would be required for him to get what he wanted.

"I am sure that you would have won regardless, Mr. Campbell. You seem to be quite adept at the sport."

"Required of a man of my station, Miss Smart." Campbell smiled broadly. "Must keep on *top* of everything."

Valerian casually belted him, wishing that his hand didn't sink right through.

"Campbell, don't you need to get ready for your race with Penshard?" Basil asked, and Valerian felt some renewed kinship with his younger brother.

They had always maintained a strange relationship. Frequently sick, Basil had been unable to participate in the games Valerian craved. And Basil had monopolized their mother. But after Thornton . . .

The duke's first son had been the perfect heir. Hard to live up to such perfection, and Valerian had never tried until he'd been forced to the role. He had disliked his older brother, who was charming when he wanted, vicious at all other times—little need to understand where he had developed that, since he had been constantly under the tutelage of the duke and dowager. But even as an imperfect brother, he had been at least completely willing to let Valerian get himself killed in some adventure, and had always promised plenty of money for such happenings. Anything to keep him out of the center of the ton, which Thornton planned to rule with an iron fist.

Valerian and Abigail had spoken of the many places they would travel. The lions they would hunt. The seas they would sail. It wasn't until he had started to notice that there was a real difference between them beyond their clothes, her damned skirts that needed to be tied or unwound from branches, that the notion of Abigail as a partner in crime had changed.

And by the time it had set in that perhaps there were different *types* of adventures to be had in the world, Thornton had died—under inauspicious circumstances—and Valerian had been thrust into a much different life.

One that didn't include all of the broken ideals and dreams of his youth.

Campbell had helped spur that. Valerian narrowed his eyes as Aidan continued to speak to Abigail, trying to coax her into further conversation before leaving to take his place in the next race. Campbell, whose father was ill and undemanding. Who didn't have the same familial expectations even though his title demanded certain obligations. Who had scoffed and laughed at the brush he'd discovered so long ago.

"There is little desire to hurry, Danforth," Campbell said to Basil. "Not when one has such a lovely lady before him."

Valerian had taken over as the de facto leader of the group a mere year after Thornton's death. He wasn't sure Campbell had ever forgiven him for that, not that he much cared at the moment—wanting to crush the man as he did—but Aidan had followed along, been a good disciple since.

And Valerian had formed a tentative relationship with Basil after the death of their mother. The two of them the last rational members of the household. It was hard to think that Basil might want him dead—but the viper's nest of their youth might have influenced his brother more than he'd thought.

"Good luck, Mr. Campbell."

"With your favor, I can't but win." Campbell smiled charmingly at Abigail and strode off for his race with Penshard. Valerian hoped he fell on his crooked lips.

Basil looked like he wanted to say something to Abigail, but he simply looked toward the finish line, the edges of his mouth tight in only a way that someone who knew him very well would be able to see.

But Basil didn't fancy Abigail. He could read his brother in that aspect, and for all of his uncertainty surrounding what Basil was up to, it wasn't for courting Abigail.

So why was Basil upset about Campbell and Abigail?

Abigail leaned back into him and a sharp shock ran through him. His hand automatically rose to her neck, massaging the smooth area where her hair met the sensitive flesh below.

Abigail Smart was someone who never sought reassurance. Who stood tall and weathered all storms with grace and dignity. Who had purged him from her life long ago—making him force her to pay attention to him ever since.

Except that wasn't true, and a niggling guilt surfaced that he had long assumed she didn't care, accepted the possibility that she was the social climber his father and grandmother had claimed her. Had ignored her notes. Had been angered by the very thought of her, even though he used the possibility that she *might* care against her in every situation.

He pressed forward against her. Just an inch, just because she was pressing into him. A nudge, a game. Nothing like seeking reassurance himself.

He had been molded into an earl, a future duke. He had gotten past his brother's death, his own part in it. Needing to live up to the Rainewood standard, and to protest it all along.

Thornton had ruled with an iron fist.

And he had become his brother.

No. He shut down that line of thought and touched Abigail again. She was one of the last reminders that he wasn't Thornton. That he had been someone else once.

He had hated her for that once. Once not long ago.

He had loved her for that for far longer.

He gripped her shoulder. And now, now he

could no longer even identify the emotions associated with her.

He had become his hated brother.

Abigail felt Valerian stiffen behind her, but there was little she could do to inquire as Basil began speaking again and the race between Campbell and Gregory cued to start.

"Be wary, Miss Smart." Basil continued to watch the race, but his low voice reached her.

"I try to be ever vigilant, Lord Basil."

"Excellent. I would just see that you do not become a pawn in something that has been going on for far longer than you can know."

She examined him closely. "Such as what?"

"Old grudges and dangerous proposals. From more sides than you are possibly aware."

"Losing patience in your houseguest, Danforth?" Stagen said from the side.

Abigail looked at the two men. "Houseguest?"

"Campbell is staying with Danforth for a few weeks. Repairs on his house forced him out," Stagen said lazily, as if he hadn't just dropped a vital piece of information in her lap.

Valerian gripped her shoulder more firmly, and she felt the pressure radiate within her. If Campbell was staying at Number Eighteen with Basil . . .

"Has he been with you long?" she asked innocently. "I know houseguests sometimes take a toll on one's good humor."

Basil smiled, but didn't answer.

"He wasn't staying with him before. I would have known of it," Valerian said behind her, his breath a whisper in her hair.

A whistle sounded and they turned to see Campbell and Gregory line up, straddling their horses. She couldn't hear what they were saying, but Campbell confidently tossed his head. Gregory's eyes narrowed and he said something that wiped the smile from Campbell's face.

The starter gave them a mark call and then jerked his hand down. The two men surged forward, pushing against the dirt as quickly as their long strides would allow. Dead even, they went over the hill at a breakneck pace. Both men put their legs up, the wheels tumbling over the terrain and making them bounce and lean forward.

They hit the bottom of the slope and headed for the finish, legs pumping again. The crowd went wild and money changed hands as final bets were placed on the outcome. It was going to be a close finish.

They surged for the line, chargers hugging together as they headed into the final stretch.

Either could win. Abigail could see Valerian's dark, flat look from the corner of her eye, but he too was watching the finish line with too much intent to be merely bored.

They closed in on the finish. Twenty paces, fifteen. Abigail held her breath at the sheer thrill of the close race. Ten paces, five.

Gregory's hobbyhorse sharply veered left and Campbell lost control as he tried to jerk out of the way. His horse overturned in a cloud of dust and Gregory's crossed first.

The crowd gasped, then surged forward, taking her with them.

Gregory dismounted and handed the horse to a

waiting servant. Campbell untangled himself and rose, brushing off his trousers in a cloud of dust as he purposefully moved toward Gregory. The crowd surged even more intensely, wanting to observe the confrontation as closely as they could.

Phillip quickly ran to Gregory's side, and Stagen leaped forward to grab Campbell, grasping the back of his jacket. Campbell's fists clenched and he strained against Stagen's hold.

"You cheated, Penshard."

"You lost control of your mount, Campbell."

"You deliberately jerked into me."

Gregory held out his hands, waving them. "I never touched you, Campbell. Your mishandling of the charger is what did you in."

Campbell's face mottled with rage. "Why you— I challenge you to—"

Stagen pulled sharply and Campbell jerked back midsentence. Stagen said something harshly in his ear. The crowd leaned in, eager to see where things would lead.

Campbell shrugged Stagen away and straightened his jacket, tugging at the cuffs. "I challenge you to the balloon race, Penshard. Double stakes. Your choice of balloon against mine."

Abigail was sure that before Stagen had stepped in he was going to challenge Gregory to something far more dangerous.

Gregory smirked. "You are a glutton for punishment, Campbell. My choice is easy. My stake will be in Brockwell's contraption."

Phillip shifted nervously as all eyes turned his way, but held his place.

"Excellent. I look forward to grinding you both

to the dust. I'll let you know my choice by courier tomorrow." Campbell slapped his hand against his trousers, sending up another cloud of dust and strode away. Stagen gave the crowd an encompassing look and set off after his friend.

Basil's brows pulled together, but he didn't go after his housemate. He turned to Abigail. "Well, exciting as that was, I must apologize for how the afternoon has turned. Shall we leave, Miss Smart?"

Valerian straightened. "I will go see if I can catch Campbell and Stagen on the way and then hurry over to the carriage."

Abigail nodded at Basil. "That would be quite acceptable, Lord Basil. And do not fret over the events—I daresay the gossip hive will be abuzz with the happenings this afternoon."

Mrs. Browning was more than pleased to be on their way. It took another five minutes to disengage themselves from the gossiping crowd, but they finally headed back to the parked carriage. Abigail walked with Basil, while her mother and Mrs. Browning trailed behind at a respectable ten paces.

"You'll have to forgive Campbell, Miss Smart. He tends to be hotheaded."

She smoothed her skirt. "He seems to have been up enough to challenge Mr. Penshard to another race."

"Yes, and a foolish wager that was too."

She peered at Basil. "What do you mean?"

"Brockwell's balloon is solid—revolutionary even. He will win easily."

"Foolish wagers seem to abound these days."

"That they do." He cast a side glance her way. She returned the glance.

"Why did you ask me on this outing, Lord Basil?"

"Curiosity, Miss Smart. And fondness for an old acquaintance and a friend of Rainewood's."

She stiffened. "We are hardly friends."

"My brother sometimes suffers from the same hotheadedness that Campbell does, but should Lord Rainewood desire to grace us with his presence once more, perhaps you should look more deeply."

"What do you mean, grace us with his presence once more?" she asked, smoothing nervous hands along her skirt as they walked. "Why would he not?"

"I don't know, Miss Smart." Basil gave her a long look. "Do you?"

She laughed wanly. "As if Lord Rainewood would tell me his plans." She saw in the distance that Valerian was hurrying back toward her. The flesh and blood Rainewood would never confide in her nor hurry back.

"I would be less surprised by other things."

She looked at Basil sharply. "Your brother and I are quite at odds, Lord Basil. You know that perhaps better than anyone else."

"Are you?" They reached the carriage as Valerian appeared back at her side. Basil held a hand out to help her up. "I've always wondered at that myself."

She took his hand and allowed him to seat her before he helped her mother and Mrs. Browning.

"There is little at which to wonder. He has made it very clear."

"Ah, but that is only when you look at the surface. You should know by now that though society as a whole does just that, many of the individuals see far more."

Valerian was hardly paying attention as he concentrated on entering the carriage. It seemed to be getting harder for him, but he was still able to do so as long as she was there.

She was glad that he was otherwise occupied.

"They see the deeper well of animosity, I'm sure."

"Mmmm," was all he answered.

Valerian successfully entered the carriage and sighed as he slipped onto Mrs. Browning. She could see the woman shudder from the corner of her eye.

Valerian leaned forward until his lips were almost at her ear. "There's something that Campbell is hiding. Something more than what we already think. And he is living with Basil. We have to search there." He tapped a finger on the back of the seat. "Leave something behind, if you can."

She tucked her wrap into the folds of the carriage seat when Basil was occupied with driving. It was tucked in just enough so that Basil wouldn't notice it upon her exit, but so that someone would find it upon inspecting the carriage. It would give her an excuse to call upon him at Number Eighteen. She exited behind Mrs. Browning and her mother.

"Thank you for the lovely afternoon, Lord Basil," she said. "It was truly a pleasure to see the hobbyhorse races."

"It was my pleasure, Miss Smart." He smiled at her, but there was a watchfulness to his eyes. "Perhaps we can meet again?"

She saw her mother watching her closely—likely trying to see if she would capture the opportunity or let it slip past in retribution. "I would like that," she answered.

Mrs. Browning frowned, but nodded to Basil. "Good day, Lord Basil."

As soon as they were in the house, Mrs. Browning spoke. "I wish to speak with you both."

Abigail dutifully followed into the front parlor, Valerian behind her. Mrs. Browning shut the door.

"Though I do not entirely approve of Mr. Penshard, either he or Mr. Campbell would make solid choices and they seem interested despite their poor display of temper there at the end. I believe that you should better extend your efforts to those that will make you an offer, Miss Smart."

Abigail raised a brow at the implication and obvious reasoning behind the statements. "Are you saying that Lord Basil will not?"

"You know that he won't"—*silly girl,* went unsaid—"the Duchess of Palmbury won't have it."

"If Abigail likes Lord Basil, then I do not see the harm in allowing him to pursue her," her mother said softly.

Abigail looked at her mother, who looked steadily back. Abigail tilted her head in acknowledgment.

Mrs. Browning smoothed her dress at the challenge to her absolute authority. "Yes, well, as I said, I think we'd do well to focus our efforts on those with whom there is a real chance. It is nice to have a multitude of choices, but let us be realistic."

"And I say that it is Abigail's choice."

Mrs. Browning's lips disappeared before smoothing. "You hired me for my advice, Mrs. Smart."

"That I did."

Abigail held her breath as Mrs. Browning's eyes narrowed on the calm choice of words—the way that her mother had just told their paid companion that for the first time her advice would not necessarily be followed.

"Very well." Mrs. Browning smiled—a sharp smile similar to those that Valerian's grandmother had perfected. "Shall we look over the guest list for the ball tonight?"

The ball had been tedious. There was too much excitement strumming through her to manage everything that had been thrown her way. Campbell had apologized to her for not winning the race and shown her that he still sported her ribbon favor prominently.

That had set tongues to wagging. Valerian had been grumpy and proprietary the entire night, making dire threats and wishes against all parts of Campbell's body and heritage.

And now it was closer to dawn than midnight, and once more she was sneaking into a house with only a ghost for a lookout. Telly would never forgive her if she found out—Abigail having slipped out after the household was asleep. Then again, if at this point Telly discovered her absence, it was likely that others would too and Abigail would be in much deeper trouble.

She ascended the stairs with the help of Valerian and found herself on a clean and orderly second floor. Voices punctuated the air further up. Valerian pointed to a room at the right. "Your wrap is likely to be in there, as will Basil's personal documents. You search. Retrieving your wrap will obviously not work as an excuse, should you be found, but at least we can work with it somehow. I'll go up and keep an eye on those two." There was something dark in his eyes before he turned.

Basil's study was extremely organized, but in a way that made it seem as if he was purposefully trying to put off someone who would be snooping. Things weren't in the exact place that a person might normally put them, but instead grouped in peculiar order. Still, once she found a pile or drawer she was able to figure out at least what she was looking at.

Chief amongst the papers was a detailed accounting of Valerian's whereabouts prior to his disappearance. A pit settled in her stomach, but then she uncovered another folder. One with reports from three different Bow Street Runners and two other investigators—all looking into where Valerian could be.

Her name jumped from the page as a suspect in his disappearance. Following that was a note that nothing had been found in her room or house. She saw the signature of the dowager duchess at the bottom authorizing the action. She gripped the page for a moment before smoothing it again. So now she knew why their house had been searched and by whom.

Her fingers encountered smooth leather and she pulled out a green book hidden between two stacks. Templing's ledger. She swallowed.

All of it explained Basil's sudden interest in her, which had started after she had repeated things only Valerian would know. The dowager had probably given her name as a suspect from the first, hating her as she did.

Basil was looking for his brother. He wasn't responsible for his disappearance.

She smoothed her fingers over the leather surface again. She wanted to take it. Destroy it.

One finger wrapped around the edge of the front cover. One peek. Just to see. To know if her fear was justified.

She pulled the cover back. Names and dates jumped out. Notes and notations. She flipped a page, skimming, trying not to absorb the scandalous writings and the temptation such knowledge might give her in a future moment of anger.

One page turned to two, and then three until she reached blank parchment.

Her name wasn't there. Relief crashed through her and she stared at the book for a moment before tucking it back in its spot. The weight of the secret still sat upon her shoulders, held for another day.

Her wrap rested by the door, but she left it there. It would be completely obvious were it to disappear.

She walked up the steps to collect Valerian and saw him leaning against the doorframe, looking inside the room, his fists curled into balls underneath his crossed arms.

"Raine will kill me," Campbell said drunkenly from inside.

She moved closer so that she could peer around Valerian and see inside.

"He hasn't shown any inclination to doing anything other than towing the family line, Campbell." Basil refilled Campbell's glass. "When was the last time you saw him?"

"The night of the Malcolm's fete." Campbell drained half of the glass.

"What was he doing when you last observed him?"

"What the bloody hell does it matter now? If he ever returns, I'm dead."

"Perhaps his state of disappearance can tell us if that is true."

"You speak as if that matters. What matters is that I'm after his bird. They've been together, Danforth, I'm telling you. Have you seen the looks when they think no one is aware?" He tilted his head back against his chair, drunkenly. "Have you?"

"Yes," Basil said softly, but much more calmly. "But there is nothing there and never will be."

Campbell pointed a finger at him. "You can't know that."

"Oh, I can be reasonably sure." Basil topped Campbell's glass.

Abigail watched, lips pressed together as the reality of the conversation penetrated.

"He will be engaged to the Malcolm girl soon. Valerian knows his duty."

"He will still kill me."

"Do you deserve it, Campbell?" Basil watched the other man closely. As much as the conversation bothered her, she couldn't help but thinking that Basil was doing a damn good job of trying to discover the information about Valerian's disappearance. "There are men after you, are there not?"

Campbell waved his hand. "A few debts. A

pittance, that is all. It will be taken care of soon enough."

"How is that?"

"No need to worry, friend."

"I learned early in life not to worry unduly, Campbell. Too many things out of one's control. But I find myself curious."

"Made a deal." Campbell put his fingers over his eyes and heavily wiped across. "All taken care of. Think I could use a nap now, Danforth."

It wasn't more than a few seconds before Campbell was nearly snoring, head tilted back on the chair, mouth open.

Basil observed him. "Fool," he said softly and rose.

Abigail stepped to the side to avoid being seen as Basil disappeared into a connecting room. Her action in the sudden silence turned Valerian's attention on her. He motioned her into a different side room and she slipped inside. Footsteps ascended the stairs, indicating Basil had retired above.

"Basil is trying to locate you." She wasted no time before whispering her findings about the documents, the search, and Templing's ledger. "He can't be the one responsible. And it sounds like he would help us. His questions to Campbell . . . I—" She swallowed. "I could tell Basil about you."

"No." The word was short and crisp.

"You wanted me to—"

"That was before." He grabbed her arms. "Before I knew what happened. You are to say nothing now, do you understand?"

"But—"

"No. I won't have that doctor or anyone else

coming for you because of this. It's my final word."
She bristled at the command, and his hand slid
down her left arm in a caress. "It is my fate that
we are dealing with."

He looked away for a moment, a sharp but sad
look in his eyes. "I don't want you punished for the
circumstances in my life."

Again, hung, understood, at the end of the
phrase.

She swallowed, something in her hopeful yet
sad, because she knew it wouldn't last. She nodded.
"What do you wish to do?"

His hands dropped from her arms. "I don't
know. I don't want you to search Campbell's room
and risk getting caught or even to go near him.
Basil we could handle, but Campbell's discovery of
you would be dire. Besides, if what you say about
Basil is true, then he has most likely searched
Campbell's things."

Abigail nodded, "I think we need to search
O'Malley's."

"Absolutely not."

"It is the only way." She turned and opened the
door without thinking—without making Valerian
look on the other side first—and stopped dead at
the sight across the threshold.

Aidan Campbell leaned against the balustrade,
trying to drunkenly maneuver down the hall.
His eyes turned toward the door and widened in
surprise.

"This is a most fortunate turn of events." Campbell smiled crookedly, "I will enjoy being betrothed
to you, no matter what Raine says." He reached
out and swayed into her.

Chapter 18

She shifted out of the way just in time to avoid the collision. Campbell righted himself and stared at her with glazed eyes. She stared back. The shifting of a floorboard above as Basil paced was the only sound in the room.

Valerian swore copiously, filling the air for her ears only.

"Miss Smart?" Campbell's bleary eyes surveyed her, taking in her too-big trousers and oversized shirt. His eyes lingered upon her chest and then dropped back to her legs.

She was doomed.

"I must be dreaming."

She blinked. Perhaps salvation was still in her grasp.

"Though how I could imagine such a thing, I don't know. Let me see." He reached out a hand to touch her and salvation slipped through the funnel. If he touched her, it would be over, she was sure.

She laughed as brightly as she could, though it emerged slightly hysterical in nature, and took a quick step away. "A Merry Christmas to you, Aidan. We can't open presents just yet, however.

We must have our feast." She gave a little bow and softly clapped her hands.

"Abigail," Valerian warned.

Campbell's eyes crossed for a second and he leaned a hand against the wall. "Christmas? But where is the holly?"

She turned in a forced jig. "The holly boughs are below. You said you wanted turkey feathers above." She pointed to a strange wreath of feathers attached to the wall. She had no idea what they really were, but all that mattered was convincing the drunk man in front of her that she wasn't really there. "Aidan, Aidan, Aidan, and his turkey feathers."

She would have died of embarrassment at her actions if she weren't so terrified of what happened if she failed.

"I didn't know I liked turkey feathers, but I do like you." He tried to grab her and she sidestepped him, forcing him to stumble.

"Not until after the feast."

"I think we should have our own feast." He reached for her again. "Marry me, Abigail Smart. I will give you what Raine does not."

She stumbled. Valerian's fist slashed right through him.

"Not before the *Christmas* feast," she said a little more hysterically, emphasizing the holiday. "The holly boughs await."

"If you were really here I would compromise you, force you to marry me. Get one up on Raine finally. Restore the family fortunes and name. Plunder your curves." He stumbled toward her to do what she could only assume was start said plundering. She danced away, trying to keep in the act and trying not to scream.

"I'm going to kill him." The calm low voice came from behind her, but she didn't turn to see Valerian's face, too concerned with keeping her eyes on Campbell.

"No rain on Christmas," she said, trying to keep her jig going in continuing motions away from him.

"Not rain. Raine," Campbell emphasized.

"Do you enjoy rain?"

"He needs a comeuppance."

She stumbled again, but continued her movement. "And did you give it to him?"

Campbell rubbed a hand across his eyes and swayed. "Not yet. Bastard always wins."

"Are you planning to do something to him?"

"Tired. Need to sleep." He stumbled forward and just made it to the settee in the middle of the room before collapsing.

"Get out of the house, Abigail," Valerian whispered harshly.

"But—"

"Now!"

She hurried through the door. Campbell made some noise behind her and then fell silent.

She took the steps none too silently as she scurried to the door—thankfully sans servants standing at watch—and tore it open to the street.

She stumbled out of Number Eighteen and onto the walk. Her borrowed boys' trousers wrapped around her legs, constricting her in a way that skirts never did. Hindering her and pointing to the absurdity of her disguise, of the plan, of her life.

She glanced at Valerian who strode next to her, full lips pinched and looking in all directions.

That had gone utterly wrong.

"You are finished. No more searching," he said.

"But Campbell sounded like he was going to confess to something—or to exonerate himself," she said as she hurried along the walk, avoiding late-night revelers and keeping her head down. People usually saw what they expected to see. Seeing Abigail Smart hurrying through Golden Square in a footman's outfit in the dead of night did not fall under that category. Still, better to be cautious then ruined.

She had almost achieved the latter back in Basil's house. She shuddered.

"I don't care. You aren't doing this again."

"What is the worst that could happen? I become betrothed to Campbell and make mother and Mrs. Browning deliriously happy?"

"That isn't amusing," he said harshly.

"I wasn't trying to be," she said bluntly back.

He stopped and looked at her, dark lines shading all of his features. "If that is what you—"

He halted abruptly and she followed his gaze. Her hands froze, followed by the rest of her body. Numb.

Dr. Myers stood across the street staring back, a slow smile working its way across his mouth.

"Oh my God," she heard someone say, even though the echo of it came from her lips.

"Move, Abigail."

But she couldn't. She didn't want to turn her back on the man—every preservation instinct once more taking hold. Myers stepped from behind the high hedges and through the gate onto the walk. Steady, even steps toward her.

She took Valerian's advice and ran.

"Stop, thief!" she heard the hated voice say behind her as she blindly ran, a parody of her own doomed chase days before.

Foreign hands reached out to catch her—hands helping a fellow patron to catch a wayward thief. One set grasped the fabric of her shirt, but she twisted and tore away, continuing to run. Unfortunately, another strong set of hands got a better grip and held tight, ripping a seam in the shoulder of her shirt.

She looked up and then quickly down again as she recognized Sir Walter.

Ruined. Utterly ruined.

"My lord, thank you. I'll take the thief from here," the hated voice said.

"He looks barely old enough to know better," chided Sir Walter. "Be gentle. Rehabilitation should be sought for the willing."

"Of course," The doctor's oily-slick voice said in response. "I will just give him a good talking to. Thank you for your help."

Dr. Myers gripped the neck of her shirt and forcefully pushed her toward the end of the square. She allowed it. She couldn't let Sir Walter identify her. She couldn't let anyone else in the square—for surely they were staring at the spectacle—see her too closely. She'd deal with Myers just like she had before.

"Oh, this is surely my lucky day, Miss Smart," he said softly as he marched her around the corner and into a darkened side street unlit by the gas lamps illuminating the square. "I don't know whether to take you home to your mother and claim immediate rights or just end things here."

He gripped her chin and she attempted to remove it from his grasp. His fingers tightened, bruising the skin beneath. "Oh, I can mark you all I want. You are outside your home. Your mother can do nothing to help—not that she would after this."

The fleeting thought that her mother might help her anyway was chased by the doctor's other hand closing about her raised wrist, his body pinning her other arm. Dark, livid marks stood out around the skin of his neck.

"Rehabilitation." He laughed softly. "Such choice words. Your rogue spirit marked me the other day, Abigail Smart. And I will make you pay for it."

She wildly looked around, but Valerian was nowhere to be seen.

The doctor followed her gaze. "I didn't get rid of him, I see. Another task to undertake when I am finished with you. You will—"

But she didn't allow him a chance to finish his sentence, she brought her trousered knee up, unhampered by the bulk of a dozen skirts, and into his privates. He doubled over and she raised her knee to his bent forehead.

She hadn't grown up with Valerian, the scourge of Devonshire neighborhoods, without learning something.

As Myers cursed and fell to the ground she spared a quick look for Valerian, but he was still nowhere to be seen. She swallowed and looked down. She needed to get home before the doctor recovered and followed her, or worse, beat her home—exposing her to her mother and the servants, who would undoubtedly gossip to Mrs. Browning and ruin her anyway.

Her mother might think her behavior too terrible. Really try and send her away for her own good. Might even finally believe Myers that she needed to be watched somewhere under his direction.

Abigail closed her eyes, thought of all the man had done to her, then kicked him in the head with her borrowed boot. He splayed across the ground and she shivered at the actions—both hers and his.

"Abigail." She nearly wept in relief as Valerian appeared at the front of the alley. "There are two men headed this way. You must leave."

She needed no extra urging and ran to the nearest cross street and hired hack she could find.

Only when they were safely in her room did she allow the shivers full rein.

Valerian put a hand on the back of her neck. She leaned into the touch.

She needed it. Needed him.

That he had turned his back completely on her once made the admission doubly painful, but there was little denying anymore that she wanted him. She was another idiotic lackey that thought the sun rose on his smile.

She stiffened, her pride telling her to pull away. Not to allow him to damage her any more than he had before.

He touched her shoulder. "My heart stopped when Myers cornered you."

She pulled away from the nearly irresistible urge to just give in and hand Valerian everything that she was. She walked forward a step and turned. "Do you know who the two men were?"

His hands dropped to his sides and his eyes darkened. "One was from the alley. The man who held you. The other I have never seen."

She tried not to let her shudder show. This was the life that her mother had thought to save her from once—a simple person on the street who had to run and connive to save herself.

"Myers is obsessed with you," he said.

"Yes." She gave a tight grin. "Hard to believe."

He examined his jacket, brushing a hand down the bottom to smooth it. His eyes briefly drifted to her dressing table. "Not so hard, really."

"Be careful, Valerian," she said, trying to lighten the sudden tightening of the mood in the room. "I'll come to think you care."

"No, perhaps you'll come to think that I never stopped."

Her body stilled and she looked at him, trying to see the joke, to watch for the sudden movement of his body or mouth that would indicate that he was being cruel.

It never came. He instead looked again to the table and moved to the bed, running a hand down the carved wood of the four-poster pole.

"So hard to admit to failure, Abigail. To admit that fear ruled my actions so long ago. Fifteen and confused."

This was the Valerian that she had once known. Willing to put his heart forward, to lower his defenses. She wanted desperately to believe that this was truly he, and not some imprint of him that would melt away.

"It was so much easier to shut it away, Abby."

Her heart lurched and her feet automatically moved toward him. She put a hand tentatively on his shoulder, rubbing along the fabric there. "That was a terrible year. Your brother—"

He tensed under her hand. "Yes, Thornton. Do you know that when I look at you sometimes I see the boy I used to be before Thornton passed. Before I took his place. Completely." The last was said almost too low for her to hear.

"No, you aren't Thornton."

He turned around and her hand dropped to her side. He lifted her chin, his eyes piercing hers. "I am just like Thornton, Abigail. I took up his mantle and wrapped it around me like it was my birthright, which it never was. I cut out everything from my life before—those things that would keep me from becoming the perfect heir."

"You were already the perfect heir."

He laughed harshly. "You defend me? Even now?"

She bit her lip. "A bit, yes. There are things that I have a hard time forgiving you. But I can't help but want to forgive the boy I knew so long ago. That I loved like my brother."

His hand dropped from her chin. "That was part of the problem, was it not?"

"What?" She asked, confusion taking her.

"You thought of me as a brother."

"I—" She bit her lip. She didn't have the guts—not with their past so murky and their future relationship so uncertain. But his hand touched the lace at her wrist cuff and she inhaled a deep breath. "I had stopped thinking of you in those terms before our disagreement. Before that one quick kiss."

Just a peck after a particularly spectacular swing they had completed with joined hands and laughing faces, the golden meadow swirling around as they'd celebrated life and friendship. Fallen into the grass, an impulsive kiss placed against rose lips.

His eyes met hers, deep brown and full of some emotion. His fingers raised to her neck and curled around the back. "Interesting, as I had done the same."

Some part of her had known it, or at least hoped. Had banked on it when she'd gone to him for help. Had fallen into stunned disbelief at his cold rebuff. "But you cut me out completely. You—"

He pressed his forehead to hers. "I know. You can't understand the confusion. The betrayal. The pull I felt in opposite directions."

"There is little pull now. You are stuck here."

"I *want* to be here."

She swallowed and looked deep into his eyes, searching for the answers she wanted. There was only what she could see in the spirit though. It had to be enough for now. "I want you to be here too."

She touched his shoulder. Shoulders that even with his thinner size projected strength and certainty. Arrogance and a hint of highborn disdain. It only made him more attractive. The lure of the forbidden. The weakness of the female mind to want the man who showed the most prowess or dominance.

Lips pressed against hers and she was lost in the almost sweetness there—though there was too much about Rainewood that was hard and sure to give in totally to sweetness of any kind.

And it begged the same question, this changing Valerian, this return to the younger and freer boy on the verge of manhood, the one who would admit fault and ask forgiveness. Was he real?

His hands skimmed down her sides and she leaned into him.

If he truly was a spirit caught in his quest, once it was over he would disappear forever. Loathsome Thornton had disappeared after his quest had been complete.

She curled a hand into Valerian's hair and kissed him back with all the passion she could muster.

What if Valerian were truly different? If his body was somewhere out there, waiting to be reunited with his spirit? Would he become the old Rainewood, ton cock of the walk, or the new Valerian who hearkened back to the boy she had loved?

A hand curved around her backside, bringing her flush, lighting all sorts of wonderful heat below.

What would happen were he never to recover his body? Would he stay with her forever? Be able to touch her and speak to her. Hers and hers alone? A seductive thought, and not one she should contemplate too hard or else she might do something stupid like stop searching for him.

She couldn't do that—not when there was a chance that he could truly come back to life.

She pressed against him, pushing in just the way she had seen a spirit wench do once. His breath hitched.

She couldn't do that to him—deny him true life. Not to the boy she had loved and the man she was starting to love again.

She ran a hand down his torso and dipped it

below the top of his trousers. Two fingers, all she could reach beneath the band, slipped across the hardness there.

His state could be used against him, just as he had initially used it against her.

"Remove your clothes," she said against his ear.

His entire wardrobe disappeared. She pulled back and watched the shock in his eyes, satisfied.

"What . . . ?"

That he didn't have enough control to keep his clothes on made her more bold and she pulled his head back to hers. Reassured that he wanted her just as much as she wanted him. That perhaps he even felt more than desire for her. To be tested, for sure, but at the moment all she wanted was for the thoughts that had collected for the past ten years to have their physical way.

She cocked her head, suddenly feeling a freedom that she hadn't in a while. No matter which way this played out, she could live her fantasy. "Shall we try another adventure, Valerian?"

His eyes went completely dark and she curled her fingers around him, using the techniques she had seen in the past. Seen but never put into practice. She slid her fingers up and smiled in satisfaction as he jutted into her grip.

"Abigail." There was a hint of warning in his tone, but as she drew her fingers back down and rotated her wrist she was rewarded with his breath catching, his body moving even further into her grip, his hands reaching for her.

She let him catch her. Let him cover the fabric above her breasts with his hands. She almost let go of him when his thumbs fell through the fabric and brushed her nipples, but she held on and continued the motion, memorizing every sound he made and each emotion that filtered through his beautifully darkened eyes. She changed her movements according to the reactions he made and was rewarded when he captured her lips and kissed her as if she were the only woman he had ever desired.

"And neither the Malcolm girl or any tarts in your past can make you shiver like this." Her lips moved to his ear. "Isn't that right, Valerian?"

He hitched her against the pole of the bed and pressed against her heat, trapping her hand between them. Moving against her so that her hand and his body rubbed against her, firing all of her blood below.

"Are you going to make me come apart, Abigail? Make me beg to be embedded inside you so deeply that we might never separate?"

He pushed her further up, the friction rubbing her against him, the men's trousers barely a barrier. He grasped her hand and suddenly her fingers were undoing the ties at the top of the trousers and with his slight move backward to allow space, the too big fabric was pooled around her feet and she was bared to the air below her freed shirt. He ran a hand down her side, under the shirt, skimming her bare hip.

"What will it be, Abigail? How much of this adventure are you willing to travel?"

The choice wasn't as difficult as it should have been given her misgivings about his state. She simply wanted him too badly and had for too long to deny the need. She gripped the top button of

her shirt and slowly started to undo each one as
he rubbed against her, pulling the shirt open when
she finished. Letting it slide down her arms and
pool with the trousers on the floor. His eyes heated
and his hand moved over her belly, slid along the
undersides of her breasts. His movements below
nudged them together and she felt so heavy and
slick as they slid together, skin to skin.

She had seen enough spirits in action. Had seen
what naked confidence did to the other party.
She tossed off any embarrassment at her assets
or lack thereof and squared her shoulder blades
back against the pole, allowing her left breast to
rise and fall perfectly into his questing hand. She
leaned into him, feeling the gorgeous sensation of
his hands wrapping around her breasts.

She wrapped her hand back around his length,
which was still dancing along the entrance to her
heat below. She pulled her fingers to the tip. "I
want to make you beg."

She was rewarded with a lunge, a growl, his
lips devouring hers, one hand lightly squeezing
her nipple while his other dropped below, curling around between them and into her. Delicious,
just as before. And this time instead of the teasing
thrusts he had made that had held her on edge and
then sent her over, he reached inside and stroked—
one long pull down a smooth slope.

She shuddered and gripped him harder, arching
back, finally understanding just why the women
spirits reacted in such a way to the stimulation, to
the encompassing feeling of passion.

"I'm going to bury myself within you, Abigail,
and you'll never be able to forget it."

She wrapped her arms around his neck and hitched her leg up, knocking his hand away and bringing him exactly in alignment with the part of her that was demanding it—the heat nearly unbearable in its intensity. "Yes, make us both beg, Valerian."

She didn't know what she expected, but when the length of him suddenly surged inside her, she nearly cried out—the feeling was so intense that only the stars covering her vision made her stop the yell, the moan, that would wake the dead. He covered her mouth with his and when he pulled back an inch and pushed inside again she gave in and moaned.

She pushed against the pole with her arched back, the wood biting into her spine. He abruptly gripped her and shoved her against the edge of the mattress, somehow keeping them connected as he followed her down to the coverlet, a deeper thrust connecting the space that had been lost through the movement.

Spirals of pure sensation radiated out and she clutched at his shoulders as he continued the pace, the driving need, almost out of control.

"Abigail," he whispered as he drove into her so deeply that she felt him embedded in her soul. She answered every question he was asking through her body, through her eyes, gazing up into his. His darkened and he thrust again, setting every nerve in her body aflame.

"Yes," he said.

And she arched against him, clinging to love rediscovered and consummated.

Chapter 19

Valerian watched her sleep. Wretchedly complicated, life. Even if he woke to this all truly
being the dream he had wished for it to be in the
last couple weeks, he didn't know if he could go
back to being the same.

No, he could. It was demanded of him.

But what price to pay?

She shifted, her rich brown hair spreading further on her pillow. So much more wild and free
than the plait her maid usually dressed it in. He
touched a strand and then withdrew his hand. She
wasn't for him. He knew it—had always known it
since he'd become the heir. It was one of the things
that he had railed against internally. One of the
reasons that he had purged her from his life, the
temptation too great otherwise.

There had been many excuses, many reasons
to live life without her. They all seemed so empty
and pointless now. What standard was he living
up to? What fear was he running from? What had
he allowed himself to become over the last ten
years?

He knew that if the real list ever became public

she would be ostracized. His grandmother would make sure of it to her dying breath.

The tug strained and stretched. There was a part of him that wanted to follow the tug, that knew that he would end up in his physical body if he just let loose long enough to let it take him. But the other part, growing stronger by the day, whispered that he would lose everything he had gained should he follow the tug.

He rubbed the silky strand between his fingers.

His betrothal agreement was already drawn up—had been for a long time now, just waiting for him to stop dragging his feet. Celeste Malcolm would make the perfect society bride. All he needed to do was wake up, sign the document, and show up at St. George's at the appointed hour.

He could continue living his life the way he had for the past ten years. Continue to be on top of the ton, strengthening that tie even. Beating Thornton at his own game.

Abigail rolled over, her cheek cradling on top of his hand.

Such an easier thing, to pretend that this was his life instead. To contemplate alternatives.

To live the life that he had denied himself. One full of love and laughter. One that demanded he splay himself forward, give her his heart, allow her the power over him that she had once had. That had cut so sharply when he thought she had betrayed him. Laughed at him. Turned against him.

He never wanted to feel that again.

He touched the strand once more. But could he go without feeling her next to him?

What price then did love demand?

* * *

Abigail woke to the early chirpers singing in the tree outside her window. Valerian was away, probably attempting to terrify a maid somewhere in the house. He always returned within a few minutes of her waking though, as if he knew the exact moment her eyelids parted.

She stretched and pulled the cord for Telly before swinging her legs out from under the covers.

Aunt Effie looked even worse than she had the day before. Crackling and blurred. Abigail opened her mouth to say something, but stopped when she heard footsteps ascending the stairs.

There was a tentative knock on her door. "Come in, Telly."

Abigail rose and was in the process of walking to her dressing table when she saw her visitor was not her maid after all.

"Mother."

Her mother softly closed the door behind her.

Abigail watched her, suddenly wishing that Valerian was near and that he hadn't gone to do whatever it was that he did in the house when she was abed.

"Abigail."

"Good morning, Mother. I was expecting Telly so that we might get an early start on the day."

"I know. I heard the bell and told her to wait."

Abigail shifted. Any deviation in her mother's routine was cause for concern.

Her mother crossed to her dressing table and absently played with the implements on top, arranging them. Abigail stiffened when her fingers touched her ivory brush. Her mother had never asked her where she had gotten it, had simply stared at it those long years ago, then moved on to another topic.

"How are you?"

"I am fine." She waited, wondering what her mother was up to.

"I sent a note to Dr. Myers this morning."

Abigail stiffened. The man had contacted her mother straightaway after all. Followed through on his threat in the alley. She hadn't thought he would be believed without proof—the natural optimism she had once possessed had been creeping like a vine into her thoughts and twisting them back to what they had once been. Dangerous to be optimistic.

She contemplated exactly what she would pack and to where she would go first. Valerian's flippant suggestion to dress like a boy and go to the continent, delivered so long ago now, was mad, but not as mad as staying.

There was a sense of calm overlying the panic. The moment she had dreaded with her mother— the end—had finally arrived, and there was some sense of relief that the choice was now upon her.

"I see."

"Do you?" She could see her mother's eyes close through the looking glass, sad and weary.

"No, you know that I do not," Abigail said as calmly as she could manage. "I thought we had come to an understanding."

"We did," her mother said softly. "I told him his services would no longer be needed. That they would never be needed again."

Abigail sat down abruptly on the bed and gripped

the lace-covered cloth, unsure she had heard her right. "You, you are not going to try to get me to accept his treatment?"

Her mother's eyes opened, shining and sad. "No," she said softly.

Abigail thought she would feel an overwhelming sense of relief, but instead she simply felt numb. "I don't understand."

"I know you do not. And it is past time I explain myself."

Abigail would have eagerly sought the explanation two weeks ago. Too much had changed, however. "Very well."

Her mother hesitated, then turned from the mirror. She walked forward slowly, as if Abigail might bolt. When she didn't, her mother tentatively perched at the edge of the bed.

"A long time ago, I fell in love with a boy. The silly sort of young love when the body and mind are first blooming."

That wasn't exactly what she had expected to hear, but she nodded for her mother to continue.

"The boy seemed interested in me too. Oh, you know the type of interest. Ready for a quick tumble—his first, and willing to do most anything to get it." Her mother seemed embarrassed for a second then raised her chin. "I allowed him to kiss me. It was magical."

She smiled briefly and Abigail's curiosity peaked. Her mother had never talked about anyone other than her father in such terms.

"And then . . ." Her hands curled into the coverlet. "And then I saw my first one."

Abigail froze—immediate understanding coming

upon her as a direct mirror to her own past. She opened her mouth but was unable to say anything for a few moments. "You saw spirits?"

"Yes," her mother whispered.

So many emotions whipped through her that Abigail had trouble identifying any of them. Relief, hope, confusion, rage. "You knew. You knew this whole time."

"Of course I did." Her mother refused to look at her. "How could I not?"

"But why didn't you say anything?" Anguish rose within her. "I desperately needed someone to talk to."

"I know," she whispered. "But I thought it easier if you just got rid of the curse altogether— the sooner the better. Before you could be beguiled like I was."

"Beguiled?"

"Yes." She looked at Abigail. "The Smart family. Our family worked for theirs. They always had a kind word for me, even in death. Shared all their secrets. Shared everything that I needed." She looked away. "I didn't want you to fall into the same seductive trap. Getting too interested in a spirit, believing in things out of your control, losing some of yourself."

"But you married father."

"Yes, but all of my knowledge of the Smarts . . . It was always there at the edges, waiting. Tempting me. I lost them when I was cured, but I never lost the memories or the knowledge."

Their real name—Travers—lost to time and the diligent erasure that her mother had put their background through. Her mother had used all her skill to marry George Travers, a nice middle-class man with moderate income, who'd then been fortunate enough to fall into an inheritance and an even better business investment. It had made them rich—and after his death, those investments had financed their entire charade as the Smarts for nearly two decades.

"Why Dr. Myers?"

Her mother's fist curled more tightly. "His father was a doctor too. Learned all his secrets from him. He rid me of the world of which I had become entirely too fond."

Abigail watched the tension in her mother's body. The dawning horror was tempered with cold certainty. "He forced you to have relations with him."

"Now, Abigail." Her mother's smile was strained. "Not forced. He showed me that it was in my best interest. It only took a few times and he was correct. The visions disappeared completely. I was cured."

"He took advantage of you!"

"Never." Her mother shook her head, her hand still clutched tight. "Of course the actions were uncomfortable, but I bore them."

Abigail had a vision of her mother's hand—unwillingly given, pulled into a room, a man with Myers's smile mounting and grunting while the woman—she couldn't picture her mother, her mind forced her to insert someone else in the vision—looked lost beneath.

"He convinced me it was for the better good. I thought later that had to be true. When you became so fond of Lord Rainewood and then had your falling out. I thought it was due to the spirits. I thought you would be happier. Dr. Myers promised me that he had other methods of treatment."

"Not the better good, Mother. What Dr. Myers's father did to you was wrong."

Her mother smoothed a hand along her perfectly upswept hair, rubbing the glossy strands. "I was a willing participant, Abigail. And it did cure the affliction."

Abigail wished she could find and kill the older Myers. She had seen the exact look her mother possessed on other women's faces. Those who allowed themselves to be manipulated because they were too unwilling to say no, to say that they were uncomfortable. Grinning and bearing it. Giving in to something that they were never comfortable with.

"You were going to let the same happen to me."

"I—" Her mother smoothed her hair again. "I—"

Her mother couldn't finish, and Abigail had sudden insight into her parent. Her mother had always refused that type of treatment for Abigail, even though she now claimed that it had worked for her from past experience. Her mother might say that she had been a willing participant, but somewhere deep inside that she didn't acknowledge she wasn't able to subject her daughter to the same.

"No," her mother finally said. "But he almost did, didn't he? He promised me he wouldn't." She closed her eyes. "He said that if I didn't want that treatment I would have to refrain from touching you until you were cured. I just wanted you to be happy."

Abigail put a hand out to her mother's arm. A bare hand extended and placed upon the skin exposed between her mother's dress and gloves. She expected her to pull away, even if just based purely on habit, but she stayed in place.

"Abigail, I never wanted, I never, intended . . ."

"I know, Mother," she said quietly.

"Oh, Abigail. I thought perhaps if you received no touch that you would be less susceptible. That you wouldn't need the full treatment." Her mother reached out a hand and tentatively touched her in return. "That is what he told me. I—" She looked down. "Was it just another lie?"

Her mother suddenly pulled her forward into an embrace. Abigail leaned into her arms, eyes closed, waiting for the quick hug and subsequent rejection. A flood of embarrassing relief and a tangle of emotions rushed through her as her mother clutched her back as strongly as she was being clutched.

"Oh, Abigail, I am so sorry. I should never have had us embark upon this path. Never thought to claim the knowledge I had of the Smarts. I—I just wanted something better for you than what I had before I met your father. An attempt at a better life."

Abigail remembered those first few years of intensive schooling. Of training to be something for which she had not been born. Manners and knowledge gained not from the casual negligence with which true members of the ton acquired it—in school, in the house, being around the people involved—but with a steadied determination to prove something to someone she had no idea truly existed.

And then they had moved to the country. Near a young boy just a few years older with already rakishly handsome features. A boy who ran wild, not having enough attention of his family, a devil-may-care attitude surrounding him.

She hadn't wanted to lose him. She had embraced the schooling with a relish she had never before possessed. Wanted those beautiful, spirited brown eyes to always look upon her with favor.

She clutched her mother more firmly and looked over her shoulder. Her eyes clashed with deep brown—eyes that had grown more intriguing but darker, more shadowed. And now . . . looked furious beyond belief.

She stiffened. It didn't matter how long he had been standing there listening. One second was too long, and from the expression on his face he had been there much longer than one second.

Her mother hugged her more tightly, then pulled back. "Abigail, it hasn't been particularly awful, has it? You have many suitors. You can choose one and retire to the country if you wish. Be truly part of this world." Her mother stroked her hair, but Abigail couldn't keep her eyes from the apparition in the corner, the one with the narrowed eyes and closed expression.

"The Smarts were a good family. They wouldn't have minded. I know they wouldn't have." Her mother touched her own hair briefly again. "And I covered things too well. No one will ever find out."

Abigail couldn't speak. Couldn't open her throat enough to choke out a response. Valerian continued to stare darkly as each newly revealed secret, each worse than the previous, spilled from her mother's lips.

"We will find a way for your children not to be cursed." Her mother hastily held out a hand. "In a different way, of course. I'm sure that you will find a way."

Tainted stock. That was what she was. Not only was she not even a proper or real member of society, but any children she had were likely to be cursed as well. Passed down through her doubly tainted blood. She could see the condemnation in the eyes piercing hers.

She willed the tears away. Her mother touched her again and Abigail resisted the urge to lurch forward and bury her head in her mother's shoulder and never look up again.

"I will see you in an hour for the first visit, yes?"

Abigail nodded, unable to speak. Her mother said something else and slipped from the room, looking lighter than she had. Abigail felt the weight of a thousand suns upon her.

She looked away, unwilling to continue to see mercurial brown eyes that had been so passionate the night before looking on her with the renewed hatred of a night so long past.

Abigail remembered that day as if it were as fresh as the morning's dew clinging to the bottom of her windowpane.

She sat on the stump of a fallen oak in the cozy wood copse, their standard meeting spot, and stared as Thornton Danforth, Earl Rainewood, stepped inside instead. "My lord." She rose.

He stopped and watched her, his sharp, cruel eyes taking her in. "I felt the pull here. It must be because of you, since you can see me. A little nobody, how perturbing."

She raised her chin. She disliked the heir intensely, more for how he treated Valerian than in how he treated her, but he was still an extremely atrocious person to be near.

His eyes narrowed further. "How extremely interesting though that it should be Valerian's pet that brings me here."

She blinked and shifted on her feet, suddenly wanting to put some space between them without showing the need to do so.

"You will help me." He continued to move toward her, stalking her.

A strange laugh bubbled from her stomach up to her chest. Hysterical in nature. Valerian's brother was speaking in a maddened way. "I see. Perhaps you might find a servant better able to offer help." She waved a hand toward the Palmbury estate.

"Abby?"

She breathed a sigh of relief as Valerian's dark head appeared through the trees.

He appeared, a broken look upon his attractive boyish face—a face that had just started sharpening into something even more appealing. She felt the urge to go to him—an urge that was growing stronger each day she saw him.

Something in his eyes lightened, though he still looked strained. "Thank goodness. You are the only one who won't hate me. I have to tell you something."

She cast a nervous glance at Thornton. "Perhaps we should go for a walk."

"No, I have to get it off my chest now. No one comes here."

"Your brother," she blurted, pointing.

His brows drew together, pain filling his eyes. "How did you know?"

She stared at him, then motioned toward Thornton. Valerian followed her movement, then turned confused eyes back on her.

"Yes, they are all at the house. Their eyes judging. I had to get away. I have to tell you—"

"Not here," she hissed.

"What?" Valerian looked frustrated, anger replacing the other more complicated emotions. "What has been ailing you lately? You have taken to turning bright colors and making strange requests."

She gave him a look full of affront. She would normally have blustered her way past the comments, even as her cheeks started to heat automatically. But he shouldn't speak with Thornton there, no matter that he seemed completely oblivious to Thornton's presence. Thornton would hold anything said over Valerian's head.

"Your brother."

Valerian's eyes went blank.

She pointed to Thornton, who regarded her with cruel eyes, smiling.

"This is not amusing, Abigail," Valerian said.

"I know!"

"Who knew that this would *be* so amusing," Thornton said. "Little Miss Nobody, lost in the clutches of her own madness."

"What? Stop talking."

"Abigail, have you taken a fall?" Valerian approached her cautiously, reaching out to touch her head.

"No, of course not! Look." She waved at Thornton.

"Tell him that it is his fault. Everything is," Thornton said.

"What?"

A warm hand slid across her brow. "You are sweating."

She swatted Valerian's hand away. "It's hot out. Now, what is happening? Better to leave and be rid of your brother's continued presence." She glared at Thornton. "Little could be more foul."

Every muscle in Valerian's body stiffened. "What did you say?"

"He'll make such a shoddy duke," Thornton said scornfully, looking Valerian over. "Completely ruin the line,"

"I can't believe they let you get away with this. *You* will make a terrible duke. You will ruin the line," she said to Thornton, with no small amount of viciousness.

If Valerian could have grown stiffer, he would have. "What?"

She gave him a look, unwilling to repeat herself or what Thornton had said. She had always found the "ignoring someone" game silly, even when they played it to annoy the governesses.

"You think it my fault as well." Valerian's tone was odd. "And you think I will make a terrible duke."

"Valerian, you are trying my patience with this

game." She motioned to Thornton in a gesture that said exactly what she thought of the donkey and any game that included him.

"I thought you of all people would support me," he said, anger coloring his tone red.

She rolled her eyes, annoyed that he was ignoring Thornton's jabs and taking his anger out on her instead. "Stop playing games." She motioned sharply toward the path that would take them away from Thornton and the estate and deeper into the areas that only they explored.

But Valerian just watched her—an expression on his face, closed and remote, that she had never seen before. "Perhaps the boys at school were right."

"What?"

"I have to go."

"But—"

But he had already turned and was striding away, pushing hanging branches from his path.

Abigail narrowed her eyes, more irritated now than when it had just been Thornton taunting her. What was Valerian's game? He had been acting oddly lately himself as well, and this was just further confusion.

"That was lovely. I couldn't have done better myself." Thornton sounded pleased and she tried to kill him with a glance.

It hadn't been until later that afternoon that she had discovered that while thinking about killing him was an admirable thought, Thornton was *already* dead—killed in a riding accident while racing Valerian.

The incident had been blamed on Valerian, but the duke and dowager had realized their heir dilemma immediately and started to hush the gossip.

Abigail had been scared witless when the spirit of Valerian's dead brother had continued to follow her around, taunting her, telling her that she had to do things for him—that Valerian would never speak to her again.

Days had gone by before she had had a chance to speak to Valerian. Completely frightened and scared—seeking her own reassurance from him. But he had changed. Gone cold. His father and grandmother hovering over him, unwilling to let the last surviving Danforth, however poorly tolerated previously, do anything circumspect. After all, it was just a matter of time before Basil succumbed to death, as weak and useless to them as he was. They needed Valerian and he seemed more than willing to suddenly bend to their will as the perfect heir.

Valerian had briefly and unemotionally listened to her tale of ghosts, of Thornton's game, called her a few choice words and then called in his grandmother to casually eject her from the house. His parting words, "You are mad. Never speak to me again," had haunted her more than his spirit ever could.

A dozen notes returned unopened. Servants firmly keeping her from the grounds. His immediate return to Eton and all holiday visits canceled. Dozens of spirits showing up, approaching her, driving her mad. Needing the reassurance of her best friend and finding cold silence instead. Valerian had abandoned her as surely as he must have felt on that day that she had abandoned him.

She hoped Thornton was burning below.

She pressed her hand to her forehead. What a terrible series of events. If only she hadn't been so young and stupid. If only she hadn't already started to tiptoe around Valerian anyway. Keeping secrets, her feelings for him changing into something much more than a friend, and her not knowing how to deal with it.

If only he hadn't been so raw to turn to his family instead of to try and seek an explanation from her—the bloom of womanhood cursing her in more ways than one and throwing up a barrier between them. The miscommunication and widening social divide separating them.

She looked up at him standing against the door. "So now you know."

"You aren't Abigail Smart."

She gave a strained smile. "I am the same person I have always been."

"Are you?"

Every foul word she had heard in society ran through her head. "Except I'm *common*."

"There is nothing common about you."

"Were you not listening?" she demanded.

His eyes darkened. "I was."

He looked beyond angry. She had always known that it was how he would react. Had always been terrified that he would discover her duplicity.

"I'm sorry." She looked away.

"I am as well. If I had known your mother planned to do such foul things to you, I would have run away with you myself."

Her head jerked up. "What?"

Telly bustled in to help her ready for the day,

and her mother walked in behind, saving him from answering, though he sent a dark look her mother's way before walking to the bed to watch.

It took a good hour to get ready. An hour in which all she wanted to do was to ask him question after question.

"Abigail, I've made us late, and we have a hundred appointments before the Malcolm's ball tonight," her mother said. "It can't be helped though."

Her mother touched her shoulder, retreated, then touched her again. "And I'm glad that our talk was the reason for our tardiness," she whispered, so that Telly couldn't hear. "Relieved that you finally know. Happy to build a better foundation for us." She straightened. "The carriage should be ready, I will see you downstairs."

Abigail nodded and waited for Telly too to leave, giving her only a minute alone with Valerian.

He hadn't been surprised about the deception. Her throat closed on a sudden rush of emotion. That really only left one question.

"What did you do with the full corruption list, Valerian?" she asked softly.

He turned away from her. "I burned it. As soon as I saw your name, I burned it."

Chapter 20

"**T**here is going to be a grand announcement tonight, or so I'm told," Mrs. Browning said as the carriage rocked toward the Malcolm's ball. "And Lord Rainewood is expected to put in an appearance finally."

Abigail's sat straighter and Valerian jerked from his seat near the window. "He hasn't been to any events in nearly two weeks," she choked out.

"Well, he will come to this one if he wants to have any say in his betrothal."

Abigail swallowed while Valerian swore violently. "That is the announcement then? A betrothal?"

"Of course," Mrs. Browning said, as if she wasn't just making the assumption. "I expect you to show the proper courtesy to the dowager duchess when extending your congratulations. I have noticed that she isn't entirely comfortable with Lord Basil courting you. Nevertheless, we will be polite."

Abigail couldn't resist. "She is barely polite to us."

"She is a duchess! You must understand that." Mrs. Browning shook her head, lips pinched. "You have never had the proper respect for the levels of society. As if you wouldn't have learned from birth where you fell in the social hierarchy!"

Abigail smiled wanly and her mother's laughter was a little too high-pitched.

"As it is, we would have been told the latest information had we attended the balloon races." Mrs. Browning gave her a dark look. "All the gossip churned there today."

"I take it the races were eventful?"

"Mr. Campbell ruined Mr. Brockwell's balloon and there was an altercation with Mr. Penshard because of it."

Abigail's hand went to her mouth. "Poor Mr. Brockwell."

"Yes, he was devastated. I would have liked to observe it all first hand. I had to get the news from Lettie. Horrible."

"Did you discover anything else?"

"Mr. Brockwell made a stunning turn around by fixing his balloon. It lifted finally and indeed won the final race. Seems to be the toast of the Young Scientist's Society because of it. Why anyone is interested in those mechanical matters though, I'll never know. A good cup of tea and a nice bit of news is a far better way to spend an afternoon. The betrothal gossip, for instance. Far more interesting."

Abigail's stomach churned, and she listened to the rest of the daily gossip with half an ear as they pulled up the packed drive.

In the interior of the brightly lit, extravagant ballroom, the spirits were even easier to pick out than usual. Abigail swallowed at their sallow tones, their crackling edges, their drawn faces. She passed two ghosts speaking to each other.

"We are about to lose another one."

The second woman patted the first on the arm. "I know, Margaret, I know. But it happens to them all eventually."

She wanted to ask of what they were speaking, somehow feeling that they would answer, but Mrs. Browning urged her forward toward Mr. Farnswourth. As she looked over her shoulder, she could see the spirits gazing at her sadly.

It made her twitch. She had a feeling that the whole night was going to cause that reaction.

Sure enough, the view of the rest of the room confirmed this notion. Miss Malcolm preened in the center of the room, appearing to indicate to all present that the rumors were true. That there would be a betrothal announcement.

"I heard that Miss Jones's second cousin, Lady Tenning, heard from her maid's friend who is a friend of Lady Marple, who heard it from Mrs. Fortening that her husband saw the document on Sir Walter Malcolm's desk. It said that the Palmbury heir was to be betrothed to Celeste Malcolm. Lucky girl!"

All talk concerned the betrothal and Valerian. A few people obviously recalled that one of his last actions before leaving had been to argue with her and they looked to her for a reaction each time his name came up. Abigail tried to keep her smile firmly in place.

Valerian had strode off upon entering the room, trying to discover what was happening. She caught glimpses of him here and there, but he only reappeared at her side when he grew exceptionally pale. She swallowed to think of it. That he was disappearing with the rest of the spirits. That their physical actions had done this and he might leave before she was ready. Before they found him.

She was on her twentieth conversation about Lord Rainewood, and about Miss Malcolm's great fortune, when the general level of the voices rose and gossip rode a wave through the Malcolm's grand ballroom.

"Did you hear?"

"No, what?"

"Mr. Campbell has been attacked! He was almost taken by villains! A constable saved him just as he was being dragged away."

"Oh dear!"

Abigail waited for the entire story to make its way to her. Mrs. Browning and her mother leaned in as well.

Lady Orton parted her fan and made a few sweeps before gifting them with the news, her eyes fluttering in satisfaction. "Mr. Campbell was walking down by the docks when he was attacked by ten men. He fought valiantly but fell beneath their combined blows. And then they were trying to drag him off—kidnap him, so it seems! Can you imagine?"

"No, poor man," her mother said fretfully. "Have they caught the men responsible?"

"No, but there is a man hunt, you can be sure. Can you imagine why anyone would want to attack Mr. Campbell?"

Valerian snorted darkly, suddenly appearing

beside her. "There are a thousand reasons, and they are increasing every day."

"No, Mr. Campbell is an upstanding citizen," Mrs. Browning said.

Abigail thought of the endless debts that Campbell seemed to owe. "What was he doing by the docks?"

The entire group stopped talking and turned to her. Lady Malcolm sniffed. "I'm sure I do not know. Walking. Minding his own business," she said, as if she wasn't gossiping endlessly about the man.

"It matters little," Mrs. Browning said. "That they attacked Mr. Campbell anywhere is beyond the pale. They need to be punished. Common folk should not touch their betters."

"It is likely they won't be caught," another woman said. "The watch are so pitiful these days. Letting scoundrels and rogues run the streets."

"But Mr. Campbell is well?" Abigail asked Lady Orton.

Mrs. Browning nodded sharply in agreement with the question. "He has been quite attentive to Miss Smart."

Abigail pressed her lips together but waited for the answer.

Another lady leaned in. "He is well. Laid low, but accepting visitors should you wish to stop by and see how he is doing."

"A fine idea." Mrs. Browning said.

"He is convalescing with Lord Basil." The woman pointed.

Basil was conversing with a group on the other side of the room—it looked as if they were actively trying to squeeze him of every last drop of information. Basil was smiling charmingly, but she knew he would reveal only what he wished. Slippery one, Basil.

Abigail excused herself to the retiring area. Halfway there Mr. Stagen appeared next to her, silently, like a tricky spirit in his own right. "Good evening, Miss Smart."

"Mr. Stagen."

"Have you heard from our erstwhile companion?"

"Mr. Campbell? No. I have heard that he was attacked and has taken ill though. I do hope he is well."

"Ah, yes, Mr. Campbell. He should be right as rain come a few days' mend and ready to be fawned over by the ladies of the ton. Do not despair."

She looked at him more closely. "If not Mr. Campbell, then to whom are you referring?"

"Lord Rainewood."

She stiffened. "He is your companion, but I do not think he would ever claim to be mine."

"No?"

"No."

He tapped his fingers against the handle of his cane as they walked. "Interesting the things you remember with age and a bit of hindsight behind you. I seem to recall him always speaking of a girl at home. One of whom he was quite fond. The boys gave him quite a bit of hell for it—especially when girls started to become a different breed to the rest of us." He smiled. "Of course, some of us have always considered them so. Raine took a hit for being friends with a girl—even one that none of us had seen."

"Interesting, Mr. Stagen," she said stiffly. "But I hardly see what that has to do with me."

"No? I seem to remember he called his friend Abby once when he wasn't watching his speech. Curious, don't you think?"

"Quite curious. Of course, there are many Abby's in this country, one would think."

"But none quite as close to Raine's notice as you."

She thought of the way the women in the group had talked about commoners. "I am far beneath his notice."

Stagen merely tipped his head. "And one recalls other things. Like the trick that was attempted at the Crupper's ball."

She remembered quite well. She had narrowly missed being the brunt of a most embarrassing prank. Somehow it had exploded on Valerian instead.

"Yes, bad luck that Lord Rainewood found himself in the middle of it." The incident had provoked a somewhat mean smile to her face at the time.

"Oh, I don't think luck had anything to do with it. It was a perfect prank, planned for the first lady in white to cross its path. I won't tell you who was in charge of it, of course, but it should have gone off without a hitch."

"Not that it wasn't quite satisfying to see V-Rainewood dripping in water instead, but what does this have to do with me?"

"Mmmm. Someone triggered the trap early."

She had assumed it had been Gregory, or maybe Phillip under Gregory's command. "Don't tell me it was you, Mr. Stagen?"

"No, not me."

The way he was looking at her, and his words, made her swallow. "You are trying to tell me that Lord Rainewood sabotaged the prank and put himself in harm's way for me?"

He tilted his head. "Yes."

"As he would for any lady, then."

"No. Not for anyone else, I should think."

He would for his betrothed. He was an honorable man once bound by something. She gave a brittle laugh. "You are mistaken."

"No. It has always been about you." His voice was musing, his eyes piercing.

She tried to wipe his words away with a sweep of her hand. "Lovely, Mr. Stagen. You flatter me. But Lord Rainewood barely knows I exist."

"Interesting, since all of his focus is on you when you are near. And Raine is the jealous sort. He doesn't take kindly to anyone else marking something he sees as his."

"You are creating fantasies, Mr. Stagen." She picked up her pace. "Besides, if this were all true, he could have ended the prank without ending up in the middle of it."

Stagen smiled. "He found out about it only a few minutes before it was due to happen. Only he is allowed to touch you."

She swallowed. "V-Rainewood doesn't touch me."

Stagen gave her a considering glance. "A strange relationship the two of you maintain, but a relationship nonetheless. Only those that are looking truly notice it, but we do."

She thought about the prank. About how Valerian had arrived, slightly winded, at just the exact time to trigger the device. She thought about the relief she had felt as she'd looked at her pristine white dress—the water would have revealed her to God and the world.

Valerian had looked so angry—but she had assumed it was because of accidentally triggering the gag.

"Why are you telling me this?"

"I just thought maybe you knew more about Raine's whereabouts than you were telling."

"Ah, yes. You and Lord Basil have been keeping tabs on me."

Stagen smiled faintly. "Neither of us believe you responsible—at least not anymore. But there is no denying that you might have more knowledge than you claim."

Abigail tilted her head. "I see." She considered him. "I will tell you this. If I knew of Rainewood's whereabouts, I would tell you. It seems as if you have his best intentions in order." She didn't know Valerian's whereabouts, however, and she didn't think pointing across the room to the invisible man roaming around, between, and through the party guests was likely to make Stagen satisfied with her sanity.

Stagen smiled. "Very well, Miss Smart. I knew that you could be counted upon."

"Why?" she asked as calmly as she could.

"Because while I watch Raine watching you, I also watch your reactions to him." He tipped his head. "Good evening, Miss Smart."

Abigail watched him walk away, a bit numb.

Valerian appeared at her side a few moments later. "What did Stagen say?" His voice was tight.

"He is looking for you. Did you discover anything?"

He shook his head, lips thinned.

"Very well. I'm going to speak with Phillip."

"Why?"

"Curiosity about something."

She needed a few answers. Needed to know if there was really a chance that the other Valerian, the one from weeks ago, had such a care for her. If there was a possibility that his two incarnations were the same.

Phillip was standing near two women who were chattering while he lifted his glass awkwardly. She walked his way and nearly smiled at the relief that stole across his face.

"Good evening, Mr. Brockwell."

"And to you, Miss Smart."

She could feel Valerian at her side, but didn't look his way. "I have a question for you."

Phillip nodded, simply looking happy not to have to listen to the women near him anymore.

"At the Crupper's ball, do you remember that prank that went badly for Lord Rainewood?"

Phillip nodded, a nervous smile playing about his lips. His previous eagerness to speak with her visually diminishing. "I do. Nasty thing meant for you, wasn't it?"

She could feel Valerian stiffen at her side. "Yes." She looked at Phillip closely. "Did you have anything to do with stopping it?"

Phillip cocked his head. "No. I'm happy that you escaped from it though."

"Thank you. What about Mr. Penshard?"

"I'm sure that he was equally happy."

"No, did he have anything to do with sabotaging the prank?"

Phillip shook his head. "No, he was with me, I remember."

"Ah, thank you, Mr. Brockwell." She cleared her throat. Had Valerian truly sabotaged it?

"They are always playing nasty pranks and creating problems," Phillip said heatedly, all of a sudden. "It is little surprise that they find themselves in trouble."

The two women seemed to clue into the discussion all of a sudden.

"Do you suppose someone could have attacked Mr. Templing and Lord Rainewood too?"

Phillip went white.

"That would explain why they aren't here even with the gossip about the betrothal on everyone's lips. How awful. But the duke is saying that Lord Rainewood is simply out of town on estate business."

"And Mr. Templing?"

"Perhaps with him? Oh, the possibilities if not. I must question Lady Malcolm."

The two women continued to chatter, but Abigail only had eyes for Phillip, who was picking at his pocket, looking increasingly nauseous.

"Mr. Brockwell?"

His eyes swung toward her and he cleared his throat. "Yes, Miss Smart?"

"It is quite hot in here, is it not?" She fanned herself, but continued to meet his eyes.

He nodded sharply, understanding at least the nature of her question. "Yes, would you care to accompany me to the refreshment table?"

"Please." She put her hand on his arm and allowed him to lead her away. She waited until they were well away before asking, "Did you have something to do with it, Phillip?"

"Something to do with what?"

"Mr. Campbell's attack."

"Of course not!"

"But he ruined your balloon."

"I fixed it. Made a better inroad with the Society over how quickly and correctly I did so."

"But I would have been quite angry, had it been me. Might even have wanted to get even with the man. Perhaps a knock on the head?"

"I didn't do anything to Campbell!" Phillip was flustered, his face changing into a mottled shade of red mixed with the palest white.

Abigail looked at him closely, suddenly realizing something. "But you did something to someone else?"

The shades instantly blanched. "I, I didn't say that."

"But you implied it, Phillip. What did you do?" She watched him. "Did you have something to do with Rainewood's disappearance?"

"Of course not." He licked his lips. Then licked them again.

Valerian swore and took a swing. It went cleanly through Phillip without making contact.

Phillip looked miserable. She opened her mouth, closed it, and then opened it again. "Oh, Phillip. What did you do?"

Phillip frantically looked around, then steered her a few feet away.

Valerian furiously followed. "Abigail, don't be stupid."

But she wasn't going to be stupid. She only let Phillip steer her out of the earshot of the others.

Phillip looked as if he might break down right there. "It was just a little knock on the head. I, I couldn't let Rainewood have that list. He might not do something with it, but his friends . . . Templing, Campbell. The bets. I had to. Edwina . . . and it . . . always like . . ." he stuttered. "But I did nothing else, I swear. I searched for the list and when I didn't find it I left them there."

She swallowed around the gigantic lump in her throat. "Left them where?"

"In the street."

"Oh, Phillip."

"They probably woke up and went to the country. Went to convalesce or drink," he said somewhat desperately. "No one would touch them. Not the heir to a duke. To Palmbury."

"You left them in a bad section of town. Any villain could have kidnapped them."

"No one would dare do anything though. I even sent an anonymous note to the watch in order to—" He broke off and gave her a queer look. "How do you know which part of town it was?"

She blinked and Valerian swore beside her. "Oh. I'm just speculating because the last place they were seen was down by a shady hell."

"Nothing could have happened, I'm telling you," Phillip stressed, the tension cracking his voice hinting that he didn't quite believe himself.

She took a breath before blurting out anything unfortunate. "Why haven't they been seen, then?"

"As I said—"

She put a hand on his arm and Valerian growled. "Phillip, you don't believe that."

He chewed his lip and looked miserable. "I had to do it. I'd never see Edwina again. Her mother would make sure." Abigail wondered in what position Phillip occupied the list. "I don't know what happened after I left, I was sure that they would be none the worse. You have to believe me."

And somehow she did.

"You are staying with your aunt on Golden Square, aren't you?"

He looked surprised. "Yes."

She nodded. "Number Twenty still?"

"Yes."

She couldn't see him, but she could almost feel the intense relief behind her that projected off Valerian in waves.

It hadn't been Basil. Nor Campbell. Nor even Gregory.

Oh, Phillip.

Chapter 21

"**I** want you to tell everyone what Brockwell did!"

Valerian had been demanding it for an hour now. Through the not-quite-announcement of his betrothal to Celeste Malcolm—the duke taking Celeste's hand and making it obvious to all that the match had his full approval, even without the showing of the future groom. Speculation had continued to be rampant, the gossip mill churning. Each uttered word had driven another nail in her headache.

She was just glad they were finally home. "Phillip didn't take you."

"He attacked us. He as good as put me in this position."

That was true. "And for that damn list. But someone else took you. Something else is at work here, don't you see?"

"That muckrakers or common thieves disposed of us or sold us to the nearest body part mill? Yes. And I want Brockwell punished for it."

"I'm not pleased with Phillip at the moment."

"Not pleased? Not *pleased*?"

She scowled at him.

"Abigail, you can't be seriously thinking of letting him get away with it?"

"Of course not. Phillip said he is going to tell someone. Probably Sir Walter. I think it has been eating him up inside. But there is nothing to be gained by hurrying up that process. He doesn't know what happened afterward."

"Maybe he is lying. Have you thought of that, wise one?"

"Of course. But Phillip just doesn't have it in him."

"He had it in enough to attack us."

"But what about the other attacks? The men in the square? The men at the hell? They were waiting for you, Valerian. From everything you've said, they took you on purpose."

Valerian opened his mouth, whether to agree or not, she wasn't sure, but he suddenly flickered and disappeared.

Valerian woke to the screams, the groans. Not Abigail's cellar this time though—no, this was the hospital, or building, or wherever he was being held. A shot of some sharp spike rushed through him and he pulled up on his clasps, turned his head toward where Templing was the last time he had seen him. But Templing wasn't there.

The reflection through the window shone through. He stared at it for half a second and internally swore. He pulled forcefully against his clamps.

A hand gripped his face and he thought frantically

of home. But instead of Grayton House, Abigail's face pulled into view. His closest confidante.

There was one thing that tied everything together. The list. The doctor. The attack.

One thing.

The hand gripping his mouth poured the vile liquid in, but he managed to spit most of it away.

She had always been his closest confidante, even after they'd parted ways he had never replaced her.

He thought of her face when she'd been ejected from Palmbury Manor so long ago, when she'd tried to speak to him.

The hand succeeded in forcing him to swallow.

He needed to go home.

Abigail paced her room, lips pressed together, heart raging in worry. Plotting how she was going to get back into Grayton House for a third time. And whether he would even be there.

They were close to finding him, or to losing him, if he had started flickering so fiercely and disappearing so easily. Perhaps she should just go after him herself.

Free him and let him go. Give in to the inevitable.

She heard the steps behind her and chided herself for not even paying attention enough to hear her maid enter.

"Telly, we are going to O'Malley's tonight. I'll need your help."

"You aren't going anywhere."

She whipped around, her hand lifted to her throat. She took a step forward before stopping. "How?" she whispered.

Valerian leaned against the four-poster looking exhausted. "I returned to my body, but then ended up here."

"Oh."

"It's not O'Malley's."

"Oh?"

"I read the sign incorrectly."

"What is it, then? We will go."

"No."

She narrowed her eyes. "Why?"

His eyes turned dark. "It isn't safe."

"Valerian—"

"No." He took a breath. "Listen, Abigail, I'm s—"

Telly bustled through the door. "Miss, are you ready for bed?"

Valerian's mouth clicked shut and he drummed his fingers against the four-poster. Sound that it still seemed only she could hear, if Telly's unchanging, expectant expression was anything to go by.

Aunt Effie flickered in the corner.

Abigail let Telly strip her of her ball garments and concentrated on the brush on her dressing table as Telly peeled one layer then another from her. She had kept the brush, always. Never quite able to part with it, even through her darkest days with him. Oh, she'd tried to toss it a number of times. Hidden it away, thrown it in the rubbish bin. But she'd always retrieved it. Put it back in place on her table.

She said nothing as Telly worked. She didn't know if fighting again would make Valerian disappear. One of these times he wouldn't reappear. She knew it, dreaded it. He would just be gone.

Whether from the mortal coil, or socially once more.

Abigail retrieved the footman's gear from the drawer as Telly folded her garments.

"Miss, are you still entertaining your new spirit?"

It was an unfavorable choice of words under the circumstances. "Are you worried, Telly?"

"A little, miss. I just wondered whether we would be going out again. The talk has been all about people going missing lately on the streets. Just up and gone. No word left."

Telly looked at the trousers and shirt askance. Abigail hadn't said that they would be going out, but pulling out the clothes as good as proclaimed it.

"I haven't decided yet whether to go out, Telly. Do not worry yourself."

"Yes, miss. I'm going to get you some warm milk while you are deciding. I will be back soon."

"Thank you, Telly."

Valerian's narrowed eyes followed Telly, then he stalked off after her. Abigail sat still for a moment, then pulled the shirt between her fingers, wondering what she could do to make things right. For herself and for them.

Valerian followed Abigail's maid downstairs and through to the backyard. A man waited for her in the shadows.

"Well?"

"I think she might go out. I will go too, of course."

"Of course." The man placed a hand at the maid's shoulder. "You are a good servant."

Telly leaned in and fiddled with his collar and shirt, actions that spoke of a familiarity more than casual acquaintances.

"She continues to speak to them, poor dear."

"You do encourage it."

"Well, I can't say anything. She is a wonderful mistress otherwise. Just because she is a bit batty, doesn't mean a thing. She gives me her best dresses when she is done with them and treats me kindly. That one I wore the other night—the one you liked so well? Beautiful, wasn't it?"

The man ran a hand down the maid's hip and gripped her rear, pulling her against him. "Anything on—or off—you is."

Telly giggled. The man ground his pelvis into hers and Telly's breath caught.

"Is she still talking to that one—the man?"

"Yes, poor dear. She has held a tendre for him forever. And now she is convinced he is with her. I hope it doesn't break her mind when he shows back up."

The man grabbed a handful of the maid's skirts, grinding against her again. "I wouldn't worry about that."

Valerian narrowed his eyes and memorized everything he could about the man.

"No? But she was always ranting about Rainewood this, and Rainewood that. And now she positively dotes on the imaginary man. When the real earl gets back from wherever he is, she won't know what to do with the imaginary one."

So the maid was oblivious. Duplicitous to her mistress by revealing her secrets, but unmindful of the dangerous type of information she was passing on.

"If that happens, you can use your 'Gypsy' ways to help her."

Telly had the grace to at least bite her lip and look embarrassed. "You know I hate when you tease me about that. I had to say something, Roland. She is a wonderful mistress. I didn't want her to dismiss me just because she is slightly mad. We all know it in the house. I just hope that she marries well. The uppers have long histories of madness. She'll blend right in."

Valerian gritted his teeth. Abigail's one support, and even she was false.

"Oh, I'm sure your mistress will be fine."

"I do hope so. I think I can talk her out of leaving tonight."

"Good, you do that, sweetheart. You want her to stay safe, don't you? Don't want the poor dear wandering around the streets."

"No!"

"Good girl. Then keep her inside tonight. O'Malley's isn't in a terrible section of town, but you'd have no idea what you were getting into. Better to stay safe." He tweaked her breast. "She still wants to go to O'Malley's, yes?"

"Yes."

He pulled more firmly against her breast, drawing the maid further in. "Good. You are the best maid she could have. We'll give her another place to search instead. A safe place tomorrow. She can get her adventure done safely. Tomorrow. Yes?"

Telly moaned as Roland pulled her into a dominating kiss.

One hand worked up under her skirt and the maid gasped and rubbed herself against him.

"If you can't convince her to wait until tomorrow though, send me a note," Roland said. "I'll make sure to keep you safe."

"You treat me so well, Roland."

Roland undid his trousers and pushed the maid somewhat violently against a hedge. "That's right. And you always come to me first, don't you."

"Yes!" The maid's head slipped back as he pushed into her, forcing her against the twined branches. Telly wrapped her arms around the man's neck and held on as he grunted and thrust, somewhat brutally pushing them both to completion.

Two footmen watched from the window near Valerian, their heads peeking above the sill, faces nearly pressed to the glass.

Valerian turned back to the pair copulating. He couldn't but picture Abigail's face thrown back in ecstasy instead. Whereas as a youth he might have found the scene before him titillating, just as the two footmen obviously did, now he just found himself wishing to be back inside. Upstairs.

The man gave one final grunt and thrust into Abigail's maid hard. Telly squealed into his mouth.

He let her slide back down and gave her a pat on the rear. "I'll be back tomorrow, if'n I don't see you tonight."

Telly nodded frantically, eyes glazed, and the man slipped over the wall. Telly returned inside, her color high and breath uneven. Valerian followed her to the kitchen, where she picked up the promised glass of milk, and then up to Abigail's room. She smoothed her skirts with her free hand and knocked.

He followed her inside and Abigail opened her mouth to say something.

"Tell your maid nothing," he demanded. "Tell her you aren't going out."

Abigail looked at him and for a second he thought she would argue, but then she said to Telly, "I've decided to turn in for the night, Telly."

"Oh, very good, miss!" Telly set the milk on the dressing table, wincing only slightly as she did. Stupid girl had twigs on her back, but Abigail's attention was elsewhere.

Telly picked up the trousers and shirt as if she were taking them to the wash. Clever girl.

Part of him wanted the maid to take the outfit. To keep Abigail safe in the house. The other part of him knew that if Abigail didn't have the outfit she would go out in a dress anyway and give herself away completely.

"Abigail," he said, calling her attention back.

Abigail turned and saw her maid. "No, Telly, leave those."

"But, miss—"

"I'm not going to use them, Telly. I just want to have them near should another incident present itself like the one with that man who came to the house the other day. You understand, correct?"

Telly looked torn.

Abigail's eyes narrowed. "Good night, Telly."

"Good night, miss," Telly said softly, backing away to the door.

As soon as the maid's footsteps echoed down the hall, Abigail turned to him. "Now what was that? Are you going to tell me?"

He opened his mouth and then shut it. He could tell her that Telly was a fake. That she believed Abigail to be slightly crazed. He could completely crush her with a few sentences.

"I just think it wise not to have her with us."

"But you were the one who wanted—"

"I know." He moved abruptly to the window. The maid had probably been giving that man information for a long time now. Relieving her knowledge of her mistress's condition. It was likely how those men had known Abigail could see spirits.

He swallowed. How they would have known who to target.

He looked back at her—strong and sturdy. Hiding the vulnerability beneath. Her maid was the only one who she thought believed her—and she had turned false. Her mother hardly counted, hiding the shame for so long.

Knowing that no one believed in her . . .

"I'm sorry for not believing you, Abby."

Her indrawn breath was reflected in the hand that rose to her chest.

Damnit if he didn't suddenly want to prostrate himself in front of her and beg forgiveness. "I'll make it up to you. Someday. I promise."

She looked bemused, but nodded, the color in her cheeks heightened, making her even more desirable. "Thank you," she said softly. Her eyes lightened and happiness began a tentative bloom within their depths.

He wanted to scream with the unfairness of it all. The wasted time.

The look on her face morphed into concern.

"Valerian, you are starting to flicker a bit again, just around the edges."

He felt it, the tug pulling. "I need to go."

She nodded and gathered her things. "I know. I'm ready."

"No, I want you to stay."

"No." She looked at him calmly. "You can't leave without me."

"I will find a way. I did earlier."

There were crinkles at the corners of her eyes as she stepped toward him. "No. You will start to lose your way."

"I know."

She put an insistent hand on his sleeve. "You might not be able to return. You might become an aimless spirit wandering."

"Perhaps. But I will return. I promise. Now you must promise me, Abigail. I know you will follow, but—" He looked to the window. "You must promise me that you will stay in the hack. That you will not follow me once we are free of the house."

"Why?"

"You are in danger."

"I know."

"No, you—" He took a deep breath. "Promise, or I will simply stand here until I fade away."

She stepped back. "No."

"Yes. Promise me."

She swallowed. "Very well."

"Good. I will hold you to it, Abigail. Are you ready?"

He watched her straighten her shoulders. "I'm ready. I have been ready."

Under what star had they been brought together? And was it a lucky or unlucky one?

"I as well."

And in that he was answering more than just one query. Her lips parted, her eyes filmed, but she simply nodded and they walked through the door.

Chapter 22

It was almost as if now that he had embarked
upon the truth and accepted it, that he was able
to follow where the tug led.

"Where are we going?" she asked.

"The Lamppost Tavern."

Abigail shot him a sharp look. "You had the letters in the wrong order."

She had always been especially quick. "Yes."

"You saw the whole sign?"

"Yes."

She stayed silent for a moment as the carriage
rocked across the stones. "In what condition were
you?"

"Still alive."

She nodded, biting her lip. "That is good."

Something pressed against his chest—wanting
to come out, but the last restraints of his stubborn-
ness pulled it back. He just nodded in return, the
tension settling upon the carriage.

"Valerian, I wanted you to know—"

"I do, Abigail."

She nodded again and the tension, instead of
dissipating, grew thicker.

They had taken great pains to avoid being followed. There had been two men watching Abigail's house—whether they had been in with Roland, the duke, or some other entity, he didn't know. But they had successfully negotiated around the watchers while well-timed distractions had taken place—a carriage overturned down the street, an argument between two drunkards on the corner.

He could only hope that there hadn't been another lackey about—or a man like Evans—who watched while no one knew.

The carriage passed the tavern and he looked across from the sign. A brick building, completely innocuous-looking, stood to the side.

But there were bars on some of the windows. Not completely unusual, not enough to cause comment if one didn't know, but now they stood out like a sign proclaiming "asylum" in bright letters.

The hack stopped a block down from the tavern, as instructed. He watched Abigail in her borrowed clothing, smoothing her trousers. Her shoulders were straight, but he could see the tension lacing them.

She calmly tipped her head.

He smiled faintly and touched his lips to hers. "See you on the other side, Smart."

He concentrated on the pull. Concentrated on exiting the carriage, and walked through.

Abigail waited for Valerian to disappear into the brick building, then pushed open the door and nimbly exited the carriage without one ounce of remorse.

She handed the driver three times the fare. "Wait here and you will receive the same compensation upon the return trip."

The driver eagerly accepted the money and tipped his hat.

She concentrated on the brick building as she walked. The bars. What she knew would be inside.

A few people passed on the street. Late-nighters returning from parties or early-morning workers dragging themselves to their jobs.

She walked up the steps and touched the door handle. It swung open an inch.

She swallowed. In any other circumstance she would run far, far away. But Valerian was inside. Both the living one and the not quite living one.

She was going inside no matter which one emerged after.

She pushed open the door. The entrance hall was dark, but a stairway lifted into the next floor and a faint light shone down.

She saw Valerian at the top of the stairs, his edges more dim than she'd seen, leaning against the wall and dipping through. He suddenly turned.

Swearing filled the hall and he limped back down the stairs, the lines of his body growing firmer as he drew nearer.

His hands wrapped around her arms.

"You promised to stay in the carriage."

"You are flickering again, Valerian."

His lips tightened. "I don't care."

Calm ran through her at his words. "You will die."

"You don't know that."

"You will stay a spirit forever or go into the beyond."

His grip tightened. "What if I want to stay a spirit? Stay with you? Will you leave then?"

The words wrapped around her, seductive in their intent. She tried to shake them away, but with each vine she peeled away, another would grip and coil.

She dipped her head. No, she knew what she had to do. "No."

"Don't do this, Abigail."

"I must."

"You are in danger."

"So are you."

"No, you—"

Voices from outside drew close to the door.

Valerian swore again. "Let me go first. And don't do anything foolish!" He darted up the stairs.

Voices followed behind. Not hurried. Measured. They hadn't been discovered, then.

And she couldn't go back. Valerian seemed to know it too, if his pinched full lips were any indication. "I have to find my body so that I can kill you myself." He closed his eyes, then waved her forward, his hand plastering her to the wall each time he heard a sound.

He led her through a maze of corridors and landings. Faint sounds followed and surrounded. Then the sounds sharpened. Moans, screams, pleas. She shut her eyes.

"Abigail—"

"No, continue." He hesitated and she pushed against his side. "Go."

They entered a long hall that contained beds

on either side, a corridor stretching through the middle.

The moans hit her as she walked down the center row of the beds. The men's wrists were strapped to the rails, and in some cases their ankles. Some had blindfolds, some had gags, while others stared unseeingly at the ceiling. One ungagged man looked up as she passed.

"Help, my child. Help me pass to the beyond."

She swallowed. Dear Lord.

"Help me."

Similar scenarios played out in her mind from the other asylums she'd been forced to visit. They clanged and converged together and she gripped her head. The spirits couldn't be separated from the poor live souls.

"Help."

With Valerian freed, he could shut this place down. Free everyone inside. She turned away, tears blurring her eyes as the man's pleas continued. A hand touched her back—a fleeting touch. She blinked the tears away and moved forward.

"Where do you feel pulled?" she asked in a low voice, hoping that her voice wouldn't break.

Valerian hesitated, then pointed to a hall at the end of the row. She nodded and walked that way, the horrific moans following her like a trail of snakes.

She could feel the cuffs about her wrists. Feel the terror of being pinned down, unable to fight. Feel the despair that no one would ever help.

She shook off the shivers. She needed to get through this. To find Valerian, escape, and send someone back here to close the place down.

She had just turned the corner into the hall when a door opened and a man stepped outside. He stopped and stared at her while she stared back. He smiled unpleasantly and his hand lifted to his head.

A purple bruise marred his forehead from where she had hit him with the plank. She shifted on the balls of her feet.

"Miss Smart, what a *pleasant* surprise," his cultured voice said and memories of him speaking while she was pressed against the bricks froze her mind. "We have a bed waiting just for you. It has been waiting for weeks now. Years really. How fortunate for us that you've chosen to come of your own volition."

Something lodged in her throat. Two men appeared behind him. Valerian shimmered.

"Grab her," the man from the alley said.

The lackey who stepped forward to do so was obviously convinced that she would be taken easily. He strutted toward her. "Come here, little filly."

She gripped behind her, her fingers closing around metal. The man reached toward her and she grabbed the bedpan and arced it up into his chin. His head jerked back and he crashed toward the floor. The other unknown man and the one from the alley rushed toward her at once. Valerian stepped in front. He planted his feet, expression tightening, and as the unknown man reached him, Valerian pushed forward with his hands. The man abruptly folded in two and dropped to the ground. Valerian staggered, but she couldn't go to his side. The man from the alley stalked toward her, though his eyes tracked to the left and the right.

"Have a little help again, Miss Smart?"

"Yes." She straightened. "Better to leave now while you can."

"Oh, no. I will deal with your helper. Our bait."

Bait? Oh, dear God.

She didn't have time to process her horror before the man continued. "In the meantime, I have a little help too." He whistled. Valerian charged him as soon as the note sounded, but it was too late. Footsteps echoed down the hall. The two of them went down, tackled to the floor. Valerian got in a punch before he clutched at his stomach.

"Abigail."

And he disappeared.

Three other men ran inside. "Mr. Evans?" One of them said.

She stared at the spot where Valerian had just crouched. She fervently hoped he was waking somewhere in the building and not either gone for good or with his spirit trapped somewhere else.

The new men stepped toward her and she squared herself to fight. She was going to lose. She knew it. But she wanted to take at least one of them to the grave with her.

Evans regained his feet. "All alone, Miss Smart? That is too bad, now isn't it?"

He took a menacing step forward, but another man stepped from the shadows, raising his hand. "Stop."

The men immediately ceased, even Evans, though he looked furious.

The man from the shadows stepped into the

shine of the lamp. Abigail's throat closed as his features came into view.

"Good evening, Miss Smart."

Valerian woke to unimaginable pain. He strained at the straps at his wrists. Abigail.

The ceiling came into view. The same ceiling that had lined the other room. The one where Abigail still remained, surrounded by men intent on harming her. He strained against the bonds again, but his muscles barely obeyed.

He heard a scream and pulled harder. He needed to get to her.

He imagined the brush on her table—one she had kept all these years, the look on her face in the height of passion, the girl that had once raced him up the tallest tree.

He twisted with everything in him and there was a clang as the bar disconnected from the bed. His restraint slid from the bar as it banged to the floor. He undid the other tie as quickly as he could—fingers numb and cold, barely feeling the pinch of the ties.

He pushed himself up and undid the ties to his ankles in the same way, relieved that he still maintained most of his clothes. The last tie shot free and he lost his precarious balance, tumbling to the ground.

He laid there for a second, stunned, before attempting to get up. His muscles wouldn't obey. He tried to grab the rail that was still attached above him, but it was too high. He turned his head and saw a stool across the room. If he could just get to the stool, he could lever himself up.

Abigail. He had to.

He pushed himself onto his stomach, reached forward, and started crawling, arm over arm, the pins and needles growing more heated as he progressed.

Another scream.

He anxiously pushed with his legs and they weakly gave a shove against the tiles. He pulled and pushed like a demented snake until he reached the stool.

He dragged himself upward, his unused muscles straining. He sat for a second, winded, then pushed himself up. He couldn't afford to rest. He shuffled toward the door, bumping into everything as he went, scattering cloths and pushing into tables.

The man who had been guarding him all this time must have been one of the ones that had been summoned.

He stumbled through the hall and into another doorway and saw a man working on a body. The shock of blond hair on the pillow stopped him cold.

The man leaning over the body moved slightly and Valerian could see Templing's face. He looked completely awful. Barely alive—if he even was. The man raised a surgical knife and Valerian gripped a shovel standing at guard near the door—for cleaning up afterward, no doubt—stumbled forward, and swung it up and into the man's head. The man fell on top of Templing and the knife skittered across the floor.

Valerian reached down, wincing, and touched Templing. He was cold, but there was a faint heart beat at his throat. Valerian unlatched his cuffs.

Another scream sounded and Valerian's head whipped up. He would come back for his friend.

He leaned down and grabbed the surgical knife from the floor using the shovel as a crutch, then straightened as fully as he could—more of a hunched-over position than anything else and shuffled back. He was almost near the door when he saw it. Two pistols in a case to the side.

A twist of the knife in the lock broke both, but he didn't care. He lifted the pistols, the weight like a dozen bricks in his hands. His eyesight would have to do if he needed to shoot someone down one of those long halls. As long as it wasn't Abigail, he didn't particularly care who he shot at the moment.

He loaded the pistols as quickly as he could with the supplies from the case and then restarted his trek.

Off to find Abigail. Off to end this madness.

Off to save the one good thing he had left.

"Sir Walter. How fortuitous that you come to be here. This building needs closing immediately. I believe that the reformers would have a fit should they see the state this jail-masquerading-as-a-hospital is in."

Sir Walter smiled faintly. "Very good, Miss Smart, but I do not doubt your intelligence."

She bit her lip. "Why?"

"Why what, Miss Smart? Do I not doubt your intelligence?" He strayed more firmly into the light, waving the other men back. They reluctantly did so. "I have studied you too long to doubt your intelligence. So perhaps instead you are asking, why am I here?"

"All of your talk of *gently* helping others." She pointed toward the hall filled with beds that she had passed through, the moans and an occasional scream still echoing through the halls. "Congratulations. You have duped us all. What a disappointment."

"Oh, no, Miss Smart." He walked forward, holding his hands out in an appealing gesture. She backed up a step, the wall at her back. "I seek to help everyone. Only by true experimentation can we glean results."

"So you are using those poor souls to do your experiments? To gain your exalted knowledge into the mind of man?"

"Poor specimens now, but they served the greater good. I started out with the derelicts, the deranged upon the streets. But I found in time that I needed something a little more. People from other levels of the social masses."

"So you picked Lord Rainewood?"

"Ah, yes." He looked her over. "Lord Rainewood. A more advanced experiment, if you will."

"He is betrothed to your *daughter*."

An emotion other than gentle calm stole across Sir Walter's face for the first time. "Is he?"

"The ball—"

"Ah, the ball. Did you know, Miss Smart, that Lord Rainewood has put off the betrothal for two years? Two years that my dear Celeste has been waiting. A diamond on display, losing her shine a month at a time."

Abigail blinked.

"I couldn't understand it. Who wouldn't want

my beautiful daughter?" He tapped his walking stick. "And then I saw him with you. And I knew."

"I'm sure you are mistaken," she said as calmly as she could. "But if you believed that, why not just find another suitor who was more ready to marry?"

"No. The Palmbury heir is the richest prize in the ton. And furthermore, once married into the family, the connection becomes untouchable."

A strange feeling overcame her. "You are afraid you are on the list."

"Very good, Miss Smart. I told you that I didn't doubt your intelligence. I looked into your past and found out everything I could about you. Fascinating."

He tapped his cane again. "I realized I could kill two birds with one perfect throw. Taking care of Lord Rainewood solved all of my problems. A purebred subject to study. A new heir to the dukedom and husband to Celeste in Lord Basil. And best of all, he brought you to me."

She couldn't catch her breath.

"Oh, yes. You were the richest prize in that sense. The driving force. A chance to study you." He stepped toward her. "Dr. Myers was kind enough years ago, over a bottle of wine, to tell me the tale of a girl who could see spirits. I had to meet you, of course."

Stars built in the back of her eyes. She blinked, stumbled, tried to keep herself upright.

"I am a patient man, Miss Smart. A man interested in humans and science—a man who began with similar origins to you—needs to be in order to succeed as I have. I simply had to set the right course and let things fall into place."

"No."

"But yes. Someone who could see spirits! Why the possibilities were endless. Imagine, being able to peer into the afterlife? To speak with them. To finally understand the answers to questions that never have answers. To use for, well, anything. To become anyone. Just as your mother did."

"The spirit world is not as scientifically sound as you make it, Sir Walter, nor as interesting."

"Ah, but I need to know." He smiled. "And you are my link. I've had to do my share of interfering in order to get you where I wanted you. Alas, that you have such a stubborn streak. And Lord Rainewood made things difficult."

"So you, you picked Lord Rainewood because of me?" She could barely get the words out, horror icing her veins.

"His link to you was one I wished to explore, and have in a most fascinating fashion." He looked from her to a few feet to her side. "I assume that he is here in some form, guiding you."

She said nothing.

"And then there were the other reasons that I stated. Lord Basil will make a much more malleable husband. Celeste has her eye on Lord Rainewood, alas, but she will adapt."

"And Mr. Templing?"

"The wrong place at the wrong time, I'm afraid, for Mr. Templing. He has been quite useful in my studies. I hadn't expected him. My men gathered both after Mr. Brockwell did his job."

"Phillip is in on your scheme?"

"Oh, heavens no. Just easily influenced. A few harmless phrases untraceable back to me—so easy to make others think ideas are their own—and he took to finding the list like a duck to water. Probably best though for him that he didn't find it."

He smiled. "So many people after that one piece of paper. Your friend Mr. Penshard. If he follows in his father's madness, perhaps I will study him someday as well. An associate of mine took on his father's case. A fine man, Gregory, if a bit hotheaded. I would have encouraged his suit of you if I thought I could have gained access to you that way, but he is too strong willed. I would have had to use his father against him in order to control you, and unfortunately Mr. Penshard tends to think on his own."

Something else snapped into place. "Mrs. Browning."

"Ah yes, a dear, distantly related cousin. But then we are all somewhat related in society, sometimes it seems. Mrs. Browning took your case at my behest."

That explained so much that if the rest of what he said wasn't so incredibly mad, she would wonder why she hadn't thought about someone putting Mrs. Browning up to the task before.

"How do you think to just cover our disappearances? I assume poor Mr. Campbell was also your doing?"

"A joint venture. Mr. Campbell owes a lot of money. I was simply taking the opportunity to help his creditor while also purchasing myself another useful specimen."

"And you'd just, what? Let the ton shrink down one by one to nothing due to your tests? What about when you want to reveal whatever knowledge these tests have gained you?"

"Ah yes. The dilemma. But I am a man who is dedicated to the sciences. To the study of humanity. I will give up my fame in order to bring about advances for society. I will gain other advantages through the links to the other side I find through you. I do not fret that anyone will truly care about the fate of the lordling and his scathing friend in a year. In fact, it will make for delicious gossip—stirring the pot, helping the others retain their need for scandal. Our society thrives on it. We will continue to flourish, even if I need to sate my urge to pick a few test subjects from the edges."

"But Phillip . . ."

"Ah yes, a simple matter of human motivation, as I said. I merely planted a few well-placed suggestions to dear Mr. Brockwell, and he took matters into his own hands. Delightful. I have made sure he will be rewarded. And he doesn't even know it. Truly a successful experiment."

"You are horrible. He will live with the guilt."

"I'm sure he will get by it in time. I will study him most judiciously while he does. He is interested in Miss Penshard and I will encourage the match." He smiled. "I am not an evil man, Miss Smart."

"No?" She looked around the room.

"No. You will be well kept. I will study you,

of course. Find out how this delightful world of spirits works." He looked eager. "Dr. Myers has explained much, but he can't tell me the specifics, the hows and whys."

"Did he tell you that he tried to rid me of my ability?"

"I told him under no circumstances would that be allowed."

"Oh?" The thought that even if she didn't survive, she could make Myers regret his own part as well was too keen. "He tried to rid me of it just a day past." Sir Walter's eyes narrowed. "Methinks you need to have a talk with your friend. He doesn't much sound like he is following your orders."

"I see. Thank you, Miss Smart."

"And if I lose the ability?" she asked.

He shrugged. "It would be unfortunate, but a dissection might help to understand the root cause. There would still be some good to come."

She opened her mouth, but nothing emerged. Her breath too caught in her throat.

A loud thud sounded and two of the men fell to the ground.

"I think not." Valerian limped around the corner carrying a shovel and two pistols.

"Ah, Lord Rainewood. So good of you to join us," Sir Walter said calmly.

Valerian stared at him for a long moment. Then he raised one of the pistols in his hand.

"Are you going to shoot me, Lord Rainewood?" Sir Walter asked, as if this too were a social experiment he was conducting.

Valerian took aim and fired. Abigail gasped as Evans went down with a ball firmly embedded in his leg. "That was for what you almost did to Abigail. Don't make me shoot higher."

Sir Walter watched his lackey writhe in pain. "A most inauspicious beginning. Are you going to shoot me now, Lord Rainewood?"

"I haven't decided." Valerian cocked his head. "I'd like to choose the most painful method of dispatching you."

The other pistol didn't waver, even though he had to prop himself up against the wall with his hip.

"I was thinking that trying you in the courts—creating a public ordeal that the masses could gobble in order to stir their need for scandal—might be just the method."

Sir Walter watched him. "Touché, Lord Rainewood. You think they would believe you over me?"

"Are you trying to convince me to put a bullet in you instead? I am amenable to that solution."

"Surely a man of your standing can see a more beneficial trade?"

"Can I? I thought I heard something about how useless I was. Surely you can't want to do business with someone as worthless as I?"

Sir Walter smiled slightly. "You always did have potential. Wasted potential, but potential nevertheless."

"I'm flattered."

"Your brother dying squashed that potential. I wonder if we could have resurrected it? Had I thought about taking you under my wing earlier . . . but your father is a determined man."

"Stop speaking," Valerian said calmly, though his eyes were angry.

"Ah, but conversation is truly the vehicle we use to understand."

Valerian watched Evans push himself back against the wall, still writhing. He kept his pistol steady and trained. "I don't seek to understand you, Malcolm. I couldn't care less about you. All I want is for you to pay for your crimes. For what you did to Abigail."

"Ah! Marvelous." He looked between them. "Once I let go of my need for you as the duke's heir, the pair of you truly became a delight to watch."

"And you are becoming irritating." Valerian motioned with the pistol. "Get moving."

"To the courts, then? I should think this should prove a most interesting trial should you actually make it out of the building."

Valerian's eyes narrowed on the man.

"Valerian—"

"I know, Abigail. I won't shoot him yet." He raised his voice. "Unless he does something to you, then I will shoot off body parts at will."

They began walking down the hall, and some of the patients quieted as Sir Walter passed. Terrified.

He walked steadily in front of them, with a certainty that bespoke confidence that he would overcome.

Pounding footsteps came from below. Reinforcements. And not ones for their side.

Abigail was just thinking on how they were going to figure a way out of this mire when one of the patients suddenly lunged up with a yell and plunged a pair of surgical scissors into Sir Walter's back. The patient tumbled from the bed and lay still upon the floor.

All cries ceased for an eerie moment, and then another patient—one who had looked comatose—vaulted from bed with a war cry and undid the straps of the man next to him. And the man after that. Bedlam reigned as the cries started again, in increased intensity as one man after another was freed. They ran in all directions, a good number rushing the men who had appeared down the hall to help Sir Walter.

Sir Walter's eyes were disbelieving. He reached behind him and felt the protruding steel. Valerian pulled Abigail back.

"Well, I hadn't quite accounted for that." He said it so calmly, that for a second she didn't think he was truly hurt. He looked at her, head tipped, eyes calm. "Do not tell Celeste."

Then he tipped forward and fell to the floor in a heap, the large metal handles appearing on an island of spreading red across the cloth at his back.

The action seemed to take the wind right from Valerian's sails. She reached for him as he began to collapse. She got her hands beneath his armpits and nearly buckled under his weight, even as thin as he'd become.

She gripped the pistol in one hand and looked around as well as she could while trying to balance him. "Valerian. I need you to help me get you outside. Just a little ways more. We don't know who is still here inside."

She half dragged, half helped him down the hall of crazed patients, some of whom were fighting the men, the other portion doing insane things like crawling on the beds, or rubbing the walls. She somehow steered Valerian through the madness, down the stairs, and into the street. Luckily no one followed them out, though she kept the pistol cocked and ready.

She hailed the waiting hack as soon as she was near enough for the driver to see. He jumped from his perch and helped her load Valerian inside.

The carriage started to move and fingers touched her face—real fingers, firm and gorgeous. "Abby, I l—" The fingers slipped from her skin and dropped to the floor.

She panicked for a moment before she found his pulse, strong beneath her fingers. She breathed a sigh of relief and held back the tears that threatened.

Ten minutes later she ascended the walk and knocked on Stagen's door.

Chapter 23

Abigail strode into the ribbon store, Telly lurking behind her. Telly had been acting strangely for the last few days. But then, everyone in the household had. Mrs. Browning had made quite a scene when Abigail had informed the woman that her services would no longer be required.

Her mother hadn't said anything in the negative, allowing Abigail to handle it. A tentative salvo in their blooming relationship. Abigail just hoped it continued.

She could barely see the outlines of four spirit women chatting in the corner. They were all vague shapes now. Even Aunt Effie was a mere shimmer.

Valerian had been holed up in his home, recuperating under strict orders from the duke, and Templing had been rescued and was recovering as well. The ton had been talking nonstop about both men and about poor Sir Walter who had been in a tragic carriage accident. Gossip was ripe with what would happen to the betrothal.

She desperately wanted to speak with Valerian about Sir Walter and what had happened in the asylum. To apologize for putting him in that situation because of her. But every time she had sent a note it had come back unopened.

All of her fears reared. Did he blame her? Had he reverted back to the old Valerian? The one who wanted nothing to do with her other than as a taunting target? What if the man he had been as a spirit was as fake and fleeting as the spirits who now flickered in and out of her vision?

Two society women entered the shop and Abigail ducked her head, her bonnet hiding her face. She didn't feel like chatting with anyone at the moment. It was likely to be all talk about Valerian and what would happen with his betrothal. The two women walked to the basket of ribbons a few down from where she stood.

"Have you heard?"

"It's delicious."

"The Smarts aren't really the Smarts after all. Fakes, pretenders, common bourgeoisie." The last was said with the relish of a light French accent.

Abigail froze, her hand clutching the black-and-white striped ribbon in her hand.

"I know. The Tynsdales or Travings, or something. Can you believe the gall? Thinking that they would not be discovered? As if we couldn't see a pretender in our midst." The woman sniffed. "I always thought there was something off about them."

Abigail tried to release the ribbon, but her fingers continued to grip it. She tried to move her feet, but they were stuck fast to the floor, as if made of slate.

Sir Walter had discovered the truth, but to her

knowledge, only one other person had known that she was not who she said she was.

"Well, we won't be seeing much of them anymore. Nothing for it but to run from London. They'll never be accepted into polite society again."

"Never. Oh, but I do so hope they try. Imagine it?" The other woman tittered.

"I hope so as well," the other woman said with a vicious titter. "Social climbers should all be put under rigorous regard, in my opinion." The snobbish tone to the woman's voice made Abigail's fingers clutch a little more tightly.

"Do you think someone will tell the Smarts before the Landmarks' ball tonight? Or will we all wait for the fireworks?"

"I do so hope for the latter, don't you?"

"Of course! Fine entertainment."

The other woman sniggered. "Yes. Let's go. These ribbons are all passé, and I hear the new store near Piccadilly has brand-new fabrics. All the rage."

"Yes. And I need a new one for mourning. I hear that with Lord Rainewood back, and poor Sir Walter in the grave, the announcement of the earl's official betrothal to Celeste Malcolm will happen tonight or tomorrow before she goes into mourning."

"Lucky girl." Envy bordering on dislike laced the words. "Such a priss, Celeste."

"Stay your tongue. She will wield too much power for us to be on her bad side."

Thunder sounded in the distance.

"Rain again. And the last few days have been so

unbelievably bright. I had hoped to go to the gardens this afternoon," one of them said.

Valerian was the only one who knew. Who had known. And all of her notes had been returned unopened. Abigail couldn't swallow around the knot in her throat. The ribbon crushed beneath her palm.

"Brighter days beckon, surely."

"I do hope so. Now about that new shop . . ."

The two chattered as they exited.

Abigail looked at her hand, the crumpled stripes of the black overtaking the white, drowning them. Anger rose to drown the devastation. She let the ribbon fall from her hand and walked to the door.

"Miss, miss!"

Telly yelled as Abigail stepped outside. A light drizzle was falling, but the steady pat of increased raindrops signaled that she would be drenched soon. She continued walking.

"Miss, your parasol!"

Abigail ignored her. Grayton House was two blocks down and four over. Then only one block down, then three to go. Telly kept moaning and fussing, but Abigail didn't care. She let the rain sheet over her, let her hair fall, plastered to her forehead and cheeks until she stepped up to the door and rapped the knocker.

A servant answered immediately, a footman by his dress, and she stared him full force in the eyes. "You will summon Lord Rainewood."

The man's eyes widened. "Lord Rainewood is unavailable for visitors, Miss—" He paused as if asking her name.

She gave a tight smile and stepped inside.

The man had obviously not thought her a threat, not even considering her bedraggled appearance, and so hadn't expected such a move. He sputtered. "Miss, you can not just enter the house."

"Summon Lord Rainewood."

"If you leave a card, perhaps I can see that he receive it."

At another time she might have felt bad for the poor man, but the fading, drab outline of the opera singer passing behind him—a reminder of this madness and its consequences—made her less agreeable. "I will not leave a card."

The man signaled frantically to another servant passing through the hall. The other servant's eyes widened and he turned and made haste in the other direction. Going to get the butler most likely. To eject her from the house through intimidation first, and if that didn't work, by force.

She walked down the hall toward the parlor without waiting for such a thing to occur.

"You can't go there." The footman tried to grab her, but she twisted from his grip.

The Duchess of Palmbury sat inside sipping tea by herself. Abigail stopped and waited, watching as the dowager's eyes turned to her, weighed her, satisfaction in their depths.

The footman bowed, and then bowed again, nearly apoplectic. "Your Grace, my apologies, she simply walked through."

The Duchess of Palmbury's mouth turned upward, her entire face reflecting malicious excitement. She waved the footman away. "The upstart come to have her last stand, I see."

"I wish to speak with Lord Rainewood," Abigail said as calmly as she could.

"I believe that will be quite impossible. What would you have to say to him? Nothing of note."

"I have something quite significant to take up with the earl."

The Duchess of Palmbury shrugged and sipped her tea. "He doesn't speak with common women."

"But he doesn't have any trouble with vulgar women, I take it? Or else he would never speak with you."

The dowager's eyes narrowed dangerously. "Nasty little trollop. Such an annoying gnat. How fabulous the last few days have been for me."

"I am sure they have been. I'm sure you will not mind me speaking to Lord Rainewood in that case. I'd like to make my displeasure over his actions known before I leave town. Your fondest wish, isn't it, Your Grace? That I leave? All accomplished, if you just let me have a word with your grandson." She shrugged. "Or else I will haunt society until I do."

"My, aren't we the obsessive little nobody. Threats? You think the watch will take your side? That the magistrates won't hesitate to make sure that you never, how did you term it, *haunt*, us again?"

"I am extremely determined. I will take your bet to see which of us succeeds."

"Foolish girl. All I have to do is hold you here and have them come to remove you."

"But you won't," Abigail said calmly. "You are far too interested in my demise not to draw this out."

The Duchess of Palmbury sipped her tea. "It is true, I want to see your face when Rainewood completely snubs you. He has been living up to my exact requirements for years when it comes to you."

Anger pulled through Abigail, but she simply nodded. "Yes, I had figured that you were behind most of his behavioral changes toward me."

"No, *dear*. That was entirely on your head. I never did know what caused it, but I was delighted to no end."

"I am sure that you were."

The dowager smiled and waved her hand. "And now I grow bored. Leave and be on your way. Exiled to wherever you choose. Though I shall delight if you decide to stay in Town and get snubbed at every turn."

"That is because you are a notorious crank."

The dowager's nostrils flared and her teacup hit its saucer with a clang. "Be gone from my house before I have you thrown out."

"Not until I have my say with Lord Rainewood. I want to tell him exactly what I think of him."

"And what do you think of him?"

She whipped around to see Valerian leaning against the door. He looked worn, but far better than when she'd dropped him off at Stagen's.

"Va-Rainewood." She squared her shoulders. "Your grandmother and I were just discussing the gossip around town."

Valerian frowned. "I find myself uninterested in the gossip at present. I'm sure it is full of more stories of forced betrothals and tawdry tales."

"Rainewood!" the dowager exclaimed. "Take that back, young man."

Valerian lifted a brow at his grandmother, then turned back to Abigail.

No attempt at an apology or even an explanation. Not even a denial and a good day.

He tapped a finger against his arm. "I take it from the pugilistic set of your shoulders and face that you are not here to inquire after my health but instead are displeased with me for some reason."

"Yes. You know well what reason that is. No wonder you returned my correspondence."

"I am afraid I do not know the reason. And what correspondence?" He moved from his reclining position against the doorframe. She caught the faint wince as he straightened. "Please enlighten me as to my new sins."

The dowager's eyes twitched at the mention of correspondence. Ah. But that didn't solve the bigger concern.

"You used me," she said, trying to keep the pain from her voice. "And then you revealed what you knew."

"What is this? How long have you known, Raine wood?" the dowager demanded.

"How long have I known what?" He addressed the question to Abigail, eyes narrowed, face unreadable.

"About my family."

Something changed in his face, but she couldn't tell what.

"What about your family?"

"Don't be coy, Rainewood." The dowager brushed imaginary crumbs from her skirt. "About how she and that vulgar mother of hers are frauds. Everyone knows."

"I see. I did not know that everyone did."

"You are saying that you did not reveal the information?" Abigail demanded.

His eyes turned icy. "I see that you believe that I did. What have I to say in my defense against such belief?"

Abigail laughed bitterly. "The slipper is on your foot now, is it not, then? To have no defense to the sure belief that someone else maintains?"

He regarded her for a moment and his expression loosened a fraction. "Touché."

"Why?" She tried to keep the pain from her voice. "I did everything I could to help, at complete cost to myself."

He took a step toward her and stopped. "I said nothing."

"You were the only one who knew."

"I said nothing."

"You embraced me afterward. Like you meant it. Like you . . ." She broke off.

"Abigail, do you want to do this in front of her?" He inclined his head sharply toward his grandmother.

"Rainewood!"

He ignored the dowager, his eyes narrowed on Abigail.

She shook her head in denial seeing nothing more to lose, nothing of her pride remaining. "I just want to know why. Why? I, I gave you everything. You might not have realized it, but I did," she finished in a near whisper.

"I know." He stepped toward her then. "I know." He tentatively reached out a hand and pulled her to him. She melted into his arms, nearly sobbing.

"Rainewood!" The strident voice echoed outside of the bubble.

"I was going to come for you," he said against her hair. "I thought there was plenty of time. And I was going to do it right. I had no idea what the gossip mill had caught," he said softly. "I will work every day to make sure that you never doubt me again."

She stiffened against his chest. "What?"

"Rainewood! Butler! Lord Rainewood is ill and this interloper is attacking him!"

She felt Valerian look above her hair. "Your Grace, I hardly think it wise to embarrass yourself so."

"Rainewood," the dowager sputtered. "You are not yourself. Let that miscreant go."

"You are talking about the woman I plan to keep permanently in my life, Your Grace."

Abigail pulled back to look at him. A drop of water dripped down her cheek.

"You cannot just take her to mistress, Rainewood."

"I said nothing about taking a mistress."

The dowager sputtered, unbelieving. "But she is a fraud. You can not do this to the family."

Valerian looked down at Abigail and wiped the drop away with his thumb. "I am not 'doing' anything to the family, Your Grace. It won't even be a blip on the gossip sheets unless we treat it as such."

"Everything is fodder for the gossip sheets."

"Not if we don't dignify it with a response and just go along as if this is the way things will be."

"We will not go along with it as the *way things will be*. You will marry Celeste Malcolm. We have already approved the match."

"I believe that you would rethink that were you to know certain truths. Besides, you need the groom's signature in order to have a fully-drawn contract these days."

"You will marry her."

"You are mistaken."

"I did not spend all of this time finding out the truth about that little wretch"—she pointed at Abigail—"just for you to disregard it and throw our lot away."

The room went still. The dowager duchess seemed to realize that she'd made a mistake. She lifted her chin defiantly. "I did it for the good of the family. For the good of society."

Valerian smiled dangerously. "If I hadn't already made up my mind, you would have just made my decision easier. Thank you."

The dowager looked confused. "So you aren't going to keep her."

"Oh, I fully intend to *keep* her and have her in my bed as soon as possible."

Abigail's cheeks went pink and the Duchess of Palmbury sputtered.

"Rainewood! How dare you say something so vulgar."

"I know. Lovely isn't it?"

"She is making you common!" The dowager pointed a gnarled finger at Abigail.

"She is making me human," he said quietly. "And

nothing you or anyone else in society says is going to make one whit of difference to my decision."

"But Valerian," Abigail whispered. "Everyone knows. I am ruined."

"Really? Well, what is social power if you don't exercise your right to control the masses every once in a while?" He lifted a brow and some of the sparkle that had been missing for years shone through. "Come, let's have an adventure, Abby. But first, I have something to give you."

He took her hand and led her to the stairs.

"Rainewood!"

"Yes, Your Grace?"

"I won't have that type of behavior under this roof!"

"I was merely going to give her something I've kept for a very long time, but you have filled my ill head with possibilities. It will be my pleasure to fulfill them. Thank you."

"Rainewood!!!"

Valerian smiled devilishly and squeezed Abigail's hand. Something about the smile loosened the last thread of worry from her heart and she squeezed back, hope filling her.

Chapter 24

The glittering lights from the Landmarks' ballroom shone up the stairs and through the doors as Abigail stepped forward in line to be introduced. The butler announced the group in front of them, a rowdy bunch who hadn't even looked behind to see who was at their backs. If they had, they might have gawked a bit.

Abigail knew that half of the people inside were hoping she'd show. Hoping for the entertainment of the night. A chance to squash the interloper in their midst.

She stepped up to the top of the stairs and looked over the sea of eager, sharklike faces spreading below.

The butler looked at the card he had been handed and cleared his throat. "I believe there is a mistake."

"No, no mistake," a warm, deep voice intoned— just a trace of haughty coldness underlying the words, demanding obedience.

The butler shifted. "Very good, my lord." He threw his shoulders back and opened his mouth.

"Earl Rainewood and his intended, Miss Abigail Travers."

Valerian smiled devilishly and stepped next to her, extending his arm. She placed hers through his, and he winked at her.

The last vestiges of nerves calmed. Seeping right through her pores as the security and love she saw in his eyes, a reflection of her own feelings, did what nothing else could. She touched the beautiful ivory comb in her hair, knowing that no matter what, things would work out. She believed that now. *Knew* it.

That even in the vat of sharks that lay below, she had a raft that would always hold her, and that she could support in return.

"Think of the adventure awaiting us." He leaned so that his eyes were level with hers, his mouth sinfully close. "And even better the one that awaits when I sneak into your room tonight."

"As if I will let you enter."

"As if I would let you keep me away."

She put her right foot upon the top step and smiled.

Next month, don't miss these exciting new love stories only from Avon Books

Obsession Untamed by Pamela Palmer

Delaney Randall is snatched from her apartment one night by Tighe, a dangerous Feral Warrior—one of an elite band of immortals who can change shape at will. He needs Delaney's help to track a dark fiend, but soon becomes wild with an obsession for her that is as untamed as his heart.

Since the Surrender by Julie Anne Long

Captain Chase Eversea receives a mysterious message summoning him to a London rendezvous . . . where he encounters the memory of his most wicked indiscretion in the flesh: Rosalind March—the only woman he could never forget.

The Infamous Rogue by Alexandra Benedict

The daughter of a wealthy bandit, Sophia Dawson once lost herself in the arms of Black Hawk, the most infamous pirate ever to command the high seas. Now she is determined to put her sinful past behind her and marry a well-born nobleman, but her ex-lover has returned for revenge . . .

Beauty and the Duke by Melody Thomas

Ten years ago they were young lovers, sharing sinful touches and desperate ecstasy. But he was bound by his promise to wed another. Now they say he's cursed, that any woman who shares his bed will meet an untimely end. Should Christine be afraid of the devil duke and his ravenous desire?

Visit www.AuthorTracker.com for exclusive information on your favorite HarperCollins authors.

REL 0709

Available wherever books are sold or please call 1-800-331-3761 to order.

At Avon Books, we know your passion for romance—once you finish one of our novels, you find yourself wanting more.

May we tempt you with . . .

- **Excerpts** from our upcoming releases.

- Entertaining **extras**, including authors' personal photo albums and book lists.

- Behind-the-scenes **scoop** on your favorite characters and series.

- **Sweepstakes** for the chance to win free books, romantic getaways, and other fun prizes.

- Writing **tips** from our authors and editors.

- **Blog** with our authors and find out why they love to write romance.

- **Exclusive content** that's not contained within the pages of our novels.

Join us at
www.avonbooks.com

AVON

An Imprint of HarperCollins*Publishers*
www.avonromance.com

Available wherever books are sold or please call 1-800-331-3761 to order.

FTH 0708